The Knight and the Rose

**Winner of the 2001 Romantic Novel of the Year Award
by the Romance Writers of Australia**

"*The Knight and the Rose* is a lovely medieval, rich as a
stained-glass window, but as complex as real life."

—Jo Beverley, national bestselling author
of *The Devil's Heiress*

"The best book I've read in many months. . . . The writing is
simply superb. . . . The plot is original and intriguing, the
characters are dynamic and multidimensional, and the setting is
vivid. The author has successfully woven the actions of her
fictional characters into the historical events of the period."

—Lesley Dunlap, *The Romance Reader*

Also by Isolde Martyn
THE MAIDEN AND THE UNICORN

The KNIGHT and the ROSE

Isolde Martyn

BERKLEY BOOKS, NEW YORK

B

A Berkley Book
Published by The Berkley Publishing Group
A division of Penguin Putnam Inc.
375 Hudson Street
New York, New York 10014

PRINTING HISTORY
First published in trade paperback in Australia and New Zealand in 1999 by
Bantam.
Berkley trade paperback edition / February 2002

Visit our website at
www.penguinputnam.com

Library of Congress Cataloging-in-Publication Data

Martyn, Isolde.
The knight and the rose / Isolde Martyn.
p. cm.
ISBN 0-425-18329-7
1. Great Britain—History—14th century—Fiction. 2. Knights and knighthood—
Fiction. 3. Married women—Fiction. I. Title.

PR9619.4.M37 K58 2002
823'.914—dc21
2001043179

PRINTED IN THE UNITED STATES OF AMERICA

10 9 8 7 6 5 4 3 2 1

For John
who liked this story best of all

Characters 1322–1327

Listed in order of appearance, real historical characters are marked with an asterisk.

Sir Fulk De Enderby "The Mallet" husband to Lady Johanna FitzHenry and a veteran of the wars against the Scots

Lady Johanna FitzHenry third wife of Sir Fulk de Enderby and youngest daughter of Lord Alan FitzHenry, Constable of Conisthorpe

Agnes her tiring woman

Geraint (Gervase de Laval) a rebel fleeing from the Battle of Boroughbridge

Sir Edmond Mortimer* rebel from the Battle of Boroughbridge, heir of the rebel Marcher lord, Sir Roger Mortimer of Wigmore

Father Gilbert chaplain to Lady Constance of Conisthorpe

Lady Constance wife to Lord Alan FitzHenry, Constable of the royal castle of Conisthorpe and mother of Lady Johanna

Yolonya tiring woman to Lady Constance

Sir Geoffrey Seneschal of Conisthorpe Castle

Lady Edyth de Enderby Sir Fulk's unmarried sister

Sir Edgar de Laverton knight in the service of Sir Fulk

DAME CHRISTIANA a holy widow and recluse under the patronage of Lady Constance

JANKYN (WATKYN) jester to Thomas, Earl of Lancaster

MILES FITZHENERY younger brother of Lady Johanna and heir to Lord Alan FitzHenry

LORD ALAN FITZHENRY Johanna's father and former Constable of the royal castle of Conisthorpe

AIDAN Lord Alan's manservant

SIR RALPH DE MIDDLESBROUGH Deputy Sheriff to Sir Roger de Somerville, High Sheriff of Yorkshire

AMICE Ranulf Weaver's wife, daughter to Yolonya

PETER Amice's son, scholar under patronage of Father Gilbert

STEPHEN DE NORWOOD proctor of the archdeacon's court, advocate to Geraint/Gervase and Lady Johanna

MAUD DE ROOS a widowed noblewoman

WILLIAM DE BEDFORD judge of the archdeacon's court

MARTIN DE SCRUTON examiner to the archdeacon's court

AVICE MERCER, MARGERY FULLER townswomen of Conisthorpe

JOHN DE DREUX, EARL OF RICHMOND* Duke of Brittany and Constable of Richmond Castle

HUGH DESPENSER THE YOUNGER* favorite of King Edward II

HUGH DESPENSER THE OLDER* Earl of Winchester, father to Hugh

QUEEN ISABELLA* Queen of England, wife to King Edward II and sister to King Charles IV of France, later known as "the She-wolf of France"

EDWARD, PRINCE OF WALES* future King Edward III, son of King Edward II and Queen Isabella

SIR ROGER MORTIMER* rebel Marcher lord, imprisoned in the Tower of London, father of Sir Edmund Mortimer and favorite of Queen Isabella

CECILIA DE LEYGRAVE* lady-in-waiting to Queen Isabella

LADY ELIZABETH BADDLESMERE* wife to Sir Edmund Mortimer and daughter of executed traitor, Sir Bartholomew Baddlesmere

ADAM ORLETON, BISHOP OF HEREFORD* supporter of Queen Isabella and enemy of King Edward II

HENRY, EARL OF LEICESTER* brother of Thomas, Earl of Lancaster

Prologue

March 16th 1322, the Feast of St. Boniface

"HOW MANY MORE TIMES MUST I TEACH YOU YOUR duty to me!" Fulk de Enderby lashed his ringed hand into Johanna's cheek, sending her stumbling back against the bedpost. She heard his spurred boots descend the stone stairs outside her door, and slid miserably to the floor, huddling beside the coverlet. The bruise down the side of her face was already ripening uncomfortably against the interwoven metal threads. Yes, how many more times?

The laughter, the joy in life, that once had been her nature had been threshed away; Fulk, this so-called worthy banneret her father had compelled her to wed, had nigh on defeated her but she still had a little courage left. Killing the old fiend might be a mercy to mankind even if they hanged her for it. Anything to escape the cruelty and the beatings.

Cob, her little hound, whined against her ankles. Johanna roused herself and gathered him into her arms, rocking his head against her kirtle. Only a matter of weeks, she thought, and she would be prepared to hurl herself from the top of the keep and risk an unhallowed grave and eternal Hell. Satan at least might have a sense of humour.

"Oh, my lady, what damage has that brute done this time?"

Her young tiring woman, Agnes, came quietly into the bedchamber and knelt beside her shaking mistress. Dried lavender seeds tumbled from the cloth tucked into the girl's waist and she smelt comfortingly of the linen press. Fulk had not taken Agnes from her, not yet.

The younger girl gently turned Johanna's face to the open shutters and shook her head sorrowfully. "This wicked place! I curse your father for sending us here. There were tales in plenty, but did he care?"

"They were wrong!" Johanna knuckled the tears away angrily.

"Who, madam?"

"The wretched jongleurs with their songs about knightly chivalry and love. All lies!"

The small dog, all paws and teeth, grew tactlessly playful, at odds with his mistress's unhappiness and Johanna set him down. "Do you think my skin will grow calloused and as wrinkled as a walnut from all these beatings? Mayhap that Hellspawn will not desire me then."

Rising, she paced to the narrow slit that served as a window. A blackbird perched precariously on the crenellation flew off, his freedom mocking her. She had uncaged every songbird in the castle; she was the only prisoner.

Her palms pressing against the insensitive stone of the walls, she stared longingly through the deep embrasure at the bleak brown-tufted hills that breasted the horizon beyond the village of Enderby.

"If only he would let me ride. Just to escape for a few hours and feel the wind on my soul."

"He thinks you more likely to conceive if you forsake riding."

"Ha, what truth is there in that? Besides . . ."

Agnes came across and slid a sisterly arm about her. "I know." The chapel bell for morning mass crossed the silence between them like a shadow. "Light a candle for me and tell the chaplain why I shall not be at mass." Coiling her fingers into fists, Johanna bruised them against the broad sill. "Oh, by our sweet Saviour, what I need is a miracle or let God send a thunderbolt."

"Aye, well, you never know, my lady, God might send both."

One

"1 'LL NOT BE TAKIN' YOU FURTHER, MASTER SCHOLAR."
Geraint awoke to a jab in the ribs, felt the weight
of Edmund's inert body across his thighs and knew
that the danger, the nightmare, was still with him.

The carter clambered down from the driving board and relieved
himself on an untidy cairn of stones. It gave Geraint the chance to
come to his wits before the fellow sauntered round to the side of
the wain and lifted up the sacks that had been giving his passengers a meagre protection against the chill damp.

Rubbing the sleep out of his bleary eyes with his thumb and
forefinger, Geraint wondered how he had even managed to doze,
awkwardly crammed in as he was between the tightly lashed barrels of Bordeaux wine and the crates of North Sea stockfish.

"Looks like he'll be wearin' a thick 'ead when he wakes," the
carter muttered, casting grim eyes over the youth cradled in Geraint's arms and wrapped chrysalis-like within a heavy cloak.
"Won this at dice, did he?" He reached out and tested the fabric
between his fingers.

In a different world, Geraint might have clouted the clod for his
discourtesy but the fellow unwittingly had carried them at risk of
his own life. They had certainly not been on the list of goods to
be collected.

"Aye, he did," Geraint muttered indifferently, tossing his fair
hair back and eyeing the wild wood that disappeared into the mist
in each direction with misgiving. "Where are we?"

They had been trundling for hours across a foggy, God-forsaken moor since leaving Ripon but now he could hear the churning of river water against crags and knew they had left the high country.

"T' road yonder hies east up t'at moors agenn and I dare say you'll no be wantin' that. Go straight on an' down the road lies Skipton. If you'd be wantin' t' nearest village, cross the bridge, take the right lane and follow t' beck along. Me, as I told you this mornin', I be bound to deliver goods to Bardon and, like as not, the Cliffords or t'constable ull give me food'n lodging, but they don't like me bringing extra travellers wi' me. Tried it afore."

"Aye, fair enow," answered Geraint. "Help me down with him then." Not for the first time, he was tempted to slide a blade between the carter's ribs and seize the wain, but he had seen so much death in the last week that he had no stomach for further killing and, like as not, if the man was known hereabouts, some gossip might recognise the horses and start asking questions. Besides, the man seemed to be a charitable fellow with a misplaced respect for poor sozzled scholars and did not deserve such a miserly end.

"Happen there might be another traveller as can take you further," muttered the carter, clearly feeling guilty at dumping them like sacks of waste from a tanner's. Between them, they lifted down the groaning, valuable heir of the imprisoned rebel, Sir Roger Mortimer. "By the Rood, he ain't no feather."

Geraint grunted. Both he and the carter were strongly built but the intermesh of Edmund's bones and flesh weighed cursed heavy. It was a veritable marvel how two humble feet could keep any healthy man upright at all, let alone in chain mail, he reflected, as he propped Edmund against a convenient milestone and straightened his aching back, striving to hide the fact that his own wound was hurting like the Devil's fire. The cold wind was already scourging him through the thin fabric of his tunic and poking icy fingers into his ears. He tugged his ragged hood forward and stamped his feet to get the blood flowing back through his limbs, stiffened from the journey.

"I ain't partial to pokin' me nose in where it ain't welcome," muttered the carter, scratching his scrubby chin. "But your friend seems right sickly."

"Pah," snorted his passenger dismissively, "if you think he looks white around the gills, you should have seen him under the alehouse board two days ago. We are supposed to be journeying back to his family," he added. "Leastways we will be if he can poxy well stay sober enough to tell me the directions."

The middle part of the freshly baked tale was certainly not a lie—that was if King Edward's armoured sheepdogs had not herded up the remainder of the Mortimers still at large.

"An' here was I hopin' he might be one of them wounded rebels what opposed the king's men up Boroughbridge way. Might be a reward for some of 'em, I shouldn't wonder." So the fellow did not have a turnip for a brain.

Geraint sniffed with what he hoped was convincing incredulity and shook his head. "Not him, my life upon it!" He was careful to watch the carter's face, hoping that the man believed him. With the flail wound weakening his left shoulder and arm, he did not rate his chances of overpowering such a brawny fellow. During the journey, he would have had surprise on his side, but face to face now with merely a knife—well, not unless he had to.

"Aye, well," the carter shrugged. "I'll be off then. God be wi' you, lad, and Christ preserve your drunken sot albeit he looks ripe for an early grave. There's a priory down the dale if you reckon sommat else is ailing him." Sensible advice except that his enemies would be sniffing around the religious houses like dogs above a coney warren.

"He will be back at the dicing table tomorrow," Geraint grinned. *If he was not dead before sundown.* "God's blessing on you and my thanks."

"Glad to have the company, young 'un, not that you said aught. But it's good to have some extra muscle if a wheel should loosen comin' over the high places an' I should not have cared to meet one of them rebels." With that, the carter clapped him heartily on his wounded shoulder then happily busied himself checking girths and hooves, leaving his passenger with his teeth clamped together, nearly passing out with the pain of it.

With relief, Geraint watched him eventually flick his carthorses moving. It was a mercy the fellow had not expected payment; being dressed like a poor scholar had its advantages. He scowled at the stained, worn tunic that served him now and waited until the cart had rumbled out of sight before he heaved Edmund into the paltry shelter of the wood.

A twitter of wrens in the thicket complained at being disturbed as he gently set Edmund down and paused to retrieve his breath. The young knight's lank brown hair lay tumbled incongruously across a patch of wood anemones that were optimistically unfurling.

Poor Edmund. Nature had spooned him out too small a dose of his father's appetite to live life to its full. Yet the lad had tried his best to act in Roger's interests and support my lords of Hereford and Lancaster against the king.

Geraint had little thought to play his nurse, but discovering their companions slain and stripped beside the campfire when he returned from seeking food and tidings, and only the lad left alive, had given him little choice. Dead before nightfall? Please God, no, but the dank, grey weather seemed to be closing in upon them again.

He felt the despair of being a stranger and the hollowness of not knowing where to find kindness that could hold its tongue. With no familiarity with these Yorkshire dales, he was not certain how far they had come from the great road north nor whether the people of these parts had heard the tidings of the battle.

He decided to scout out an empty barn loft, warm with animal breath, where he could bestow Edmund at dusk. His clothing had already blessed him with a kind of sanctity, so it seemed but a simple matter to pass himself off as a footloose schoolmaster and cozen a crust or two from a housewife. And with God's providence, there might be a laundered sheet left out upon a hedge that he could pilfer to dress their wounds.

The ashes and hawthorns, still unbudded, yielded no cover so he hacked free some nearby coppice to make a shelter of sorts, interweaving a mesh of foliage byre-like around Edmund's body. It would conceal the youth's presence and shield the upper part of his body and, with God's good grace, keep the wind from chilling him further. Not that it seemed the young knight was even aware enough to be troubled.

Setting out to return to the crossroads, Geraint took the village lane, which ran cheek by jowl with the wood as far as he could see. Accustomed to riding, he felt disoriented and vulnerable out of the saddle, or maybe it was because his wounded shoulder throbbed with every step, his belly was pleading to be fed and the freezing wind was slowly addling his mind.

Furrows of mud sucked at his feet so he picked his way instead along the matted grass at the road edge, trying to avoid slithering into the ditch that kept him company. It was an effort to keep the memory of the battle and its aftermath from repeating like a continual rallying trumpet in his head, and to staunch the anxiety that he could be hanged or worse. Dazedly he floundered on, blowing on his fingers and trying to concentrate on his footing.

Pounding hooves and the jingle of harness drove the weariness from his mind. God forbid they were bounty hunters! Cursing, he sprang into the ditch and crouched against the mess of ivy and nettles. A half-score of men-at-arms, their surcotes too far off for him to recognise, came thudding into sight heading towards the village.

Pressing his body hard into the bank, he crossed himself, offering more rash promises to St. Jude as the ground pounded with their passing, or was it his heart, frantic lest they drag him away for interrogation before they hanged him?

The saint must have heard his desperate prayer. With his damp hose muddied further and his hands prickling from nettle stings, Geraint eventually clambered back onto the road.

If the soldiers were searching the village or drinking at an alewife's, he would be better to seek his help from some more isolated villeins, so he struck south through the wood, his arms hugging his body against the wind-hurled raindrops. Were they bounty hunters? Would they search this far for fugitives? All about him the lichen-encrusted trunks grew hostile as if they shared some sinister secret. Unease crawled down his spine. The telltale slap of startled pigeon wings confirmed it; he was being hunted.

IN THE SOLAR AT ENDERBY, JOHANNA TOOK THE LETTER HER HUSband held out to her, cursing that she had never been given the opportunity to learn what the confusion of black marks meant.

"What does it say? Oh, for our Lord's sake, tell me!"

Eager as a young dog to please, her mother's comely, fair-haired groom, who had just arrived from Conisthorpe bearing the letter, butted in: "My lady, your father is dying, and your lady mother beseeches you to come home straightway."

Sir Fulk de Enderby twitched the parchment from Johanna's fingers and turned a face towards the groom that usually bespoke punishment for his own servants. Realising his offence, scarlet faced, the young man fearfully pulled his forelock and inspected his toecaps as if he had suddenly grown alien appendages.

"Does he speak truly?" Johanna asked swiftly, diverting Fulk's wrath and anxious to know what else her mother had written. There were more lines marching across the letter than that brief summary had warranted.

Her husband gave a curt nod, folding the missive and tucking it beneath the safe custody of his belt. No sympathy lay behind his cold smile. Had Fulk been in Jerusalem at the time of the blessed Christ's crucifixion, he would have been one of Pilate's household knights ramming the crown of thorns harder on Jesus's brow, and wearing that same coercive expression.

Discipline and conformity were everything to Fulk. Which was why she, his young third wife, had failed every test. Above all, she was barren, her womb unresponsive to his seed and her husband could not forgive her for it. He had tried to beat obedience and pump fruitfulness into her until she was bruised both outwardly and inwardly, but still her mind and body had refused to conform.

And her father and mother, rid of her, had remained indifferent even though she had dispatched them word of her unhappiness. A sympathetic visiting friar had clandestinely carried them tidings of her misery, but no answer had come. Though a baron with Norman ancestry and of higher rank than her husband, her father, Lord Alan FitzHenry, had not bothered to admonish his old friend Fulk. The ties between them as companions-in-arms were clearly more important than helping his once beloved younger daughter.

"Well, wife, what is to be done? You are of a sudden unusually tongue-tied."

Johanna swallowed nervously, glad that the veil hiding her injuries also screened her from Fulk's interrogative stare. Please God, she could play this aright. She tightened her lips stubbornly as she chose her words.

"My father can die without me," she declared. "I have no wish to set eyes upon his face again." Turning towards the cushioned windowseat, she crossed her fingers within the shadows of her sleeve and waited for his temper to take flame.

Her husband grabbed her by the shoulder and spun her round

to face him. "Why, what ignoble attitude is this? You shame my name, wife."

Beneath her veil, she winced at his touch. "I will not go."

He turned abruptly on her mother's messenger. "Wait outside!"

Fingers, fierce as talons, fastened into the soft flesh of her upper arms. Fulk loomed over her. If ever Death the Great Leveller set aside his hooded travelling cloak and scythe to dress for dinner at a bishop's table, she would wager he would have the appearance of her husband—tall, gaunt, hoary-headed and bereft of pleasure in humanity.

"You shameful bitch!"

Vixen, she hoped, might be nearer the truth.

"*Go?* With *this?*" she hissed, setting back the gauzy tisshewe to show where he had hit her. "I curse my father that he married me to you! He may die alone and unshriven for aught I care."

Fulk, as always, was unmoved by guilt or shame. "Curse all you please, woman, but your father still has not paid the balance of your dowry and I will have it." He thrust her away, and paced towards the brazier. Turning, he jabbed his forefinger towards her. "I say you shall go. You will reconcile yourself with your father and plead on your knees for what he owes me. Tell him you are with child."

"By *you!*" she scoffed, hating him with the loathing that Our Blessed Lady must have felt towards Judas on the morning of Christ's passion.

Hurling insults at Fulk's age and childlessness were the only weapons in her arsenal save cunning. She voiced them seldom, fearing too much use would blunt them. But today the victory must be hers.

With one stride, he grabbed her chin and forced her to look at him. She trembled at the fury in those joyless eyes, afraid lest she had gone too far. If he beat her senseless, she would be too ill to travel.

"I had a foul bargain in you, girl. How many beatings will it take to make you hold your peevish tongue?" He stroked his fingers down her throat and she froze, her gaze averted from the pale, lined flesh, the steel blue eyes. Take away my looks, she prayed. Make me loathsome so he will set me away out of his sight.

"I thought your youth and vigour would swiftly nourish my seed, but you are disobedient, Johanna. You do not give yourself to me like a good wife should." Not now, she prayed desperately. Not here, with my mother's servant beyond the door.

"I will not go!" she hissed. "So what will you do? Tie me to the litter?"

"Escort you there myself and stand behind you to see you grovel on your hands and knees for your inheritance."

"*You* go and do the grovelling. I care not."

His thumb and finger collared her throat. "I think I will devise some new punishment for your waywardness. A public humiliation. A scold's bridle perhaps." He was bluffing. No knight would shame his lady in the common gaze although privily he might well humiliate her in front of the servants. "Or would you prefer the hair shirt and scourging once again?"

For an instant longer, she showed him no fear.

"I mean it, wife. Or perhaps you would like me to dismiss your beloved Agnes?"

"You Hellspawn!" She hung her head, seemingly defeated.

"Excellent, I see we understand each other at last." He let her go and flung open the door.

"Return to Lady Constance, fellow, and tell her my lady her daughter will set out at first light. Will you not, my heart?"

Johanna sent him a sullen look and turned her back. As the door closed behind him leaving her alone, she at last dared to smile in triumph.

Two

GERAINT LEANED AGAINST AN OAK TO CATCH HIS breath and listened, wondering how many bounty hunters there were. He tensed, ready to catch his stalker by the throat, but only the tap of an industrious wood-pecker and the constant swearing of distant nesting rooks reached him. Perhaps his mind was playing him tricks. He could not leave Edmund for much longer. God forbid their enemies had already found him.

He staggered on and at last stumbled onto a well-used bridle-path that climbed and twisted awhile before bringing him down to rough-hewn planks across a beck. Beyond, the track disap-peared round the hillside. An ideal place to jump a man. Edgy, certain that he was pursued, Geraint half knelt, feigning to drink, and unsheathed his knife. Dead bracken rustled. He rolled aside as a cudgel came hurtling towards his skull and sprang up to face a thickset, black-maned lout grinning at him from behind a tangled beard. Relief flooded through Geraint. This was no bounty hunter from Boroughbridge for the scoundrel wore neither haubergeon nor a scrap of stolen armour. This was nothing more than a scurvy outlaw.

"My purse is already cut," he growled in English, covetously eyeing the black sheep pelt the brigand sported.

"But your knife and boots would do me right well, stranger," the rogue chortled, not in the least deterred by his opponent's larger frame.

Geraint braced himself but the attack never came. Instead, the man cocked his head, listening, and sucked in his cheeks. The clomp of hooves came from along the path.

"Better pickings coming!" the outlaw chuckled softly. "I will split the winnings with you. Pax?"

The sudden reprieve astonished Geraint but before he could protest or run, the rogue concealed himself behind a tree.

It was a crinkle-haired cleric leading an ass who rounded the corner. The aged churchman took a horrified look at Geraint and his knife. There was no time to warn him before the outlaw came at him across the planks. The little priest gave a roar of defiant outrage and jabbed the end of his quarterstaff into his attacker's right eye. Then, twirling it with the skill of a Scots war veteran, he sent his assailant tumbling backwards into the water. Before Geraint could protest his innocence, the priest hurtled across the planks, thwacking the staff into his side and then wounded shoulder with the precision of a rotting cabbage hurled at a pillory. And the world went black.

HIS HEAD STILL REELING, GERAINT OPENED HIS EYES PAINFULLY AT the huff of hot breath on his mouth to discover that a hound's black nose was investigating him. He could still hear the ripple of the beck but there was now a soft murmur of voices and the fidgeting of horses' hooves. Someone had propped him against a tree trunk, but his wrists were tightly tied and he became aware of three pairs of feet.

"No sign of the other one," someone said, and a fourth pair joined the others.

Several people seemed to be assessing him like sworn jurors, but none of them he recognised save for the priest, and there was no sign of the outlaw. Had the priest been travelling ahead of the rest?

Fortune had certainly played the whore with him; he was not used to gazing on the world from the dirt like some penitent villein. Even if these people knew naught of what had transpired at Boroughbridge and that he was an escaped rebel, they would assume he was an outlaw. He might as well have turned himself and Edmund in to the nearest sheriff.

"He is wounded. I never did that." The old churchman's blue gaze studied him with interest.

Geraint stared down at the darkening patch on his breast while a second man, a knight grey haired and grizzle bearded, knelt down before him, unbuckled his belt and lifted the thin tunic to inspect the damage. The man grimaced, his breath hissing.

Their prisoner blinked at the scarlet, bloody mass that was part of him from collarbone to belly and moistened his parched lips. For a moment Geraint was shocked but reason assured him that the fresh blood spilling out more than covered the true extent of his wound.

"It should make an interesting scar, do you not think?" he commented huskily in Norman French, trying out his most appealing grin, desperate to convince these people that he was no uncouth, rank-smelling ruffian but a wandering scholar. It would buy him time and mayhap he would escape the noose.

The knight glanced up at the churchman in confusion, clearly not sure what kind of beast they had snared. "Aye, if it is attended to straightway," he answered Geraint. "Have you more of these?"

Their prisoner lifted his bound hands. An ugly gash descended for a span width below his elbow, half-hidden by the ill-fitting sleeve.

"You reckon these might impress my grandsons if I live that long?" His bravado was returning.

A bright blue skirt with a gris hem swished forwards. Geraint became aware that the knight's lady was staring down at him— an older woman with the girth that came from childbearing and a laden table. He gave her but a cursory glance and looked past her to watch the knight's face. Therein lay his fate.

Judging from his appearance, Geraint's captor was not overly wealthy. The man wore no gold and his woollen tunic had seen much wear albeit his sword scabbard and belt were of excellent craftsmanship. He would certainly seek payment if he guessed King Edward might reward him for a fugitive rebel. But thankfully his expression was concerned rather than suspicious.

"Yolonya, have we anything that will staunch the bleeding?" the lady asked over her shoulder. There was a rending noise as someone's underkirtle was generously ripped.

An even larger woman, clad like a servant and with arms the size of mutton joints, crouched and thrust a wad of linen against his wound and ungently threaded another strip under his arm and bound it tightly.

"Now, what are you doing on my land?" It was the lady who spoke.

Geraint swore inwardly at his stupidity and reappraised her. Her eyes were too shrewd, damn it! He could tell she was weighing how she might profit from his capture. Her gaze took in the neat cut of his hair and evaluated the reasonably costly boots that he had refused to abandon, which were so at odds with the fraying tunic that strained across his broad chest. She pointedly studied the finely wrought horn handle of his knife that the priest was holding before looking back down at him for an answer. Oh yes, too shrewd by half.

"It saddens me to say it, young man, but I really do think you should abandon your aspiration to play Robin Hood. Save it for May Day, hmm? The recklessness is there but..." She gestured apologetically, as if she was sparing him a more cutting comment.

"—But I am inept," he finished for her. "Yes, it would appear so." He was conscious of his stubble, that his fair hair was tousled and in need of a sousing. Clean and well clad with sweet breath and good teeth, he could usually net a woman's heart with his smile. He tried now. "I am a poor scholar of Oxford, my lady, and I pray you for charity to give me a few pennies and some food and I will be away from here as fast as I may."

"And your injuries? Never tell me the masters of Oxford hurl words at you with such leaden ferocity." Although he liked the amusement in her voice, he did not dare share a morsel of the bitter truth with anyone.

Smiling painfully, he shook his head. "True, madam, but I was set upon as I was about to drink by the rogue who attacked yon priest. You were impressive, Father. Is the outlaw also trussed so deftly?" They did not answer him nor produce the wretch. Geraint moistened his lips nervously. That was unfortunate; the fellow could have been forced to corroborate his story.

The lady exchanged glances with the others. It seemed as if the jury was still considering, but she did not have the patience to await a consensus.

"Oh, free him, Sir Geoffrey." She folded her arms and regarded Geraint sternly, as the knight—evidently not her husband since he had made no contribution to the decision—loosened his bonds and helped him to his feet. He must have tottered precariously. Not only did his head swim viciously and his wounds throb but now his other side also ached damnably where the priest had whacked him.

"Please, I beg you, have you any food?"

Mercifully, she nodded to the churchman. After much fumbling in the pannier strapped behind the ass's saddle, the priest drew out a pot. Was that all the man could manage? No bread and cheese?

The lady caught Geraint eyeing it ravenously and set a hand upon the priest's arm, delaying him from unsealing it. "Who was it set upon you?" she demanded, taking the pot delicately between her gloved fingertips as if she was about to bestow a jousting trophy.

"Good dame, for the love of God." Geraint held out his hand for the nourishment but she withheld it. "Should I have asked his name, madam, before he hit at me?" Her mouth tightened angrily at his sarcasm and he cursed his temper. "I beg your pardon. I should not have spoken so."

Hugging the vessel possessively against her bosom, the lady tyrant circled him, inspecting him as if he was a villein up for hire. "What are you called?"

"Ger . . ." By Jesu, he needed a name. It was necessary but difficult to think fast, given his addled state, but he was used to dissembling. He chose one he was at home with. "Gervase de . . . Laval." God willing she had never crossed the sea.

Satisfied, she handed him the stone jar. Lifting out the stopper, he jabbed his fingers in. Honey. Better than nothing. He hungrily scooped out some of the sticky mass, swiftly licking it off his fingers before it wasted on the ground. The dog plonked itself in front of him, wagging its tail hopefully. The lady, anticipating his other need, gestured to the leather bottle on the knight's belt and Sir Geoffrey handed it reluctantly to him.

"Thank you, sir. God and all his angels bless you, my lady." He raised it to her before he drank. The ale ran down his dry throat, pleasing him better than the finest of wines. He wiped his mouth with the back of his hand and stopped the pot. "I beg of you may

I keep these?" he asked gravely, too proud to lace his voice with pleading.

They were watching him with an excess of curiosity, and he cursed inwardly. It was tempting to ask their help for Edmund, but far too dangerous. He needed to be quit of them. Going down shakily on one knee, he carried the lady's hem to his lips. "I am a poor scholar, my lady, and I thank you for your act of charity. God be with you." He rose and turned to go before he remembered they had disarmed him. "Would it please you to give me my knife?" he asked humbly.

That too was handed him and he touched his forehead to the lady, bestowed a wry mutter of thanks on the rest and hobbled off in what he hoped was the wrong direction.

It took a cursed while to find Edmund for he picked a circuitous path lest the outlaw should follow him, but no panicked bird or snap of twig betrayed unwelcome company.

"Edmund, Edmund! Can you hear me?"

He felt for a pulse at the side of the youth's neck. It was faint beneath his fingers but still there, thank Christ. His beloved cloak, soft leather, waxed against the weather, had kept the drizzle off the young knight from neck to calves, and he was right glad that he had made the sacrifice. Gently he loosened its folds, praying that the bleeding had stopped.

"Is he still alive?"

Geraint spun round, drawing his knife with an oath, but it was the priest who had come up behind him, his tread soft as cats' paws.

"It were best you had kept out of this, Father. Now I shall have to kill you," he growled, but the thin little wafer of a man came closer still.

"Kill me?" A wry smile twisted his lips. "I have bested you already, I recall." The priest's glance fell meaningfully upon his wounded shoulder. "You do not have the mien of a murderer, my son, and my lady will unleash her hunting pack to track you down. Here is better work for me." Not waiting for an answer, the older man crouched beside Edmund, reaching out a compassionate hand, tributaried with veins, to feel his forehead.

Even as he cursed inwardly, Geraint was glad of the comfort of another human being. If Edmund was dying, at least his soul would not be sundered from his body unshriven.

Shifting round, the cleric set back the cloak and inspected the bloodied shirt beneath. He frowned, not liking what he saw, and swiftly covered him again.

"There is a healer, a holy widow, dwelling on my lady's demesne west of here. We have presently come from there. Your friend will not last long without her skills."

"How far?"

Brushing the leaves from his habit, the priest clambered to his feet.

"We can have him there by nightfall if we sling him on a litter with my ass and another beast aft and back. I will fetch them hither as fast as I may. Keep him as warm as you can and say your prayers." He lifted his face to the sky, assessing the clouds, and then returned his glance to Geraint's hesitant face and the blade still naked in his hand. "Or would you rather he die?"

"Could you not fetch her here?" Surely the woman could not disobey the priest's summons?

"Her? Not Christiana." The cleric studied his face, adding, "You fear I will be indiscreet? Is that what concerns you? I know battle wounds when I see them, *master scholar*. And I heard that a rebel army was on the march from the Trent with King Edward harrying them."

Geraint averted his gaze. Dear God, the man knew too much for his own good. "And these are the Mortimer lions unless I am mistaken." The priest stooped and fingered the embroidery on the edge of Edmund's shirt collar showing where the cloak ties had slackened.

"You are mighty omniscient," Geraint answered coldly, grasping the weapon more firmly. Certes, he would need to use it; the man had just written his own death warrant. Yet his curiosity was whetted. "We are dangerous company. Why should you wish to help us?"

"Because . . ." The churchman's blue stare rose from the lad's face to gravely examine Geraint's. "Because King Edward has broken the laws of God." He took another interested glance at the prostrate knight. "Edmund, I heard you say, eh? Not quite so comely as his father. Yes, I think I can guess whose son this is.

Trust me. You have little choice." As if he read suspicion rampant
still on Geraint's face, he continued, "Oh, I know a Mortimer when
I see one. Three of Sir Roger Mortimer's brothers are priests, and
Walter, rector at Radnor, is a good friend of mine. Was not Sir
Roger arrested down in Shrewsbury in January on the king's or-
ders?"

Geraint stared at him, further amazed that he was so well informed. "Aye, arrested after being promised a safe conduct to King
Edward at Westminster."

"Is Sir Roger still alive?"

"For the nonce. The king has him mewed up in the Tower of
London."

"Then I suggest we do everything we can to ensure his heir
lives." He stood tensely waiting for Geraint's decision, as if he
faced a snarling dog with its hackles up.

It was necessary to be pragmatic. Geraint's grip on the haft
eased and he slowly sheathed the knife. "We rode out to rescue
Sir Roger on the road from Shrewsbury to London, but there were
too many soldiers for us. That was two months since."

The priest took a deep breath, as if in relief that his life was no
longer in peril, and answered, "Fortunate, I would say, otherwise
you and Sir Edmund also might be in the Tower or hanged from
Shrewsbury gibbet by now. We have heard some rumour of a skirmish north of York. Is that where you have come from?"

"*Skirmish!*" So they knew little as yet. "Bloody slaughter, more
like. My lord of Hereford is slain and Thomas, Earl of Lancaster,
is claiming sanctuary in Boroughbridge church."

"God protect him!" The priest fervently crossed himself. Even
though the weapon was put away, he raised his eyes to Geraint
with new respect and a great deal more apprehension. "Do you
know who else led the rebel lords, my son? Was Sir Roger Clifford
among them?"

Of course, *down the road lies Skipton*. Geraint realised he was
hard by the demesne of the Cliffords, the great lords in these parts.
Surely then the king's men would search all the harder in these
dales. Clifford and his men—any of the fortunate wretches who
survived—might flee this way.

"Clifford is a man of massive height, taller even than yourself,
married to my lord of Hereford's daughter," the priest was saying.

"I believe he was with my lord of Hereford, but whether he escaped..." Geraint swallowed painfully. "I fear the king will wreak sore vengeance on all those taken prisoner. God's mercy, we only escaped by the skin of our teeth and then our company was set upon by bounty hunters just east of Ripon. If Edmund is caught and accused of treason, it will go ill for his father in the Tower."

"Then better he lie low at the healer's... if he lives out the night. You also, young man, you look as though a sparrow could topple you, big as you are." Or an ancient priest might!

"This holy widow, can she be trusted?"

"As God is my witness, yes. And if any mortal can mend him, she can." The cleric's heavily lidded eyes glittered with sagacity now. "You will have to trust us, won't you?"

Three

THREE DOGS IN A VARIETY OF SIZES HARANGUED HIM and sniffed suspiciously at his heels as Geraint warily followed the priest Gilbert into the dwelling of the woman Christiana. The inevitable smoky smell that met him surprisingly carried no obnoxious tallow vapours and it was reassuring to see that the earth floor was clean. The only extravagance was the costly beeswax candle, no doubt a gift from the faithful, squatting stolidly on a small table. Vellum and quills were neatly set out around the candle holder.

Before he had a chance for further observations a scrap of a woman stepped out from behind the door. Grey braids on either side of her head, neatly coiled like a noblewoman's, showed beneath the folds of a blue headdress as clean as those in any painting of Our Lady, and her kirtle, dark as yew needles, hung in sober folds. A simple silver cross, the length of a finger, rose and fell upon her bosom.

"How is a body to write her revelations with continual interruptions?" she demanded, brown eyes, round and shining like wet river pebbles, glaring at her visitors. Geraint's jaw slackened. Revelations! This Christiana must rate herself immodestly high to have the temerity to set herself such a task. A literate woman!

As if she sensed him judging her, the old dame sucked in her cheeks and lifted her chin in challenge.

"Why are you back, Gilbert? Come to see if I practise the black arts by night, have you?" And as if to add a macabre quality to her humour, a black bird flapped from the rafters, startling Geraint into crossing himself. "Ha, this is Jack. You have frightened the handsome young man, Jackie." The jackdaw fixed one eye speculatively on Geraint as it settled on her shoulder and then scratched its grey nape thoughtfully.

Father Gilbert chuckled. "Well, you have familiars in plenty if ever I want to petition the archbishop," he countered, firmly stopping her from latching the door. "I am here because this scholar needs your healing and we also have a wounded man out there slung between our horses."

"Excellent," muttered the widow shrewishly. "That must have done his hurts a power of good. Special, is he?" She took up the candle. "Did my lady bid you come?"

The men followed her out. "She knows of this, yes." The priest instantly sensed Geraint's angry reaction and swiftly set a reassuring hand on his good shoulder, adding, "But we require your discretion, Christiana."

"Do you now?" She marched across to the pole stretcher where they had lain it on the ground. "He is not her leman, is he?" The priest gave a grunt of disapproval but Christiana continued undeterred. "No?" She surveyed Edmund by the candle's light. He was swaddled tight as a fly in a spider's web. "Hmm, too green a codling, from the look of him. Well, do not stand there like drones, the pair of you. Fetch him in."

Once they had laid Edmund on her palliasse, she gave Gilbert the candle and ran gnarled hands exploratively over the young man. "Hunting accident? Or has there been a battle?" Her gaze, thick with curiosity, swung from the priest's face to the stranger's.

Geraint met her piercing inquisition. Given the light, feeble though it was, it was necessary to try for an honest expression. "I would prefer not to have to lie to you, good dame."

"Can you save him?" Father Gilbert interrupted. "My lady would be pleased if you would care for him and the lad here."

Christiana's antennae must have sensed Geraint's irritation at being referred to as a lad. "Hunting accident for you too, *boy*?" she asked, her harsh voice larded with sarcasm, and, not bothering for his answer, pressed her fingers against the side of Edmund's throat. "Hold the candle here for me." Then her eyes flickered over Geraint once more. "Care for the pair of 'em? Oh, no, of course not," she added waspishly. "Let her magnificence send the king and his court as well. What matter if it pleases me not one whit. I request to be left alone yet every stray dog, two-legged and otherwise, comes whining. Bring the poxy light closer!"

" 'A soft answer turneth away wrath,' " snarled Father Gilbert. "Have done with this prattle."

"Do not dare quote at me, sir priest! Have I broomed these boys from my threshold? No, I have not." She pulled down the skin beneath one of Edmund's eyes and inspected its colouring.

"Well?" asked the priest as she finally straightened up.

"I will do what I can." She swung round on Geraint. "You, get your shirt off! What are you gawking at, lad? Over there, move the skull off the stool."

Geraint lifted what had probably been the inside scaffolding of a badger's head and set it beside the hearth next to two other skulls. Did she grind them for potions, he wondered, as he sat down with a weary sigh.

"Well, uncover yourself, scholar, or are you expecting me to play your nursemaid?" He felt the blood heating his cheeks and fumbled at his belt. The effort of freeing himself from his tunic made him swear and Father Gilbert came to his aid.

"You should minister to my companion's wounds first, dame."

"Nay, boy, let me see what mischief you have suffered. I want you to gather wood and stoke the fire. We shall need hot water to cleanse the pair of you."

"I shall do that." Father Gilbert lit a taper from the candle, grabbed a wicker basket which stood by the hearth and went out.

"My eyes are not so good by candlelight, but I will do what I can."

Geraint surrendered to Christiana's skilful prodding like a tired child, relieved to have someone else make the decisions for a little space.

"When did this happen?"

"Two days ago, I think." Was that all?

"Like that, is it, my handsome? Well, a good night's sleep will sort you out and cleanse your memory. I am sure you will think up a good tale to tell me in the morning." Her voice lost its levity. "What was it damaged your shoulder? You can lie through your fine white teeth but see sense; if I know what I am dealing with, I might be able to heal you faster."

Geraint hesitated. "The gash on my arm is from a pitchfork."

"And your other wound?"

"A flail," he answered softly.

Christiana gave an unladylike whistle. "Sits the wind in that quarter, eh? Plenty of enemies out there, have you?"

"No, that was done by one of my own side." He trapped her hands, forcing her to look him in the face. "Will my companion live?"

She wriggled her fingers free from his grasp.

"No," she answered. "I very much doubt it."

BEFURRED AGAINST THE CHILL DAMP, HIS COLLAR RAISED LIKE A DE-mon's hood, Fulk signalled for the portcullis to be raised and handed Johanna into the litter that was waiting in the courtyard. He made no effort to tuck the coney fur rug about her thighs as if he was a dotard besotted with a young wife, but gave his hand to his youngest sister, Edyth, who, with her usual smug expression, seated herself beside Johanna.

"You never told me she was coming," Johanna blurted out. It would be a journey planned by the Devil; her sister-in-law's collared pet squirrel was already scrambling up its mistress's shoulder, cowering from Johanna's dog.

"Edyth will remind you of your duty, madam. And do not stay away long. I want you back the moment your father has agreed to dispatch the remainder of the money he owes me. Make sure my sister witnesses his consent." Johanna made no answer, ignoring him as she turned her little dog's attention from the squirrel and made Cob cosy upon her lap.

Fulk looked across her at his sister. "Remember what I told you, Edyth! Have others there besides. We may need them to give testimony."

"I am not a fool, brother," Edyth answered sharply, her glance directing Fulk's attention meaningfully to the dog.

"This creature stays." The tiny hound yelped in pain as her husband violently snatched him from Johanna's hands and flung him to the wet cobblestones where he cowered whimpering.

Johanna clenched her fists futilely and swallowed back the tears. Were there no depths that Fulk would not sink to? Last night and this morning had been further humiliations. She would have given the throne of England to scour his face with her fingernails in front of his servants, but Agnes was sitting pillion behind one of the escort ready to leave, and she did not dare risk losing her as well.

"Do try to behave decorously, Johanna," Fulk admonished, pinching her cheek with a nasty leer. "But you will not have much choice, will you?"

"God rot you, Fulk!" she whispered. It was all she dared.

He laughed and let fall the litter curtain.

"Lead on, Edgar." Another scourge to her back but one of which Fulk was probably unaware. Ever since she had arrived at Enderby, Edgar de Laverton, one of his knights, had been wickedly eyeing her like a polecat watching a squirrel. Damn Fulk! He was sending half her problems with her, but at least she would be free of him.

The litter swayed uncomfortably as the horses were whipped forwards and the squirrel, caught unawares, snagged her veil, landed unwelcome on her lap and bit her gloved thumb. It could have been a portent, thought Johanna gloomily, but as she heard the hooves of the packhorses clop behind them across the drawbridge, her spirits started to soar. It was like leaving Hell.

No one ever leaves Hell, her intellect reminded her. *If your father recovers, he will send you back. Only Fulk's death or yours will free you from this bondage. You are no better off than a villein.* No! Johanna protested silently. There has to be a way. *Men make the laws,* persisted the practical voice, adding pettily: *Besides, Fulk has your dog.*

Johanna lifted her chin resolutely as the wooden planks of the drawbridge were winched up behind them. Whatever it takes, she vowed, I am *never* going back.

GERAINT RAISED SURLY EYES HEAVENWARDS BEFORE SCHOOLING HIS gaze into a proper semblance of gratitude and humility at the arrival of the Lady of Conisthorpe next morning. He turned towards her, his arms spiky with kindling wood, feeling unkempt in her elegant presence.

Smiling, she set back her fur-lined hood with a hand gloved in Moorish leather and let her horse prance round towards him, delicately picking its hooves across the spangled grass. The sun glittered on the gemmed caul which held her hair close to the nape of her neck. A few strands of silvery hair glinted among the mass

of auburn pulled severely back into the snowy linen which framed
her high-boned cheeks and wilful chin.

"I said how is your companion?" she repeated, gazing down at
him from the saddle with all the grandeur of a formidable goddess
of plenty. "Is he mending?"

Geraint sighed, temporarily unloaded his armful into the lee of
the cottage wall and returned dutifully to take her palfrey's bridle.
"No, my lady, but he lives yet."

The lady made no answer but swung herself out of the saddle
and briskly strode towards the cottage, leaving him to play the
groom. He tethered the horse reluctantly, his mind bristling with
anxiety. Did she ride unaccompanied? he wondered, glancing uneasily round for her servants. How many knew of his presence?

He hastened after her, determined to have some answers and
found her giving Edmund a cursory inspection.

"So, you have kept him alive," she exclaimed, studying the
youth's face while giving the old dame's crinkled cheek a peck of
a kiss as if she was an ancient aunt. Perhaps she was.

"Just, God be praised," muttered the old woman, unmoved by
the perfumed embrace.

"I take it, if he recovers, he will not be fit to travel for a while."

"No, child."

"Excellent."

"*Madam?*" Geraint clenched his jaw.

She looked around the cottage as if making an inventory, but
her thoughts were obviously elsewhere. "I may have some work
for you, Gervase," she exclaimed, tapping her riding crop impatiently against her silken surcote, as if anxious to be gone. "I will
return tomorrow. Have you everything you require, Christiana?"

"Ha, apart from peace and solitude, you mean? More clean linen
for the dressings would be a blessing and healing moss too."

"Yes, of course, Christiana, I shall send a manservant for it and
you shall have your supplies by Father Gilbert's good grace after
noon."

"Madam." Geraint hastened out after her into the sunshine. She
was waiting for him to untie her horse for her. "I . . ." He wanted
to plead that she keep a still tongue.

"Yes?"

"Sure . . . surely it is perilous for you to ride without an escort, my lady. That outlaw who—"

"Oh, him." Her eyes sparkled, lingering on Geraint's still unshaven chin. "Do you take me for a fool, master scholar?"

"No, madam."

"My servants await me hard by, never fret." She looked back towards Christiana, waving her crop to encompass the cottage and the trees beyond. "You know what this place is?" Geraint shook his head, having observed little in yesterday's dusk. "It is a park for our deer. I have given Dame Christiana permission to dwell here where she may be in seclusion and devote herself to prayer and meditation. And since she detests visitors, my people have orders not to disturb her. My chaplain, Father Gilbert, who brought you here, comes to administer the Holy Sacrament to her twice a week." So she had fathomed him. "Does that set your mind at rest, *master scholar*?"

"Yes, my lady."

"How is your shoulder?"

"It mends, I thank you, but I fear my arm fares worse." Linen strips hid the inflamed flesh.

"Fortunately it is your left arm. I thought that since you claim yourself to be lettered," her gaze rose assessingly from his bootcaps to his collarbone, "you may assist Dame Christiana to write down her visions. Her hands often pain her, poor soul, so it will be a way for you to repay her for her charity. I take it that will be no difficulty?" From her tone, she thought him to be barely literate.

"No, madam." He saw surprise glitter in her eyes.

"Scholar indeed," she murmured. "Well, well, there is more to you than meets the eye. Your hands, sir."

He stared at her perplexed and then realised she was waiting for him to cup his fingers so she might place her foot on them and mount. In the saddle, she smiled down at him silkily and, with a flourish, unstrapped a saddle roll and tossed some clothing into his surprised arms.

"These will be a better fit, I trust."

He blinked at the tawny tunic and leather hose but before he could thank her, the palfrey was in full gallop up the path.

"A law unto herself, that one, now that his lordship is afflicted."

Christiana stood beside him, her hands on her hips, stretching her back.

"Afflicted?" Somehow it had not occurred to Geraint that Lady Constance was still a married woman. Could she have told her husband about himself and Edmund? "What is wrong with her lord then?" Leprosy, the crabs, the crippling stiffness that came with age?

"Seems Lord Alan has been smitten by God. Lost his speech completely, she reckons, besides the sense all down his right side."

"How long since?"

"A week, maybe less."

"And is there aught you can do?"

Christiana shook her head. "God's will. These things happen." She poked a bony finger into his back. "Now neither you nor I have time to waste in idle gossip." She peered up the track that Lady Constance had taken. "Keep your nose out of it, that's what I say, master scholar. Let Lady Constance mind her own affairs."

"Aye, and not mine," Geraint added fervently.

FOUR

T HE ENDERBY ESCORT, WASP-LIKE IN THEIR BLACK and yellow livery, sounded their horns as they approached the archway of the Conisthorpe barbican and the castle clarions answered shrilly. Pulling back the litter's curtain, Johanna was heartened to see that the drawbridge was already lowered to welcome her home.

In the blink of a tearful eye, the inhabitants of the great jumble of dwellings within the bailey emptied into the courtyard like bees from a smoked treetrunk so that by the time Edgar de Laverton had dismounted and was assisting Johanna from the curtained folds of the litter with his predictable leering smile, a crowd of Conisthorpe servants, tasselled by an untidy row of jumping offspring and a garlanded pig, was waiting to receive her.

Amazed that her mother had preserved the pig for sentimental reasons, Johanna held a friendly gloved hand to its cautious snout, chucked one of the cleaner children under the chin and received a fistful of bruised primroses. She badly wanted to share her euphoria at being back with those familiar faces, but it was necessary to behave soberly and she was ashamed of setting back the fine Laon veil—she could barely see out of her left eye.

What alarmed her too was that the castle seemed to lack a sombre mien. God forgive her for hoping that the mighty Constable of Conisthorpe was still ailing to death. It was selfish, despicable and she would fall into Hell faster than a penny down a well, but her bruised face throbbed and she knew if her father's health had returned, he would send her back to Enderby—without the remainder of her dower.

"Sweetheart." Her uninhibited mother was hurrying down from the steps of the new hall as fast as her skirts would allow. Most noble ladies waited by the door to be kissed unemotionally but the Lady of Conisthorpe made her own laws. She threw her arms about Johanna and then let go, masking her dismay, as she sensed resistance.

Johanna desperately wanted to feel her warmth and strength, but not a word of compassion had been sent to her during the exile at Enderby and her mother's silence had left her cautious and resentful.

"What is the matter?" Constance whispered, stepping back.

"Oh, it is good to be home." Johanna's voice was brittle. Lifting her skirts, she mounted the steps ahead of her mother and then turned.

Her mother stood transfixed on the lower step, unusually bereft of words, staring at her as if she had suddenly sprouted wool and a pair of curly horns. Perhaps she was wrong, Johanna thought, mayhap her letters had never reached Conisthorpe.

"Johanna." Pearls of moisture formed and sparkled on her mother's lashes. So she had been missed.

"I feel as though I have been away a millennium, madam," Johanna offered softly as a concession.

Encouraged, her parent took a step up and stretched out a hand to lift away the barrier of fabric.

"Not now," Johanna said swiftly with deceptive lightheartedness, glancing meaningfully at the litter to distract her. Forehead puckering, Lady Constance obediently turned to have her attention instantly snared by the emergence of Edyth, complete with squirrel, into the courtyard.

"By all the Saints, did you have to bring *her*?"

In less fragile humour, Johanna would have enjoyed her parent's expression.

"Oh, *he* sent her to report on me. She is like a dag of mud, sticking to my life. Perhaps we can find a bucket somewhere."

Her mother raised an eyebrow, took a deep breath, rearranged her features in a vacuous smile, and sailed down to greet Edyth somewhat fulsomely.

It was wonderful to have an ally again; since Edyth was not expected and there was no bedchamber to tidy her into, Johanna's organising mother deftly manoeuvred the Conisthorpe chaplain, Father Gilbert, into conducting their guest around the gardens, giving orders that he was to point out the features, *all* the features. Then, after conducting Johanna to one of the bedchambers built above the new hall, her mother hastened off to deal with the remainder of the visiting entourage and to warn them they were expected to return to Enderby next day.

Wanting to feel herself a maid again, Johanna unlooped the cream silk barbette that tethered her pearled headband, discarded her veil and unpinned the dark plaits from her aching head.

"Shall I rebraid it loosely for you, my lady?" Agnes asked hopefully as her mistress restored anarchy to the regimented tresses.

Johanna shook her head and opened the casement. She stood idly watching the river below tumbling over the broad fall. The cold breath of wind from the soaring moors that gilded the edge of this little world was a physical reassurance. She was home, the comforting familiarity of Conisthorpe no longer an insubstantial dream before waking. Tears might serve now; words were beyond her. Nor could she sum up in any way how much she valued this innocent, haphazard concurrence of hill and dale stretching before her from the steep cliff. It was not just the poetic grandeur of moving shadows of cloud dappling the hillsides which filled her soul, the land's prosaic aspect gave her pleasure: the narrow timber bridge with a queue of mules and carts on the town side deferentially waiting for her father's bailiff to ride across and the uncontrolled scatter of weavers' houses beyond. Even the wire interacing of winter branches necklacing the river banks pleased her.

But the comforting peace before her could not yet erase the suffering of the last months. She was safe here, but she could not drive the thoughts of her little dog and those who had served her well at Enderby from her mind. Who would have a care for Cob? And what of Barnabas, the little page who was always incurring Fulk's wrath? At Yuletide when the child had clumsily spilt the best Bordeaux over her husband's finest clothes, Johanna had grabbed the other end of the stick and refused to let him beat the boy. Only by agreeing to fast for two days as penance for the child, had she managed to persuade Fulk to spare him.

Behind her in the bedchamber, Agnes busied herself unpacking the few kirtles brought from Enderby. To have packed all would have aroused Fulk's suspicion.

"Johanna?" Her mother, returning, spoke from the threshold without her usual certainty.

Her daughter latched the casement, closing off the valley behind the translucent lozenges of cloudy glass, and slowly turned. She saw the horror of her appearance reflected in her mother's appalled expression.

"God Almighty!" exclaimed Lady Constance, crossing herself. She came across to Johanna, one hand clasped to her mouth. "Oh my darling," she whispered, "is it hurting?"

"Every bit of me is hurting," answered Johanna coldly. She came swiftly to the crux of her resentment. "Why did you not write?"

"But I did." Constance raised a hesitant hand to touch her daughter and let it fall unwelcomed. "You are assuming—" She paced away and turned, "Indeed, you should have had, let me see," she tapped her fingers against her skirts, "yes, half a dozen letters. I dictated them to Father Gilbert. Ask him if you do not believe me."

Her daughter shook her head in despair. Fulk or Edyth must have prevented the letters reaching her.

"Oh, lambkin." Her mother, understanding, opened her arms and Johanna threw herself into them, the tears gushing up as if she simmered inside with sorrow.

"It has been dreadful, madam, dreadful. Ask Agnes. If only you knew how good it is to be home, to be free."

"Aye," Agnes sniffed, "will you look at my lady, madam, thin as a bodkin and nigh blinded by that excrescent."

"Excrescence, Agnes," corrected Lady Constance, distractedly patting her daughter's back.

It was wonderful to be held by loving hands. For a little space, the demons in Johanna's life were muzzled and she wept out the anguish. Eventually she stilled and drew back, mopping the tears away with a sodden kerchief.

"So, is he dead yet, the tyrant that yoked me to that fiend?" She watched her mother wince at the bitterness in her voice.

"You mean your poor father?"

"My father who always swore he loved me. I suppose he thought I exaggerated in my complaints. It is a pity he had to be dying for you to bring me home."

Her mother's defensiveness gave way to self-congratulation. "But I have managed it! You are here, are you not?" Johanna stared at her resentfully and Constance went on hurriedly: "As God is my witness, child, I tried before, but my lord brushed aside every reason I could find: 'The marriage must be given time to work.' " she mimicked. " 'You have turned the girl into a milksop. It will do her good to learn obedience, she is too wilful.' You know what he is . . . was like."

"*Was!*" Johanna stared at her. "Was? Then, in God's Name, tell me what ails him! How close is he to making Satan suffer his abominable company?"

Lady Constance saddened. "He is not dying and yet—"

Panic streaked again through Johanna. If need be, she would lock this chamber door and take her own life. Her fingers curled into claws of frustration. "God give me strength!" she exclaimed, addressing the stars daubed on the whitewashed ceiling. "Surely you are either dying or you are not."

"No, you see, my darling, it is some kind of visitation. It was . . ." Her mother shrugged, her palms open and lifted as if she trusted the Almighty might just deposit the right words into them. "Johanna, it . . . was as a thunderbolt. One instant . . . What *is* the matter?"

Conscious that she was staring openmouthed at her parent, Johanna pressed her lips together and tried to suppress the desire to grab up her skirts and rush to the chapel to give God an exuberant thank-you.

Her mother's one-must-make-allowances expression dissipated. "Your father had been riding all day with the new bailiff—some trouble with one of the villains at Kirkbridge—and he came back in good humour well before supper, striding into the hall calling for ale, hale as you please one moment, and in a thrice he had collapsed. There was nothing we could do. I sent to Skipton for the Cliffords' physician and the fellow came as soon as he might. But he said there is nothing to be done."

"So it is not a frenzy?"

"No, nothing of that sort. He is paralysed down one side and cannot speak."

Christ forgive her for being pleased but she could not mourn the loss of a loving father who had metamorphosed into a ranting tyrant and forced her, poor fool, to believe that marriage with the wealthy Fulk was better than imprisonment and daily beatings.

"Can he write?"

"What an odd question! I should not think so. Basically, my darling, it is not easy to know if the poor soul understands a word we say to him, and, to be honest, we have not thought of trying him with parchment yet, but his sword arm is certainly useless. Perhaps he may be capable of scratching a cross with his left hand eventually—if he makes any kind of recovery—but I doubt he will understand what he is doing. Oh, I have hardly come to terms with the situation myself. It happened but a week since and there has been so much to do. I wrote to your sister Petronella and Sir John but I expect she is too far gone with child to travel and I have not heard back from Sir John yet, but that is to be expected. And I assure you I sent for you straightway."

Johanna, feeling guilty for ever doubting her mother, reached out a hand and drew her close.

"Thank God you did, *Maman*," she whispered, bestowing a kiss upon her cheek, "and with such a message! Nothing else would have moved Fulk. I am only allowed back in order to acquire the rest of my dowry. That is why that wretched Edyth is here—to make sure I return with laden packhorses. Damn them both! Go and spy out where she is now, Agnes. That cursed woman is a cat on human legs."

Her mother sat down on the high bed with a sigh. Johanna paced to the window and stood stroking her finger down the carving. "You have to help me, *Maman*. I *cannot* return. Should my father recover his wits . . ."

Her mother lifted a kirtle from a half-emptied coffer, one that carried her own stitching, and absent-mindedly fingered the soft silk.

"*If* ever he does. Dame Christiana reckons it might take him years, if at all. Mind, she has not seen him, but the physician said the same." She laid the garment upon the bed. "You shall not go back, I promise you."

"But what can we do against Fulk? He will send for me within the week or come himself to see why I have not returned. Do you think if I ride to the Benedictine nuns at the Priory of St. Clement in York, the nuns will give me protection? I will gladly take holy vows there. If I never set eyes on another man as long as I live, it will not bother me."

"Oh, Johanna, you addlepate, that will not serve. Did not Fulk remark at your wedding feast that the prioress, Agnes de Methelay, is some distant kinswoman? Of course there are the Cistercians but if you have truly set your heart on the cloister, you would be better to go to one of the great abbeys in the south out of Fulk's reach. What better than Shaftesbury? I know the abbess, Margaret Aucher."

"Then, please, no time must be lost. Pray, could you write to her this afternoon on my behalf?"

Her mother paced to the door, her fingertips a steeple at her lips. "Yes, I could do that, certainly, but I have another notion. You may not like the sound of it but I . . . I believe there is an alternative way, except it will require another's help."

Not all her mother's enterprises worked, but Johanna was now a creature tumbled into an unmapped marsh, grabbing at any lifeline. She sped across and gently shook her mother's shoulders. "Tell me of it then, *Maman*. What must I do?"

Lady Constance set her aside. "Give me until tomorrow noon— Oh!" The door ring turned in her hand, lifting the latch, and Edyth marched in unannounced, an embarrassed Agnes at her heels. She lifted her pointed chin at Johanna.

"Skulking, sister? Should we not go and see your father about what is owing? The chaplain tells me that he is not to be shriven after all and . . . Oh, madam, I . . . ."

"Did you think my mother was a tiring woman to be opening doors for you, Edyth?"

"My lady, I—I beg your pardon." Edyth managed an almost apologetic obeisance.

"I think it inappropriate for you to trouble Lord Alan at the moment, Edyth. Perhaps tomorrow before you leave." Lady Constance waited a heartbeat for their guest to soak in her meaning and added sweetly, "It was kind of you to accompany Johanna, but I am sure you are needed at Enderby to play the chatelaine in my daughter's absence."

Her words were like drops of water on duck feathers; Edyth was not at all ruffled. "Oh, I have already discussed that with my brother and it is decided that I shall stay here until Johanna is ready to return."

Her sister-in-law bit back a retort and lifted an eyebrow at her mother.

"Excuse me," answered Lady Constance, sweeping round Edyth in a stately manner. She paused and turned, framed like an altarpiece in the doorway. "I have just had a good idea," she told Johanna, "and . . ." She hesitated, smiling broadly at her unwelcome guest.

"And, madam?" Edyth prompted, frowning.

"And I have to find a bucket."

LADY CONSTANCE SEEMED TO FILL DAME CHRISTIANA'S DWELLING with her restless presence. A few moments earlier Geraint had started up from Edmund's bedside, drawing his knife at the sound of hooves. Now he was relieved to learn it was only the Lady of Conisthorpe. The disruption, however, was tiresome; he had spent the morning happily carrying out chores for the old lady, trying to forget that there was a world beyond the deer park, a world where he was hunted.

"Dame Christiana is out herb-gathering, madam. Do you want me to give her a message?"

The lady prowled, glancing at the parchment he had been working on earlier and prying into a stoneware pitcher but her gaze eventually returned to him. She studied him thoughtfully and then declared, "I mentioned yesterday that I had work for you. Is he any better?" She lifted her jaw indicating Edmund.

"No, madam." How much did she know? Had Father Gilbert told her of Edmund's parentage?

"Come, let us go outside. All these skulls, ughh. Oh, Dame Christiana, you are back." She helped the old lady free her arms from a basket laden with nettles and hedge parsley. "How can you possibly tolerate all these bones? What is that? A sloughed snake-skin?"

"Vipers are no worse than some as is living."

"I hope you are not including me, you old besom, for I will not be sending you some of the latest batch of cheeses nor a firkin of ale if you are. Come, Gervase, we have matters to discuss."

"Do not go inviting the lad to your bed," cackled Christiana, "he will wear you as thin as a poor man's soles. Bah, go and be secretive, see if I care."

Geraint reddened as he followed Lady Constance out. The bawdy exchange at his expense was disconcerting. Dame Christiana's protectress was sufficient in years to be his mother and she certainly eyed him with an older woman's brazen freedom.

The lady led him beyond eavesdropping distance of the old dame who fetched out a stool and plonked herself down on it in the sunshine, watching as if to chaperone them.

"That tunic fits you better." The lady's green eyes teased him. He might have known she would ask more than gratitude.

"So, how may I serve you?" he asked brusquely, hoping his tone might dampen any ardour on her part.

"Oh, not me," she answered softly. "I have a daughter. Four, in fact." Geraint groaned inwardly. Not more women. It was bad enow dealing with a scolding mystic and this capricious lady of the manor without further mischief.

"My youngest daughter has a problem."

Do we not all? he thought, witheringly. "*Is* or has, madam?"

She ignored his sarcasm. "Well, it used to be *is*, but she is now wed to a stonyflint who abuses her right cruelly."

Already unstabled by Christiana's bawdy jesting, Geraint's thoughts galloped to an unwelcome conclusion. "I hope . . . I trust you are not . . ."

"Suggesting that you *amuse* her, master scholar? Oh no, more desperate than that." Her voice lost a little of its humour.

"Desperate?" It was necessary to make his position plain. "I do not hire myself out like a stallion, Lady Constance."

To his relief, she laughed. "Climb off your high horse, master. I thought you a humble bookworm and here you are making far too many assumptions." She held a cautioning forefinger up to silence him. "Do not premeditate me further. As I said, her husband, Sir Fulk, is very cruel to her. I love Johanna dearly and I cannot bear to see her suffer. I want to sever these marital fetters and to do this I require a man who is, like yourself, unwed." He felt like hiding his hands but she had already observed he wore no betrothal ring. "To come to the point, Gervase de Laval, I want you to swear before an ecclesiastic court that you plighted your troth to my daughter before she married Sir Fulk."

Geraint was rarely short of an answer, but she had winded him. "Perjure myself, you mean?" he spluttered finally.

Why did this have to happen? He was in trouble enow without this added complexity.

She smiled. "I require merely words not deeds, young man. Are a few extra weeks in Purgatory too costly? Not only will you be freeing another soul from a present torment but you will emerge with your celibacy intact."

He would be saying no, of course, but it did not hurt to prolong the conversation or sate his curiosity. Besides, he might have heard of the husband. It would give him some inkling as to where the danger might lie in this shire. "Tell me more about this Sir Fulk."

"Sir Fulk de Enderby. His demesne lies a day's journey on an ambling horse from here. Not as wealthy as our family. His castle is older than Conisthorpe. Round keep, you know the sort, built around the time of the first Henry. He is older than my Johanna by some thirty years. He was a companion of my lord's in the wars against Scotland yet a dissembler. I thought him amiable but . . ." Her voice dropped, "Johanna always was wilful but he beats her daily."

"I feel sorry for her but it is not against the law for husbands to chastise their wives."

"Do you doubt my judgment?" He read the steel will in her eyes; she did not like to be thwarted.

Geraint shook his head, wary at her sudden change of tone, but he would be damned if he became embroiled in her scheme. God protect him! The High Sheriff of Yorkshire, not to mention every bailiff and bounty hunter between Berwick and Bristol, was scouring every cranny that might hide a rebel from Boroughbridge. No! If she shot at this target from every angle, the arrow would not stick.

"What would you have me do, madam? Walk into this Fulk's

hall and say, 'I am a poor scholar who took your wife's maiden-head before you married her and I have just remembered I want her back'?"

"Something like that, but far easier. She has just returned to Conisthorpe."

"With her husband?"

"No." She raised a hopeful eyebrow.

"No, my lady, I am sorry but it will not wash. Dear God, madam, I am just a scholar. The husband will skewer me like a fish before the matter even reaches the nearest bishop's ears."

"A few days of dissembling is all I ask. The archdeacon's court is due in Conisthorpe within a week."

He gazed at her in horror. "You cannot be serious, lady. It is a case for the bishop. No archdeacon would dare touch a marriage dispute between the nobility." He ran a hand through his hair. "By all the Saints, madam, your whole notion is incredible. As if your daughter would mire herself to wed a schoolmaster with no prospects."

She tried again. "It could work. You are a stranger, that is crucial, and of pleasing appearance—enough to turn a young woman's heart. And I am sure you are learned enough to plead your case. There is no one else I can think upon and if I do not use this chance that God has sent me . . ." She shook her head sadly, pacing away from him. Then she turned. "Johanna threatens to take her life if I send her back. You are our only hope. God has sent you for this purpose, I know it." Her eyes glittered with unshed tears, her mouth twisted beseechingly.

"Well, the Almighty never consulted me," muttered Geraint. "And my answer is no."

Lady Constance took an angry breath and he braced himself. Now that the cajoling had failed, he expected her to have an arsenal of threats ready to catapult. God in Heaven! If this cursed woman only knew who he really was, she would not have the audacity to rattle on.

"My lady, there are matters you do not understand. I would help you if I could, but . . ."

"You would leave the shire afterwards, of course. Johanna would not expect you to remain. All we need is for the church to dissolve this marriage. A week and an oath is all we ask of you."

"If it were within my power . . ."

The face she turned to him was adamantine. "I know who *he* is." She jerked her head towards the dwelling. "And you, whoever you are, why, you are no more a scholar than I am a fisherwife. Let me be plain, young man, unless you do as I ask, I will send a messenger posthaste to the king. I believe he stays at York. It is not very far."

Geraint took a deep breath. "I have a knife, my lady. I will kill to keep the heir of Sir Roger Mortimer safe and I shall not hesitate to take your life and the old woman's."

"You will not travel far with a dying man and my palfrey will be recognised."

"I will have to risk both."

"Oh dear," she said gently. "But what if he dies before tomorrow? Will you change your mind? You shall be paid handsomely. Costly tastes, hmm?" Her glance provocatively slid over his boots.

He regarded her unhappily. Women were supposed to know their place; they were supposed to be ineffectual, gentle creatures, bearers of babes and, well, chattels that must be protected. The last thing he wanted was to have to kill this lady and the healer in cold blood. By Christ, if he did, every man within the shire would be hunting him before sunrise.

"What is the penalty for treason against the king?" she prompted softly. "They will half-hang you, then they will cut you down and draw out your entrails—"

"Exactly. And what is more, if they catch me, they will take Edmund. If they convict him, they will take his father outside to Tower Hill and—Dear God, my lady, would you have the hanging of so great a man as Sir Roger Mortimer on your conscience?"

"Would you have my daughter's death on yours?" He turned away from her, his arms folded sternly. "Please," she pleaded, all pride and menace emptied from her voice.

Geraint swallowed. A pity Edmund was not close to recovery. He needed time. If only he could get the lad safely away.

"I will think upon't, my lady. Give me a day to consider. I cannot run far with a dying man."

"But you can run far on your own." Her voice sank to a whisper, "If you abandon him, I swear I will turn him over to the high sheriff, alive or dead." Her expression grew more adamant with every heartbeat. "You have no choice! You have to do it!"

Five

"MOTHER, ARE YOU OUT OF YOUR WITS?" Johanna sank onto the linen chest in her mother's chamber after midday dinner, her thoughts whirling like blown windmill sails. She regarded Lady Constance scathingly. "Am I to understand that you opportuned some man of unknown origin in the wild wood this morning and offered him money to be my husband! Jesu, madam, the knave might be blabbing the tale out to half the shire by now if he has sufficient ale to make his tongue gallop. What possessed you?"

"Your wellbeing for a start," muttered her mother reproachfully, "and I did not opportune him. We first met a few days ago when he tried to rob Father Gilbert."

Johanna's eyes widened further. For an instant, she could not find words to clothe her feelings. "Only *tried*!" she exclaimed. "Jesu preserve me, now you are admitting he is not only an outlaw but a stupid one as well."

Her parent sniffed defensively. "He is a poor scholar and he was desperately hungry." Was that supposed to make her feel more comfortable about the fellow?

"And a failed one, by the smell of it." Johanna rose and paced between the bed and door. Lady Constance of Conisthorpe was not usually so reckless. Certainly she ordered the demesne as skilfully as Lord Alan ever had and for the most part she chose her servants well. But had this outlaw a silvery tongue and a cheerful eye? She would wager he had cajoled his way into her mother's goodwill.

"And another thing." Johanna swung round. "Why is this scholar of yours not tutoring some rich man's sons or employed honestly as a schoolmaster? What was he doing apart from trying to rob old churchmen? Poaching our deer?"

Catching Johanna's hands in hers, her mother exclaimed, "I am not such a fool as you think me. This man will serve our purpose, trust me. Where else can I find a stranger so swiftly, one who is willing to swear that he married you before Fulk did?"

Johanna tugged her fingers away. "Do you truly realise the enormity of what you are saying? You have asked some incompetent trickster to come and pose as my husband. Think about it, madam. Why would a woman of my status have espoused myself to a poor scholar?"

"You could swear you fell in love. Besides, you have yet to meet him. You are judging the wine before you taste it."

"Of course I am." Johanna flung up her hands like birds panicked into flight. "I would not even buy this vinegary wine in the first place." She gave an angry sigh and gathered up her sewing and silks.

"Supposing I were to arrange for you to meet him, Johanna?" Her mother reached out a staying hand. "No, listen, go and bathe your face at St. Robert's spring early tomorrow morning. This young man can meet you there. *Then* tell me yea or nay."

"What, go to the wood to be assaulted? Out of one cooking pot into another."

Her mother met Johanna's outraged glare undeterred. "Father Gilbert can accompany you. He knows the scholar already."

"The chaplain is embroiled in this?" That reined in Johanna's galloping indignation. She folded her lips, pensively gathering the embroidery to her breast. What harm might it do? The old courage in her struggled for air. "I was thinking of visiting the holy spring anyway. It may help my bruises heal faster." Then she sighed, "But it will not do. Edyth will insist on accompanying me like a shadow."

"I will warn the man." Lady Constance began to unpin her veil. "I had better make haste if I am to let him know this afternoon. I hope he will agree to this. To be honest, he is not exactly enthralled by my plan any more than you are." That was scant relief.

"But the jingle of gold, of course, is loosening the straps that bind his conscience."

"You are probably right, lambkin. Where is my cap?" She searched though the untidy pile of garments on her bed. "I am thankful you are being co-operative at last. This man will be perfect for our purpose, and let us face the facts, Johanna, we are beggars and must ride whatever horse we can in this matter."

"Mother, he is a beggar and will ride us if we let him."

THE FIRST THINGS GERAINT NOTICED ABOUT THE MAN WHO HAD SUDdenly materialised out of the forest to annoy Dame Christiana were that the span between his shoulders and head could be hardly called a neck and that his skin was the hue of a brown egg. In fact one could suspect God of having pressed his thumb on the fellow's head to stop him growing an extra span before dropping him into a dyer's vat.

The knave was almost dancing before the old dame as she sought to circumnavigate him and reach the peace of her hut. Geraint could have easily made his presence felt and sent the wretch sprawling on his way with a cuff on the ear, but he was curious to see who would best whom in this encounter. As well, a strong instinct told him that he had seen the fellow before in some market place, probably seducing housewives into buying lotions that would mend anything from sore breasts to styes. The rogue's maturity—he must have seen some thirty winters to judge by his thinning brown hair and the ploughlines of his brow as he removed his beaked hat—not to mention his tenacity and particularly good clothes were sufficient to proclaim his character, and such a charlatan was the last kind of traveller Geraint wanted to see straying over the holy widow's doorstep or poking his nose into others' business.

"Give me employment, sweet madam," the man was pleading. "I chop wood exquisitely, herd cows according to the laws of Pythagoras, discuss metaphysics with sheep, juggle, tumble, recite scurrilous ballads and I have an uncommon hand." He waggled it, and then as if it were an embarrassment, hid it behind his back with an apologetic shrug.

Christiana's glance could have scythed him. "Can you tie knots

in your tongue?" Like partners in a dance, they reached the dwelling's threshold together.

"No, good dame."

"Pity." Christiana closed the door fiercely on his piked toe.

"Ow! For shame, mistress, a crust of bread and I will be gone
in a trice."

"Nay, feed you and you will hang like a bad smell in the air
for days." She tried to push the door closed but the man kept his
foot in place.

"Sweet mistress, surely, living here on your own, you lack for
company and those hands would be fairer for another's labour.
Ouch!"

The woman now had the rogue by the ear but he was wriggling
hard and Geraint moved into view, reluctant to reveal his presence, but he could not chance the dame receiving any hurt.

His large and sudden appearance stifled the fellow's bravado,
but only momentarily. "For pity, master, bid your wife let me go.
My mother said my ears were long enough."

"Wife!" exclaimed Geraint and Christiana in unison.

"Is she not your wife, sir? For I never saw such a fair and comely
wench. Desist, my lovely one. Ow!" Another clout caught the
knave's ear.

Geraint started laughing as the man sank to the ground with
legs crossed, his hands cradling his head to ward off further blows.

"What are you, besides a good-for-nothing?" Geraint asked as
he set his arm protectively round the old dame's shoulders. He
was appreciative of the man's wit. Give the creature his due, nothing else had made him smile since Boroughbridge.

"I would be flattered if you thought me a fool but alas, sir, as
you say, I am good-for-nothing, a vagabond."

"So what can you truly do besides let your tongue run amok?"
Christiana folded her arms and inspected him.

"Do?" exclaimed the fellow, falling onto his knees with a hopeful doglike expression. "I grovel, I plead, I say prayers that God
will send generous, charitable folk to succour me and keep me
from the Devil."

"Where are you from?" Geraint asked, his curiosity aroused.
The man's dialect was southern, Kentish perhaps.

"I was born in the shadow of the Conqueror's tower, master, and have truly walked in shadows ever since, aping my betters."

"Ah, send him on his way, lad," muttered Christiana to Geraint, tossing her hands in the air. "You will never get an answer out of this one that is not tarnished with falsehood. You worm, be gone!" She disappeared into her cottage. The door closed emphatically.

The man climbed to his feet, fastidiously brushing the dags of dirt from hose that betrayed no mending. The gesture stirred a memory. Had he said "fool?"

"By Heaven, now I know who you are," exclaimed Geraint. "You are my lord of Lancaster's jester!"

The man's head jerked up in terror and he would have taken to his heels had Geraint not grabbed him more swiftly.

"How dare you accuse me of consorting with rebels!" shrilled the man, wriggling worm-like to free himself from the hold on his cape. "What would a jester be doing in this God-forsaken place? As for Lancaster, the world knows him as a traitor."

"Be still, you scoundrel!" snarled Geraint. "Do you think the king's men are bothered with the likes of you?"

"King Edward would readily shackle any who fought at Boroughbridge so I am told." The glares between them weakened into an understanding and Geraint slowly let him go although he was poised to prevent the fool's escape. Only the smaller man's hands writhing like mating adders betrayed his fear.

"The earl is an honourable man," Geraint commented softly.

The jester gulped and was silent, his gaze wandering like a blind man's fingers over his enemy's features. The fight seemed to go out of him and his shoulders sagged. "Oh, good sir, I went into battle for Lancaster, twice fool that I am." His voice was burnished with sorrow.

"You did?" Geraint grabbed him by the cape again. "What news of your lord then? Is he taken south to London and stowed with Sir Roger Mortimer?"

The small man stilled, his brown eyes fearful of his interrogator. "Has the news not whistled through the forest like an arrow?" he asked, swallowing nervously. "My master is taken in irons by boat to the king at York. They dragged him from the church at Boroughbridge, set my fool's cap upon him and hauled him up the high street to the river."

Geraint let him go with a mixture of disbelief and amazement.

The fool's glance zigzagged Geraint's stature from boots to collar. "I see the news displeases you, master."

"I too have come from Boroughbridge and if you have been less than honest with me . . ."

The jester scowled at him. "An excellent but foolhardy revelation worth much gold perhaps. You are a bigger fool than I to tell me so." Then he added gravely, "I thought none escaped, even those who shed their armour and stole women's skirts off hedges."

"Why did they let you go?"

He sighed. "The Carlisle men would have beaten me right sore in the churchyard when they took my fool's cap and bells but I made them laugh and they relented."

"In God's name, man, what were you doing in the battle lines?"

"I followed my lord like a faithful hound, but I'll not speak of it further." He gave an exquisite shudder.

"Oh yes you will if you want to keep body and soul together."

"Not this moment," pleaded the jester, and he sprang back, shedding his wistfulness like a wet dog shaking itself. "Let us blow this ship in a different direction. You are not what you seem, great one. Mayhap you need a servant."

Ah, there was a thought. The jester had yet to hear of holy springs, wilful wives and the formidable, scheming Lady Constance who had come riding in yet again after noon demanding Geraint's unquestioning compliance.

Seeing the wolfish grin, the fool was of a sudden disconcerted. "You do?" he asked, wary now.

"Oh yes."

"How do I look?"

Jankyn, the jester, pirouetted like a whore in a Southwark bathhouse. Geraint's discarded black hose, washed free of mud, were drawn tightly over his head and the ample scholarly tunic was belted round his middle.

"A true rogue," clucked Christiana. With slits cut for eyes the improvised hood looked sufficiently malevolent. It hid the fool's distinctive lack of neck and gave him a few extra inches. Not that he was puny, but if he was going to play an outlaw, he needed to look the part.

"And I?" asked Geraint, pulling down the black hood which Lady Constance had brought him.

"An improvement, sir."

"If we borrow the good Christiana's dagger and stick that in your belt as well, Jankyn, it might suffice."

"What, two daggers, sir? I will look like a cutler's stall."

Geraint shrugged. "Have it your own way. You are, of course, built like a Colossus and no one could dream of mistaking you for anything but the Robin Hood of Wharfedale." The withering remark was a mite unfair, but Jankyn of course did not know of his earlier baptism into outlawry and his humiliation at Father Gilbert's hands. He had decided to let the jester take the forward part. It offered him a better chance to observe the female bane named Lady Johanna, and the fool had a dexterity with words that would not go amiss.

"Thank you," declared Jankyn, ignoring the insult and waving his hand pretentiously in the manner of the king's favourite, the younger Hugh Despenser, only to find his new ally's right hand encompassing his throat.

"Have a care, man! I know who you ape. You could be gutted for such a jest."

"Aye, true, but then both you and I could be hanged for aping outlaws. What if we prey upon some other brigand's turf, that other woolly pelted wretch you met? And if some other strangers fly into our web, shall we rob them for practice?"

"We run—like the deer do."

"YOU INSISTED ON COMING, EDYTH, SO DO NOT GRUMBLE," JOHANNA cried over her shoulder, urging the mare faster with her heels. She deliberately left her two companions several lengths behind on the woodland track and turned off to the river path, anxious to be earlier than the stranger. St. Robert's spring was a magical place to her, one that she hated sharing, least of all now with Edyth. Although it was safer to have company, she desired a few moments of peace to pray in solitude.

Spiky wild garlic and sorrel dappled the wooded slopes and to her right the willow fronds fronting the river were trying to decide whether the sunlight was sufficient to risk their tender leaves. A few paces more and the well-trodden path narrowed. She dismounted, startling a pair of bramblings, and led her horse along to the small cleared glade where a fallen tree had been cut to make a foot bridge across a beck joining the river. It was an exhilarating feeling to be on her own, however briefly, but there was no time to dawdle. Swiftly tethering her horse to a beech sapling, she rewarded her with a withered Lenten apple and, lifting her skirts, crossed the bridge pigeonfooted.

As if in defiance of this holy place, some early toadstools had burst up, born unseasonably of the moist night, and these Johanna treated with respect, heartily wishing that the Queen of Elfland might carry her off to be her tiring woman. No, perhaps not even a comely Elfin king could heal her invisible scars but Saint Robert might listen. It was said that the hermit had seen a vision here in his wanderings as a youth before he became a monk at Fountains. His cave beside the Nidd at Knaresborough attracted pilgrims, but this holy spring was little known.

The path led down to where the river narrowed through a chasm and there the sun sparkled on the sacred gill bursting out of the bank. A withered garland of summer flowers, left over from dressing the well the previous Ascension Day, still clung to the tangle of undergrowth above the spring and there was a scattering of white petals fallen from the blackthorn thicket higher up the slope.

A local mason had carved the saint's head upon a stone slab and set it up beside the spring and here Johanna knelt to cup her hands, offering an unspoken prayer to the saint. The holy water was icy enough to freeze the bruises off her so she methodically splashed it up under her veil, then gasped in surprise as a man's arm coiled around her ribs and a palm came down across her mouth before she could scream a warning to the others.

As Edyth and the chaplain turned the corner into her view, a second, shorter man, hooded like an executioner, sprang out onto the path behind Father Gilbert, blocking their retreat.

"Here's sport, look you!" the shorter rogue declared in a Welsh voice, prodding the chaplain forward to where the path widened beside the spring. "What have we here? Ladies come to pray to Saint Rob to take away their pimples and give them beauty. But vanity is a sin, they say. You will look better without your jewels, demoiselles."

Edyth turned on him. "Cowards! Brigands! Attacking defence-
less women and a poor old priest."

"No wedding ring, my darling? Now I can see why you have
come to pray for beauty," lilted the Welsh voice. "Ask the saint
for the gift of silence too and you might find a brave husband,
look you." He was grinning broadly at his fellow ruffian.

This rough handling was not called for. And there were not
supposed to be two of them. What fools to pose as masked outlaws. She would not be able to make a proper judgment. Cursing,
Johanna drove her elbows backwards but her captor was tall
enough to evade her flailing fists. The Devil take him! The man
was made of rock. She could feel his body, hard as steel, pressing
into her back as she wriggled to free herself.

Geraint was enjoying the feel of the girl. This must be Lady
Johanna he was holding. The breasts that rested upon his forearm
were pert enough to keep their ripeness through childbearing but
of sufficient fullness for his taste and she fitted excellently against
him. It was a pity that the veil hid the lady's face. Thanks be to
the great multitude of saints that the other scrawny unwed woman
was not Lady Constance's daughter.

He swiftly revoked the prayer as the lady Johanna kicked him
hard in the kneecap with the heel of her boot and he almost kneed
her headfirst into the holy spring. He insinuated his right leg between hers so that she could not easily repeat her assault. That
halted the wench's squirming but then her fingers started unaccountably scrabbling for his dagger. With little choice, he freed the
lady's mouth so he might slap her hand away from his belt. The
dagger he drew himself and held it against her breast.

Johanna froze, not only terrified of the evil blade but also too
aware of the firm thigh and muscle pressing against her legs
through her kirtle. She would agree that the outlaws must not
arouse Edyth's suspicions, but this was unseemly.

Contending not only with a struggling wench, Geraint also
watched Jankyn anxiously. He had warned him about Father Gilbert's reputation with a staff, but the priest carried none and now
looked as mild as a lamb in a painting of the Nativity.

"Down, both of you, facedown." Jankyn waved the sword.

Father Gilbert fell to his knees, crossed himself and then lowered his forehead to the ground.

"No!" snapped Edyth. "I am not prostrating myself before any Welshman."

"Do it or Black John here will kill the wench."

Johanna stiffened as the man holding her thrust his dagger higher so that its tip was now pricking against her throat.

"Do as he says!" she squeaked, barely able to speak. She was of a sudden convinced that the man holding her might be a genuine outlaw.

Edyth sullenly prostrated herself and the short leader gleefully planted a foot on her back. "Would all English women behaved so." His eyes grinned at Johanna through the slits. "And you, sweetheart, now you."

The wretch was jerking his sword menacingly at the ground, indicating that she should grovel and it pleased her not one whit. How could her mother have bargained with such a rogue?

The great rapscallion holding Johanna let go of her. She backed away from him. Dear God, but he was huge and menacing in the hood. And—pox take him—who was he, this second man?

"What say you, Black John? Bind the priest, shall we, and let's have some rare sport."

The second man, who had held her, was studying Johanna through the sinister hood slits with an intensity that she found uncomfortable. Too flustered to stare further, she tumbled to her knees, swallowing anxiously. This was definitely not going as she had expected. The Welshman might be behaving boldly because of Edyth's unexpected presence, but the evil faceless appearance of the pair of them was whittling away her courage. She had expected to sum up her prospective bridegroom from his face and demeanour. Her mother must have been taken in by the rogue or maybe he had run away and these were real brigands.

"I had rather you killed me than raped me," she declared with a bravado that might evaporate in a thrice.

The shorter ruffian grinned at his companion before his eyes leered down at her. "Or we do both, look you." His swordpoint teased at the folds of her kirtle. Suddenly whether he was an authentic outlaw no longer concerned Johanna. His impudence was intolerable and there was no way in the world she would consent for him to play her husband.

"Go on, kill me!" she hissed. "I would welcome it. There is nothing to live for."

The leader seemed nonplussed for the moment, then he rallied. "Show us your face, lady, or are you as ugly as this one?"

Edyth gave a growl of protest but he toed her in the shoulder-blades.

"Oh, I need the holy water," Johanna declared vehemently, throwing back her veil.

The man lost his Welshness for a second in a ripe Anglo-Saxon exclamation. He stared at the disfiguring bruises, slackjawed, and looked to the one called Black John, who stood dumb as a scare-crow. She had shocked them. There was an uncomfortable silence.

Johanna bit her lip. Her mother's poor scholar was definitely out of his element and the other taller fellow was merely waiting for instructions.

"Here," she snarled. She tugged off her rings and tossed them at his toecaps. "Take my rings. I have no use for them. Any of them!" The wedding ring bounced off Edyth's back and rolled to a standstill at the large brigand's feet.

His gaze never wavering from her face, the Welsh outlaw stooped and scooped them up. The large ruffian ignored the golden band.

"And you might as well take my life too."

"No, my darling." The man had recovered his Welsh character. "It looks as though some English rogue attempted that. There is still some chivalry in this forest, look you. Let me see you to your horse."

Johanna struggled to her feet ignoring the fellow's proffered hand. In the glade, out of hearing of the others, she whirled round on him.

"Never tell me you are my mother's poor scholar."

Her tone was scathing. The short knave gulped beneath her glare.

"We come in all shapes and sizes at Oxford, my lady."

"This has been an utter waste of time and, besides, you were hopeless back there. You were supposed to rob us, not play the braggart."

The man called Black John came running down the path and

muttered something incomprehensible in Welsh, jerking his thumb to the trees rising up the hill.

"And you pick an empty-headed gormless fool for your accomplice," Johanna hissed. The large man's head jerked back as if she had struck him. "Leave Yorkshire! I do not want your services. Sell my rings. I will tell my mother I have paid you off. You could not convince a wench you are a man, let alone an archdeacon that you are a husband. Go!"

"Johanna." Edyth's voice reached them.

The big man took to his heels.

"Pardon, my lady," the Welshman muttered. "But—"

"Leave me, you fool. For the love of God, go!" He disappeared between the trees after his large companion, running nimbly.

"Johanna, are you unharmed?"

"Yes, Edyth, my wondrous beauty saved me."

"Johanna." There was almost contrition.

"Yes, Edyth." Johanna waited for the sympathy that might redeem Fulk's sister.

"You brought those beatings on yourself." It was disappointing. She had hoped a few days away from Enderby might give Edyth a fresh perspective. "And did you have to give those brigands your wedding ring? They might have been content with less."

"The Devil may have my rings and good riddance. Where on earth is poor Father Gilbert? Why did you not stay for him?"

"He tried to rise and swooned."

"Then in God's name, why are we tarrying?"

Johanna prayed as she gathered her muddied skirts and ran back to the spring, hoping the priest had been trying to delay Edyth and the turnsickness was but feigned. It was a relief to see him on his feet, but she still took his arm to steady him.

"I am well." He patted her hand. "The rogues did not harm you?"

"No, cowards both. They scampered the moment Edyth reappeared."

Yes, she was well rid of them. Inspecting the ground, she noted without regret that her wedding ring had disappeared. That was the only good portent.

Holy spring! She glared at the innocent bubbling water with

reproach. The saint had not been much help, for it was clear that her mother's plan could not possibly succeed.

GERAINT ATTACKED DAME CHRISTIANA'S FIREWOOD WITH SUCH FE-rocity that she asked if he was trying to reopen his wound and kill himself with his anger. She did not stay for an answer, but left him wiping the sweat off his brow with his sleeve.

Gormless, was he? Well, he would show her. No, he would not! He would leave Lady Johanna to wallow in her trouble rather than be entangled in the deceit and falsehoods. But the memory of the girl's cruel injuries and her shame at her hurts stayed with him. There had been truth in her plea for them to kill her and yet an instant later she had been scornful, abusing them. This Johanna had some courage even if she was too forward for a woman. May-hap her tongue had provoked her husband to lash out at her and yet she no longer cared for temporal things. *Take my rings*, she had said. Few women would have made such a gesture, but then she knew they were not outlaws. And yet . . . and yet.

When he had finally piled the wood outside the door, he stood, feeling empty and exposed as though he was a pot scourged with sand. Free me from this, Lord God, he pleaded, just as he had prayed in the monastery long ago for a way out of the dark future that had faced him.

The cottage door opened behind him. "Must I wait all day?" Dame Christiana snapped. He had forgotten his promise to be her amanuensis. "Have you made up your mind yet or are you going to hack the entire chase into firewood to vent your temper?"

"I will not go through with it."

The recluse made concaves of her cheeks. "Young Mortimer is too ill to shift, but certes you are fit to leave."

"I know . . . yet . . ." He kicked at the doorstep. "Do you think Lady Constance could carry out her threat?"

"Who knows what worms wriggle around in the compost in my lady's head? What of the daughter? Comely, is she not?"

"Not that I could see. Do you know her then?"

"I knew the maiden and I would not have wished her matched to Fulk of Enderby. Is her spirit broken yet?" For an instant she peered into his eyes as if seeking out his soul. "But what matter in the hour glass of time? Come in and seat yourself. Let us divert ourselves to spiritual matters. I have some quills sharpened for you."

He had been writing to Christiana's dictation for nigh on an hour when he heard the whinny he was dreading. Lady Constance's horse always made the sound when being tethered.

His hostess cursed beneath her breath. "Will I never finish this? Her ladyship always comes at an ill time. More trouble for you, master, a post-mortem on your outlawry, I'd say." She rose to open the door.

"Hopefully, the *coup de grâce*," muttered Geraint.

Lady Constance swept in. Behind her, Father Gilbert set down a wicker basket containing a rumble of feathers and beaks that proved to be two disgruntled chickens destined to mollify Dame Christiana's testy humour.

The lady strode across to the table. "Less lily-livered with a quill, I see." The loft creaked above her head. "And this must be the Welsh cockerel."

Jankyn, freshly woken from his nap, swung down too eagerly from the loft ladder and upset one of the resident pitchers, much to the old woman's annoyance.

"Or," Lady Constance raised an eyebrow, "are you the gormless one?"

"Acquit me of that, goddess," the fool exclaimed and knelt, grabbing a fistful of her embroidered hem to his lips.

The lady threw a sagacious look upon Geraint as if she guessed he had given his companion encouragement to meet her. He had; if God were kind, she might accept Jankyn as a bridegroom. But no . . .

"Uuugh!" exclaimed Lady Constance, removing her gloved hand from Jankyn's enthusiastic kisses, and frowned at her earlier choice. "It seems your thieving technique has not improved. My daughter says you were both hopeless and that she even had to urge you to rob her. Is that true?"

Geraint laid down the quill. He rose respectfully with an apologetic sigh, but confident of dismissal. "Aye, madam, that is the right of it. Jankyn lost his Welshness and I became somewhat tongue-tied. I will be on my way as soon as Sir Edmund is mended."

"But I am still available." Jankyn perched on the table before her, licking his finger and smoothing his eyebrows. "However, I charge a higher fee since I am extremely experienced at pretending to be better than I am."

"Introduce us," she ordered Geraint wearily.

"Madam, this is Jankyn, jester to Lord Thomas of Lancaster."

Jankyn's breeziness burst like a pricked bubble. "That was a confidence," he protested, bouncing off the table. "I do not want the lady delivering me to the sheriff."

Lady Constance eyed him derisively. "I think the reward would be hardly worth the wear on my horseshoes. Besides, Master Jankyn, my daughter thinks you are the man I asked to play her husband and in no ways considers you up to the part."

"I can be *up* to any lady," refuted Jankyn, wriggling his hips, "if I so wish, but neither of the wenches offered much inducement."

"Blathering numbskull!" Dame Christiana snorted, causing an end to the conversation and much affront to Jankyn.

"Madam, your daughter commanded me to sell her rings by way of dismissal payment, but would you like them back?"

Constance eyed Geraint shrewdly. "How honest of you." She appeared to give the matter some thought and added, "No, leave them hidden with Dame Christiana for the nonce. By the way, what did you do with her marriage band?"

"I cast it to St. Robert. Mayhap it is still there if she desires it back. I hope you find some more worthy stranger than I, madam." He strode to the door, opened it and bowed, waiting for her to leave. Father Gilbert gave him a nod and stepped outside.

Lady Constance seemed amused at the dismissal. "I have decided that there is no reason that my daughter would have fallen in love with a poor scholar. She is too headstrong for that. You will make an excellent knight, I think. Your armour will be delivered tomorrow." With that she swept past him like an empress.

The jauntiness fell from Geraint like an unbuckled belt and he stepped back in astonishment, banging his head on one of Dame Christiana's many wall crucifixes.

The lady meantime swung herself into the saddle.

"Madam," he protested, making a grab for her bridle but she directed the horse round, her eyes brilliant and hard like lodesterres.

"My daughter may have dismissed you, but I have not." And she touched her heels to the horse's side.

"You were sent by God, remember," murmured Father Gilbert. He clambered onto his ass and bestowed a blessing that included Dame Christiana, who glowered at him and disappeared indoors in her usual abrupt manner.

"A curse on the lot of them!" Turning away, Geraint angrily smote upon the nearby apple tree with his fist. A shower of water droplets cascaded onto his head and shoulders and he swore loudly.

Jankyn skipped around him and tweaked a withered leaf off his mantle.

"A vow of celibacy perhaps before the loving reunion."

"Oh, roast in Hell!" roared Geraint.

Six

EDYTH GAVE A SHRIEK AND JOHANNA HALTED IN mid-sentence, her lips parted in astonishment at the apparition on the threshold of the great hall. For a moment she was frozen in shock, just as Sir Gawaine must have been when the Green Knight, huge and arcane, arrived uninvited at Camelot.

Formidable and warlike in his full armour, the golden-haired stranger looked unnaturally tall as he stared about him. A crested helm faced her malevolently from the crook of his arm and this he relinquished imperiously into the hall steward's astonished arms as his gaze, arrogant and tense, slid along the high table and fixed on her, like a wolf selecting a vulnerable ewe. His mouth tightened in satisfaction and he waited.

Her world was out of control; Johanna felt the panic rising in her. This was not the Welshman she had met in the forest, it must be the larger man, his companion, the ruffian who had held a dagger to her throat.

She rose to her feet, glancing at her mother who narrowed her eyes swiftly, urging her to speak. Of course, he was waiting for her to recognise him. "I . . ."

Dear God help her, they had not even settled on his name. Anger and impatience glinted in his face as he stood there, and she felt his rising irritation aimed at her like a drawn bow. "S-sir . . ." she began again but pieces of the stranger's armour were glistening like stars. A blue curtain came down, shielding him from her sight, and as if someone had hauled away her foundation stone, Johanna crumpled gracefully to the ground.

Damn the wench! Geraint cursed as he was left standing in the midst of the hall while a rabble of exclaiming women carried his so-called wife out. Was he supposed to clank after her and cast himself on his steel knees, professing love and demanding forgiveness for abandoning her? Or had they purposely left him to tell his version of the marriage to the rest of the household?

It was Father Gilbert who stepped down to meet him, his clasped hands held serenely within the deep sleeves of his habit. Here at least was an ally, but the chaplain wore the expression of St. Augustine about to convert a pagan Briton.

"You are a stranger to us, Sir . . ."

"Sir Gervase de Laval." Geraint curtly nodded his head with the polite but undeferential manner the upper nobility seemed to adopt towards churchmen. "I seek my wife, Johanna, daughter of Lord Alan FitzHenry."

"Your wife!" The priest's right hand untwitched from the sleeves and drew a swift cross over his habit before he turned with a finely judged consternation to include those seated above the salt. "This is a very serious assertion you are making, Sir Gervase," he answered gravely, his voice loud in the hushed hall. "My Lady Johanna has been wed to Sir Fulk de Enderby almost a full year."

Geraint stared at him in feigned amazement.

"But the lady and I were made handfast some two years ago before a priest." He swung round, glaring at them all. "Where is your lord? Let me speak to him this instant!"

There was a rustle of ill-ease among his audience; they were wading in deep waters. One man on the dais stood up reluctantly and Geraint saw with relief it was the stocky seneschal, Sir Geoffrey.

"Ahem." The knight ran a hand over his grizzled moustache as if in a true dilemma and evaded the apparent predicament by offering appeasement. "Sir Gervase, will you not sit at our board until Lady Constance may rejoin us? We must look into this matter."

"My lady's mother?" Geraint spoke disdainfully. "Is her father not here?"

Again the hedging, the exchanged looks as to who should answer.

The seneschal cleared his throat. "Lord Alan is indisposed, sir. Pray you, sir knight, come and be seated."

Geraint grudgingly allowed them to show him to the high table. That itself was a victory. It was the lady Johanna's place where they bestowed him. A fresh winecup and a trencher were hastily set before him.

A fuming, smouldering look upon his face, he accepted the meat from the carver and then forced himself to calm somewhat. With luck, he might be able to stall any explanation until Lady Constance or his so-called wife deigned to reappear. He did not dare examine the faces of those along the table that he must soon put name to. Instead, he gazed thoughtfully at the rest of the household cramming the long tables below, and they stared back as if he had escaped from the king's menagerie.

THE WOMEN MUST HAVE CARRIED HER INTO THE SOLAR, JOHANNA decided, as the chatter of her mother's pet ape penetrated her returning wits, but it was the sudden, strong smoky smell which fiercely jerked her back among them. Yolonya, curse her, was smouldering feathers under her nose, and her mother was ushering Edyth and the other women out. They had made her comfortable on the recessed seat beneath the window with a cushion beneath her head.

"She be back with us, my lady," Yolonya exclaimed joyfully.

"I cannot feel any bumps." Her mother's fingers came to scuffle in her hair. They had removed the barbette and veil.

Johanna's head swam as she tried to sit up and Agnes's hands forced her back again with soft murmurs bidding her rest. She smelt the rosewater, fragrant in her mother's samite kirtle. "So that is why you look so fine tonight," she muttered with a glare. "Why in the name of all the Saints did you not warn me you were going to ask the other outlaw?"

"There is nothing like genuine emotion." Her mother's cool palm descended on her brow. "The armour fits quite well, I think."

"Is he still there?"

"I hope so."

"Oh, dear God, what did you say to him?" She struggled to sit up and then put a hand to her forehead. It was not dizziness but cowardice that assailed her and she sank back with a groan.

"Nothing yet. I trust that was a genuine swoon?"

Johanna scowled, her eyes squeezed shut, wishing the world would leave her alone, especially the large outlaw.

"By Our Lady, you have never done that in your life afore," muttered Yolonya. "Agnes, 'as she been eatin' proper like?"

"Johanna, look at me!" Her mother shook her sternly. "Are you sure you are not with child? What were you using, sponges in vinegar? Upon my soul, Johanna, if you are, we will be done with this endeavour at once."

"No, no, I am not!" Johanna snapped but she opened her eyes in momentary panic. Dear God forbid! A babe by Fulk! Misery made her lash out: "And if I was, madam, what would you go out there and tell him? 'Oh, you have the wrong household. You must mean Lady Johanna Fitz*booth*, hers is the fifth castle on the left of the king's highway facing north, but watch out for her husband, he is vicious with the lance.' "

"Johanna!" Her mother's desperate voice made her subside. "Hush, use your wits! What *am* I going to say to him?" She darted a questioning glace at the door.

Agnes, with an ear to the wood, giggled. "There's naught amiss going on. I'd say take your time, my lady."

There was no escape. Johanna pressed her fingers to her temples, trying to think clearly. How should she behave? "If he married me two years ago . . ." Then her quicksilver mind reasserted itself. "Ha, I know. This is what you must go out and say."

"Dearest!" Her mother's eyes were as round as millstones as Johanna finished. "I cannot . . ." She paused, her eyes narrowing with mischief and understanding, "Yes, I can," and beamed admiringly at her daughter, before she moistened her lips and braced herself to face the hall.

"YOU CAN IMAGINE WHAT A SURPRISE THIS IS TO US ALL." THE CHAPlain had moved a sullen boy, clearly of noble birth, out of his place next to Geraint, giving their guest some space to protect himself on his left flank.

"I warned Johanna that she must have patience," Geraint de-

clared irritably, hoping he was not overdoing the part of angry
returned husband. "I told her I would return."

"Ahem, this would appear to be some folly of our Lady Johanna. She was ever a scapegrace as a child," commented Sir Geoffrey, perching himself on the carved arm of Lord Alan's chair on
his right. The elderly knight's Saxon blue eyes were almost too
bright with amusement, lending him a hobgoblin mien.

"Folly!" exclaimed Geraint, slamming his goblet down so that
the great salt holder wobbled. "She pledged her obedience and
body to me before a priest. Is the blessing of Holy Church in these
parts gorwn feeble?"

He must have overcooked his withering tone for Father Gilbert
muttered tersely, "Have a care, young man. We have only your
word in this matter and I assure you we shall acutely examine
your allegations and the lady Johanna's testimony in this right
thoroughly." Geraint saw the priest's glance sweep along the table
to the familiar, scrawny woman glaring at them both. It was the
lady Jankyn had set his foot upon. With rising dread, Geraint wondered is she could recall the height of Jankyn's accomplice.

"Pardon, Father, what did you say?"

"I said Sir Fulk de Enderby will have something to say in this,"
Father Gilbert repeated pointedly.

"Indeed he will!" The woman—Edyth, was it?—leaned forward, her chin jutting angrily above the dewlaps of her gorget. "If
I were you, whoever you are," she sneered, "I would leave here
and forget any promises, that is, if any were made."

Geraint raised his eyebrows at her as if surprised that anyone
would have the insolence to address him so, especially a woman.

"Who are you, dame?" Unwed, he remembered. No man worth
his salt would want to take such a scowling broom handle to his
bed.

She was not put off by his disdain. "I am Edyth de Enderby,
you upstart, and I tell you that my brother was wed to Lady Johanna in front of fifty witnesses before the chapel door in this very
castle. If I were you, sir, I would ride from here this very hour, for
by the Saints, when my brother hears your falsehood, he will
thrash you for your lies."

Geraint met her evil look without flinching. "If I speak false,
then by all means let him try, lady." For the first time, he smiled,

as if her demeanour pleased him, pretending to note the dark-lashed, piercing eyes. That her gorget was parting company where it was pinned to her hair coiled about the old-fangled wadding on the left side of her face he also observed briefly. "You do right to defend your brother so bravely."

Dear Heaven, the charm worked. Disarmed, the lady lowered her eyes modestly, her mouth smug. But he was not finished.

"Tell me, chaplain," he said calmly. "Is it permitted that I settle this matter by combat? If so, it is easily resolved." It was the last thing he intended but it was the knightly thing to suggest.

The woman's pointed chin rose aggrieved again. "And my brother will win." But she spoke less tartly, challenging him, as if believing that he might admire her courage.

"No!" The priest waved his hands as if to end the dissension. "This is a matter for Holy Church." Father Gilbert's expression was admonitory for more than one reason, Geraint realised, and cursed silently. He had been wrong to mislead the woman Edyth. He was here to rescue Lady Johanna from a hateful marriage; to do good, not wreak further mischief.

The tardy arrival of his makeshift esquire saved him further answer as down at the distant end of the hall there was willing shuffling to make room for Jankyn on the bench, no doubt to grill him with questions. The former jester grinned up at his master and raised a tankard. He only hoped the jackanapes would stay sober and keep a still tongue. Not for the first time, Geraint heartily wished he was a hundred miles away.

All heads swivelled as the small door to the lord's withdrawing room behind the high table whined open. Lady Constance closed it carefully behind her and stood for a moment, as if to regain her composure. Then she took a deep breath, her eyes seeking him out.

He and the other men at the table rose. She gathered her fine russet skirts up and glided majestically across to Father Gilbert, laying her hand for support upon his sleeve as she addressed Geraint.

"In truth, you have cause to be here, sir." She turned to include the others at the high table in her gaze, but her words were intended to carry further. "Behold me both confused and dismayed.

It seems we have all been misled and should have heeded my daughter's protests against her marriage to Sir Fulk."

A great babble of consternation broke out and Lady Edyth's bosom, what little there was of it, rose furiously, as she jumped to her feet and brought her fist crashing down on the board.

"What, are your heads addled? You fools! I suppose any moment some other tourney freelance will saunter in and you will believe him too."

"Well, he won't be asking for you," muttered some wit, faceless on the crowded lower benches.

Edyth ignored the cut. "Lady Constance, are you telling us that your daughter did have a liaison with this jay?"

Jay! Geraint's jaw slackened at the insult, but before he could retort Lady Constance waved an angry hand to silence Edyth. "Let me be heard! I will have no more interruptions in my own hall. You, sir!"

"My lady." Geraint bowed.

As he straightened, the lady made sure she did not meet his gaze squarely as she flung a shaking hand toward the great door. "My daughter bids you leave, sir. She declares that you left her a bride for a full two years and nary a word since, and she is now wed to another. She considers you a knave and a braggart and will have naught to do with you."

Geraint gaped as if she had planted her fist into his belly. He had not been expecting this. Of course, a sharp parry to his offensive. The clever little shrew! Or was it her mother who had thought this out? It would serve the pair of them aright if he did march out across the drawbridge.

"We will see about that!" he snarled and started towards the solar. Lady Constance put up ringed hands to bar him.

"Step aside, my lady!" Geraint thundered. "I have not ridden from Westminster to be set aside like a pair of worn shoes. The lady bids me leave, does she!"

A hiss of awe greeted the mention Westminster.

Predictably it was Lady Edyth who flung herself in his path as he reached for the ringhandle of the door. Her shoulders were thin and bony against his hands.

"Two years?" It was a scornful hiss. "Get you gone, we do not want you here! Stop him!" she shrieked, her fist aiming for his face as he swiftly set her aside.

His hand on his sword haft, he swung round with a grin. "Come, who is the brave heart among you who will stop me. No? I thought not."

HE WAS REAL. JOHANNA HAD NOT IMAGINED HIM. HE FLUNG OPEN the door and stood there, humbling the lintel by his stature, as displeased as an heir told that his inheritance has passed to another.

From the spurred sabatons on his feet up to the meshed coif flung back upon his broad shoulders, every inch of his great stature was clad in steel. Johanna recognised the fabric of his surcote as having come from her mother's workbasket, but now, stretched across this stranger's armoured breast, the silken panel dominated by an upthrusting sword hilted in sable was menacing.

Johanna's hands coiled anxiously into fists at her sides. If she had ever expected either outlaw to take her mother's fee, it would have been the shorter one, whom she had imagined dark and swarthy, but this man had golden hair to his shoulders and blue translucent eyes whose gaze unsettled her. Christ protect her! This was the impudent scoundrel who had held her against him at the holy spring and pressed his dagger to her throat. She had enough of woe with Fulk and now her mother was putting her future in this rogue's hands. Indignation and another older emotion that she did not recognise shortened her breath.

No wonder he had stared his fill at her by the holy spring. He was doing it again now. Unblinking, the disconcerting stare slid from the half-loosened braided hair, over her parted lips, down the bracken-dyed kirtle towards the darned toe of her stocking— she swiftly hid her foot under her skirt—before rising slowly again to grimly study her swollen face. Then insolently he folded his arms and raised his eyebrows questioningly at her mother and Agnes, flanking her like two loyal men-at-arms.

"They tell me you have married another, lady. How can this be? I married you!" His voice, strong and well-spoken, shook her like an overhead rumble of thunder.

She should say something but no bucket of words rose at the

turning. Her voice was gone. She could only stare in disbelief at this warrior advancing on her like a huge scaled monster.

Geraint cursed; the contrary wench was leaving the talking to him. The young tiring woman might be sending little covert glances at him as if he was St. George come to supper, but Johanna FitzHenry was treating him as if he was the dragon.

Without her headdress, the young woman's face, the whole-some side, was unnaturally pale against hair almost as dark as Whitby jetstone. He tried not to be conscious of the ugliness of the bruises and yet he could not ignore them. He searched her face, imagining her unmarked and liked what he saw—dark-lashed eyes and a sweet mouth that should not have been so unkindly used. Gervase de Laval was supposed to have cozened this wench into a betrothal and now he was back because he loved her still. Yes, it was possible. When her hurts were healed, the lady Jo-hanna, judging by her undamaged cheek, would prove exceeding fair. She had spirit too, as she had shown at St. Robert's spring, but why was her courage ebbing now? Why did she not answer? Had her mother not warned her of his arrival?

"Johanna!" he exclaimed sternly, halting but a step from her, and she quivered beneath his furious gaze as if she was truly afeared of him. Was the pretty maidservant privy to the secret? Could he drop his guard? No, better to be cautious and keep to his part. What next? Presumably he should demand to know who had disfigured her, but there was more meaty matter to be chewed first. "Lady, did you or did you not marry me two years ago?"

A slap and a scuffle behind the door thwarted her answer. Before the hefty Yolonya could keep the door shut, the woman Edyth forced her way in and half a dozen disembodied faces, including the seneschal's and Jankyn's, crammed the entrance.

Geraint ignored Edyth and scowled at his supposed wife. *Come on, curse you!* he fumed, *Answer me!* The lady Johanna swallowed, her fingers fluttered at the small golden cross that rose and fell above a cleavage that would be alluring if there was more flesh on her. She managed to nod feebly then she sank back against the cushions, her eyes flickering closed. Voices behind him muttered. Now what was he to do?

A smile barely upon his lips, he surveyed the women languidly as if they bored him. "Lady Constance, pray order your people out again. I have something to say to my unfaithful wife and I certainly do not intend to shame her before the common gaze."

He understood the uncertainty that flashed across Lady Constance's face. As a stranger, he had no authority to be alone with the lady Johanna. Conscious of their audience, the mother now stepped forward, her eyes blazing. "You lay a hand on my daughter and I will have you booted across the drawbridge, knight or no."

"Lay a hand on her? No, but I will choke the life out of the whoreson who bruised her face. By all means remain if you insist, madam, but the rest shall go. Leave us!" He strode towards the doorway and the watching gargoyles instantly shot back.

Lady Constance made a show of deliberating. She bit her lip and then slowly nodded at the other women. He waited insolently as they all trooped past him. The fair maidservant curtsied deeply. Forward-thinking, that one, and shapely too.

The stick-like Edyth predictably stood her ground. "I certainly will not leave. She is married to my brother."

Geraint turned a gaze upon her that had quelled many an impudent servant. "Then I will have a message for your brother. *Later!*" He circled her, as a wolf might a lamb, until she was between him and the door. "Later!" he repeated sweetly and moved forwards like a great wave against a coracle. She retreated, holding herself rigid and he shut the door in her face. He was left with Jankyn who had squeezed in and looked hopeful of remaining.

"Outside!" ordered Geraint. "See we are not interrupted." The fool staunched his disappointment and with a salute let himself out.

Geraint turned, changing his grin to a glare. "By St. George, precious little help you gave me, my lady."

Provoked, Johanna sat up. "Your arrival was foolish!" His expression made her add hastily, "But very effective."

"What was foolish?" The stranger's voice was a dangerous purr.

"No one warned me that you were going to appear like that in the middle of dinner." Her voice grew smaller. "I mean, to have to greet you in front of everyone. I do not even know your name. I had no idea w-what to call you. I . . ."

By Our Lady, where had her mother found him? This man

looked not only as unmanageable as Fulk, but he seemed just as surly and full of conceit as the rest of his gender.

"Gervase de Laval at your service, madam wife." The rustle of a sleeve reminded him that Lady Constance was still with them. She glided between them now as gleeful as an earl about to invade France.

"You are a miracle, master scholar," she exclaimed. "And so delightfully huge in your armour. I am glad it fits so well. How clever of you to arrive so fully attired."

Scholar! *This* was the scholar, not the other man? Had this rogue deliberately chosen to be the silent outlaw so he might mark her behaviour?

"It is only just beginning," Johanna cautioned her mother softly, frowning at the stranger. "I am not laying wagers yet." How much had her mother offered him?

"Could it have been better?" Her mother whirled upon her. "I doubt it. Your swooning, the armour, and your answers to each other. Excellent, excellent!"

The man set a hand on the wall above the hearth, his body losing some of its rigidity. "Was it honest, your collapse, or do you practise it once a week?" Clearly the scoundrel's curiosity needed sating, but his tone was sarcastic. Surely he could have seen it had been too ungraceful to leave room for doubt?

"My swooning? As genuine as a miser's love of gold. And there are bruises to prove it," Johanna added reprovingly, finally rising from the cushions and hiding her toes in her leather mules. "I probably have a perfect set by now—like jewellery." He gave her a cursory glance and looked away, but not before she had glimpsed the disbelief in his face.

"Why are you here?" she asked him waspishly. "I thought you had decided against helping me. I presume my mother had to raise the price—or is the armour thrown in as an extra bounty, *Gervase*?"

"Johanna!" hissed her mother.

The so-called scholar dragged his attention from the hearth to her toecaps and allowed himself another perusal of her. The iron gaze that finally met hers was haughty and dismissive.

"That is between your mother and me. The money will suffice for now." He paced to the windowseat and swung round on her in a creak of steel and leather. "Was I sufficiently *gormless* for your purpose?"

So that had stung him, had it? Johanna suppressed her inward glee, hoping he had simmered a whole day thinking about it. For once, she had found a hole in a man's hauberk to slide home an insult and she could not resist provoking him further.

"You could have told me it was the goosehead that you had bargained with, madam," she exclaimed to her mother.

His gaze clashed with hers momentarily in a suppressed fury, but her remark never drew verbal blood for although he raised arrogant brows, his mouth twisted in faint humour. It surprised her; there might be more flavour to this dish than she had suspected. And not so gormless either, but it was obvious that like all men this one was puffed up with his own conceit.

"Peace, daughter, will you bite at the hand that helps you?"

"Your pardon, master scholar." Johanna turned her head away at her mother's scolding, cursing that she was expected to be grateful to this rogue. Perhaps the reproof was justified but the man was being paid. The silence between the three of them grew uncomfortable and she broke it with practicalities.

"Since it is still several days to the hearing, what do we do in the meantime? Now, for instance?" She indicated the waiting hall.

The stranger moved towards her with a rasp of steel. "Now, lady? Why, you and I must concoct the tale of our so-called love." His tone was insolent.

Johanna felt herself blushing and lowered her gaze. He was right, damn him. "Yes, I suppose we must." She subsided once more onto the cushioned windowseat.

That had deflated the little vixen, Geraint grinned inwardly. Goosehead, was he? But he was inclined to be merciful and count his blessings. At least Lady Johanna had the intelligence to see sense. He could have found himself compelled to pretend love to a spineless, vapid creature who merely bewailed her fate the whole time. He half-turned to Lady Constance. "Would it please you to send for some victuals, my dearest *Mother*." There was a predictable snarl of outrage from the Lady Johanna as her parent blinked at him, taken aback. He bestowed his most charming smile upon Lady Constance. "I have no wish to face yon Edyth again on an empty belly."

"Of course." The older woman recovered. "I will return instantly. Johanna, behave!" she admonished and let herself out.

Maybe the food would put him in better temper. Geraint ignored the sullen female back directed at his notice and sighed inwardly. This adventure had better be worth his while. At least there was no shortage of money to pay him, judging by the chamber's furnishings. Cushions of scarlet boasted panels of blue taffeta with catkin edgings and embroidered coverings capped the stools before the fire. The stallion wall-hanging pleased him—the noble beast, free and unharnessed, milk-white upon a slaty background—and around its edge the maker had deceitfully harnessed gilded leather strips to give a clever semblance of a golden frame. Fur hides were scattered across the floor and a small murrey carpet a pace square was set before the lord's chair.

To see a book open on the lectern was gratifying, but its pictures proclaimed it was merely a bestiary. He scowled. A woman's picture book. Was it all a distaff demesne now? Certes, there was no evidence of any man taking leisure here. A wooden tapestry frame showed an altar piece barely started, while anchored to a great candleholder behind the chair was leashed a pretty-faced ape, probably worth its weight in gold, if you liked that kind of creature. Work baskets overflowed like miniature haberdashers' stalls with mending and sketches. A boy's tunic sleeve trailed from one, its embroidered cuff half-finished.

A tapestry depicting the judgment of Solomon faced him from the opposite wall but the two kneeling women looked as though they had the king flummoxed. He swung his gaze away and discovered at last one man managing to take the lead in this infernal place. Here was a painted hanging of Orpheus, lyre in hand, looking gleefully on his wife Eurydice as the demons dragged her back to Hades. Fortunate fellow! He imagined the lady Johanna sinking anguish-faced into a large badger tunnel and discovered that the wretched wench was watching him.

"Is this your handiwork, lady?" His glance indicated the stool cover nearest him, with its three blood red lions rampant echoing the coat of arms carved upon the chimney's hood.

"No, but the horse is mine." It surprised him. "Assessing our ability to pay you?"

He readjusted his shoulders against the wall and regarded her with ill-concealed irritation, making it clear that he was loathing the entire business.

"Yes."

"What price?" she hissed, springing to her feet. "How much?"

Alone with her, it was hard to turn the conversation. It had been agreed between him and Lady Constance that there should be no mention of Edmund Mortimer to her daughter, but it left him posing as an unscrupulous adventurer. He addressed the air beyond her right shoulder, his tone cold and impertinent. "How much is your happiness worth, lady? You wish to toss in some interest and lower your mother's fee?"

A lascivious blue gaze brushed across her face. Johanna felt the blood rushing into her cheeks and turned away, hiding her anger. Better to give him the benefit of misunderstanding. He might be merely using the words as armour against her. Since this ribald was clearly proud, no doubt he resented taking her mother's orders.

Common sense must prevail, she decided, regaining mastery over herself. If her mother's plan was to work successfully, there had to be some sort of truce between them. Clasping her hands firmly before her, she swung round to face him. His appearance still disconcerted her but she was being illogical; size should be no bar to learning.

She took a deep breath for it was necessary to be businesslike. "Let there be no misunderstanding, master scholar. I do not like this . . . this perjury any more than you but I am grateful to you for agreeing to take on the task. We must be as efficient and as thorough as we can so that you will not be delayed any more than necessary. As you rightly point out, we must spend the next two days discovering exactly what the archdeacon's court will need to know and making sure that we tell the same tale."

The stranger looked relieved at her matter-of-factness. He straightened up from the wall. "What I do not understand is why we do not go to a bishop and have done?"

"Did Mother not explain? The bishop is in my husband's pocket." He swore and she added, "I agree, it is usual for people of *our* status to have the matter settled privately and the archdeacon's court usually hears cases from the common people, but Father Gilbert thinks it might be even better this way. Everyone will hear of the matter and the decision will be harder to set aside when my husband disputes it."

"Very well, so be it," he muttered grimly.

"Now we have to consider the next step. You have returned after two years. You are furious that I have remarried. I am bitter that you never sent me word. What should we do now?"

A rare smile curled about his mouth. "Use your imagination, my lady. I know very well what I would want to do if I had been away for two years." His look swept down over her breasts with calculating impudence.

"Yes, of course," exclaimed Johanna, pinkening. "But I am still very angry with you."

"You are?" The charm, fierce as a crossbolt, would have whammed pigeons from the sky.

"Please stop teasing me," she snapped. "You would try and—"

"Kiss you? I would not *try*, madam, I would—"

"—do it?" She swallowed beneath that devastating smile. "No, you must remember I have a very sore and tender face."

"My lady, if you forbade me your lips, then I should concentrate on the rest of you."

"Oh." The lady sat down again, thinking about it with so grave a frown that Geraint was in danger of putting aside his ill-temper with the whole business and laughing at the absurdity.

"Here is your repast, sir." Lady Constance swept in, followed by the woman Yolonya carrying a tray of food, and let down a cup board from the dark oak aumbry. Yolonya set the repast there, then she dutifully lit a taper from the hearth and touched it to the candles in the wall cressets.

"I thought you might need this, Johanna." Searching in her belt-purse, Lady Constance triumphantly produced a smallish onion. She seemed put out by their surprised stares. "To help you weep, of course."

Johanna took it and shrugged at the undernourished vegetable. "So thoughtful," she said dryly. "Why am I supposed to be weeping?"

"Is it not obvious?" Her mother, poised to reveal her plan, halted. The stranger clearly was too hungry to listen. Without a by-your-leave, he strode across to the platter and bit into a pastry, savouring it before he loftily inclined his head.

"Yes, pray tell us, madam. For my earlier suggestion has fallen wide of the target." His cool stare goaded Johanna. She ignored the jab, her attention fully upon her mother now.

The older woman waved her hands. "Oh, you must quarrel loudly and then you, Johanna, slap his face." Two astonished pairs of eyes turned upon her. The man looked outraged at the suggestion, the food halfway to his mouth. "And you, Gervase, must leave for the nonce. I cannot permit you to stay here tonight. It would not be seemly, after all."

Ripping the bread, he scooped up some sauce with it, swallowing the mouthful before he answered. "Seemly! Madam, the lady is supposed to be married to me." He smoothed away a morsel of food clinging to his lower lip and turned his haughty gaze on Johanna. Oh, he would be slippery as an eel to deal with, this one, she thought as she sensed her face redden tiresomely beneath his study, but her mother's logic was sound.

"I will not slap you hard," she reassured him, her expression impertinent as she tossed the onion nonchalantly behind her into the cushions. "I know what it feels like."

"You will not do it at all, lady." He carefully wiped his fingers on the napkin before he raised eyes hard as jewels. "You were supposed to have been foolish enough to marry me for love, remember."

The conceited wretch! Oh, she would delight in bringing this man down to earth with a thud from his elevated view of himself. When the case was won, then . . .

Lady Constance's hands shot up between them. "Peace, the pair of you. We have to play this cautiously. I have to decide whether to believe you, lad, and until then I am not letting you under my roof."

Johanna watched him bristle beautifully at the insult.

"What am I expected to do? Go back to my lodging?"

"Oh no, you must never go there again, not until the hearing is over. Put up at the hostelry in the town and come back tomorrow for our answer."

He thought about it, sipping his wine slowly. "Aye, there is sense in that."

"I think you should leave presently. But be careful, Sir Gervase. No doubt Lady Edyth will send word to Enderby at first light and her brother will be after your blood. He can ride right swiftly when he has a mind to it. Now, on with your masks, the pair of you."

For an instant they glared at one another defiantly like fighting cocks flung into the ring.

"Let us have this over with," he suggested condescendingly, as if she was a child about to be spooned some unpalatable dose.

"Oh dear, where is the onion?" Her tone was intended to draw blood but he merely jerked his head at the windowseat. Cursing under her breath, Johanna hunted it out from the beneath the cushions and tore at the papery skin with her nails, anxious to have him gone.

"Here, let me." His voice was impatient as he reached out and took it from her, but the mere brush of his fingertips stole her breath away. She watched him wield the knife swiftly through it, then with a mocking bow he held out the oozing half to her as if it was a moonstone in the setting of his fingers.

"W-what shall we say in quarrel?" Johanna took it from him with a shyness she had never experienced before. The eyes watching her hardened like a hawk's.

His fingers suddenly grabbed her wrist and jerked the onion up to her nose. "Think on the man who spoilt your face, lady. You would lash out at him for his ill-treatment. Your beloved Fulk. Breathe deep."

She did not need him to coax anger from her at the mention of Fulk but, by Heaven, it worked. "Pretend I am him, my lady. Imagine him wanting to kiss you."

He snapped his fingers in command at her mother, twitched the onion from Johanna's fingers and hurled it into the corner. Lady Constance flung open the door and ran out distraught with her knuckles to her lips.

"Go away from me!" screamed Johanna. "How dare you!"

"Whore!" snarled Geraint, backing through the doorway.

Unjust, shrieked Johanna's common-sense side as she enjoyed advancing upon him. A whore was she? He was going too far and she grabbed the dish of food and flung it at him. The gravy made rivulets down his shining breastplate and clotted the knit of the hauberk.

The arrogant man blinked down in genuine astonishment at the turgid liquid congealing in the steel mesh, but as he looked up a jug of wine hurtled its contents into his face before he could retreat further.

"Deceiver!" Leaving the support of the doorway, she smacked her palm hard across the left side of his face.

Gervase reeled back, his expression so shocked that she nearly burst out laughing.

"I will be back, madam!" he rasped, knuckling away the wine droplets, and he strode through the hall, redfaced with genuine embarrassment as the household gaped at him in silence like a congregation overawed by a sermon.

Johanna slammed the door closed and flung herself onto the cushions, her shoulders shaking.

"You wretch, that was wondrous!" Her mother's skirts brushed her thigh. Then an arm encircled her shoulders. "Dearest?"

Johanna sat up, her fingers scraping away the tears.

Her mother gasped. "I thought you were laughing. What is the matter?"

"He called me a . . . whore, Mother. And I will be, having sworn obedience to one man and then wedding another."

Her mother sighed. "Oh, lambkin, if you want to eat an egg, you have to break the shell. Do or do you not want to be free of Fulk?"

"Yes, but, *whore*. That is what he thinks of me. And . . . and he said, if we really had been married, he would want to hold me and . . . oh, *Maman*, I cannot bear the thought of any man touching me so ever again."

"Hush, my dearest." She let her parent rock her in her arms. It was small comfort. Even her stalwart mother had not been able to prevent the marriage to Fulk and now it seemed she, Johanna, would be at the mercy of another man's whims. If they did aught to displease him, Gervase de Laval could abandon them and disclose their lies.

"I am so frightened," she whispered. She dreaded lest he return; she feared he would not.

As if she read her thoughts, her mother whispered, "He will be back. He has no choice."

Seven

"RECONCILED TO YOUR DESTINY YET, GREAT ONE?" Jankyn, with folded arms and concave cheeks, was contemplating Geraint like an artist poised to make his first sketch of the martyrdom of St. Sebastian.

The keeper of the hostelry in Conisthorpe's marketplace, with a tyrannical sagacity the Emperor Nero might have recognised, had booted two merchants, one horse dealer and a scruffy pardoner out of the best room in order to accommodate the dubious son-in-law to Lady Constance. Which was why Geraint was sitting gloomily upon a hastily vacated bed, wondering, amongst other things, if the previous occupants had carried extra passengers.

"What choice have I?" He roused himself. "What about you, Jankyn? If you want to thieve the pony at first light, I will shovel words over your tracks for a few hours."

The jester shook his head. "Where to? My friends, such as I had, are scattered like shards of a broken pissing pot all over the kingdom. I suppose I could journey south to Redhill to see if my Lady Lancaster—leastways she was until she ran off to de Warenne—might give me work." He shook his head, "Nay, ten to one they'll have their own fool. What say you to employing me further? Have I efficiently served my few hours apprenticeship?" He seized hold of Geraint's boot.

"By all the Saints, man!" Geraint bellowed, grabbing the mattress before he was jerked onto the none-so-clean rushes. "I was grateful for your company tonight, but do you really want to share a noose if they spur the horse from under me?"

"Master Gervase, I may as well throw in my lot with you for the nonce. Being an esquire is simple work. Putting drunken knights to bed, kissing them goodnight, cleaning the bloody gouts off their swords, sponging the vomit off their tunics, telling them how the ladies adore them when they are in the dumps. And where I fail, you may instruct me further." He looked up, his dark eyes shining. "Be honest, you will need a fool at the end of each day as a butt for your anger and, believe me, my absolution comes cheaper than a whore with crabs."

"True." Geraint slowly smiled.

"As for the noose, Lordy, I saw friends skewered on swords at Burton and Boroughbridge. Cheer up, we are more likely to be clobbered over the head with an unchained bible and excommunicated. And what of that? Priests are but men when all the ceremony is done. Curses hold no fears for me. Verily, God and the Devil look after their own." He held out his hand, "Done, then? Shall I be Watkyn as I was last even?"

"Aye," Geraint spat on his palm and slapped it into Jankyn's. "Done!"

GERAINT LEFT FOR THE CASTLE NEXT MORNING, HUNGRY TO BREAK his fast, and laden with more anger and hardly less trepidation than he had the day before. He had slept ill; the heavy rain lashing the shutters all night and a multitude of night demons, his own fears, had kept him tossing. But washed and shaved, facing a lamb-like March wind which betokened more rain, he felt somewhat restored. At least he was garbed more comfortably today and his borrowed armour was stowed on a packhorse led by Jankyn. The yeasty smell of fresh-baked bread lacing the woodsmoke and sea coal added a still sharper edge to his appetite, and he cursed as a platoon of squealing bacon pigs, driven in for the market, delayed their crossing of the square.

A half-dozen stalls were already trading beneath the butter cross, gaining a march on any merchants' apprentices who were tardy in unchaining the shop boards that doubled as shutters for the lower windows and heaving out the panniers of goods to be arranged upon them for the day's trading. The ale brewer was up a wooden ladder fixing a fresh garland over his door to the instructions of a broadbeamed woman who was inexplicably distracted by Jankyn's progress across the thoroughfare. The jester blew her a kiss.

"Hmm, if that is your taste, it is a wonder you are not rolled out thin as pastry," commented Geraint.

"Bah, I go for drum towers. Those little turrets the lady Jo—" He yelped but Geraint lowered his fist abruptly, aware that a priest, bordered by the inevitable zigzagged Norman door of his church, stood watching, twisting his hands against the morning cold.

Geraint muttered a crisp expletive, barely avoiding a barrow hedgehogged with leeks. Certes, Jankyn's company was going to be a qualified blessing. It might be useful to have an ally within the castle, but the man would have to keep a stopper on his babble. His waking quips had clashed with Geraint's ill-tempered grunts, but then he was not about to face his in-laws.

"They are flying the pennons for you," observed Jankyn cheerfully as their horses trotted up the street leading to the castle. "Should you have bought some flowers?"

"Probably," growled Geraint tersely. He justified his omission muttering that Johanna had done nothing to deserve them so far and he was not going to brave the bad-tempered pigs again to reach the butter cross.

"When the lady's face is mended, she may prove sweeter tempered," Jankyn answered soothingly.

"And I am the rightful king of England," retorted Geraint.

"Look on the bright side, sir. She is still young and could be pining for a charming lover. Mind you, this Fulk de Enderby, they say, was the scourge of the Scots. They still call him. 'The Mallet' by all accounts."

"What!" His horse shied at the sudden tug on the reins. "The Devil take you, Jankyn. Who told you that?"

"The loquacious alewife, between fertile kisses."

"Pah, some *mallet*! Any man who has to beat his wife shows weakness."

"That is a remarkably philosophic observation in this age, sir, though not one to be spoken aloud in an alehouse, I am thinking." Jankyn was too viciously cheerful. "I learned a great deal last night and not all of it gossip." The dark crescents beneath his eyes added meaning to his grin. "The alewife told me that the Lady Johanna was a right bag of mischief." He received a snarl from Geraint and added swiftly, "Not that the good wife spoke ill of my lady's virtue, quite the contrary. She reckoned it took Lord Alan years to find the young demoiselle a match. Too finicky she was and would have none of 'em until her father lost patience and her to the Mallet."

"I wish you would stop calling him that," fumed Geraint. "Where was the alemaster while you were pleasuring his wife?"

"Indulging the hostelry tapmistress, I believe." Jankyn parried the insinuation with another verbal assault. "Should you have worn your helm this morning? 'Twill be better at withstanding flying tankards than your forehead."

"You," muttered his new master, "may sit outside the stable and pick the peas out of my hauberk."

"Well, I count myself fortunate. Spending a morning scraping off the gobbets of food that still cling to your knitted steel will be preferable to breaking fast with a shrew." Jankyn swiftly urged his horse sideways, nearly knocking himself stupid on a fletcher's sign sticking out from a jettied upper storey before Geraint could grab him by the ear. "I will wager you a silver penny she calls you a goosehead again before the day is over."

Geraint refused to answer the gibe, and though he felt daunted he had no intention of returning to the inn to break his fast. His belly was rumbling and, judging by yester even, the board at Conisthorpe was generous. He was not going to spend good money on poor alehouse gruel when Lady Constance would supply a heartier repast.

His name at the barbican raised a chuckle of laughter.

" 'Tis a marvel you be comin' 'ere once more, sir knight. Cleaned your armour yet?" Unseen, the speaker was full of bravado, but once the drawbridge rumbled down, the bald-headed porter saluted him respectfully. "My lady Constance expected you back, sir."

"A wonder that I am," Geraint snorted, frowning up at the louring towers of the keep.

Beyond the gate, a stableboy skidded to a halt before him and led their horses through a veritable village of dwellings and workshops to the far side of the courtyard. It was a greater castle than he had realised yesterday, and a prosperous holding, seemingly well maintained. The thatch of each building was in good repair, neat as an expensive barber's cut. No shabby shutter half-hung from a single nail, and while there was the usual stink of manure and cooking smoke, familiar in any castle, the stench of the latrines was missing. Mind, the wind was blowing the other way.

By the time he dismounted at the small flight of steps to the hall, he had collected an entourage of some twenty gaping spectators. The steward, summoned to meet him, clapped his hands to dismiss the crowd and brusquely removed a girl child who was untidying the first step, picking her nose pensively at the strangers.

Observed in the watery sunlight, the raised hall was of recent construction. Instead of an old-style central louvre, smoke rose from ornately capped chimneys, and the broken edges of ancient shells still stood out clearly on the limestone walls. Supported on an undervault, it had been built out from the curtain wall on the cliff edge, facing west overlooking the river. Large traceried windows of grisailled glass had been set into the walls and the uppermost floor—presumably the private apartments of the FitzHenry family—had generous casements to let in the light. The shutters and lower light of the solar, or great chamber, were wide open and Geraint wondered if Lady Johanna was watching for his approach. Somehow he doubted it. More like, a servant lighting the morning fire with green timber could have filled the room with smoke.

Setting such useless thoughts aside, he followed the steward up into the porch and gave his sword and cloak to Jankyn's care. From beyond the nail-studded great doors an agreeable aroma of fresh bread reached him. Driven by hunger rather than enthusiasm, Geraint took a deep breath and strode in. He waited while the steward hastened to the high table to announce him.

By day, the hall was cheerfully light and pleasant, its flagstones dappled with sunshine, and well swept. A manservant, leaving through the serving entrance to his right, turned and made obeisance to him, while another hurrying in with a small bowl of potage inclined his head in courtesy. So the household was being cautious.

The comely maidservant who had swished her skirts at him in the great chamber rose from one of the lower trestles and scurried out the serving entrance, no doubt to warn her mistress.

Only a handful of people were eating at the high table. Sir Fulk's sister was mercifully absent, but Geraint recognised the boy.

Lady Constance was halfway through her sops in wine. She eyed him with feigned perturbation and gravely came down into the body of the hall to greet him. She made her voice carry.

"So it seems I did not dream last evening, Sir Gervase. You are back here to confront us."

"It is a serious matter, my lady," he growled, bowing over her hand. "I would scarce journey all the way from London for a trifle."

"Then I suppose you had better join us at the board. This matter must be resolved with all speed."

He followed her to the steps of the dais and asked gravely, "And where is the bane of my life? Still abed?"

"No." So the lady had been waiting. Lady Johanna materialised from the doorway behind him, dainty as a statuette of a hollow-eyed Holy Virgin. This morning, as was the fashion among women of her standing, she wore a sleeveless cote, open at the sides so that much of her kirtle, red as holly berries, showed beneath. Narrowly cut, the dark blue overgown's embroidered border drew his attention to Lady Johanna's curves. She could have done with more flesh on her, but for all that she had a figure that tempted touching. He was displeased that she hid her lustrous black hair. He had noticed yesterday how the dark tresses had crept forward appealingly, half masking the damage. Now both her hair and face were shrouded by a veil and it was hard to tell her mood. Was she hiding from him? The barrier of fine linen irritated him as if she had deliberately set a wall between them.

The hall watched and the burble of conversation slackened. Imperiously, he held out his wrist to her. "Come! I would break my fast."

For an instant he sensed the waywardness in her, but the chin framed by the snowy barbette lowered demurely and she glided forward to set her hand meekly upon his sleeve. Then she faltered, raising her head, as if her glance swept round the expectant faces in the hall beyond his back.

"It is easier not to look," he advised kindly, mollified by her obedience. He was hoping that nervousness rather than mischief might render her more malleable this morning, but he could not resist adding provocatively as he conducted her to the table, "I was waiting for you to curtsey in apology. My servant is still grumbling."

She mistook his humour but the poke of language awoke her voice.

"Be glad that your face is more resilient than mine," she retorted, her tone disrespectful for a wife, the veil rising and falling with her breath. He did not answer her effrontery. Like salted herring, she would keep.

A page materialised at his elbow with a ewer and napkin and, thankful for the formality to mend the silence, he dabbled his fingers in the perfumed water and hoped that everyone would stop looking at him as if he had six heads and a demon's tail.

Lady Constance waved him to be seated and the tension eased. Somehow both the ladies Constance and Johanna conveyed the sense of keeping the lid on a bubbling broth. The household discreetly received the message and gradually the rumble of conversation resumed, softer of course—they were all straining like spring grass shoots towards the sun to hear what he was saying.

Freshly perturbed by the stranger's return, Johanna was startled to find he was just as large without his armour and quite as unpleasant as the day before. With her composure in utter disarray, she watched in astonishment as Gervase de Laval, without hesitation, unbuckled the baldrick carrying his sword and complacently slung it upon the back of the only chair as if he belonged in the castle. It was her father's chair of estate.

Her mother was taking a risk in accepting the gesture so meekly. Forgetting her veiling, Johanna sent her parent a querying look, but Lady Constance, unable to see it, sat down stonily, pretending she disapproved of the entire matter and could not do a thing about it.

To do him credit, Johanna's supposed husband courteously saw her seated upon his other side before he calmly made himself comfortable. She perched tensely on her stool, wondering how the man beside her could be so much at ease if he was a poor scholar. In his shoes, she would have been apprehensive of her manners, but this rogue was enjoying every instant of it, swanning like a true knight. Perhaps it was the clothes that made the difference to a man's confidence.

He had discarded the chainmail, gauntlets and other protective bits and pieces that knights strapped on for the gorget of dark blue and the soft fustian tunic of madder dye that Yolonya, the speediest seamstress among them, had been secretly labouring upon in her mother's bower two days before. The hood was lined cunningly with tawny taffeta, so too were the hanging scalloped sleeves, reaching to his calves. But it was not all borrowed splendour, she conceded, for he had also taken pains with his person; his chin was shaven skillfully without a cut and his fair hair, unsettled about his face, had been freshly washed.

Now if she had exchanged marriage vows with a man such as this two years before—no, what was the use of such imaginings, of maybes, when Fulk's cruelty lay encrusted like a festering sore upon her spirits. Firmly, briefly, Johanna closed her mind against the memory of the beatings and endless haranguing, rationalising that this arrogant scholar might be just as great a tyrant in the bedchamber. All men were. Many a time she had heard her father berate her mother behind the bedcurtains. No, she would trust no man, especially not this upstart. And he, curse him, was glancing about with a very smug air.

This pleases me well, Geraint was thinking. The respect he saw in people's faces was very satisfying and the chair felt comfortable against his back as if it had been carved for him. After all, if he really had given his vows to Lady Johanna, with Lord Alan incapacitated and the boy he assumed to be the heir still a minor, this castle was his to command. And—he paused, his alecup halfway to his lips—to carry matters to extremes, if the archdeacon's court approved this so-called marriage, he could dig himself into this burrow permanently. The thought amused him, but beside him Lady Johanna fidgeted with the food set before her and he changed his mind. In any case, he was not going to abandon the Mortimers who had given him employment since he had fled the monastery, and the sooner he was out of these women's clutches, the better.

Lady Constance cleared her throat. "As you can imagine, Sir Gervase, I slept little for worrying about this matter and my head truly aches from thinking on it, so I have asked our chaplain whom you met yesterday to hear what you have both told me." She sighed, drawing her fingers down her face with seeming weariness. "It is my opinion that you have each spoken the truth, but I will follow Father Gilbert's judgment . . . and, of course, your wishes, Johanna, in this. I am informed there is an archdeacon's court session due this week, so if my chaplain agrees that you are in the right, you, sir, will have to bring a petition before it against Johanna."

"Who is this man?" Before he could answer her, the dark-haired boy pushed in between them. The glass buttons marching down a fustian cote-hardie and the oak-leafed oversleeves confirmed Geraint's impression that this must be Lord Alan's son and heir, though what he was doing still at Conisthorpe at his age was questionable. "Why is he in my father's chair?" he demanded shrilly. "You said I could not sit in it though it is my right, so why may he?"

He looked about twelve years old, but to measure him by his manners instead of inches, the brat must be somewhat younger than his height suggested. Lady Constance slid an arm about the boy's waist but he shrugged her off with unconcealed embarrassment.

"Not now, Miles," muttered Johanna. "Go and finish your bread."

"I said who are you? I have not seen you before," the boy persisted.

"No, but I have," snapped Johanna, "and that is enough. Madam!" Lady Constance calmly sent him back to his seat, where the child sat petulantly, glaring at Johanna.

"I will find time to talk with you later in the day, young man," Geraint offered recklessly. "After I have had speech privily with your sister and the chaplain." Hopefully that would staunch the imp's questions for now, else he would be bound to ask what no one yet had dared to.

"My elder brother, Hal, God rest his soul, died on the field of Bannockburn." Johanna sadly crossed herself, adding "That is why Mother spoils Miles."

"Yes, I can see she has not learned from her mistakes," he answered. Clearly not used to banter, the lady was not amused. "No, do not throw wine over me this morning, my love," he added hastily. What would it take to make her smile? He raised his cup to her, drank and then challengingly turned it so she might drink from the same place.

He watched her hesitate, like a swimmer caught between Scylla and Charybdis, obviously hating the intimacy of the gesture but conscious that the household was watching them as keenly as dogs slavering for tidbits. She lifted the cup, however, and, raising her veil economically, appeared to take a sip.

Now what was expected? Johanna wondered, unused to the part of loving wife. The silence lay between them like a mother-in-law. The stranger made no effort to break it, merely attacked the bread with white, strong teeth. In fact, thought Johanna enviously, it looked as though he had most of them. He certainly was one of the most comely men she had ever set eyes on. However was she going to manage him? She gave him another pensive glance from beneath her lashes. That nose was unquestionably the sort that she imagined had landed with the Conqueror. As for his strong jaw, she wagered he would not take insults lightly.

Insults! What was wrong with her? she chided herself. She should be drooling over him with gratitude, but instead she found him alarming. Oh *Maman*, she thought apologetically, she and the scholar had no more chance of pulling this cart along together than a lamb yoked with a donkey.

She realised he had been staring openly at her with a mixture of amusement and irritation. Of course, being her long-mislaid husband, the wretch could bestow his stares wherever it pleased him. Dear Heaven, she thought, this rogue might soon abuse the situation.

"I am most displeased you called me a whore last night," she told him softly with dangerous sweetness.

The blue eyes studied her unblinking. "For what you did, lady, you are fortunate that I did not set you across my knee before your servants."

Johanna panicked, recoiling as though he had struck her and would have risen had he not grabbed her wrist.

Damn her! Geraint had not realised how genuinely sensitive she was. "Pardon, my lady." With contrition, he turned her hand over and pressed his lips to her palm.

Johanna fumed inwardly. Yes, he was supposed to behave like this to convince everyone they had been in love, but the knowledge that he despised her made his every gesture an affront. Well, it needed two for a tournament. She had bested him last night and she would win this also. Jerking her hand away, she sprang to her feet, her voice tearful and loud.

"Where were you when I needed you? No one believed me. Two years!" She cast her gaze towards the high beams. "What was I supposed to think?"

The servants, hurrying through the body of the hall, halted in mid-stride, agog at the entertainment provided by their betters. Her brother's jaw dropped like a portcullis whose rope has frayed.

"I am here now, lady." Her father's chair scraped back as Sir Gervase rose and towered over her. "I gave you my word I would return."

As if mollified, she slowly lowered herself onto the stool, dabbing a napkin beneath her veil.

Geraint returned to his repast, wondering whether he would prefer to strangle her now or later. He ate, as if in sulky silence, but not sure what to say or do next. His supposed wife was giving him no help whatsoever.

With relief, he saw Father Gilbert striding up to them. Exchanging greetings with Lady Constance, the priest nodded to them. "Sir, my lady, if you would both accompany me to my cell after your repast, I shall be happy to hear your testimony."

"That pleases me well," exclaimed Geraint wholeheartedly, summoning the page with the ewer. His fingers cleansed, he thrust out his hand for the shrew to take. "Come, madam," he barked.

The lady huffily rested her fingers on his wrist. He did not know that behind her veil she put her tongue out at him and wished he would suffer a plague of boils before the week was out.

FATHER GILBERT'S CELL SMELLED OF WAX AND INK, QUITE DIFFERENT from the apothecary aroma which Geraint had been expecting. There was a narrow room leading from the chamber which was simply furnished with a trestle and forms. A small illuminated tome, propped on a stand, lay open on the table and the low stub of the candle explained the priest's tired look. Beneath the mullioned window a stone sill boasted an array of plants, a saucer of galls, a pair of scales and a pot with "Copperas" scratched upon its paper label in spindly writing.

"Now, my children, I will leave you and say my prayers. Use this time to think back on what happened between you two years ago. When you are resolved, we shall go through it together as if I was the archdeacon's officer."

Not for the first time, Geraint wondered why the chaplain was helping them, but the priest met his suspicious glance with the sort of beatific smile that only a few churchmen manage to acquire, and closed the door of the inner room, leaving them alone.

As if a master of the tournament had tossed the cloth to begin, Johanna began the gallop.

"How very sensible," she applauded, flouncing past the shelf of plants. "Well, sir, the hunting season is now upon us and we may privily tear each other to shreds since we are both reluctant to be part of this mummery."

Geraint frowned. There was little time to make their plans, and he would be cursed if he would give her his blessing to quarrel further. It was necessary to keep to the essentials.

"I am in your hands, lady. This is your demesne. You must tell me how and when we met." He sat down on the form resignedly, which creaked in objection to his weight. "I take it you have given the matter *some* thought?"

Ignoring the jibe, Johanna paced around the table. "Mother and I decided on two years ago because that was just before our parish priest died and we could pretend that you and I took our vows before him. It would have been—"

"Do you think you could take off that ridiculous veil?" he interrupted testily. "And stop pretending to be a horsemill. My head is not on a swivel."

His remarks brought her to a suprised halt. "I . . . I do not like other people seeing my bruises."

"I am not other people. It irritates me. For the Lord's sake, lady, it is like talking to a curtain blowing in a draught."

"You think it does not annoy *me*?" she growled, but she rearranged it over her parted hair, tucking it behind the crespine. As there was only one form, she reluctantly sat down at the other end of it.

To her dismay, he shifted closer. He was on the bruised side of her and it startled her to have him take her chin in his hand. "I would keep the bruises ripe for the court and in the common view if I were you. It will help our case." He inspected her hurts as if he were calculating their worth.

Johanna's breathing swiftened at his proximity and the unpro-
voked familiarity. She did not dare to look into his face but she
could smell the pleasant musk he wore and a warning went off in
her mind like a bird shrilling danger. She mistrusted the way this
man had an impact on her senses. Lifting her face haughtily from
his fingers, she answered, "True. I will try to find the courage to
do without it. Would you prefer that we change places so you will
not have to look at my bruises?"

"That bespeaks vanity. But, yes, if it pleases you." He slid back
to the other end and stood up.

In an embarrassed silence Johanna wriggled further along the
bench. He sat down in her former place, moved the bookstand
back so he might prop his elbows on the table, and spoke, not
looking at her, but running his forefinger along the rough grain of
the trestle.

"I realise you are very sensitive about your appearance, my
lady, but try to forget about it now. We have much labour before
us."

"Very well," she agreed.

In profile, Geraint was disturbed to discover that she really was
quite beautiful, like a coin that was freshly minted on one side and
bludgeoned on the other. It gratified him too that she dressed with
care. Now that her veil was set back he could see her glossy raven
hair was neatly braided, not tightly but with a gentle fullness that
emphasised her femininity. He was amused to note her skin grow
right rosy under his study and chivalrously let his attention fall
upon the chaplain's leatherbound tome instead.

"Let us continue, my lady. Pray, describe the priest to me."

With a rabbit of thought to chase, Johanna became less inhibited
at being closeted alone with the stranger.

"The parish priest's name was Father Benedict and he was about
three score in years. He had sky-blue eyes, and three warts—here,
here and here." Aware of the man's eyes upon her face again,
she pinkened further and lowered her gaze modestly to the table.
"He . . . he had wispy white hair round the back of his head, the
rest was bald. His hands were veined, even more so than Father
Gilbert's." She continued to itemise the priest's appearance and
then made him repeat it, counting off the points on her fingers.

"When did we meet?"

"In the wild wood. You were making camp. You had come to St. Robert's spring because you had heard the saint performed miracles and you had a very bad rash and feared it was leprosy and a friend of yours had his skin trouble cured by the saint so—"

"Dear God preserve me," Geraint crossed himself.

"And you fell in love with me at first sight and decided to become better acquainted so you stayed two more days in the forest and waited for me each afternoon."

"And how was it you managed to contrive our meetings, my lady?"

"Agnes, my maid, told everyone I was indisposed."

He sighed. It sounded feasible.

"I borrowed her hood and kirtle for a disguise."

"Could we not have met in London or somewhere else distant from here? In another household? At the king's court?"

"I visited the household of my lord Despenser when King Edward and Queen Isabella were there, yes, that was over two years ago."

The man's shoulders stiffened for an instant. "You meant the castle at Caerphilly?"

"No." She looked puzzled. "Ah, you are talking about his son, Hugh Despenser the younger. No, I meant the older Despenser. He has a fine house in Bristol, but perhaps you—"

"A remarkable coincidence. Yes, I have actually been inside the older Hugh Depenser's house in Bristol, and his messuage in London too. I once did some notary work for him."

"For a scholar, you are much travelled." She gave a little sigh of envy. "But I have been to Westminster too. We were at that Feast of Pentecost when the king was shamed by a strange letter and—"

He cut her short. "I think we are making progress at last. So perhaps Sir Gervase met Lady Johanna in Bristol when the king was visiting. Was there an opportunity for dalliance while she was there?"

"Oh yes, there were feasts and entertainment. Perhaps he fell in love with her at first sight and had the courage to write a poem to her and bribe her maidservant to conceal it beneath her pillow and she was so delighted that she spoke with him and . . . Oh, it is so much easier saying this impersonally." Her self-consciousness returning, she lowered her eyes again modestly. "Your pardon, I ran away with that bone but does it sound reasonable?"

"It sounds more believable, and so, with a headful of deplorable poetry, he tracked her back like a hunter to her home." Surely that must have happened to the lady Johanna? She was lovely enough. Had no man made her giddy-headed with a poem?

Johanna glanced sideways at him. Despite his male arrogance, she appreciated the effort he was making to be constructive. Yes, this man might convince the court of his tenacity. He definitely would hunt down the object of his desire.

Heartened, she continued. "Ah, I know, he sent her a letter that he was dying of love in the wild wood and only her presence would succour him. She could not resist. It was a mission of mercy. Yes, I like that." She clapped her hands. "Men can be so foolish in love that they will traverse kingdoms to seek their beloved." Suddenly remembering her reluctant audience, she coloured and added in a sad whisper, "At least, so the ballads say."

She darted another peep at him. For an instant, she had foolishly forgotten her mistrust of him. But he was actually smiling and it looked genuine.

The temptation was irresistible. "Have you ever been that lovesick, master scholar?"

There was weight in that catapult, thought Geraint, his good humour with her fast disappearing as he caught her coy glance. Because he did not answer her, she seemed to realise the ground was hazardous. He watched her fingers play nervously with the hem of her veil. "I beg your pardon, sir, but it would help me to know. I mean you no malice." There was no flirtatiousness in her voice, but he could pay her in equal coin.

"Yes, I have felt the affliction very badly. Have you?"

"No!"

It was wise to urge the story forward since the sudden silence had become as uncomfortable as the wrong-sized saddle. He rose to pluck a dead leaf from one of the chaplain's pots. "So this rebellious maid met a stranger in the wild wood. Thrice?"

"He wooed her and declared his love. Being foolish and inexperienced, not to mention rebellious, she believed him." Talking to this man's back was far easier than facing that hard, intelligent gaze.

"How old would you have been, my lady?"

Discovering her age? A probing question, though valid.

"Sev . . . about eighteen," she answered truthfully. "And you?"

"I suppose, two-and-twenty." He idly flicked at a cobweb. "So she managed to give him kisses instead of visiting the sick. I would wager he merely desired to lie with her."

"No, he loved her," Johanna insisted, twisting her hands in her lap. "They took their vows."

He turned and leaned forward emphatically, his hands gripping the table edge. "But he never came back."

"He did! You have!"

Their eyes locked like hounds' assessing each other before a brawl. Jesu, his instinct told him weaving this fabric of falsehoods with her was going to become a torment. His breast rose with a sigh as he straightened. "Yes, I have."

Her heart beating somewhat faster, Johanna spoke rapidly.

"They made their solemn vows before Father Benedict. Sir Gervase promised her he would come back one day but he warned her that he would be required to serve his lord when he got back from his pilgrimage."

"Pilgrimage, what pilgrimage?" he asked testily. Another of her flights of creativity.

"Rome? Jerusalem?" she suggested hopefully. "I am trying to think of reasons why he would be away so long."

He had his temper bridled again. "I have been to Compostela but no further. Let it simmer for now." He paced and swung round. "Forgive the indelicacy, lady, but this matter must be aired. Did he lie with her?"

She would not look up. "Oh no," she answered too quickly, colour flooding her cheeks.

"She is lying." He folded his arms. "Of course, she lay with him. No sane man would let the opportunity past."

"He was noble, chivalrous, upholding the virtues of courtly love."

"Fie on that, lady, save it for dreamers. The reality is adultery. Chivalry does not exist outside the stories. The real world is Fulk de Enderby."

Eight

JOHANNA SPRANG UP LIKE A PANICKED WILD THING AND would have bolted, but the stranger caught her arm before she reached the door and furled her hanging sleeve about his other hand.

It was like taking hold of an unbroken mare, thought Geraint, one that might kick him, but he persisted. "Sir Gervase must have lain with her, my lady. They had the blessing of Holy Church."

"Let go of me!" she squealed, flailing out at him. "Do not touch me!"

"In God's name, my lady, be silent!" He thrust her down on the bench. Thank the Lord, she subsided, but her breathing was fast and her hands were still clenched into fists in her lap.

"Whatever—" Father Gilbert burst out of his room and halted as Geraint flung up a hand to stay him.

"Be calm, Father, there is no harm done."

Johanna's breathing grew slower but she was close to tears as she regained mastery of herself. "I am sorry." She put her fingers to her temples as if there was pain between them. "This ship will founder. I know it will. Go, sir, before we drown you with us."

"May I ask what this is about?" The priest fixed Geraint sternly.

He answered readily, "Oh, worldliness, a true marriage in the sight of God. If Gervase de Laval married this lady two years ago, they would have lain together to consummate the match. It would lack validity otherwise, yes?"

Father Gilbert perused Johanna's averted face. "Ah."

With a wary eye on her, Geraint explained. "Let me offer you a hypothesis, Father. If Holy Church has given its blessing to a man and a woman, there is no hindrance to their lying together."

"But we are not talking hypothetically, my son. We are referring to your behaviour, are we not? Do you mean now or two years back?"

Geraint watched Johanna's green-grey eyes grow large as cart wheels.

"Either." He knew the answer but he needed the priest to convince her.

"There is no hindrance in either situation."

"She wouldn't have!" The lady jumped to her feet. This time he was ready, but careful not to touch her. He barred the way. "I need to think, sir," she protested. At least she held the reins of her emotions now.

"Is there time for that, my lady? If you want to outwit Sir Fulk, you have to pretend to yourself that you confirmed your marriage vows *de facto*, not merely *de jure*."

The priest nodded. "Such is the way of the world, Johanna. My son, perhaps you would like to step outside and ask your servant to fetch us a hot posset from the kitchen? My room is cold and my bones are stiff. It is a small vanity, I fear."

Geraint accepted the errand like a drowning man thrown a rope.

Johanna sank gloomily onto the bench as the door closed. "How very tactful of you, Father. See! He is a dog that cannot wait to be let out." She slapped the table. "God help me, I do not know if I can proceed with this further. I suppose you overheard most of this through your prayers."

Her sarcasm fell off him like raindrops on duck feathers. "You are making headway, daughter. It can work if you are diligent." He half-sat himself on the table. "Let us be honest with one another. Your mother tells me that anyone who remembers your willful nature as a little maid will not be surprised at this secret marriage."

"I would. If I met that maiden again, I would not recognise myself in her." Johanna trailed a finger down the side of the book's leather cover. "I have changed, Father. The woman I am now would never have met that man in the wild wood. And even two years ago I was never a harlot. Headstrong perhaps, but never wanton. I have always tried to obey God's commandments, every one of them."

He sat down beside her and took her right hand in his. "But that is not at issue. You must forget how you feel *now* about marriage. To win your case, you must convince the jurors that you married this man, who was landless then, secretly because you loved him so much that you were willing to risk your father's wrath. You wanted to bind him to you with holy vows and, in return, you offered him your love, your duty and your body."

She tensed. "Yes, I see that. But I do not want to think of this man in those terms. It is hard for you to understand as a priest and I do not think I can even begin to explain what I feel or," she set his hand free upon the table, "perhaps it is what I have never been able to feel."

His face was compassionate. "Daughter, do not let the bruises Sir Fulk has put upon your body remain like scars on your soul as well. Two years ago, you must have believed that love was possible. Two years ago, you would have let this handsome stranger lie with you because you loved him and believed in his fidelity. You must resurrect this belief, child. Cleanse your heart and believe that you could have loved."

How could he understand how damaged she was—that marriage to Fulk had been like living with grey embers that any instant could flare into an evil fire that scorched all within its path. "Remember that our beloved Lord said one must be like a child again to enter the kingdom of Heaven. Try to see it in those terms. To free yourself of this marriage, pull down the fences you have set up and begin afresh."

She stood up, desiring some solitude to make sense of herself before she faced the stranger again, but the chaplain's expression disturbed her. Father Gilbert was trustworthy, but there was a smugness now about his mouth.

"Why are you helping us with these falsehoods?" she asked. "You, a priest, are encouraging this man to perjury and advising me to set aside vows made before God. It does not make any sense. The archbishop would not approve, would he?"

"Why, child? Because I want to see you free of Sir Fulk before he destroys you completely." She turned away unsatisfied, knowing that he was completely dependent on her mother for his livelihood. Was it merely to please Lady Constance that he was being pliant? After all, age and its accompanying laziness would make him reluctant to face the labour of seeking a parish benefice.

"You think to spur the horse in a different direction by asking these things, Johanna. If you do not understand yourself, how can you understand me or any other human being?" He stood up and stepped behind her like Satan in the wilderness. "Since your return I have glimpsed the desperation in you, watched you contemplating an unhallowed grave." Her head jerked up at that. He had read her so clearly. "You can put your life to better worth. Give yourself to God. Do not baulk at this hedge, my daughter, or else you will be ensnared in a living Hell forever."

"Oh surely I am guaranteeing myself a mattress in the real Hell either way," she countered. "Well, no matter. But will you be there to lead me in when the Devil bids us welcome? My falsehoods tarnish you and Mother. Is that just?"

His face tightened. Oh, the hammer definitely hit the anvil but still he outmanoeuvred her. "I perceive the hand of God in all things, and I do know this: after your mother and I prayed to save you, Lord Alan was smitten by God and the stranger appeared in the forest."

"A miracle and a thunderbolt. How very comforting." She hated the cynicism in her tone and relented with a sigh, "Yes, perhaps, you are right, Father."

"Child, let us return to this issue which dismays you so. You have to admit to having had carnal knowledge of this man Gervase, or the archdeacon's court will not believe you." He held up a hand to staunch her protest. "I have been in love. I understand its power, my daughter. Love would have made you risk—will make you risk—anything to be in the arms of this man you met two years ago. And, Johanna, you would not have behaved like a harlot then, you would have behaved like a wife. Look at me, my lady. Trust my judgment."

She read the pity in his eyes and knew she lacked healing.

"What is it like being in love for a man?"

Pain lanced across his face as if she had thrown cold water at him. "No, please forget I asked that, Father. I had no right to pry." But he had confirmed her suspicion. Loving hurt. Because she loved her little dog, Fulk's ill-treatment of it left her vulnerable.

"My child." The chaplain put a fatherly arm about her shoulders and sat her down with him again. "I was once the happiest and most unhappy man on earth. If my love smiled at me, I walked on air, but if she scowled, it was as if all delight in the world was gone. I knew carnal lust. I burned for her like a soul in Satan's fire."

"Did you . . ."

"Lie with her? No, I was green as a new shoot, and she was wife to a young lord. No, I did not dare touch her."

"Did she love you?"

Father Gilbert smiled and Johanna sensed it was a foolish question, but he still answered her. "I doubt it, but I thought of her the whole time until I understood how much I was betraying God. So I prayed for our dear Saviour's help and He gave me courage to leave that household. And yet I am glad I felt Love's arrows, for all their pain. You see, it helps me understand why people in love behave so. And you, my daughter, have not yet felt those darts."

"Why does God curse us so?" She rose and waved her hands as if the explanation might fall into her fingers like a ball. "Oh forgive me." She paced away and then spun round on him. "Why are we such a mess of emotions? Sometimes I wish myself a simple woodland creature that feeds and ruts according to the seasons." She slammed her fist into her palm. "I need to find some other way out of this."

"It is too late for that. You are in the saddle and so must ride." A new proverb! The canny churchman—tactfully avoiding the adage about making a bed and lying in it.

The latch rattled. "Ah, daughter, here is refreshment."

Geraint returned with a scullion at his heels. They were interrupting too soon to judge by the priest's expression but the possets had already cooled crossing the yard and he had glimpsed Lady Edyth prowling. There was little time to waste. He closed the door when the servant left and took up his beaker, setting a booted foot upon the bench. Father Gilbert scowled at him and he removed it.

"So, does our story progress, Father?"

The chaplain did not appear happy. "I will catechise you before mass, so back to your labour."

Geraint handed Johanna the posset and watched her savour each mouthful.

Cradling the drink, she raised an amused eyebrow at him as if reading his face for weather signs. "Do you want to put your armour on again? It might make you feel safer until I have finished drinking."

He regarded her unsmiling, although she could have sworn a very faint muscle twitched slightly at the side of his mouth. "Perhaps I will keep mine until you have emptied yours. So let us recommence, my lady. We have the reasons, we have the priest, although that will need further colour—"

"The vows are important," Father Gilbert interrupted, setting his empty cup down. He ran a hand through his narrow waves of greying hair as he warmed to his argument. "Every word is crucial. You see, Sir Gervase, if you had said to Lady Johanna, 'I will take you' instead of 'I will have you' or 'I will espouse you,' the court could argue the intent was there but not the deed, and that you merely meant to cajole the lady into sin."

"So tell us the rightful wording, Father," Johanna said brusquely. The talk of ifs and buts—especially as to whether or not she would have lain with this man—was wearying her.

" 'Ego volo habere te pro uxore mea quantum vita mea durare poterit': I, Gervase, will have thee, Johanna, as my wife for the rest of my life."

Her supposed husband repeated the Latin softly, his presence, huge and real, somehow relieving Johanna's painful memory of the same vow Fulk had made beside her at the chapel door.

"And I suppose I would have said the same?" she asked.

"In Latin?" the scholar queried sceptically, looking to Father Gilbert.

"Do you think because I am a woman that I am totally ignorant?" Johanna countered.

Gervase de Laval's indifferent blue gaze did not falter. "Yes."

Johanna swirled to the door snarling a Latin curse at him.

The priest rose. "Where in God's Name did you learn that, child?"

She read the astonishment in both their faces. It was terrible of her to shock poor Father Gilbert but her mother's poor scholar was wearing a grin as wide as the west portal of a cathedral.

"Do you know what you just said, lady?" he asked.

"Yes," she lied stoutly. The stranger folded his lips trying not to burst out laughing and failed. "Oh, very well, master scholar, what did I say then?" Hands on her hips, she faced him like a market wife.

He eventually wiped the tears from his eyes: "The translation is: 'A thousand demons take me, I have forgotten to pack my dinner in my saddlebag.' "

"Oh!" Her disappointment seemed to please him.

"Wherever did you learn such a wondrously foul oath, lady?"

"From Father Benedict," she answered huffily. "I once heard him say that when I was a child. He crossed himself most vigorously afterwards so I always thought it was something very profane."

His disarming grin somewhat settled her ruffled feathers even though it was at the cost of her pride. And the smile seemed kind, not merely skin-deep.

She sat down again and grabbed the bridle of the conversation. "I thought maybe Sir Gervase could have written his love a letter to meet her at Father Benedict's house, but—"

"You cannot read, can you?" Gervase interrupted. She shook her head regretfully. "Then, mayhap, I shall have to teach you."

"It pleases you to mock me," she snapped and instantly regretted it, for he was a scholar and must value learning, but it was rare for any man to make such an offer.

Father Gilbert clapped Sir Gervase on the shoulder. "An excellent notion, but you have no time to be tutoring. A letter, well, that would be a fine piece of evidence. Old Father Benedict would have had to read it to her. Let us do it now." Fishing a key from the neck of his habit, he asked the scholar to reach down a wooden coffer. "I need a document two years old," he muttered, evicting half the contents.

Johanna exchanged a puzzled glance with Gervase as the priest peered at each document at arm's length.

"And would my lady prefer a letter that merely requests a meeting place or would she like it to contain a rhyme likening her to a gazelle?" A sinful quicksilver had replaced the cold steel blue in the scholar's eyes.

"No need to mock King Solomon, young man," clucked the priest.

"Perhaps a blend would be appropriate," declared Johanna

gravely, lowering her eyes at his teasing. "I am sure you have had plenty of practice. What about Sir Gervase offering to meet his love at Father Benedict's and there make an honest woman of her? Father, we need a calendar for the saint's day."

"First things first. No, none of these will do. I may have to ride down to Bainham Priory." He stared at their blank faces. "I need to cut a strip of vellum from a document written two years ago. Fresh vellum will be too new. Fortunately I have a bottle of old ink which might suffice. Yes, I think I will have a word with Brother Ambrose."

"Whoa, good father," Gervase set a warning hand upon his arm, "the fewer folk who know, the better."

"Nonsense, Brother Ambrose replaces all the priory's documents if any are damaged or stolen. I shall not tell him the purpose."

"But that is—" Johanna's indignant glance met Gervase's surprised expression above the priest's head. "I did not know of that practice," she ended, deciding it was better not to voice her thoughts.

"Father Ambrose could write the letter for you if you give me an example of your hand. I would take you with me, my son, but it might be safer for you to remain within the safety of the castle. In any case, you would not wish to be parted from one another so soon."

"No, I will write my own love missive, thank you." Gervase sat himself down on the bench again, bringing up his ankle over his knee, and looked indifferently across at her. As if to appease the chaplain, he added in a less disagreeable tone: "Your advice regards the vellum, Father, shows great foresight."

"Good, good, do not forget to calculate the day that you were wed."

"Not to mention when and where we consummated our marriage." Testily, Gervase was on his feet again and looming above her like some threatening raptor. "In God's Name, my lady, do you think you could possibly manage to stop blushing like an abbess every time I mention the matter? Anyone would think you had never been wedded and bedded."

Johanna reddened further, but with undiluted fury and lapsed into a sullen silence. He ignored her sulks and began to discuss with Father Gilbert the practicalities of where he might have de-flowered her. Since the rogue was a stranger to the locality and the priest was not in the habit of seducing baron's daughters, they eventually reached an impasse and both looked round at her as if she was finally entitled to comment.

She ignored them, her fingers folding and refolding the edge of her veil. Father Gilbert's hand came down reassuringly on her shoulder.

"I have to go and prepare for mass, child. Try and think this matter out and who stood witness, then you must both come and kneel together for God's guidance."

The latch had barely fallen behind the priest when the upstart scholar, fattened with self-conceit, sallied in on the attack: "When you have come out of your sulks, my lady, perhaps you would care to contribute something useful to this discussion on our sup-posed coupling."

There were times when words were inadequate. Johanna grabbed her beaker and slammed it down on the table.

He was laughing at her. "Do you want to quote Latin at me again?" he teased and then flung up his arms in a pretence of terror as the lady squared up to him like a tiny terrier confronting a wolfhound. Too late he realised he had blundered.

"I have had enough! Mock me and snigger, if it amuses you, you arrogant upstart, but understand this! Discussing the consum-mation of our so-called marriage is anathema to me. I have been raped by Fulk de Enderby more times than I care to remember. Now either come to terms with that or get out of my sight. Look at me, God damn you!"

The grin was wiped from Geraint's face as though her words had physically struck him. He forced himself to study every inch of her bruised face anew. To have looked away now would have been cowardice and brought shame upon them both.

He swallowed eventually, fumbling for words. "Will you accept my profound apology?" Dear Jesu, all he could muster sounded pitiful and inadequate.

Her gaze freed him at last, as she turned away. "Words are but meaningless puffs of air. They must be, else you would not be willing to perjure yourself."

"My lady . . ." Even his tone fell short.

"This is not a game, scholar. I have vowed to take my own life rather than suffer such humiliation ever again."

He ran a finger around the neck of his shirt as if it choked him. "I . . . I do not know what recompense I can make. You know I did not want to be—"

"—part of this foolery. We all have our price and my mother knows yours."

"My lady, you wrong me!"

"Ha! Never tell me you are also doing this in the name of the chivalry you so despise. Rescuing a damsel from a dragon? How noble!"

He looked away, unable to tolerate her scorn, and unleashed his own anger. He was not going to take this from a woman, no matter if she had been raped by half the kingdom.

"You do not know the half of it," he snarled. "There are other kinds of suffering. You do not have the monopoly." She had not been at Boroughbridge; she had not found her companions with their throats cut, lying in puddles of their own blood. Nor would he ever tell her why he had fled from the monastery or speak of the leering faces salivating as they had scourged him.

Some pain must have showed in his face for the wrath suddenly went out of her and she sank down, her face hidden in her hands.

"My lady," he said softly, seating himself down on the bench beside her as if it were a stile. "I can see that you and I will fight all through this. It is in our nature so let us accept it. Perhaps our guardian angels glare at one another, brandishing flaming swords."

She straightened up and looked at him through eyes swimming with tears. "I suppose so," she sniffed.

His hand came down, like a lion's paw, encompassing hers with a reassuring clasp. "Be cheerful. With God's mercy, this may be over in a week's time, and you will then be free of both your husbands."

She nodded, smudging away the droplets. "I suppose we had better go to mass together."

He reached out and with surprisingly gentle fingers lowered her veil, then he stood and held out a hand to her.

"Truce?"

Nine

"FORNICATORS! YOU ARE NOT FIT TO ENTER GOD'S house!" Edyth pounced as they were about to enter the chapel with the ruthlessness of a half-starved cat lying in wait for her prey. Her face was twisted in fury. Lank brown hair was already escaping untidily from her two long plaits and the ribbons woven in them looked like they had been caught there accidentally. "You disgusting harlot!" She spat at her sister-in-law's veiled face.

I should have been expecting this, thought Johanna, setting back the spattered veil with a calmness she did not feel.

"Do you want to hit me too, Lady Edyth? Your brother does it constantly." There was a supportive mutter from the household officers gathering around them.

Edyth ignored her and jabbed her pointed chin in the air at Gervase. "What, have you abandoned your stained armour so soon, fornicator? Say your prayers for I have sent word to my brother."

Johanna's large companion seemed outwardly amused. "At what hour do you expect him, lady? He shall find me ready. Does he come to admire his handiwork upon my lady's face?" He astonished Johanna by brushing his fingers down her bruised cheek with such unexpected kindness that she could have wept. It gave her new heart to face down her sister-in-law's malevolence.

Edyth's fingers flexed into claws. "Oh, you will rue this, you hellspawn! If Lord Alan was in his wits, he—"

"What are you about, my children? Is no one coming in to

mass?" Interrupting her, Father Gilbert's hands came down firmly on Edyth's shoulders as he stepped quickly through the arched doorway.

"Excommunicate them!" shrieked Edyth, as if she felt the strength of Holy Church behind her. "They besmirch us by their presence."

"There are always a great many gathered here who are in need of the Lord's forgiveness," replied the chaplain diplomatically, firmly setting her to one side. "Do not cast stones, my daughter, we are all sinners."

"What!" Edyth rounded on him, wild eyes blazing. "You, a holy father, believe their pack of lies?"

"Demoiselle!" Lady Constance's voice rang out and the throng parted for her. "Cease this unseemly behaviour! If you wish to join us for mass, do so! If not, remove yourself. I cannot have my household idling."

Edyth's shoulders jerked in fury and she marched ahead into the chapel as if she was leading the fifth crusade to save Jerusalem.

Johanna felt like running to her bed and dissolving into tears except to flee would have been a sign of guilt and cowardice—but the hand holding hers gave it a reassuring squeeze. Or was it merely a let-us-be-moving-we-cannot-stand-here-all-day command? Curious, she glanced up, but her supposed husband's face wore an indifferent expression as he led her inside.

She was beginning to realise that, when it suited him, this reluctant ally could be a difficult man to read, and for all she disliked and mistrusted him, she grudgingly admitted that perhaps he might carry this off after all. That was if they could avoid the armed malice of Fulk and his kin and the hidden traps of canon law. Oh, by Heaven, she needed to pray for help. The thought of Fulk galloping up after dinner with his men-at-arms was making her innards turn to a poor man's gruel. Did the rented scholar realise the danger he was in? Did her mother imagine that Fulk, of all people, would be pacified with a calm discussion about the weather over a plate of oatcakes?

Prayers did not come easily; suddenly the entire household seemed to have undergone a surge of religious devotion. Even the most loutish of the stablehands, who usually had to be rounded up by Father Gilbert, was gaping at her. Johanna had hoped to have time during the service to resettle her shaken feelings, but she had not anticipated being incessantly scrutinised. She tried to pray, but the man beside her was chasing all thoughts from her head. He did not seem to be listening to the Latin either although his hands were pointed at the shrouded altar cross.

Standing gloomily in the crowded chapel, Geraint tried to ignore the wall painting of the temptation of Adam. It reminded him too much of his own situation. He did, however, manage prayers: for his dead companions; for the Mortimers; that Edmund might recover his wits; for Thomas, Earl of Lancaster, to be pardoned; and a thank-you prayer for Dame Christiana before his mind slid easily to a plea for his own survival and how soon he might escape Conisthorpe, not to mention the wrath of Fulk de Enderby and the tantrums of a wench who started like a frightened doe every time he touched her.

Indeed, he had recovered somewhat from the shrewish Johanna's verbal battering and was beginning to lick rationale into his wounds. Her behaviour, he decided, confirmed the opinion of men all over Christendom—women were definitely the weaker vessels and totally unable to control their emotions. Yes, he would have to be more cunning in his handling of all the women in this accursed place or there would be more squalls inside the castle than raining on its battlements.

Opening his eyes again, he observed that only Father Gilbert appeared to have his mind on prayer; everyone else was watching Johanna and himself as if they were a pair of fistfighters with money wagered on them.

"This must be one of the greatest entertainments Conisthorpe has had in years," Geraint muttered to Johanna as they left the chapel. "Do you suppose I might manage to toss you in the air and catch you as an encore?" He almost brought a smile to her face.

Instead she asked, "Are you intending to inspect the kitchens?"

His stride faltered at the square timber-framed building before them, umbilicled by a covered passageway to the buttery at the rear of the hall. "No."

"Then where would you like to go?"

"I have not the slightest notion. Somewhere my antics cannot be watched as if I was your mother's pet monkey. What about up there?" His glance skimmed the ramparts. "Or would you prefer to introduce me to your blacksmith?" Johanna became aware that the muscular, leather-aproned smith was standing, legs astride, outside the forge, watching their dithering.

"You are concerned about our defences?" she countered.

"Me, never think that. How many are we expecting to come battering at the gate?" Concerned? He was hoping a rope would descend from Heaven and hoist him across the Channel.

"Fulk lost three men at Boroughbridge." Her hand was dropped as though it scalded him.

He was silent for an instant and then replied, "To the walls then, with the permission of your lady mother." Johanna turned, following his gaze. Lady Constance was still outside the chapel door, listening to Father Gilbert, while Edyth hovered behind her pretending to instruct her maidservant, but it was clear from the cock of her head that she was trying to eavesdrop. "I think, my lady, you should advise your mother to have your sister-in-law watched at all times else she might prove too handy with a windlass. Should you not send for your cloak?"

Johanna resented the man giving orders but he was right; Edyth would certainly raise the portcullis if she could, and, yes, it might be chilly on the walls.

She spent the rest of the time before dinner following the upstart scholar like an obedient dog as he roamed the battlements assessing the castle. Occasionally he questioned her as to the number of the garrison, their training and what weaponry and food they had in store. Because she had been away from Conisthorpe, she did not know all the answers; that was now her mother's or Sir Geoffrey's demesne. He curled his mouth in irritation whenever she could not provide an easy answer and then the wretch began to lecture her about defences. It had to be the schoolmaster in him.

No, she was being unfair, for he actually explained rather than lectured and he did seem to understand castle defences extremely well for a poor scholar. Of course he could have been bluffing and merely putting on an authoritative tone, as men often did when their listeners were conveniently ignorant, but he did seem to make sense and she rather enjoyed the learning, though the purpose behind it filled her with foreboding. She hoped Fulk would not be-

siege the castle and force them into eventually eating rats, her tame
pig and her mother's ape.

Her new companion also wanted her to explain all the rooftops
that filled the courtyard.

"So the keep is little used by your family," he concluded, studying the great three-storeyed edifice with its straight walls and tur-
reted corners. "Not one of Hamelin Plantagenet's then?"

"No, King Henry II's. He ordered it to replace the old wooden
fort. The former hall has been made into a guardroom and the
upper floor chamber is where we store the muniments. And there
is a well in the undercroft, which can be drawn on as high as the
first floor and we do have another well in the inner bailey. We
passed it, near the east wall. But I have not been in the keep since
my return. I never feel warm there and it is so dark and miserable.
The new hall is lovely. Having the chimneys and great windows
makes such a difference."

He had made himself comfortable, half-sitting upon a crenel,
careful to avoid any fresh droppings of the inhabitants of the
nearby dovecote.

"Your family sleeps above the hall?"

Johanna was not going to stand before him like a schoolboy
reciting Ovid so she leaned her elbows back upon the wall and
tried to seem at ease. A couple of courting doves landed in a whirr
of feathers on the spattered paving. The lady dove inspected Johanna's toe beaks hopefully while her amorous pursuer stretched
out his neck, spread his magnificent white feathers in a half-fan
and tried to coo his feathery mistress into compliance. It would
have been a good omen for the less cynical; such a pair symbolised
blissful marriage.

"There is a bedchamber above the great chamber and below that
a vault where spices, medicines and costly bales are stored. We
have another guest bedchamber above the pantry. You probably
did not see the stairs behind the serving entrances."

"And where does your seneschal sleep?"

"Sir Geoffrey has the old solar in the keep and—"

She had lost his attention. He had observed a servant carrying
out a pannier of crumpled bed linen from a tower in the west wall.

"Who dwells there, my lady?"

"I . . . it is where they keep my father." The scholar's expression showed no interest, but he said softly, "Tell me about him."

"H-he cannot talk or do much for himself. He has a servant to cleanse him and spoon in nourishment. The man crops his hair and pares his nails but . . . well . . . God forgive me," she crossed herself, "I cannot say I am sorry."

"I should like to see him." It astonished her, but in his feigned role it seemed an appropriate courtesy. "Now, if it pleases you."

"As you wish. It is time I visited him again out of duty."

She led the way back down the steps, and then waited for him further down the path while he disappeared into the latrines set into the castle wall for common use. She was glad of a few minutes respite from his questions. Much of his conversation during the last hour had been skillfully devised, not only to make her more easy in his company but also for contingency. If there was an attack, as the most senior in rank, he would be expected to take charge of the garrison.

The scholar rejoined her. "Let us to your father then," he directed as if she had delayed him.

The small tower where her father lay overlooked the castle garden.

"There is a private chapel below, but my father is incapable of using it," Johanna explained as they followed Aidan, her sire's varlet, up the short flight of steps to the middle floor.

The Lord of Conisthorpe's chamber was shuttered, the air fetid with the overuse of lavender and sandalum. A feeble taper glowed halfheartedly in a corner.

"Is he asleep, Aidan? Ouch!" Her shinbone collided forcefully with a stool in the darkness.

The attendant hastened to remove it. "Hard to tell, my lady."

It was Gervase who threw open the shutters. There was no movement on the bed but her father stared at them, the inner circles of his eyes dilated. For an instant, she imagined a flicker of wildness, frustration, in the once handsome green eyes. Now his head was bonneted, like an old man's, in a white coif buttoned beneath his chin, and the dark hair, so like her own in colour, sat lacklustre and close-cropped above a sagging face. His belly was a large mound beneath bedclothes drawn up beneath his chin, and an undignified dribble of spittle trickled from the slackened right corner of his mouth.

"This is my husband, my lord father," Johanna announced, relishing every word. "This is the man I married secretly before you forced me into bondage with your despicable companion-in-arms. See again what Fulk did to my face, Father." She lifted the veil and leaned close.

"Have you told him of the other cruelties you have suffered?"

"Oh, yes, I came to see what God had done to him and I sat alone here in the darkness and told him what Fulk had made me suffer. It assuaged some of my bitterness but he could not hear me, so what was the use?"

Gervase was inspecting Lord Alan as though he was a strange, patterned stone thrown up by the plough. Physician-like, he peered closely at her father's eyes.

"He can blink," he observed, his strong voice driving Johanna's demons into abeyance.

"Yes, but the sounds he makes are ill-formed and he has no use of his right limbs.

"Does he take much nourishment?" he asked Aidan.

"Not much, sir. A little sweet barley water with liquorice in it and Flemish broth."

"I knew a household where a woman had been smitten so. Her daughter always hoped she might recover her wits and used to sit the poor soul in their hall beside the hearth so she might watch what was going on around her."

"Did she ever recover?"

He straightened up, shaking his head. "She never regained speech but sometimes I reckoned you could read gratitude in her eyes."

"Well, Conisthorpe is a happier place without him." Anxious to leave, Johanna held open the door, but he tarried, staring thoughtfully at her sire. "I suppose your father is still alive and hale, sir?"

"My father?" He raised his head slowly. "Oh yes, but dead to me. Would that matters had been otherwise."

Johanna tactfully resisted questioning him further. Mayhap he was a bastard and never knew his father's name or else he had resisted his sire's attempts to mould him and had been disowned, but there was compassion in his face as he leant forward and mopped the dribble away from her father's chin with the sheet.

"I give you good day, my lord," he told the pathetic heap beneath the coverlet and with a courteous bow stepped back.

Clearly, the stranger's deference was not done to obliquely reprove her but it made Johanna guilty that she could not yet forgive her father.

"Leave the shutters for a while," she ordered Aidan. "From now on, open them for an hour each day if the weather is mild." She sensed the approval of her companion and was ashamed that she had issued the instructions for the wrong reasons. *Give me time, dear God, to forgive him*, she prayed. *Let the love that was between us come again.*

"What is up here?" The heels of the man's spurred boots jingled up the spiral steps and she chased after him up through Aidan's chamber. He had unlatched the outer door onto the ramparts. Not more defence tactics, thought Johanna reluctantly, her belly gurgling with hunger. He turned so abruptly that she almost walked into him. He was eyeing their position as if marking it as a sentry post.

"I suggest you stand within my shadow with your back to the crenellations and put your arms just so." He lifted her hands to his shoulders.

"W-what do you think you are doing?" she spluttered, her voice frothed with suspicion. His back was masking her from the inner bailey.

"Convincing your household that we are lovers without embarrassing you."

Peeping around the stranger's shoulder, Johanna realised that Aidan, roping up a pail of water from the well, was staring at them, not to mention Father Gilbert who was showing an unprecedented interest in the clouds, and Bart the smith and his apprentice who were making a great show of inspecting a broken spade.

Her practical side overcame her indignation, especially as he folded his arms so that he was not touching her. The movement firmed the muscles beneath her fingers even further. She kept her eyes strictly on the blue gorget of his tunic, but her body was remembering the feel of this man against her thighs when he robbed her of her rings.

"How long must we stay like this?" she asked eventually, her voice muffled.

He sighed. "A little longer."

She was trying to look anywhere but at his face, and the beaks of her shoes became boring. "Are you married, master scholar? I should have asked you sooner and Mother never said."

Geraint's fingers swiftly braceleted her wrists, freeing himself from her. "Ha, now your conscience pricks, does it?" He testily turned away, grimly studying the meadows stretching up from the steep river bank. "Would it bother your lady mother if I was? I doubt it. No, I am too poor to have a wife as yet." He looked round for a reaction, expecting her pale cheeks to be tinged at her impudence, but the lady appeared to be unaware that such an intimate question was forward.

"I suppose a mistress would be as expensive," she observed so gravely that he was hard put not to laugh.

"Yes. Would you like to apply?" Her greenish eyes responded with fury. "No, do not kick me again, lady, or I will retaliate, I promise you."

Perhaps, Geraint considered, he was lacking in manners to remind her she had behaved so indelicately, but clearly certain things had to be said. She seemed to think so too.

"When this is over, sir," she told him firmly, patting her palms against the thick stone wall, "I am taking a vow of celibacy."

Aware that they were still attracting interest from the courtyard, Geraint moved close behind her as if to shield her from the wind. Those watching might think he hugged her against him.

"Not before?" he teased. The corners of his cape were wrapping about her in the strengthening westerly.

She glanced up solemnly, examining his face, but with an effort he visored his amusement and kept his stare fixed indifferently upon the misty hills. "Lady, you may take a lover if you win the matter."

Johanna jerked her face away, chin up, shoulders tensing. "I am not interested in that sort of thing."

It was dangerous but he had to say it. "Probably because, as you admitted earlier, you are ignorant of the delights of the bedchamber." He held his breath, expecting a furious volley of arguments, but this time she kept a haughty control.

"There are no delights, master scholar, merely conquests, and I will not believe otherwise."

So there were other matters he might teach her besides the alphabet. An interesting challenge that, but far too perilous. Besides, the time was insufficient. God willing, he would be gone from Conisthorpe the moment the matter was settled and Edmund was well enough to bestride a horse.

"I am hungry," he sighed, and left it at that.

HE WAS PLEASED TO SEE A FAINT HINT OF COLOUR IN LADY Johanna's cheeks now as they reached the high table. Anyone could see the girl was too pale for her years; she should be glowing with vitality. A waif. Well, it was her problem. Perhaps she was one of those women who ate like a wren. For his part, Geraint was ravenous and slid easily into the lord's chair, hoping there would be no delay in serving the repast. He was wrong. The demoiselle Edyth marched into the hall and came to stand before him.

There was a sigh in Lady Constance's voice. "Lady Edyth, if you require to eat with us, be seated and do so in silence. I will not be chastised by you in my own hall."

"*Your* hall, Lady Constance? There is a conspiracy here to gull you. If you give this stranger credence, he will take all your goods from you and from your son." Edyth might have expanded her theory but Geraint rested his chin upon his hands and regarded her with a mocking smile. It threw her momentarily.

Lady Constance signalled to Sir Geoffrey who rose looking as though he had been condemned to bread and water for a week.

"Demoiselle," he leaned forward across the board, "my lady wishes you to leave the hall."

Edyth sniffed. "Oh, I will not eat at this table without a food-taster. Watch what you eat, boy," she warned Johanna's brother. "Some here would not like to see you grow much older."

"Edyth, how can you say such lies!" Johanna exclaimed, springing to her feet with such vehemence that her stool crashed backwards. Gervase righted it.

Miles's mouth turned gooseberry-shaped. "What is she blabbing about, Johanna? This is my hall. *I* am going to inherit, not you. If you have a son, he will get Enderby, but Conisthorpe is mine, do you hear me?"

"I do not want Conisthorpe," Johanna proclaimed loudly, thinking that it was about time someone explained to him that his father was merely the constable, holding the land from the king, "and I am certainly not going to poison anyone. Sir Gervase has lands of his own in . . . in Laval.

"Quickly, for the love of God, where is it?" she muttered, as she lowered herself back beside him.

"South of Normandy but . . ."

"Normandy!" she exclaimed to Miles.

"Not Normandy, south of—"

"South of Normandy actually, Miles. Now be quiet!"

Sir Geoffrey cleared his throat, stroked his beard and carefully addressed Lady Constance. "Lady Edyth has touched upon the matter that is perturbing me also, my lady. It would appear that Sir Gervase, if his story proves true, while he remains here would have right of command of the garrison."

Johanna could tell that her mother had not thought of this for she swished her lips sideways, one of her mannerisms when irritated.

"Yes, Sir Geoffrey."

"Say you are going to take me away to Normandy when this is over," prompted Johanna beneath her breath.

"But I am not," Geraint growled through teeth clenched in a smile.

"Yes, but . . ." Her elbow was effective.

"Lady Constance, Sir Geoffrey, you have nothing to fear from me. The only item I am claiming is this lady." He slid his arm around Johanna's ribs, and hugged her excessively. The insolence and deliberate intimacy both infuriated and perturbed her, but she dared not wriggle free. It was too unfortunate that his hand would feel her heartbeat galloping like a runaway horse. Her only consolation was Edyth's disgusted look.

Lady Constance rearranged her own expression gracefully, like a woman being forced to smile by the dagger at her back. "You see, Lady Edyth. You say these things merely to cause ill feeling."

"Pah, you are trusting fools, all of you." Derisive comments followed her as she swept out of the nearest doorway.

The high table was left in uncomfortable silence. Johanna ignored her brother's glare. "I am not an item, sir," she told Geraint firmly, unwrapping his arm from her. "And the claim, sir, is long overdue."

"There will be trouble before curfew tomorrow," Sir Geoffrey muttered. "Are we to let Sir Fulk in if he requests it?"

"Pray let us enjoy this repast, Sir Geoffrey, without further troubles. We will speak about this later." Lady Constance signalled to the servants to bring the platters in. Conversation resumed fitfully, but eventually it was running in steady furrows.

"You are not eating enough, my lady." Geraint loathed fastidious noblewomen who did not appreciate good food. Because they had been given a plate to share as if they were newly wed, he was forced to watch Johanna being as fussy as a lapdog.

"Yes, indeed, Sir Gervase," agreed her mother.

Johanna sighed. It was hard enough pretending to be the man's wife, but now he was criticising her like a real husband. "I am trying to achieve a more spiritual state by fasting, sir." Her answer was honest but she did not add that there were other reasons too, though less profound. "Holy Church seems to only respect women who—"

He refused to let her finish. "I think you should abandon such foolishness. Since you are coming to Laval with me, and I require you to bear me a healthy heir, if God wills it so, I can hardly see that fasting for the rest of the week serves any purpose. Was Sir Fulk starving you into compliance?" he added in a whisper.

Johanna froze, blushing. Bear him an heir indeed! Insufferable impertinence! Unwilling to look at him, she stared at the untouched food before she finally answered with dangerous sweetness. "I forgot that there were some things about me that you never understood, sir. We had so little time together since you insisted on leaving so hastily." She raised her face in challenge only to have him slip a morsel of eel between her parted lips.

"Eat, my lady. I want to see the roses in your cheeks again."

She could not very well spit the food back out into her hand and was compelled to swallow it. Lowering her eyes coyly, she snarled so only he might hear. "Do that again and you will rue it."

"You are a fool to starve yourself. Have you no mirror?" he growled, and instantly wished he could have snatched the words back.

Her answer was bitter as gall. "Had I been uglier, sir, Fulk would never have offered for me, and if I thought it would stop him coming here to demand me back, I would rip my face ragged with my nails."

His hand came down on hers, his voice sufficiently audible to be heard further down the table. "Let us have no more talk of ugliness, my lady, for it would be a profanity for any hand to harm your beauty. I merely speak out of consideration for your well-being." No doubt she would have snatched her hand away, but he had snared it like a mouse beneath the paw of his fingers. "My dear love, do not be angry with me. I have not suffered our parting for two weary years to be denied the touch of your hand." She was forced to let him carry her fingers to his lips. He let his gaze warm upon her averted cheek, fortunately the sound one that deserved homage, aware that they were still watched and would be, curse it, for the rest of the week. He wished he could be done with the disguising. Friday could not come soon enough. "I cannot wait to have things settled between us." His voice was a purr but his fingers bit into hers.

"Nor me, sir." She enthusiastically echoed his double meaning and kicked him. How he kept a ripe curse from escaping was a miracle of control.

"For two lovers," he said very softly so only she might hear, "I fear we are too controlled. Now that you are over your anger, you should be somewhat softer, more yielding in your demeanour."

"I am not over it yet," she lifted her face, but her lashes veiled her eyes like a maiden. "Could you stop provoking me? An heir in Laval!"

"Provoke you, Johanna?" He rubbed his sore shin. "That was only the beginning."

Ten

JOHANNA BURST INTO THE GREAT CHAMBER LIKE A VIKING into a nunnery.

"I will strangle that man!"

"I doubt it," replied her mother calmly. "He could throttle you with one hand. Anyway, I think Gervase is doing surprisingly well. Had you not better go and keep him company—hang about his neck or something wifely?"

"I have had enough of that." She picked up her embroidery and flung it down again. "*Gervase*," she mimicked sourly. "You try being his wife."

"Now there's a luscious thought, but it would not be seemly. Which reminds me, where is he going to sleep tonight? I cannot send him back to the inn."

"Well, not in my bed."

"Then—Oh, Sir Gervase, pray come in."

"I am interrupting?"

"No." Her mother waved him to be seated; typically, he stood. "My congratulations! It is going exceedingly well but now that you and Johanna have stated your positions and are reconciled, would it be possible for you to be a little less—how shall I put it—restrained with each other?"

"Oh, we have done that," muttered Johanna.

"I very much doubt it, dearest. You should be closer, as if . . . as if you cannot wait to . . ." She gestured helplessly and then added crossly, "Stop looking at me like that, Johanna."

"Ah well," Gervase spoke without smiling, "it looks like it is the ramparts for you again tonight, my lady." He turned his head to Lady Constance. "Is there a full moon, madam, or am I supposed to embrace her under a cresset?"

"I am not embracing you anywhere," muttered Johanna. "In fact, I have forsworn embracing from now on. All you get is bad breath and . . . fumbling." As Gervase looked like a dragon about to take off and burn a town, she added hastily, "I do not mean that personally. This morning was quite adequate. As I explained to you then, I do not like that sort of thing."

"Nonsense, Johanna," breezed her mother. "We all have to make sacrifices. It is very important that the whole of Conisthorpe knows you are in love."

"Why?" They almost asked in unison.

"We need the goodwill during the hearing. If everyone sides with you both against Sir Fulk, the archdeacon's officer and the proctors will nose it out. Oh, come in, Sir Geoffrey."

"Mesdames." The seneschal's expression was more anxious than usual. "Sir Fulk de Enderby's party has been sighted crossing the bridge."

"God ha' mercy!" exclaimed Lady Constance. "Already! How many horses can he have ridden to death to reach here so soon?" She rose, smoothing her skirts to hide her agitation. "I think it best if Sir Geoffrey and I deal with him, Johanna. And you, Sir Gervase, had best keep out of sight. We do not want you hit by a stray crossbolt."

Johanna tried not to show her inward panic. "Are you sure you can manage, *Maman*? And what shall you do about Edyth? Lower her over the battlements in a basket like St. Paul?"

"Well, we could keep her as a hostage for her brother's good behavior. No, I see the notion will not wash with you, Johanna. Perhaps you would like to send her packing."

"With the greatest of pleasure."

Geraint could not resist hanging back to argue with his so-called mother-in-law. Lying low stank of cowardice, although he could see that it might be as well if Sir Fulk did not learn how to recognise him, but his words fell on rank earth. Leaving Lady Constance to compose herself, he waited for Lady Edyth to emerge into the bailey.

"They are waiting until you are across the drawbridge before they parley," he informed her as she made her way down the steps of the hall.

"Afraid?" she retorted, not bothering to help her maidservant who was staggering after her loaded with an ill-packed pannier.

"No, my lady," Geraint replied coolly. Gallantly he took the burden from the grateful maid and hastened after Edyth.

"The Scots fear him, have you heard that?" She tossed the gobbet at him over her left shoulder like salt to ward off Satan.

"Yes." He finally blocked her path but she circumnavigated him and he was forced to stride along beside her. "Listen to me, demoiselle, do not hate Lady Johanna. Have some compassion for her. If anyone is to blame, it is I for leaving her to the mercy of her father. We were wed lawfully, you really must believe that and inform your brother so."

Her eyebrows rose disdainfully. "Save your breath!"

"My lady, I am petitioning the archdeacon's court and will abide by its ruling and I trust your brother will do so too. If the verdict goes against me, I . . . I will leave Yorkshire immediately."

"Amen to that!"

There was little else he could say, so with a curt bow he reloaded the maidservant and left them at the postern gate. Already he could hear Sir Geoffrey's voice up on the roof of the keep. If he wanted to observe this Mallet of the English through one of the cross-shaped firing slits, he must not tarry.

The off-duty guards, clustered round the embrasure in the hall of the keep, sprang to attention, red-faced, as he entered. No joy there, he thought, seeking somewhere more private for his observation. He paused halfway up to the next floor and saw through the arrowslit that Johanna was crossing to the chapel with Father Gilbert. It was clear from the way her fingers writhed that she was fearful. He hastened up the next flight but the door to the second floor was banded with iron. Johanna had been right—it still served as a strongroom—but he found an embrasured landing in the stairwell which gave him a fine view of the street.

A company of eight armoured horsemen was approaching the drawbridge. The livery was unfamiliar to him—yellow with a notched sable band slashed diagonally and a single black roundel pelleting the panel on either side.

The leader, presumably Sir Fulk, had his helm beneath his arm.

Tall and gaunt in the saddle, his steel-coloured hair barely covering a balding pate, he looked even older than Geraint had expected. Although it was hard to tell from such a distance, the old
man had the pale skin that turns as red as a cock's wattle in anger
and he was red now, both with fury and exertion. A mallet? Yes,
it was possible to believe. Geraint had known company commanders and abbey officials who had that same unbending quality
and lack of compassion. Such men betrayed the principles of chivalry and their manhood; debasing others to make themselves feel
powerful was an insult to human nature. It would be easy to hate
Fulk. Part of him righteously rejoiced in opposing such a man, but
the darker half of him that had suffered as a youth wished that he
might avoid the confrontation. He had enough enemies already.

It was impossible to hear what Lady Constance was calling
down to him, but Fulk's horse fretted at the taut, angry grip on
its reins. He spoke to the younger man at his elbow, a fellow with
ginger hair and moustache, who was running his gaze along the
battlements as if seeking someone. Surely this could not be the
man's son? He would swear that Lady Constance had said that
Fulk was childless and Johanna had been selected as his third wife
for her youth and vigour to beget a male heir. Poor wench. The
thought of Fulk straddling her was not a pleasant one.

The horsemen backed away. Geraint felt the rumble of the rising
portcullis reverberate through the stones beneath his feet and
heard the slam of the drawbridge landing flat.

Sir Fulk and his captain rode forward and Geraint could just
see the coiffed head of Lady Edyth facing them. She was forced to
jump forwards as the drawbridge began rising again and there was
a kerfuffle as her maid sprang clear and the pannier rolled across
the cobbles, scattering its uppermost contents. The serving wench
suffered a kick and hurriedly collected Edyth's possessions, while
the brother and sister appeared to be having some kind of argument, and then Fulk spurred his horse back down the road. His
men took off after him, leaving Edyth lonely as a leper; Johanna
would be overjoyed.

Geraint waited until Lady Constance and her small supportive
entourage had descended past him before he joined them. Johanna's mother looked as though she had survived a mental tempest as they emerged into the daylight.

"Oh, madam, is he gone already?" exclaimed Johanna, hurrying to meet them. "The king should send you to negotiate with the Scots."

"Sir Fulk will submit a counter-libel to the court on Friday, but then I expected that. He says he is going to complain to the high sheriff and is threatening to send a man to York to browbeat my lord archbishop's officers. If the matter is moved out of the archdeacon's hands, then our ship is sunk."

Father Gilbert patted his employer's arm. "Have faith, madam. Archbishop Melton and the archdeacon are old sparring partners. Now with your leave, I have business at the priory and the weather is like to turn foul again methinks."

"And Lady Edyth?" asked Geraint, and received a look from Johanna which questioned his sanity. "Well, I doubt the lady is waiting out there for a passing suitor."

Johanna swore, "Oh no, I suppose that fiend has left her here to spy on us. Do you think our gatekeeper might manage to become deaf for an hour or so or the windlass might need oiling?"

"Oh, why not," sighed Lady Constance, and Johanna swiftly crossed to the postern just as Edyth's maidservant began knocking.

With relief, Geraint sought out Jankyn in the stable.

"What think you, sir? Will this gnarled and venerable old Mallet make sufficient dent upon your buckler?"

"He looks as though he worships at the shrine of War and would willingly sacrifice the lot of us on its altar. Lady Johanna tells me he was at Boroughbridge, pray God that—why are you pulling that absurd face?"

"You have a visitor, sir."

Gervase glanced over his shoulder to discover Johanna's scowling brother skulking in the doorway.

"Well," he whirled round on the boy, clasping his hands together gleefully, "what poison would you like, Miles? A vile-tasting potion that will make your tongue turn purple and loll out as you collapse writhing? Or something viler still that could take about three weeks, slow and subtle, but not very impressive—they might think you died from an ague."

"Neither."

"Neither. You spoil my sport! The castle expects it and Lady

Edyth will be so disappointed. She has returned especially so she may say prayers for you."

"That old crone." The boy did not smile, but at least he was not taking Geraint's humour as gospel.

"At least we agree over that. Perhaps you are right, Ja . . . Watkyn, this boy may have intelligence lurking behind his sullen disposition."

The boy came further into the stable. Geraint noticed that the grooms and stablehands were suddenly carrying out tasks in the immediate proximity and doing it very quietly.

"Are you really Johanna's husband?"

"Yes, have I your approval?"

"Well, I suppose you are better than the old man. Why do you want to marry Johanna again anyway? She is so boring."

"I am not marrying her again. I *am* married to her. Mind, I admit she is one of the most aggravating women I have ever met, and I do feel some compassion for you having to be her brother. However, I do need a son. Not, I might add, to supplant you here, but I cannot manage to acquire one on my own."

The air went very still indeed save for one of the horses kicking out at its stall.

"Do you have to have *her* to get a son?"

With a stifled cough, Jankyn turned away, his sleeve to his mouth.

"She will do as well as the next woman." Geraint shrugged, with a grin at his audience who were no longer making a pretence of shovelling muck or filling feedingbags.

"Surely better, sir," exclaimed Jankyn, in control of himself again and taking advantage of the attention. "You see, little lord, you have to look at their haunches." He pointed to the flicking tail of one of the mares whose mouth was buried in the manger happily munching. "You need a female broad enough to drop a foal successfully. Check their teeth too. Remember that when you choose a wife, young man."

"Have you checked my sister's teeth then?" The boy glanced up to his new brother-in-law, veiling his insolence with his dusky lashes.

Geraint glared at Jankyn before bestowing a solemn glance on the lad. "Yes—two years ago, of course—and her haunches."

A burst of male guffaws startled the horses.

Miles, aware that he was being excluded from some adult jest, flexed his high-ranking muscles. "I want you to leave here. You are insub . . . insubnaught."

"I think he means 'insubordinate,' " Jankyn offered helpfully. "And who put that word in your mouth?"

The child ignored the esquire and scowled at Geraint. "Well, you are, are you not?"

"Yes," exclaimed Geraint. "I make a practice of it, just like you. Tell me, Miles, how long is it since your lord father was smitten?" He met Jankyn's grin. They were both thinking the boy was bored and without a mentor. It was customary for lads of his age to serve as pages in other lords' households, but Miles was still at home.

The boy shrugged.

"Quintains!" exclaimed Jankyn and the boy's eyes turned round as coins. He was having trouble following the mercurial conversation.

Geraint's glance met Jankyn's thoughtfully. "Better than a rod mayhap. Aye, I take your point, man. Show me to the castle carpenter, Miles."

"Designing your own gibbet?" The boy stuck his tongue out and before Geraint could grab him and toss him into one of the barrels of feed, he scampered.

"The brat needs a father's belt upon his arse," muttered Jankyn. There was a murmur of assent from the others.

"Very true, but your first suggestion is better. We will wear him out with kindness instead."

"There used to be a quintain, my lord, some years back," said someone. "Sir Geoffrey might know."

"Then find him and ask him, if you please. The garrison could all do with the exercise by the look of them. Can any of you tell me why Lord Alan's son is still here?"

"He was sent away to Helmsley, sir, but there was some sickness there and they sent him home."

"Aye, thankful to get rid of him," chortled one of the grooms.

Fortunate Miles, thought Geraint. At least he was welcomed by his kin, not banished like he had been.

There was at least no distaff interference in setting up the quintain. Lady Constance was reposing in her bedchamber, Johanna had disappeared and Edyth was still outside on the drawbridge like a bowl of cream left out for the fairies.

Sir Geoffrey proved to be as enthusiastic as his nature allowed and the carpenter abandoned the spare coffin he was working on in order to mend and plane the apology for a wooden horse which the seneschal resurrected, cobwebbed and splintery, from the west tower. Meantime, one of the grooms strung up a sack of manure with a shield fixed to it, remarking under his breath that it resembled a knight in every way, and the men-at-arms had their horses saddled waiting to show off their prowess.

Johanna reappeared to investigate the gusty cheering and discovered that, except for the destriers, the castle had taken a feast day. The men had cleared an area in the centre of the bailey free of chickens, infants and a wain with a broken wheel and set up a quintain pole. A bulky sack hung from one side of the wooden stand and on the other dangled a metal ring on a rope. It was a tournament practice device; if a knight or esquire failed to lance the ring, the sack would swing round to jolt him like an enemy's weapon.

To her amazement, her father, coiffed, hooded and pastried in half his floor coverings, had been propped out of the wind in a patch of sunshine to watch, with Aidan beside him on a form. Her annoying brother was there too, his young face tight with fierce concentration, being bumped along on a wooden monster, drawn by two of the grooms, with a pole under his arm, while her supposed husband was bawling instructions at him. The rogue saw Johanna and waved. Was this all his doing?

Having been jolted backwards off his equine vehicle by the impact of the sack, Miles subjected meekly to a lecture from his new brother-in-law. Johanna knew the feeling.

"He will be allowed to ride his pony at the quintain when he is more diligent." Gervase joined her, beaming back at his handiwork.

"I suppose it is harder than it looks," she murmured, watching one of the men-at-arms riding at the target.

"You want to try?" She glared at him for mocking her, but to her amazement he summoned his esquire to lead over his horse. Before she could protest he had tossed her into the saddle and

swung on in front of her. There was a roar of laughter around
them as someone handed him a wooden practice lance.

Why in the name of all that was sane and sensible had he done
this? Geraint wondered. His shoulder ached enough already. God
willing Johanna would take it as merely a jest and dismount, but
the lady seemed to have caught the exhilaration of the crowd.
True, she held herself back somewhat so that her thighs were not
encompassing his, but her compliance was encouraging. Perhaps
he could manage to coax her between the sheets before the week
was out. No, the fight to cleanse the kingdom was more important,
yet . . . Any further scurrilous thoughts were smashed aside by the
jolt of pain as Johanna clasped his left shoulder. Who was the
patron saint of fools? It was impossible to set her back down in
front of their audience without a loss of honour to them both.

"There will be less of a jolt if you hold my belt, my lady."

"Sir Gervase, I must protest." The seneschal puffed across and
set a detaining hand upon the bridle. "The lady Johanna could be
injured."

"Of course, Sir Geoffrey," he agreed with a calculated sigh.
"Pray help my lady down."

"No!" exclaimed Johanna contrarily. "I will be perfectly safe.
There is no law forbidding a woman to ride against a quintain."

"No," huffed Sir Geoffrey, "but, by the Rood, there should be.
Be it on your own head, madam!" He tossed the horse's reins away
in disgust and retired to stand with arms folded, glowering at
them.

Geraint grinned like a good-natured fool and diverted his attention to the bundle of tense femininity behind him. "No, better
tighter," He adjusted her hold so that her arms were about his
waist. "At least you will feel the sensation."

Sensation, certainly. Firmly clasped against the stranger's body,
there was an inexplicable excitement filling her. It was wrong, of
course; she could sense Father Gilbert's censure from the chapel
even though he was not there, but surely she needed to behave
like a woman reconciled with her lost lord even if it was Lent and
they were not supposed to enjoy any pleasures? The stranger's hair
smelt sweet and clean and the scent of musk as well as sweat filled
her breathing. She panicked, jerking against him. No, Sir Geoffrey
was right. She should not be doing this.

"Sit still!" Her knight in glittering armour was replaced by an irritable man—that was reality.

"Please, you do not need to do this. I am being foolish," she protested, as he kneed the horse round and took it to the end of the yard. If he missed, the sack would very likely knock them both out of the saddle.

"Afraid?" She was relieved to hear the laughter once more in his tone.

"No, but my mother will be furious if we are unable to attend court on Friday. Have you done this before?"

"With a woman? No, my wits must be addled. There will be an impact. Brace yourself."

She could not answer for he had lined up the steed and the men were roaring encouragement. Johanna caught her breath as they hurtled at the sack. So this was what it felt like to ride in a tournament. He hit the quintain full centre and was jarred back into her as he let go the pole and reined in the horse. It was over in an instant and he was lifting her down to laughter and cheers but there was a strained look beneath his tanned smile. Being a scholar, he must have had little if any practice and it had been a challenge to him too. A man of extraordinary talent, she thought suspiciously.

Though she too had winced at the impact, she felt wonderful, like a child given a whole dish of sweetmeats. How outrageous of him to have taken her up, yet no one looked disapproving save for Sir Geoffrey. It was all very bridegroomly since Gervase kept his hands on her shoulders and stood behind her as the garrison knights gathered round them with banter about other ways to use his lance. He let them wash over him, giving orders that Miles might have a turn at tilting on the pony.

Her little brother, who obviously resented her intrusion into this masculine business, smirked as the attention shifted back to him. He missed the quintain when the pony did not run true, but Gervase's odd esquire caught him.

"Again!" yelled Gervase, and Miles, shame-faced, was forced from pride to mount back up. He made a better show of it the second time, although the pole missed. Then one of the men-at-arms demonstrated the angle once more.

"We shall leave them to it." The scholar signalled his esquire to bring his overtunic and belted it round his hips. Tossing his fair windruffled hair behind his ears, he set his blue liripiped hat once more on his head. "Come, we have business of our own." He had her purposefully by the elbow. "Your turn for a lesson."

The laughter in her turned to raw suspicion. He had dared to free the entire castle from their chores without her mother's permission and now proposed some other mischief.

"Lesson?" hissed Johanna.

"Have we not agreed that I am going to teach you your letters?" Could he read the struggle within her? She did not want to be instructed by him and yet she was avid to become literate.

Before she knew it, he had propelled her to a sheltered, still sunny patch of river-sand path that meandered from outside the great hall to her mother's herb garden, safely enclosed within the castle walls. He lifted a wooden form from beneath a budded pear tree and set it right across the walk. Johanna, mystified, sat down while he searched around and returned triumphant with a stick. He seemed so determined to educate her. No man but a scholar could be that enthusiastic, Johanna decided, letting her uncertainty pass.

"I fear the dust will be your slate for the nonce. Now . . ." He sucked in his cheeks thoughtfully as he began to draw the vowels in the sand, trying to remember his own tutor's early methods and behave like the schoolmaster she still thought him.

After she settled into her role of pupil, Johanna did not seem to find his instruction confusing. For a woman, the lady learned quickly, soaking up his words like droplets of water on an expensive sea sponge. It was hard for her not having the letters in ink before her, but sufficient for a beginning. If he could at least teach her to sound out the letters and remember the shape of certain words, she might have some building bricks to play with after he was gone. It would need more than a week, but he was confident of teaching her the rudiments.

At length she shivered. Time to end. His shoulder was aching damnably, the shadows were lengthening and the promised rain was due. "Here is a Latin word for you." He drew *Amor.*

She managed the first three letters and had to be told the last, blushing. "Remember it for it will be in the letter that I sent to you two years ago."

"What else?" she asked impishly.

He shrugged and stretched. "I am not sure. I have yet to write it."

"I have never had such a missive so I cannot help you." She rose, shaking out her skirts.

"No matter," he answered, heaving the bench back to its normal position, "I have had a lot of practice."

"What is it like being a scholar?" she asked as he squired her back towards the gate. A foolish question, she supposed, but he seemed not to think so. He paused pensively and then warmed to his answer, striding on again.

"It is being as industrious as an ant one moment, the next as wild as a grasshopper, and the last, as drunk as an over-honeyed bee." He had a plausible story already made up for her. "I was fortunate. A bishop was impressed by my wits and left sufficient gold in his will for me to attend an abbey school, and then I was given a place at Merton." She looked puzzled. "It is the college at Oxford," he explained.

"And what did you study?"

Jesu help me, he thought, searching his mind for recollection of what he had heard of Oxford. "The trivium and astronomy, arithmetic, geometry, divinity *et cetera*."

"Oh, I wish a princess or an abbess would set up a college for lay women."

"Are you out of your mind, lady? For what benefit?"

"For women scholars, of course. Why should men have a monopoly of learning? Ha, I know why men do not want women to be educated. If I could read and write, I would understand everything better. Let me see." She began counting the advantages on her fingers. "I could send and receive letters, read holy text, check the rent roll—"

"Write letters to your lover," he interrupted.

She ignored him, continuing: "Draw up a contract, practise law and divinity. By Heaven, I could be the equal of a clerk and—"

The lady needed dampening down lest she set the world ablaze.

"Whoa, madam, it is your duty to bear children, command the servants and consider what stores must be set aside for winter. Who else would govern the household? That is why we have men and women, lady, we each have our duties."

Bear me a healthy heir, he had said. Why was it that when this man spoke so it made her body grow warm and yet those words, pounded incessantly into her by Fulk, could make her shake with fear?

"What is the matter, lady?" Gervase had been looming over her sternly, albeit his eyes showed amusement. She was very aware of how powerful he was. That was the trouble. Where a man could use might, a woman was forced to use cunning which gave their sex a fickle, deceitful reputation, or so men reckoned.

She cleared her throat nervously. "Well, I was thinking that the lady Eve betrayed womankind when she agreed to her lot."

"But for the lady Eve, we should still be in Paradise." His gaze was lazy and provocative. No, she was not going to be drawn on that point, Johanna resolved, deciding that his blue eyes held light wondrously within them like chalcedony, and wishing at the same time this schoolmaster would stop staring at her as if she were a manuscript to be studied. To her relief, a peevish voice from the other side of the wall distracted him.

"It sounds as though someone has finally let the lady Edyth in."

COMPOSING THE LETTER TO JOHANNA WAS HARDER THAN GERAINT had anticipated. Had he been burning with unfulfilled lust, it would have been simple. He sat sucking his left thumb knuckle. The words must be right before he made a final copy on the precious rectangle of two-year-old vellum torn from the bottom of an abbey document donated by the sinful Brother Ambrose.

If you will become my own and match deed to word . . . No, too dry.

If you are indeed my own true love, then pledge yourself to me tomorrow. Uncertain and tedious.

An hour on, he was still lacking a formula and the stolen kidskin lay unblemished, so by the time Jankyn sauntered into Father Gilbert's cell, he was in the foulest of tempers.

"It is pouring fit for Noah's ark out there," exclaimed his esquire and was cursed for shaking himself like a dog too close to the vellum. "Do I see nature's raindrops or the pearls of labour upon that noble brow of yours? What, are you labouring at it like an ox drawing a cart of coin? Insane thoughts of desire ought to be rippling from your quill by now."

"And my fist will meet your teeth in an instant."

Jankyn sat astride the bench. "Is the good father in his cell?"

Geraint shook his head and threw the quill down in disgust.

"Excellent. Close your eyes and imagine you are looking at the lady Johanna from the unbruised side. Now in your thoughts slide down the sleeve of her gown to reveal a beauteous shoulder and imagine her breast, sweetly free for your handling. Its rosy nub— Ow!"

Geraint clouted him, laughing. "I can manage that, you wretch, but I cannot say so in this letter."

"No, not in this letter. We do not want to remind the judge of what he should have been missing all these years, but surely such lascivious imagining might inspire appropriate wording. It must come from the loins, so to speak.

"My own and most beloved lady, I long for the moment when I can hold you in my arms as my own true wife. Whatever fortune might befall us, I will swear fealty to you till death part us. I cannot wait to pay homage to your delicious . . ." Jankyn's utterance gave out and he spluttered into laughter.

"Hush, man," whispered Geraint, rising and checking the courtyard. "You will have the castle wanting to share the jest."

Jankyn cradled his face in his arms on the table, his shoulders shaking.

"Even though your father shall rage like a tempest and seek my life, I vow you shall be mine in the sight of God and Holy Church," ventured Geraint.

"Now it comes," Jankyn applauded him, continuing, "Your sweet lips beneath mine tell me I have your love." He pouted his lips rosebud-like and kissed his hand.

Geraint ignored him. "Lady, be not fickle but as steadfast as the northern star and . . ."

"And I will have your maidenhead
On Tuesday e'en when we're in bed."

"I give in, damn it!"

"No, the lady will have given in." Jankyn held the quill out to Geraint. "What you have said will suffice. Write it now, friend, for by the morning the words will be flown like swallows after harvest home."

Drenched from the heavy rain, the chaplain returned before Geraint had finished and mercifully gave his approval to the text.

With a sense of achievement, Geraint and Jankyn resorted to the pantry at the back of the hall, woke the pantler and bested the contents of a firkin of ale. Having forgotten to ask where he was to sleep, Geraint curled himself into his cloak beside the hearth in the hall with Jankyn at his back and two of the dogs huddled against his calves.

He awoke stiff and befuddled. A voice which sounded like Johanna's complained to someone that several people had been banging a pot lid and singing loudly beneath her bedchamber. Geraint drew his hood over his ears. What a fool he was to listen to Jankyn! He hoped to Heaven they had given no secrets away.

"Should he not have been in your bed, lady?" Something that was Jankyn muttered and rolled away, leaving his master's back chilled.

Geraint reluctantly opened his eyes to find Johanna, neatly plaited as a bell rope and disgustingly ablazon in her hollyberry red, standing over him. He sat up with a groan.

"Your pardon, but the sheriff's officer is about to arrive to see you," she told him sweetly and a jugful of icy water hit him in the face.

Eleven

FROM THE STAIRS IN THE GREAT CHAMBER, JOHANNA watched the scholar, unshaven and crumpled, stride upstairs to her mother's bower, his expression taut and furious at the regal summons. He pulled the door noisily to behind him and Johanna, sending Agnes and Yolonya about their business, unashamedly tiptoed up and set her ear to the door.

". . . carousing with the lower ranks, and in Lent too," sneered her mother. "Not to mention your effrontery in presuming you had the authority to set up a quintain and have my lord brought down to watch."

"It seemed a good notion at the time," he countered, his voice nonchalant and sleepy. "I am sure he enjoyed it."

"Gervase," her mother sounded more like a nurse addressing an infant, "I was trying to keep the seriousness of his condition hidden. It is fortunate that hardly anyone noticed him, muffled as he was, thank God. No, they were all too entertained by the appalling spectacle of you cavorting with my daughter. She and Miles could have been gravely injured."

"I thought I was supposed to cavort with her, and considering that Miles's contraption went no faster than a hobby-horse . . ."

Johanna, imagining that determined jaw thrust up arrogantly, jammed a knuckle into her mouth to stifle her laughter.

"That is not what I saw from my window. Now please remember to behave like a member of the nobility in future. I want no more student romps though," her tone would have sheared the edge off sword blades, "you never were—"

"Johanna, what are you—"

"Sssshh, Miles!" she straightened, red-faced, and came primly down. "Say naught or I will tell Mother you put a frog in our father's bed last night."

Her brother folded his arms. "Tsk, tsk!"

The door handle above rattled. ". . . no more. Now go, sirrah!" Sweet Heaven, her mother was dismissing the man as if he were a convicted villein at her manor court.

"Quickly!" Johanna grabbed her brother's hand. She managed to reach the door to the hall where, with Miles at her heels, she swept ingenuously forwards again as Gervase stormed out from the stairwell like a thunder-cloud looking for somewhere to unload.

"Would you like me to order a bath for you, sir?"

Geraint, irritated at meeting anyone, glanced down at her suspiciously. Was that supposed to be an apology for her acquiescence in yesterday's sport or an effort to have him sober and spotless before the deputy sheriff inspected him?

"Thank you, no, madam," he answered brusquely. "I have had enough water from you for one day."

"Sir, sir, can we use the quintain again today?" The boy jumped, catching hold of his left arm and swung onto it with his full weight.

"God in Heaven!" Fierce pain streaked up his weakened arm and he flung the child off roughly.

Miles landed heavily on his backside, blinking up at Geraint in terrified surprise.

Johanna recoiled from him in horror. "You . . ." Words failed her and, grabbing her skirts, she fled. His reputation in shreds, Geraint turned remorsefully to the child and offered his swordarm to help him rise.

"I am sorry, Miles. I injured my arm yesterday."

"Th . . . that's all right," muttered the child and manfully took his hand.

His supposed brother-in-law patted him reassuringly on his skinny shoulder, and wished heartily for the sound of Dame Christiana's sharp tongue and a fresh dressing for his wound.

"I'll tell you one thing that has happened since your arrival, sir."

"Oh, you varmint, and what is that?"

"My sister laughed." The boy cocked his head on one side, grinning up at Geraint. "And I think it was at you."

THE HIGH SHERIFFS AND THEIR MEN WERE THE WHEELS OF KING EDward II's chariot; the entire kingdom ran upon their loyalty. They kept his peace and garnered gossip and information so that taxes might be levied efficiently. Not only that, they enforced fees and military service, rode into battle for the king, and hanged men for treason. It was therefore necessary to treat them with respect.

Swiftly shaven by Sir Geoffrey's varlet—Jankyn's hand was not steady this morning—fortified by a hot posset of Yolonya's that nearly removed the roof of his mouth, and now buffeted by the churlish wind between rainbursts, Geraint stood to attention behind Lady Constance outside the portal to the new hall as Sir Ralph de Middlesbrough, deputy to the High Sheriff of Yorkshire, rode in with some twenty men-at-arms behind him and the castle dogs barking alarum a safe distance from the hooves. Geraint was not feeling charitable towards the Lady of Conisthorpe—taking a tongue-lashing from a woman had grazed his pride somewhat— but sulking was not part of his nature. His conscience acknowledged the rebelliousness of yesterday as foolhardy and today's man was too scared for his skin to misbehave, so he stood beside her decorously in his newly stitched finery and tried to look like a dutiful son-in-law wagging a tail for the visitors.

"God protect us," whispered Lady Constance, as the men dismounted with the clank of steel worn to impress and terrify. "I do not like the smell of this." Nor did Geraint. He wished profoundly for a clearer head and hoped that Jankyn would have the sense to keep out of sight.

Sir Ralph, a man of sturdy girth, clad in a hauberk surmounted by a silken cote of scarlet stitched with grey chevrons, panted up the stone steps and set back his metal coif, exposing hair the hue of trodden snow.

"I have not seen you in these parts, sir." He puffed bluntly, after an exchange of greetings with Lady Constance. He stared at Geraint with candid curiosity but ignored his proffered hand.

With no show of embarrassment at the rebuff, Geraint stuck his thumbs in his belt. "Yes, Sir Fulk holds me a usurper but since he has never set eyes on me, he may hold anything he pleases, except my lawful wife. Come in to the hearth, my lord, and judge for yourself how he has treated her."

Sir Ralph looked somewhat confused at this speech but allowed himself to be ushered inside.

With a screen on a turned pole to protect her unveiled face from the heat and one of her mother's most ancient dogs snoozing belly-up at her feet, Johanna was sitting on the dais beside the fireplace, working at her embroidery frame with such deceptive serenity that no one would have suspected she was not on speaking terms with her hired husband. She had discarded the scarlet kirtle. Dainty in a gown as green as fir needles with a surcote of russet edged with coney fur, she rose and gracefully curtsied to their visitor.

With a prayer to St. Cuthbert for protection against women who jumped to conclusions, Geraint held his hand out, palm upper-most, to her, and with a hesitancy that could pass for coyness to the unobservant, she placed her hand in his. He felt her fingers quiver and understood her fear of him. Damnation! He was not a violent man, but now was not the time to change her opinion; he had a bellyful of his own worries especially if the high sheriff's officer took him for questioning. Well, it was necessary to be convincing. Trying to make amends, he stroked her bruised cheek caressingly with the outside of his forefinger and reluctantly turned his attention back to Sir Ralph.

Johanna, confused—frightened at his earlier cruelty to Miles and overwhelmed by this public tenderness—tried to rally her courage.

Lady Constance snapped her fingers for mulled wine and came to the point. "Have you come to look him over like a horse thief, Sir Ralph?"

Her frankness gave the older man a fit of the sputters. "Nay, my lady."

"Oh come, as the king's man you must be honest. The scandal is regrettably true. My daughter married Sir Gervase two years ago when he was but an esquire. It is well known that she baulked at marriage to Sir Fulk, and my lord husband locked her up and used the rod to gain her compliance."

Sir Ralph was blinking at the trio of them as if they had the frenzy. "I . . . I . . . God's honest truth, madam, I came here for quite another reason." He peered at Johanna's injuries, clearly flummoxed. "I will look into this business later. Who did you say you were?" He gazed at the young man as though he were a rope that might heave him out of this insane quagmire.

"This is my true husband, Sir Gervase de Laval," Johanna explained, entwining her arm around his. She could see her mother pulling a face by the deputy sheriff's shoulder. "Oh . . . then . . . then you have not received a message from my . . . from Sir Fulk, my lord?"

He shook his head. "No, madam, I have been on the road constantly since leaving my lord the king and the high sheriff at York and am on my way to Skipton. You have heard the tidings, of course?"

"We have heard there was a battle, sir," Lady Constance answered swiftly.

"Yes, up at Boroughbridge. Lancaster, God curse him, was trying to outrun the king's army up to his stronghold at Dunstanburgh, going to talk those Scots heathens into an alliance against the king's grace. Any rate, all is well. Sir Andrew de Harcla, the Sheriff of Carlisle, arrived in good time and we were able to hold the bridge and send a detachment to prevent any of the rebels crossing at the ford."

Johanna wondered if it was imagination that the stranger's fingers tightened briefly in hers. She looked up and received a thin-stretched smile of reassurance.

"Ah, chaplain, good morrow to you." Sir Ralph held out his hand to Father Gilbert. The priest joined them, clearly keen to keep abreast with the tidings, as their visitor continued, "Where was I . . . aye, the rebel, Sir Roger Clifford, was wounded leading the enemy charge at the bridge and some bright little Welshman on our side hid under the planks of the bridge and drove his pike up into that traitor, the Earl of Hereford." His hearers involuntarily clenched their teeth at the imagining. "Then it was a rout. Poor bloodied fools at the bridge were leaderless. Some of 'em went running across to the ford where Lancaster was trying to force a crossing with his horsemen but he was driven back. Our man Harcla did not have the numbers to take him then and there but the outcome was sure. For the rebels, it was every man for himself. Lancaster took himself into Boroughbridge church for the night, claiming sanctuary, but in the morning, with the place surrounded, he gave himself up to the king's mercy. If he ever is at liberty to lay hands on Sir Andrew de Harcla, whew . . . Oh, but this is tedious for the ladies."

Not tedious exactly but . . . Johanna noticed Father Gilbert was watching their captive scholar as if rating his chances of passing as a knight.

"And what is become of Lancaster then?" asked the priest.

"Taken down to his castle at Pomfret, and the king's there now with Hugh Despenser the older and the other lords."

Gervase, pale and addled from the night's carousing, let go her hand, looking somewhat discomforted, and her mother started impatiently tapping her foot, glancing round for the servant bringing the wine.

Johanna tried to make up for their lack of enthusiasm. "And have the rest of the rebels been rounded up then, my lord?"

"Plenty of 'em, my lady. A lot of the small fry have been sent to my lord Archbishop's prison in Ripon and the king has authorised a bounty for any dead rebels brought in as well. Mind, I tell you it is a mite hard to tell which are rebels and which are not when the corpses have been stripped mother naked. And, my lady, you would not believe the amount of booty brought in—not just horses and armour but beds, furs and buttons, a haunch of venison, even a couple of bacon pigs. No wonder the poxy fools never made much speed."

Johanna was aware that Gervase was standing still as stone while her mother was fanning herself as if to indicate that such conversation was inappropriate in mixed company, but the older man blithely continued.

"Most of 'em panicked. Some knights hacked their hair short so they would be mistaken for lower ranks. Even seized women's gowns, some did, an' would you believe they found one man dead of cold from hiding in the river behind one of the fisher's cottages."

"God have mercy on all their souls," Father Gilbert murmured.

"So, in a nutshell, Lady Constance, I am here with orders from York for Lord Alan to arrest any strangers on his demesne. You may be sure that there will be a few of the cunning devils still in hiding, lying low until matters quieten down. What would you do in their shoes, Sir Gervase?"

Johanna observed that Gervase's eyes had turned as hard as lodesterres. He seemed in no hurry to answer, as if he was giving the matter much thought. "Make for Whitby perhaps," he replied finally, "or some other port. Anywhere there is a plethora of taverns and stews along the quays that would shelter a man and ask no questions providing he has sufficient coin to buy off curiosity."

"Aye, good point, sir, but you may be sure the king will have officers poking into every dark hole from Tynemouth down to Winchelsea." The wine finally arrived. "Choice Bordeaux, eh? Ah yes, our lord king has had enow of treachery and wants every poxy rebel stifled once and for all even if the entire kingdom must be searched. The leading traitors are to be sent home to their shires for hanging."

"Do you know which rebels are still missing?" Johanna asked.

"Aye, now the interrogations are over, we do, although there are a few we are not certain about. Take Sir Roger Mortimer's heir, for instance. We know he brought a company to Lancaster's side at the Trent so chances are he headed north as well. There is a price on his head for the nonce." He took another mouthful of wine, scratched his nose and continued. "Like father, like son, eh? In my opinion, Sir Roger is fortunate to have been in the Tower this last week. Had the rogue been at large, my life upon't, he would have thrown his hand in with the rebel side and now stand to lose his head—Oh, Lady Edyth, I did not see you." He bowed over the proffered hand.

"I am very pleased to see you, Sir Ralph. I assume you are here to search out the outlaws who are terrifying women and robbing Holy Church in these parts, and I take it my brother notified you about this other disgraceful business—"

"You are interrupting, Edyth," Lady Constance admonished swiftly. "Our guest is far more interested in beating the Borough-bridge rebels out of the thicket than rounding up a few scurvy outlaws. More wine, Sir Ralph?"

Edyth tossed her veil back over her shoulder. "Well, perhaps Sir Gervase is a rebel. He only arrived two days since."

Johanna gazed at the woman in horror. Like a hangman at a public execution, Edyth clearly enjoyed tightening the noose. "It is an interesting coincidence, do you not think?"

"Since your brother's interests are in enmity to mine, I think you are speaking out of malevolence, Lady Edyth," Gervase answered calmly, his glance seeking a man-to-man rapport with the deputy sheriff. It was brilliant sangfroid on his part considering his voice ought to be echoing in his head like a bell clapper.

"Where *have* you come from, Sir Gervase?" Edyth countered and flashed an exultant look at Johanna.

Geraint made his displeasure audible. "As I said before, Westminster."

Perhaps that had been a foolish choice but he could not go back on it now. The Saints protect him! Was Sir Ralph invited to dine? The servants were setting the trenchers on the high table and the Conisthorpe knights were gathering in the porch with Sir Ralph's men. If he had to make an escape, by what means? Up the staircase to Lady Constance's bower where at least he could pick them off one by one as they mounted the stairs. Perdition! His sword was still in Jankyn's care. Had there been any weapons on the wall of the great chamber?

"Indeed?"

"Your pardon, Sir Ralph?"

"I said 'indeed,' sir. Westminster, eh?" The deputy sheriff's interest had clearly deepened. He sniffed, his moustache twitching. "So, with Lord Alan temporarily indisposed, shall you be performing his knight's service for him, Sir Gervase? My lord the king has ordered us to recruit knights for a summer campaign against the Scots. I do not know if you are already acquainted with the High Sheriff, Sir Roger de Somerville, but I assure you he would welcome any experienced knight right willingly."

"Does he embrace experienced traitors too?" hissed Edyth.

Geraint ignored the jibe and drew Johanna closer to him. If he dragged her up the stairs with him as a shield, they would not risk harming her. "This request places me in a ticklish situation, Sir Ralph. You appreciate the delicacy of my circumstances with my marriage in dispute."

"The case is yet to come before a court," Lady Constance explained.

The high sheriff's officer returned to his purpose. "Aye, but this sort of case can be heard in your absence, sir knight, and it would be as well to earn the king's favour."

Was that a warning? He must convince this officer he was a man in love. "Had this been a matter of civil law, Sir Ralph, my lord high sheriff's company would not lack my presence, but I have been in performance of knightly service ever since I last saw my dear lady here." He gave Johanna a squeeze that nearly knocked the breath out of her ribs, and kept her tight against him. "And I do not think it were politick to leave her again." He set a finger beneath her chin, and before the lady could draw back, impulsively brushed her lips with his.

Startled, witnessed and therefore compliant, her mouth was soft and enticing, her breath sweet. Although it was the merest touch and he was in danger of his life, Geraint found ridiculously that he had enjoyed it. If Sir Ralph had glimpsed the look of lusty satisfaction in his face, it was to the good. He might be offending the older man's sense of propriety, but he was supposed to be in love.

"No," he declared, "I shall not go. At least, not until the dispute with Sir Fulk is lawfully resolved." He rearranged a blushing Johanna, who had gone stiff as a cloth left out in the frost, against him so that his arms enfolded her and tried not to wince as she stealthily ground her heel into his toe, hard.

"You see what a smooth tongue this imposter has," Edyth snarled. "He should be in irons. 'Twere a pity that not more time is spent in maintaining law and order in this shire rather than mustering men-at-arms. A usurper can stride in here and lay hands on another man's lady and out there in the forest a virtuous woman can be assaulted and—"

"Assaulted!" exclaimed Johanna vehemently, discreetly struggling to break free. "If you are referring to that pitiful attempt to rob us by those two numbskulls, Edyth . . ."

Abruptly, Geraint let go of his armful, aware that Fulk's sister might suddenly see his similarity to a certain outlaw if he continued holding Johanna that way.

"Lady Edyth speaks wisely," he agreed swiftly. "I intend to ferret out these brigands."

Edyth looked mollified at his support; it blew some of the vindictiveness out of her sails.

"Did either of these outlaws make any attempt on your person, my lady?" Sir Ralph inquired of Johanna.

She hesitated. "They took my rings."

"One of them held you indecently," her sister-in-law prompted.

"Yes, that is true," Johanna agreed, her blushing deepening, and remembered to glance with apologetic sweetness at her supposed husband. She would deal with him later; by the Saints, how dare he kiss her on the mouth before all this company.

"Indeed, I will thrash the rogue when I catch him," Gervase uttered coldly.

"But I did manage to kick him," she boasted proudly, adding, "Could *they* have been rebels?"

Fulk's sister snorted. "Lord, only a fool would think so. They were far too cowardly to go within a league of any battlefield."

Lady Constance glanced uncomfortably about her. "Dear me, I find this talk of outlaws very alarming. I just thank God that those wretched Scots have not ventured down to raid us yet this year."

"You forgot to include the rebels, madam," Edyth reminded her waspishly. "Or are some of us trying to steer that boat in a different direction?"

"That will do, Lady Edyth," Lady Constance admonished. "Since you are here on sufferance, kindly keep a still tongue from now on."

Their guest tactfully took charge of the conversational boat, but evidently some of Edyth's remarks had kindled his suspicion.

"So tell me, Sir Gervase, where did you first meet Lady Johanna then?"

Her supposed husband gave her a fond glance. Thank God they had resolved that, his eyes told her.

"At my lord Hugh Despenser's house in Bristol, my lord."

The deputy sheriff's gaze examined the patterned transom of the window to their right. "Ah, near St. Thomas's church."

They were being tested. At least Gervase was confident. "No, sir, you mean St. Nicholas's."

"Was the burgage with the arras of King Arthur in the great hall?" Oh, this was most definitely an interrogation.

The scholar hesitated and Johanna, now on ground she knew, answered, "No, not when I was last there, but it has an arras of Judith slaying Holofernes—"

"Yes, you are right," Gervase exclaimed, "and was there not a

smaller wall-hanging of a hart and hunters to the left of the min-
strels' gallery?"

Sir Ralph began to lose his solemn look.

"And it has a very pretty garden," Johanna added. "Remember
the trellised arches and that secluded pathway behind—"

Their guest coughed. "Hmm, well, I do not think we need to
dwell on that."

"Do we not?" Geraint decided it was time to be more assertive.
"A private word, my lord, with my lady's permission, of course."

Lady Constance nodded graciously and Geraint, amazed at his
own audacity, drew the older knight down the dais and across to
the long stone bench that ran beneath the windows. The rumble
of laughter among the knights had grown louder and Sir Ralph's
men were eyeing him with curiosity.

"Do you not believe us, sir?"

"No, no." The older man waved his hand. "It is not that at all,
but—"

"Let me be plain, Sir Ralph, I have returned in the nick of time.
You can see with your own eyes that Sir Fulk has made Lady
Johanna's life a misery. I will own she can be wilful at times,
but to beat my darling so cruelly because she cannot conceive a
son . . . Surely God's punishment is evident. The man is still childless because it was a false marriage and now my Lord Alan is
stricken also."

"Stricken?"

He had not meant to be so explicit. "Well . . . not exactly strick-
en . . . but ill."

"Yes, I see he is not here. My lady will think me rude that I
have not—" He grunted at the sudden hand delaying him.

"My lord, I beg you, do not ask to see him, not today. My lady
has been at great pains to make him rest. Now as to the dispute
betwixt myself and Sir Fulk . . ."

The other looked reluctant to be drawn into the domestic brawl
or make a rash comment on God's way of handling the business.
"Aye, well, I know Sir Fulk and his reputation. I should not like
to be the one to decide this matter."

Geraint stared down gravely at the older man. "My lady is fearful that Sir Fulk may use force or venal means to influence the

law." As luck would have it, Johanna looked the part at that very moment, standing watching the two of them, her brow furrowed.

Sir Ralph raised a tolerant eyebrow. "Since it is a matter of canon law, young man, I cannot speak for the honesty of the church. As for mine own part, I try and see justice done—in all matters." His eyes perused Geraint thoughtfully.

Enough said! "Come, wife!" It was a relief she came to his side with seeming meekness.

"Wife! You are living now as man and wife?"

Johanna stole her arm around his waist and tucked her fingers into his belt. "No, we await the court's decision but, upon my very life, my lord, Sir Gervase was my husband in word and deed before ever Sir Fulk sought my hand." She peeped up at him and nestled closer into the protection of his arm. "Now I have my true lord back, I want no other."

Perfect. Geraint lovingly rested his chin against the pearled crepinette which covered her pinned braids.

"If the court should decide against you—"

"How can it when we speak the truth?" Geraint answered.

Sir Ralph noticed Edyth glaring down at them from beyond the high table. "You never mentioned where you have been serving these last few years, Sir Gervase." Again, the explorative thrust.

"Overseas, my lord."

"What will become of Thomas of Lancaster, Sir Ralph?" Lady Constance had swept down to join them, cutting across the bows of the conversation as if it was of no consequence.

Geraint expelled a quiet breath of relief and cleared his throat. "Aye," he asserted, "it is an unfortunate business, Sir Ralph. I will warrant there is not a man in England can deny that the earl had served England well for the most part."

The knight was mercifully diverted. "Certes, but to lift his sword against the king, cousin or no cousin. You cannot have that, Sir Gervase. Next instance you will have any lord reckoning he can rule more ably, or even worse, the Commons might decide they can govern better than our lord king. Imagine that gorgon's head of hissing snakes. They would all want their say and never agree."

"But, for hypothesis, my lord, what if you have a king who is ill-counselled?"

"You rid yourself of the advisers just as we did with Piers Gaveston."

"Forgive me if I seem to play *advocatus diaboli*, but surely that was what my lord of Lancaster proclaimed he was doing, ridding the king of his evil counsellors."

"Ah, I can see you enjoy a good argument, young man, but there is a fine line between treason and what is best for the kingdom."

He had to ask it. "What is the difference between the rebel Lancaster ridding the world of Gaveston and his taking arms against the Despensers?"

Lady Constance stiffened, her gaze not exactly a glare but the deputy sheriff wobbled with laughter.

"Method, my lad. To go into battle against the king is treason, but to arrest his favourite when he is not with him is not."

Geraint smiled, albeit it pained him much to do so. "I retire from the lists, Sir Ralph, you have unhorsed me there."

Johanna was absorbing all the arguments avidly. "But it is all greed, is it not?" she exclaimed.

Unexpected, her words fell with a thud between the two men. For an instant they regarded her like an interloper and then her so-called husband deigned to smile benignly as if he had just remembered to keep looking besotted.

"Go on, my dear." The tone was patronising.

"Thank you, sir," she answered dryly. "It seems to my humble understanding that it is those in the king's favour ranged against those who are not in his favour, and surely if my lord of Lancaster had felt that the king would listen to him, he would not have taken arms against the Despensers, and if the Despensers were also willing to listen to my lord of Lancaster at counsel and not monopolise the king then—"

"It is not that simple, dear heart." The ungrateful louse gave the older man a forgive-her-she-is-just-trying-to-understand glance and the cursed deputy sheriff beamed indulgently at her.

"Quite so, quite so, Lady Johanna." Then he had the effrontery to change the subject. "Now, where were we, Sir Gervase? Overseas, you said. Who—"

"Sir Walrand de Carentan." Johanna hurled it into the conversation before Gervase could bumble out an answer.

"I can answer for myself, dear heart." Oh, he could barely keep his anger sheathed. Well, serve him right.

"Do you know him, my lord?" she asked the older man sweetly.

"No, never heard of the fellow. Norman, is he?"

"Ah, here comes my steward to tell us dinner is ready." Lady Constance swiftly raised her hand to set it on Sir Ralph's wrist. "Pray let us take our places. There is Sir Geoffrey come to join us."

As the tiny procession moved up the side of the hall, Geraint was at last able to give Johanna a look of intent to throttle.

"A moment, lady," he snarled, setting a delaying hand on the wench's arm to make sure she was out of all others' earshot. His fingers pretended to tidy a wisp of hair beneath her headdress. "Who in God's name is Walrand de Carentan?"

"I have not the faintest notion. Had you a name ready, master scholar?"

He was staring over the top of her head as if he was fascinated by the dead fly at the base of the windowglass. "Yes, of course, I had," he said through his teeth.

"But surely Carentan is in Normandy?"

"Yes, hard by Cherbourg, so to speak, but . . . Hell and dam-nation, lady, who has been advising you?"

"Father Gilbert."

"I have to be thankful you have not spoken to the entire gar-rison on the matter. I am severely displeased with you, madam. If you wish me to carry on this mummery, you will resolve these matters with me first."

Johanna's face was defiant but her body flinched. Geraint stared at her in disbelief; she kept as still as a mouse beneath the moon shadow of an owl and he was the danger. God forgive him! Was that how she saw him, as violent as Fulk? His pompous words were now a bitter, shameful aftertaste.

"I did not mean to harm Miles," he muttered huskily. "The quintain . . ." he broke off. Her sea-coloured eyes had misted. "But that is not the issue, is it?" There was an infinitesimal shake of her head.

For at least ten heartbeats, he could not answer her. "By my mother's soul," he said finally, choosing his words as if they were gemstones to purchase, "no, I do not want to hit you, my lady. I have never in my life hit a woman." He held out his hand to her, his expression rueful.

Johanna placed her hand upon his wrist, conscious of the prickle of golden hairs beneath her fingertips, and graciously swept along beside his knightly stride. "*Are* you a rebel as well as a scholar?"

For an instant, his step faltered. Tossing his golden head, he looked down at her, his eyes now glittering with lethal malice. "Say one more word and I will be a murderer. Would you like me to leave—*now?*"

The rebellious girl beneath the bruised exterior trembled but this time it was with amusement.

"No, master scholar," she said. "Not until after Friday."

Twelve

IT WAS NECESSARY TO PUT STONES OF KINDNESS AND REC-onciliation in the breached wall between himself and Johanna, Geraint reflected, after the deputy sheriff, his belly replete, had been farewelled. Although the wench had been as unmanageable as a wildcat, he was so relieved to find his wrists unshackled and his person still at comparative liberty that he was ready to make amends.

Lady Constance, too, looked as if a burden had been lifted from her. In compliance with the orders brought from York, she commanded Sir Geoffrey to take the garrison knights out on a brief search for rebels, as much to exercise and wash them as to honour the deputy sheriff's request. It was unlikely they would stay out long. After all, it was only March and the foul weather was closing in again.

With a brief word of praise and an admonition that they needed to be better prepared for the court hearing, Lady Constance left her hireling with her daughter and swept off, sighing, to count the emptied ale barrels.

"If they find a rabbit, let alone a rebel, it will be luck not judgment," muttered Geraint scathingly to Johanna, as the last of the deputy sheriff's men-at-arms galloped rather wildly over the drawbridge.

"No, they will go and molest some poor woman who will not be able to get justice for her complaints nor a silver penny for the babe that one of them plants in her womb."

"If you are still in a foul temper, lady . . . but come, before we are soused with rainwater."

Johanna glanced up at him warily but, well fed and wined, the tall scholar standing beside her looked malleable, although there was still a drawn expression behind the now amiable grin as he offered his hand to lead her back across the courtyard.

"Ha! If? I am always at fault. Sir Ralph did not want to listen to what I was saying any more than you did."

"But he did not want to listen, my lady, because you are right, and the truth depresses him. He is the tip of the king's sword in these parts. What can he say to you?" He glanced over his shoulder. "Why is there a pig following us?"

Johanna ignored the parry. She was trying to keep the silken veil scarfing her shoulders in order. "You do not need to pretend I am a case for your newly coined charity, master scholar. It is clear that I am not allowed a voice and my mother just stands and says nothing. I tell you this: I have a great admiration for the Countess of Buchan and those Scots noble ladies who supported Robert the Bruce. He listened to them!"

"True, and our late king put my lady of Buchan in a cage and slung it over the castle battlements at Berwick."

She snorted. "To make cowards of the rest of us. What a noble example of chivalry by Edward Longshanks. She was so brave."

"And foolhardy."

"She survived."

"Emaciated."

"And she had a husband who hated her because she put her love of Scotland before her obedience to him. At least our present king showed her compassion and freed her from that monstrous cage."

"True," he answered grudgingly, halting so that she was forced to stop. So did the pig. "You have not explained this beast." He waved his arm in dismissal at the creature, but it only stared at him with an expression which in a pig might pass for blankness. "Is it besotted with you? If it is lovesick for me, I tell you I am shifting my allegiance to another household."

"It is my pig." She dived a hand into the purse on her girdle and drew out a hard oatcake, shook the fluff off it and delivered it to the beast. "I reared him and he has remembered. Now please will you explain to me about Boroughbridge."

"Why?" he asked with so torpid an interest that she would have ordered the pig to charge him, had it understood Norman French better.

"Why?" she repeated, grabbing the veil's corners. The wind, with male sympathy, had blown it against her mouth. "Oh, dear Jesu protect me, you are not going to say I do not need to know, are you? Yes, you were. How insufferable!"

"So you are now a mind reader, madam. I am quite willing to tell you my understanding of Boroughbridge but not now."

"*But not now*," she echoed his tone. "Your impertinence is only exceeded by your arrogance, you upstart. It would please me *now*, master scholar."

"I think you should rid yourself of the habit of calling me either of those names, my lady. Sooner or later you will do so in the common hearing and this pretence will have been an utter waste of time. I pray you give me leave a while. We are getting nowhere."

"Then get out of my sight! I am going to see Father Gilbert. At least he is supposed to listen." She knocked loudly on the door of Father Gilbert's cell.

Perversely, Gervase leaned against the wall and folded his arms. Johanna glared at him suspiciously, uncertain whether it was amusement or anger that curled his mouth.

"Perhaps one day, master scholar, I shall meet a man who is capable of speaking to a woman as if she has a brain. We were taken from Adam's rib, you know, not his big toe. Perhaps the Lord God had it wrong the first time, maybe the second attempt at a human being was closer to what *He* had in mind. Maybe He should have tossed out the first attempt."

The intelligent blue eyes warmed at her argument. "You think the gender of Holy Christ was also an error?" he queried and left her.

"Ohh!"

"Perhaps you should avoid these kinds of discussion, my daughter." Father Gilbert's tone was stern as he let her in. He had been unabashedly listening in.

"If you want me to be a nun, Father Gilbert, I should have

thought it was exceedingly relevant," she muttered, watching Gervase striding away.

The chaplain stared after him thoughtfully. "The Lord God may give you a second chance, Johanna, do not abuse it."

"I asked that upstart to explain Boroughbridge and he refused. He was so haughty that I grew angry with him."

"Why did you ask him about the battle?" The chaplain sounded inexplicably surprised and not a little irritated.

"I am tired of being treated like an addlepate because I am not a man."

"My lady, sometimes you should not take matters at face value. I believe our scholar knew some of the rebels who were killed at Boroughbridge. He did not say so exactly to me the other day but I received the clear impression that one of his closest friends died there."

"Oh! Then why did the wretched man not say so?"

"I expect he does not wish to speak of it. Remember the adage, 'That which is rooted in the bone, rarely comes out in the flesh.' Sir Ralph's opinions may have set him on edge."

"I suppose that next you will be wanting me to apologise."

"No, my daughter, I should not dare to suggest that."

AFTER SIR GEOFFREY'S COMPANY HAD DISAPPEARED GRUMBLING INTO the mist, Geraint found the stables were mercifully empty save for Jankyn who was whistling as he polished the haft and quillons of Geraint's loaned sword, his legs tucked under him like a tailor.

"You want absolution, great one? We are alone unless you count the pig."

Geraint cast his eyes heavenwards and turned malevolently. "Grrrrr!" The pig, confronted with a huge man waving his cloaked arms like a giant bat, retired looking bored.

"It probably sleeps on the bottom of her bed, guarding her virtue."

"You survived?"

"Thanks be to God, and I take it you wisely avoided our visitors."

Jankyn nodded and breathed on the metal. "Any tidings of my lord earl?"

"Lancaster? Only that they have taken him south to Pomfret.

Do not be thinking of going down there, will you? It would not be wise yet." He did not like the thoughts scampering like possibilities across the jester's face. "I shall need that sword now, my friend, and may I borrow your cloak as well? I am going to Christiana's."

The fool sheathed the sword and gravely held up the leather scabbard to him in a ceremonial gesture. "They say that swords and fools go together."

"No, they do not!" Geraint went down on his haunches in front of him, checking once more there was no one within earshot as he informed him softly: "God preserve us, Jankyn, it is what we expected. The deputy sheriff's men have orders to bring in any strangers and there is a price on Edmund Mortimer's head. I need to find out how our friend fares. If the worst has befallen him, I will be out of here as fast as a rat from a flaming thatch."

His esquire untangled himself and stood up. "Jesu, man, if there are any keeping a watch out there, you will lead them straight to their prize. If it must be done, let me be the one who carries the risk."

Geraint straightened and buckled the scabbard onto his baldrick. "Thanks, good friend, but I need the blessed dame to have a look at my wound, and in weather like this I doubt there is much peril." He winced at the rain sheeting down, turning the courtyard into a puddle large enough for a giant's foot. "Besides, I need to escape this infernal castle. The moment the drawbridge comes down to let Sir Geoffrey's party out, I am stealing off. You will need to keep the porter distracted. Can you manage it?"

Jankyn nodded, scowling. "I do not like it. Heads, you'll be arrested. Tails, you'll die with lung rot. In God's name, be cautious!"

"Harken, Jankyn, the deputy sheriff's men are off to sniff for Clifford's men around Skipton and if I come across any strays from the Conisthorpe company, I shall tell them I am doing my own investigating. Old Sir Geoffrey is a good fellow but as mild as watered mustard. As for fearsome Fulk, if any of his men are hanging about fouling the air and they can even glimpse me through the rain, not one of the rogues knows what I look like."

"Aye, but there's sufficient around here who have seen you.

Free ale always loosens a poor man's tongue. You are not a small man, friend."

"Stop clucking like a mother hen. I will be careful."

"Aye," Jankyn shrugged, raising an eyebrow. "That is what all the youths say to their damsels but there are always a huge number of swelling girdles afterwards. What if one of mesdames sends for you to amuse them?"

His companion winced. "I employ you for your creativity."

"How is, 'Ah yes, sweet Lady Johanna, he is up in the hayloft bussing pretty Agnes'?"

"Oh to be a fly on the dung. Lady Johanna will probably pinion you to the wall with the hayfork while she investigates. Keep her out of my hair, Jankyn, or all Hell will break loose."

BEFORE HE REACHED THE WOOD, GERAINT STOPPED AT A WAYSIDE shrine to offer prayers for the souls of his dead companions-in-arms and for Edmund's recovery. Guilt that he had not been able to keep the lad out of danger overcame him again as he stood in the puddles staring at the Christ in passion on the small rood. He had owed Sir Roger Mortimer and his lady, Joan de Geneville, that at least and he had failed them, an ill payment for a training in arms and a solid roof over his head these many years.

Poor spoilt Edmund. Considering Geraint's own upbringing, it had been a penance at first to fetch and carry for the younger youth, but one that he no longer regretted. Entering the Mortimer household at Ludlow had been paradise after the purgatory of the monastery and its cursed master of novices with his predilection for chastisement and young boys. But that was past. Now with his strength of arm and confidence, had he chosen Geraint might pick up the lecherous Father Matthew by his cowl and toss him at the wall, but he was not a vindictive man. He had seen enough of cruelty and injustice. The world needed to be put right, the realm cleansed and he would set at liberty the man to do it.

"My Lord Saviour, if Edmund fully recovers," he promised before the cross, "I swear that I shall do everything within my power to restore Sir Roger to freedom." Then he genuflected before the shrine, gave his horse an apology and a caress for the foul weather and rode on.

He saw no one in the woodland save for a brace of sodden

charcoal-burners, miserably idle on account of the rain, squelching towards the town for a drinking sojourn. Only a small herd of Lady Constance's fallow deer lifted their heads as he unlocked the padlock into the park, and swiftly disappeared fleethoofed among the coppices in case he was thinking of raising a bow at them.

"Ha, so you are back like a stray tomcat." Looking decidedly smug, Dame Christiana let him into the blessed warmth and actually managed a smile for him, although with most of her front teeth missing, it lacked beauty to the less appreciative. "All is well. He is restored, lad. Thanks be to God."

"Thanks indeed!" he exclaimed, crossing himself and certainly not regretful of the oath he had just taken. "And His blessing on you, good dame." He whirled her up and sat her on the table. "You are a marvel! Wondrous tidings!"

"Stand apace, ribald. You are dripping on to my revelations!"

Profoundly sorry, he immediately stepped back as she eased herself back onto the floor. With doglike obedience, he hung his cloak on a nail and combed his fingers through his dripping hair. "Now may I see him?" He would have pulled aside the sacking curtain which closed off the palliasse where Edmund lay, but she caught his hand.

"Let him wake in his own time. Will you take a cup of mead?"

"Aye, though I cannot tarry long." He inspected the parchment pinioned under the candle while she unscrewed the leather bottle. "How are these progressing?"

"Not at all, thanks to Mortimer's cub."

"Regained his eloquence, has he?"

"Has he ever!" She spat. "Peevish brat. Been squawking for you all this morning like a pampered fledgling."

"God be praised! That sounds like Edmund. And so there is no other damage?" He took the leather cup of mead from her.

"You'd best judge that, lad. Nothing to write home about. Nay, let him wait an instant longer. How does your shoulder?"

"Ill. That is the other reason I have come, good Christiana. It needs new dressing. I thought it better to keep the wound concealed at Conisthorpe. I am under enough suspicion as it is."

"Then let me see to you first." She glanced in at Edmund. "He's still in a slumber but it's a fine sleep, mark you. Now, we'll need more light."

She lit another candle and inspected his wounds as well as she could. "The skin is healing but there's infection beneath where the flail has taken out the muscle. An abscess, see." He could not. The patch of swollen flesh was too close to his neck. "Any other discomfort?"

"I felt an unaccountable sweat last night and my heart started racing."

"Aye, that is part of it. It needs a knife taken to it to exude the pus and then you must pack it daily with moss to fill the cavity, keep it drained and make sure you do naught foolhardy." Bleak words.

"Then lance it now," he muttered, clenching his jaw. "And swiftly, I pray you."

"Nay, I am loath to do it hastily and in such poor light, especially if you are like to get your shoulder sodden afore you get back to the castle. I will give you more padding though to keep your apparel from chafing it."

"Good dame, I beg you!"

"No, lad. Charm little Johanna into playing your nursemaid. She could manage this." As if she sensed his disbelief, she continued, "I had lief have her on my side in trouble than the rest of them at Conisthorpe."

He shuddered as she began to cleanse his wound. "Why so?"

"Oh, the girl has a steady hand and a cool head and does not flinch at the sight of blood like other noble-born wenches. For one thing, 'twas she who stitched the gash in young Peter Weaver's leg. I was living by the river then. They brought him to me but my fingers were too stiff to hold the needle. She did it though. Used to take alms to those as needed it, she did, and never turned her nose up neither." She set a wad of folded linen across his shoulder. "What think you of the wench?"

Geraint grimaced, "A veritable basilisk, her glance is perilous."

"Aye, well, but reserve your judgment a while yet. Did not King Alfred say, 'Believe nothing of what you hear, and half of what you see'?"

"And the way folks talk, the same could be said of you." He received a clout on the ear.

His exclamation drew a feeble sound from behind the curtain. Though awake, Sir Edmund was still horizontal, as Geraint expected, but from the small amount of failing daylight crawling in through the wall opening, he was relieved to see the young knight's complexion had lost the frightening grey pallor that betokened death.

The heir to the noble house of Mortimer was overjoyed to see Geraint—as much as Edmund was capable of being joyous. His voice lacked a healthy vigour, but he had his wits back and Edmund had never been taciturn. Though his speech was gasping, the words still came in abundance.

"Where in Heaven have you been, you whoreson, leaving me in this dingy hovel, at the mercy of that old scold?"

"Be thankful to her, Edmund, she saved your life."

"Well, that may be, but I wish to be quit of this place."

"Bored are you, sir? Upon my soul, you would willingly hang on to such boredom if you knew one half of what I have been at."

"I doubt it. The pain has been . . . unbearable."

"I can believe it." He hoped that the old woman still had a generous supply of poppy extract to dilute Edmund's whingeing. "Dame Christiana assures me your bones are knitting well."

"So she says, but they ache. Pain like Satan's fire. When are you going to get me out of here?"

"When your legs can manage it and then, believe me, we shall be gone from this place as fast as a lightning bolt."

"You liar, Geraint, you look as though you are living in Fortune's lap. I have never seen such embroidery." He poked feebly at the stitching around the pristine shirt cuff.

"Ah, that is my wife's doing." A small lie.

He was pleased to see Sir Edmund's face resembled a fish with its gills stuffed.

"Wife! You had no permission to marry."

"Calm yourself. I am not married, merely pretending to be married."

Edmund's brow creased censorily and he huffily looked away at the wall. "I cannot believe this. You are prancing around having garments sewn for you and enjoying the services of a woman while I am glued here, weak and ill, to this wretched pallet, with that old crone berating me as if I was a naughty infant. Where is your loyalty, man?"

His companion pulled up a stool. "I am actually doing it for your sake."

"Mine, a fine lie!" The Mortimer blue eyes bore into his sullenly. "The old hag tells me it is several days past since you brought me here. Why here, you ribald? We can afford better than this. Is there no abbey hard by?"

"Do you remember the battle?"

"Vaguely, but . . ." he frowned. "The last I recall is that you said all was lost and—and our company had better flee but then . . . Where are the others, Geraint?"

His face betrayed the dire tidings. "What happened shall be told but not now, time is too precious."

"*Dead!* Every one of them?"

"Be still and listen, Edmund! I came to warn you." He unpeeled the lad's fingers from his sleeve. "In God's name, harken for your own good. You are safe here. Even though the lady of this demesne recognised you, she will say nothing. The king has offered a reward for all rebels, alive or dead, and there is a price on your head so—"

"How much?"

Geraint did not know, but he made a modest guess and Edmund's nose wrinkled. "Is that all?"

"It is enough. After all, you were not one of the commanders."

"Does the king know for sure that I was at Boroughbridge."

"Oh, the high sheriff knows. But the crux of the matter is that the lady has vowed that if I do not dance to her piping, she will hand you over to the king—for lopping, no question."

The sick youth's Adam's apple moved as he swallowed. Although the Mortimer heir was not a coward, he was more careful of his own skin than his father. He was thinking matters over and, as usual, assuming that self-interest drove everyone else as it did him. "So although I need you here, you are . . . pleasuring this woman like a dog when she whistles for it to save *my* skin."

"No, not her, her daughter, and it is not a pleasure."

"So she is not in the least comely?" Edmund seemed to take some pleasure in that.

"One half of her face is pleasing enough, but her real husband has beaten her so hard that her other cheek is woefully bruised. She is spirited but has a tongue like a joiner's file. And now there is another force to be reckoned with, if the husband gets wind of you, Edmund, uugh." He drew a finger across the lad's throat. "It is a fine old story, I can tell you, and right perilous, getting worse each day. This morning there I was, pretending to play the husband, when the deputy sheriff arrives and starts questioning me. I have fobbed him off for the time being, but that is why I am here to warn you. They are searching for rebels and outlaws."

"Outlaws too!"

"Well, actually, I am the outlaw they are looking for," Geraint informed him as if it was an everyday matter, "but there is a brigand called Black Nick out there somewhere. I doubt he would set foot in the chase though, and he would not dare harm Dame Christiana or else every man from here to Knaresborough would be after him with cudgels."

Edmund would have no doubt cast his gaze despairingly to Heaven, but since he was prostrate already, he glared at the sooty roof.

"I do not believe this! Are your wits addled, Geraint? You are sitting there babbling about wretched outlaws and people's husbands coming after you. In God's name, man, I am . . . as feeble as a kitten still. What do I do if anyone comes searching for *me*? Can you not stay here to help? I cannot comprehend why you cannot move me somewhere where this Lady whatever-her-name-is and the husband cannot find us and then as soon as I am hale enough, we will make our escape."

"Sir, I am doing my best. I would need a wain to move you any distance and struggling to do so on my own will weaken you again. You need to keep as still as possible. Be cheerful. Dame Christiana has a pit beneath the floor here that you can hide in if the need arises and her dogs will give plenty of warning."

Edmund sniffed sulkily, his fingers plucking at the coarse blanket. "This is most unsatisfactory, you knave. Where is your sense of duty, man? You should be here defending me while I am incapacitated. Wife indeed! And what about my wife, Elizabeth? Have you sent to her yet?"

"You think I do all this in jest, sir? No, I have not had the means but I will do so as soon as I can. I am watched on all sides. My lady is fearful of me abandoning her cause, her daughter's husband is after my blood, and the deputy sheriff will come nosing again soon." He stood up abruptly, needing air. The lad in good health was hard enough to take, but, ailing, was enough to drive any sane man out of his wits. "I must get back. Even coming here to check on your well-being was dangerous, save—God willing—they are hardly likely to be tracking me in such a foul downpour."

Reading his scowling face, the youth sank back shaking his head miserably. "Is there any news of my father?" he muttered.

"Still in the Tower, as far as I know." Geraint watched Edmund close his eyes in a thankful prayer.

"And Thomas of Lancaster?"

"Taken to Pomfret as a prisoner."

"To be shut in his own new tower, doubtless."

"Aye, the Saints defend him. We are leaderless at present, that is for sure." He grabbed his still-dripping cloak from behind the curtain. "Fare you well, sir."

"Geraint, for pity's sake, must you go?"

"Yes, else I will be missed." He leaned down and put a reassuring hand on the knight's. "Try not to fret. I promise you I will return the instant it is safe to do so." At the curtain he paused and swung round with a grin. "Did I mention the Earl of Lancaster's jester is acting as my esquire?"

Predictably, Sir Edmund's jaw dropped.

Dame Christiana escorted him to his horse, holding a leather cloth above her head against the rain, and waited in the shelter of the stall while he untethered the stallion.

"I listened to what you told the lad. Bad business this and the king worse than he should be."

"Aye, certes, that is the crux of the matter." He bent down and gave the dame a kiss on the cheek. "Thank you for what you are doing there. Edmund is not normally so cheerful."

Dame Christiana chuckled. "Doesn't take after his sire, does he? His da' would charm the birds out of their nests, even the two-legged ones."

Geraint was amused at her lack of respect, but it was no laughing matter.

"His 'da' is in great danger, I fear. The king could hurdle him out to execution for high treason at any time if he so pleases."

"True, poor devil." She shivered as if a ghost had wandered over her grave and grimaced at the heavens. "More foul weather is on the way, mark my words. No men-at-arms will venture out tomorrow."

"Aye, I hope so."

She sniffed the air uneasily like an old doe sensing hunters. "No, truly, lad. Seeing as you are the lord here for the nonce, ride back by the river road and see the state of things. There is a feel to this rain that bodes right ill."

THE FADING LIGHT IN HER BEDCHAMBER MADE JOHANNA LAY ASIDE Father Gilbert's chasuble, which she had been mending as a self-inflicted penance for her impertinent interpretation of the Book of Genesis.

"Sir Geoffrey and the men will be truly sodden by the time they return," muttered Agnes. "Shall I light the candles, my lady?"

Johanna shook her head and peered out into the misty wetness. Below the castle walls, the river sounded angry.

"Dear God! The weavers! Come and see! If this weather continues, they will be caught atwixt the river and the beck."

Agnes joined her. "Evil looking, ain't it, but they surely can fend for themselves, though their head man's not got much sense. Ranulf's a cursed, stubborn tyke!"

"Is he headman there now? Oh, Agnes, I would Sir Geoffrey were back. I had best ride down and warn them."

"No, madam," protested the maidservant, catching her arm as she turned. " 'Twould be folly for you to leave the castle."

While Johanna dreaded falling into Fulk's clutches, she could not stand by as the danger of flood increased. "It would be greater folly to idle here while others perish. They are our people and must be ordered to safety. I shall leave at once."

"Then, for Jesu's sake, take Sir Gervase and his esquire with you. 'Tis their duty to protect you."

"Ha!" But as it was, she had little choice. Her mother, anticipating trouble from Fulk's men, had ridden out earlier with two of the reeves, Yolonya, and the grooms for escort to the villages north of the town to forewarn their villeins and collect overdue rents.

Johanna found the esquire Watkyn in the stable saddling the remaining horse, a shabby hackney. The man's instant guilty colouring told her that some mischief was afoot; the stallion lent to

Gervase was missing. "He has left, has he not?" she hissed, and cornered the fellow, surprised that his uneasy gaze kept sliding sideways to the variety of pitchforks angled against the wall. Sweet Jesu protect her, did the coward mean to threaten her with one of them?

Watkyn edged away from the implements, flapping his hands gently in the air as if to calm her. "Quietly, I b-beg you madam, the lady Edyth could come in at any moment."

"And you are about to slink off too!"

He cowered. "N-no, my lady."

"Liar! Where has he gone?"

"S-Sir Gervase?"

"Who else? My pig? Cease hedging, Watkyn. I am not a pea-brain. Has the coward run away?" Had it been her mother's harsh words that morning or her own contrariness? God forgive them both for being so stupid.

"No, my lady. I-I . . ." He swallowed and glanced in the air, as if searching for a story that would appease her.

"Oh, a pox on this!" She was not deceived by the silly sheep expression. "Well, I shall have to make do with you. We have to warn the weavers and fisher folk. Strap on a pillion seat quickly, man. There is no time to be lost."

Gervase's man looked horrified as he took in her determined stance. "But you can't, my lady," he spluttered, unhooking the wooden seat from the wall. "If Sir Fulk—" He drew breath and tried again, "My lady, I beg you to remain here in safety and let me do your errand."

Oh yes? Well, she would not believe that. Insolent jackanapes! As to his master, he could roast in Hell! And if the pair of them thought they could sidle away in the rain, Gervase de-cursed-Laval would rue the day. She would hurl the entire garrison after him. No, the Devil seize him, she could not! The public shame of her first husband being dragged back to her side after he had already abandoned her for two years would be too humiliating to bear and certainly lose her the case.

She drew the cered, hooded cloak tightly round her, and waited for Watkyn to help her onto the unpadded pillion.

"Hurry, Watkyn! Let us go! NOW! Take the high street down to Bridgegate!"

There was no occasion for further argument, even at the gate-house, for the porter kept well within his shelter and did not even attempt to delay them with his chatter as he windlassed up the portcullis. But the weather was merciless, the rain cruelly slashing into them as they crossed the drawbridge.

Tucking her head behind Watkyn's back, with her hood well down, Johanna was saved the brunt of it, but before they even passed the church the hems of her surcote and kirtle were dripping from the driven rain and the muddy spray kicked up from the puddles. Every jolt was a further assault on her already humiliated flesh.

Her companion wisely took the hackney at a careful pace down the steeper cobbles. Wiping away the drips that were tumbling off the tip of his nose with his sodden cuff, Watkyn muttered, "I just hope your true husband is not lurking around here."

As they passed into the lower town, the wind grew wilder. No lights showed in the growing gloom outside any of the dwellings in the street or alleyways, for the gusty wind was fickle enough to rip a feeble lantern free and hurl it into thatch.

"Madam, look!"

She wiped the rain away from her eyes and peered where he was pointing. Gervase's horse was tethered at the bottom end of Bridgegate outside the alehouse with the worst reputation in the shire. Johanna sniffed balefully, disappointedly, her heart sinking. What more should she have expected of a common schoolmaster with silver to spend?

"Shall I go and fetch him out to you, my lady?"

Ignoring the proud shake of her head, the esquire patted her hand, slid out of the saddle and splashed across.

Dismounting, Johanna led the horse closer to the alehouse wall, seeking shelter, but the water was gushing from the overhang like some broad fall on the moors.

"Well, here's a piece of luck." She had not heard the man ap-proach. For an instant she thought it was one of her mother's ten-ants, but he was on horseback. It must be one of Sir Ralph's men, she decided and then, cursing, recognised the red beard of Fulk's man, Edgar de Laverton.

"Watkyn!" she shrieked. *"A moi! A moi!"*

Thirteen

IN PANIC JOHANNA CLUTCHED AT THE REINS, TRYING TO mount, but Edgar struck the hackney. It shied. Screaming, she let go the bridle to miss the crashing hooves. Pray God someone heard her! But the wind tossed the sound away and, above her, high on the cliff, the beautiful windows of the new hall mocked her with their brilliance.

Why did Watkyn not come? Watching her enemy, she edged along the daub wall but Edgar, kneeing his horse between her and the ale brewer's door, laughed and lunged. She wriggled out of his grasp and slithered, falling onto the mud on her elbows and knees. With an oath he dismounted. It gave her time to draw her dagger.

"Sir Fulk will pay highly to have you back, lady," he bawled.

"And I will pay you more to leave me be."

Crouching, she rubbed the rain out of her eyes with her left cuff, cursing her clinging skirts. Protected by a haubergeon, he could easily overpower her if he managed to get past her blade.

"On your back, lady, that's my price. I can give old Fulk the son he wants."

"Never!"

He tore in under her guard, seizing her wrist to shake the knife haft from her grasp. With a fumble for her throat, he sought to get his arm across to half-choke her and stop the shrieking. The precious blade went spinning from her grasp.

Covered in mud, she was eel-like, but the man wore steel and the sharp mesh grazed her knuckles as he evaded the blows she aimed at his nose and eyes. Her leather toes made no bruises upon his hard boots. She fought with nails and teeth; Johanna FitzHenry was not going to be carried back to Fulk tethered across a saddle, mired and defeated, for further humiliation.

Her breath was ragged, her strength ebbing. Steel pressed into her flesh from every side as he flung himself over her, trying to snare her threshing wrists. Sobbing, she snatched up a handful of mud and flung it into his face. Some found its mark. His hold weakened somewhat. She yelled again like a demented creature but the wind, wild and vile, howled back, casting every loose bit of debris it could snatch up.

"Satan's arse!" Her assailant flung up an arm to protect his head as a hurdle of hazelwood came lunging at them. Chickens, squawking and flapping, half-tossed by the wind, came absurdly after it. Her hackney reared in terror and took off. She tried to fling Edgar from her but, swearing, he hauled her up and gave her a blow on the side of the head that sent her falling back almost senseless. With rough hands he dragged her up by the forearms, tossed her over his shoulder and went staggering towards his horse. She kicked the beast and sent it skittering from them. Cursing, he staggered after it while she aimed blows at his belly and prick.

Then suddenly people spilled out of the brewer's like ale from a tumbled leather bottle. A crude male guffaw came from the crowd. No one helped her; they were enjoying the spectacle. Not a man jack of them had recognised her. Then there was an oath and a scuffle and someone gave Edgar a kick at the back of the knees that sent him sprawling across her, knocking the breath out of her. Strong hands seized her assailant and lifted him off her as if he were a lightweight.

Gervase's face was a devil's mask of fury and delight as he spun the fellow round and gave him a powerful blow in the jaw which sent him skidding across the muddied track and crashing into the hovel wall opposite. The rogue did not stay for more but clutched at his horse's bridle and was off as if the Devil was after his soul.

Her rescuer set her on her feet. "Did he harm you?" When she shook her head, he turned angrily on the spectators. "Why do you tarry gaping, you fools! Do as I told you!"

He put his arm about her, tugging her hood forward and hiding her from the stares in the shelter of his breast as the crowd scattered running and bellowing to the dwellings in the lanes below.

People began bursting out of the homes and bawling at one another. A clutch of children tumbled out into the mud, and lined up huddled against the meagre shelter of the wall like skittles, wild-eyed while their mother frantically fetched out her babe.

Gervase pulled the esquire loose from Johanna and glowered down at them.

"In God's name! Watkyn, take this lady back to the castle. I know not what folly—"

For an instant, aching and sore, she gazed up at him in disbelief.

"Folly!" she echoed. *"Folly?"* she repeated indignantly, shouting above the wind. She forgot her discomfort and the frenzied air wrenching at her mud-caked skirts. "There are nigh a dozen families across the bridge who must be marshalled to safety, and the fisher folks downstream have more sense but . . ."

"Very well!" he snapped. "I shall see it done. Take her back, man!"

Johanna dragged her wet hair from her eyes to glare at him. "No, *you* go back and warm your hands! They are my people and I am here to—By Christ!"

A roof had detached itself. She screamed a warning as it bowled towards them. Gervase gripped her and flung her into the safety of the alehouse wall, his body shielding her back as the panel slammed past them into the neighbouring hovel.

The wench had courage, Geraint admitted, as she turned within his arms and faced him defiantly.

"As you will, lady!" he said, before she could abuse him further. "Take my horse and load it with the children. Watkyn, go over with her!"

She ran down the steep street, tugging and coaxing the baulking animal after her. The street, empty just a short while before, was now a panic of people struggling to get their goods to higher ground.

The bridge timbers were slippery, the water perilously high. A small branch just missed her, hit the torrent and disappeared, swept away swiftly by the murky swell as she dragged the protesting animal across, cursing as its hooves skidded. Staggering up the mud of the road, she made out the weavers' hovels. The small scatter of crofts on the rise above the river meadows had been there ever since she lived at Conisthorpe. If the small tributary beyond them rose, it would make an island.

Watkyn was already bawling urgently at one door.

"Pah!" The thickset weaver who flung it open listened with ill humour and for thanks gave the esquire a blow on the shoulder that nearly toppled him. "Flood! Ne'er heard of suchlike. Ain't flooded here in livin' memory. Even se'n years ago when harvest failed, there were no trouble wi' river here. Go to, you fule!"

"Get your family across the bridge now, Ranulf!" Johanna snarled in English, steadying the smaller man.

"An' who might you be, you dirty slut, givin' me orders?"

"Leave him!" Watkyn yelled in her ear and tugged her away, making for the next hovel.

"My lady! Your face!" Yolonya's youngest daughter, Amice, the weaver's wife, recognised her in horror. Evidently, sufficient mud and excrement had washed away.

"The water's rising, mistress," Watkyn yelled. "Get across to the town!"

Amice, thank God, had more sense than her husband. In a thrice she dragged off the straw where her children had been nestled in piglet togetherness.

"Rouse the others, Watkyn. I will look after these." Johanna took the hand of a child of about four years and hiked a younger one into her arms, while Amice ran with the esquire to stir her neighbours.

The children began wailing at the muddy, soaking apparition trying to coax them out into the foul weather and the weaver ignored her, cursing, but he began bundling needles and the small items of his craft together.

The road was loathsome slithery, the stones sharp beneath Johanna's soles. As she and the children reached the crossing, she was thrust out of the way as Amice's large, bedridden old mother-in-law was carried onto the bridge by four of the townsmen. Two had made a crossover of their hands beneath the old woman's vast rear and two more carried a leg each as if they were hauling a barrow. They stumbled up the bank cursing, the old hag's voice shrill, fearful lest they tip her into the river.

Johanna's arm was aching with the unaccustomed weight. The

writhing child refused to sit upon her hip and the little girl, intelligent enough to perceive the danger, hung back, quivering and
terrified, as a whip of willow leaves, ripped free, slammed at her
face. More debris of leaves and twigs pelted them maliciously like
slung stones.

"Get going, you fools!" An old villager, nearly bent double with
his spiky load, swore at the children and pushed forwards into
them, forcing them onto the slimy planks. Johanna nearly lost her
footing.

"Give us a hand there!" one of the men who had gone ahead
with the old woman demanded as she reached the south bank
again and the old crone's bundle was dropped against her skirts.
Johanna, lady as she was, stood stunned for an instant, then
shrugged, heaved it onto her back, readjusted the infant in her
arms and took the hand of the older child who was hanging back
shrieking for Amice.

"You will be safe," Johanna promised in English. "If I ask my
lady to let you see your face in her silver mirror tomorrow at the
castle, will you come?" Everyone has their price.

She tugged the tiny maid out of the rain into the doorway of
one of the stone dwellings and shouting, tried to make out Amice
in the straggle of people labouring up from the river.

"My lady!" Yolonya's daughter recognised her voice.

Johanna dropped the bundle from her shoulders. "This is Ranulf's mother's." The woman hoisted it up and took her infant.

"We are that grateful."

How fortunate that Amice had not seen Lord Alan's daughter
brawling in the dirt. But Johanna had grovelled enough to Life.
She would show a schoolmaster that she could shoulder her family's responsibility.

"Ask for your mother at the castle, Amice. Tell the porter I sent
you and, pray you, let my lady mother know where I am."

Thank God there were torches sputtering and moving upon the
battlements now.

GERAINT, HAVING SEEN THE EVACUATION FULLY UNDER WAY AND
finding that Jankyn had lost sight of his supposed wife, had a
moment's pause to feel guilty that he had ordered her about like
a common peasant and not checked to see if her attacker had

harmed her. Why had her mother not sent her servants down to order the villagers to safety? Had no one save Johanna the wits to anticipate that the lower tenements of Conisthorpe would be awash by morning?

The weavers were struggling to get their looms across the bridge. He cleared the way for them and gave a hand. Most of the rise dwellers and fisher folk were across now, but there were a few dawdlers and people who had returned for more of their possessions. He waited on the far side of the bridge, examining the faces of the women who stumbled past, their shoulders hunched against the driving rain as they clutched their meagre possessions and led their struggling animals, then he began in mounting panic to berate himself in full measure. Where was she?

It was increasingly hard to see now that darkness had fallen. Torches flared feebly and gave up their ghosts. One horn lantern was a small beacon across on the town side, but little use otherwise. He lifted a child from its mother and sat the infant on his right shoulder. A pair of little arms wrapped around his forehead like a sweatclout and he felt useful, needed. He crossed the bridge and recognised a voice issuing orders and rounding people up like a shepherd—Johanna was there.

He found her holding a young baby in her arms while the infant's mother, one of the fisherfolk, adjusted her load—a bedraggled waif, save the proud stance of her shoulders betrayed Lord Alan's daughter.

"You look very homely," he said. "Looking forward to becoming a nun?"

"The babe is pulling my hair something cruel, the second one this evening!" answered Johanna. It was also squalling with frustration and nuzzling into her front like a piglet in search of a teat. "You will make St. Christopher jealous, sir," she exclaimed, noting his passenger.

"I cannot have that." He unhooked his unusual living headdress and bestowed the little mite on one of the half-grown girls come down to gawk, then he pulled his temporary wife aside, wishing he might see her face.

He felt like abusing her—for putting herself at peril, for causing him anxiety. Instead he found himself holding out his hand and giving her another labour. "Shall we go back and search the hovels?" Perhaps he was expecting too much of her but Sir Geoffrey had not yet arrived.

Johanna followed him back over the water-lapped planks, absurdly pleased at being considered useful and capable of acting in harness with him.

"I caught one of them looting," Gervase shouted, his arm about her shoulders as they headed up once more towards the hovels, "else I should have come seeking you sooner. Father Gilbert is here and the town priest, did you see them?" He had found a piece of sacking and was battling to hold it over her.

She took the other side but Geraint could feel she was already pitifully drenched to the skin and shivering. He needed to get her back, but not without himself or Jankyn as protection lest her assailant was still lurking.

"Make sure we have everyone." They had reached the rise. "Take care of the wind blasts. Some of these will be flattened ere long. I will take this side of the road. You do the other." Mercifully she did not argue.

"Yes, sir." Her tone implied she was pulling an imaginary forelock impudently at him.

"Johanna," he caught her arm. Wrung out, her sleeve would have filled a beaker. "Take care!" He meant it.

The search was worthwhile. Johanna found an old man snoring, his breath reeking of ale. He clutched at her loins hopefully and felt her fist in his face for his pains. That woke him. She sent him scratching and sleepy into the rain where his sudden oath would have made a mercenary blush. She left him to totter towards the bridge and ran back down to cross it.

Watkyn joined her and although he would have been no match should any have tried to molest her, she was glad of his company. Not that anyone would now; they were too intent on saving their own skins. Dear God, she had never seen a tempest like this in her whole life.

"You should return to the castle, my lady." They stood now on the town side of the bridge but she was looking back towards the weavers' dwellings.

"No, not until Sir Gervase is here."

"I am here." His voice was comfortingly strong. "You did well, my lady." His strong hand curled upon her elbow. "Let us return to the castle."

"*A moi!* For the love of God!"

Behind them, Father Gilbert was kneeling on the bridge, struggling to pull a boy out of the torrent.

Johanna ran back after Gervase. The bridge quivered beneath his weight.

"He slipped. I told him he was carrying too much. Hold on, Peter!"

"It is Yolonya's grandson," Johanna exclaimed, kneeling to help as Gervase crouched down in the chaplain's place.

"Grab my hand, lad!" Gervase flung himself flat and put an arm down. "I will haul you out, trust me."

The boy had managed to seize hold of the greasy planks of the bridge but the icy torrent was hurtling between the piers, pounding his thin frame. He was screaming, almost too terrified to let go, but as he made a grab for Gervase's hand, his courage failed.

"He will drown." Johanna beat her fists despairingly into her sides as Gervase scrambled to his feet.

"Take this!" He thrust his sword belt into her hands and jumped. The bridge lurched as he leapt.

Watkyn grabbed Johanna's arm. "Christ save us, my lady! The bridge!" He urgently shoved her after Father Gilbert to the nearest bank and ran back to stand helplessly ankle-deep, anxious for his master.

Freezing water took Geraint's breath away and he grabbed swiftly at the timbers. The boy, spluttering and choking, still had an arm around a bridge support.

"The bridge! Let go!" bellowed the jester from the side.

The terrified boy would not loosen his hold and Geraint sliced at his wrist with the heel of his hand. The water hurtled them away and it was only a miracle that Geraint was able to snatch at an overhanging branch, barely visible. He fastened the lad's failing fingers to it and shouted to Jankyn who came scrambling down into the water, one arm curled around the branch.

"Be hasty, boy!" He bawled at the lad. "When the bridge goes, its timbers will come at you like battering rams."

The boy needed no second bidding. Father Gilbert and Jankyn heaved him between them up the bank. Geraint dragged himself along the branch. The boy lay gasping in the mire. His rescuer staggered out after him and knelt supporting himself on his elbows, his lungs at bursting point. He heard the crack as the crossing planks surrendered to the torrent. Like the bridge, he was exhausted.

Small hands beat at his shoulders. "Get up, come! Here is your sword back. Rouse up or the cold will destroy you!"

Johanna, curse her, was not going to let him lie there like a piece of washed up timber. He stumbled, shuddering, to his feet. A pox on it! The town with its warmth and shelter mocked him beyond the rising water. They were on the wrong bank.

Five of them, marooned like silly sheep. He straightened, assessing their situation. The rain had lessened somewhat but the roar of the running water was greater, its full wrath still to come. His companions would be colder than him, less fleshed as they were. They must seek shelter with all speed, but he doubted the remaining flimsy dwellings would hold much longer.

"Sir, the man who attacked my lady was one of the Enderby men. They are camped this side, about half a mile upstream."

Johanna's voice quivered. "The rain is easing. You think they will come for us now?"

Geraint shook his head. "Not in the darkness, but they may try to cross the other stream and seize us come the dawn." Fulk's men would have their own worries with the weather unless Johanna's attacker demanded they return tonight.

"We need shelter and dry clothing," muttered Jankyn, "else the cold will kill us."

"Do not worry on that score about me," Johanna muttered but Geraint could hear the chattering of her jaw and saw that she had her arms crossed over her breast. She might know of a safer haven but he doubted it. Could they risk trying to cross the further stream and journeying to the nearest bridge? That was, if it was still standing.

As if she was reading his thoughts, she said, "There is only a f-ford down river and that will be impossible now. Jesu, look!"

A procession of torches was coming fast down Bridgegate. Sir Geoffrey's voice hallooed them from the other side, angry and concerned for Johanna's and Father Gilbert's well-being. Lights glinted on the glistening leather of the harnesses and danced across the wicked torrent.

Geraint estimated the width of the swollen river and came to a decision.

"Search the hovels for a rope." He cupped his hands and bawled, "We are going to try and cross, God willing!"

It was Jankyn who finally found them a rope long enough for the purpose, together with some abandoned loom weights. Geraint ran his fingers along it, testing for flaws. Satisfied, he started to thread the stones on.

"Here! This is quicker." Johanna tugged off her ragged veil and they knotted the stones in it, leaving two long tails to tie round the end of the rope.

Geraint whirled it around his head and slung hard. It missed the opposite bank, and he cursed and hauled it in to try again. On the fourth attempt, it made land. He moved along the bank following the direction Sir Geoffrey was tugging the precious rope, keeping strong hold. It was not easy for either of them to find a sturdy tree. Most had been coppiced or else were too broad, but eventually Sir Geoffrey made the rope fast.

"If it was taut enough, I could walk across it," Jankyn muttered proudly as Geraint tethered it on their side.

"Well, it will not be, *Watkyn*," his knight replied warningly, "but you can test it first."

The jester shrugged. "I did not sign any articles with you for this but so be it. Say a stout prayer, Father."

Although it was knotted well above the river's surface, Jankyn's weight immediately taxed the rope lower. The water surged around his thighs. He was as agile as a monkey, swinging himself along, jumping his legs out of the water as much as he could. It was wise to send him first. The lad Peter, myopic and awkward, would have had no inkling.

Terrified, the boy hung back but Geraint taunted him. "Would you rather I sent my lady first to shame you?"

The lad made heavy going of it, fearful lest it suck him down.

"You may have saved a future bishop there, my son." Crossing himself, Father Gilbert rose from his knees to venture forth. Lean and small-boned he might be, but his priestly habit was cumbersome.

Johanna tried to pray for his safety, but her lips were trembling and her body was shivering hard. The Devil was at her elbow, whispering that it would be easy to let go in the water and end it all. *You do not want to be a nun,* the persistent voice said, *and the man Gervase is anxious to be gone from you. God gave you to Fulk. He and Edgar are out there waiting. End it now!* Preposterously she thought of practicalities. There would be no dilemma for Father Gilbert as to whether to coffin her in unhallowed ground. Strangers would find her water-battered body and some other priest would bury her in a churchyard she had never visited. Death by drowning was not an honest death, men said. *How do they know? Forget the world,* whispered the Devil. Only a cheer on the other bank ended the plausible reasoning.

"Now, you, my lady! Move like Watkyn did, not like the others. They were too slow." Gervase grabbed her chin and bestowed a kiss upon her rain-wet mouth. There was no sensation, it was a gesture.

She was too chilled now either to feel bereft or waste her diminishing mental strength with curses as she waded out gingerly into the freezing water, her hand tight on the rope. As she felt the sound land fall away, she grasped the lifeline with both hands and began that frightening journey.

It was her wretched skirts that dragged at her, catching in the water, pulling her into the torrent. The icy water against her belly snatched her breath away. She could not swim and the rope was slippery to hold.

End it now! screamed Satan above the deafening torrent.

"Keep moving, Johanna!" roared Gervase. "By Christ, woman, look out!" A log, as long as a man, was hurtling straight at her. With a prayer, Johanna put all her strength into one last effort to move along. It jolted her, grazing her side with its splintered end, swinging round to continue headfirst downriver.

The shock of it revived her spirit and painfully she slid her left hand along again and again. Her arms and shoulders were aching to perdition before Sir Geoffrey blessedly hauled her in. Amice was on the bank to put her arms about her, and despite their difference in rank, they clung together sobbing. It was only when she felt the tension in the woman's hands about her forearms that she knew

Gervase had begun the crossing. But she was wrong. Suddenly the men around her were roaring at the top of their lungs.

"Merciful Christ!" For an instant she thought that her scholar had been attacked by Enderby's men, but she could see now that it was just one swordsman on horseback who was slashing at him. Edgar de Laverton had not gone to join his men. He must have been skulking in the shadows like a wraith. Thank God Gervase had taken his sword back from her. It was her fear for him that cleansed Johanna's thoughts and the Devil finally fled from her. The Lord had not finished with her yet nor would she let Him abandon Gervase.

And God had mercy. Gervase managed to pull the man from the saddle, then sent him sprawling backwards, and leapt for the rope. But their cheers were short-lived for he was a giant compared to the previous passengers and the line, though stout, tensed as though he was a drawn arrow at the centre of an almighty bow. His huge weight had him into the river up to his armpits and although the buoyancy of the water relieved his heaviness, the torrent sucked at him, urging him to let go. Of course, he was stronger and more determined than Johanna, his powerful fists edging him along, but the tethering began to feel the strain, the rope biting further into the tree. Several men took hold to ease the friction.

"Watch out, sir!" Watkyn roared, jumping up and down, waving his arms frantically and pointing. Johanna gasped, her knuckles to her mouth. Edgar was back on his feet and hacking at the rope with his sword. Gervase turned his head, saw the danger and shifted his grip along as fast as he could. He was halfway across when it gave, swinging him out into the centre drag of the river, but he had a coil around his wrist and swiftly took hold above it with his other hand as he tried to free his left hand. For an instant, he disappeared from their sight and then as Johanna ran along the bank shouting, his head emerged from the water.

The men on the bank hauled at the rope, their heels sliding in the mud, finding little anchorage. It was Gervase's determination and strength that got him ashore downstream from them and he heaved himself up by his own efforts, one hand favouring his shoulder.

The sputtering torches, as the hallooing men gathered around him, showed the rope burns on his forearm. He modestly fended off the thumps of congratulation. God save him, but the man never stopped giving orders. He commanded Sir Geoffrey to return to the castle with all speed and Johanna found herself being flung up onto a packhorse with Father Gilbert behind her. She was cold and as sodden as a vat of soaking washing, but something had changed inside her, as if in the risk of losing life she had gained some purpose. It was she who insisted they take up a small child in front of them from one of the slow crocodilus of weavers and fisher folk trudging up to receive shelter at the castle and friary.

Her supposed husband rode up, his face shiny and cheerful in the cresset lights as they arrived at the open portcullis to a concerned castle. The dogs were barking as if they had been forced to keep silence for a week.

"Tha's not something else they haven't been tellin' us about, is it?" Johanna heard the porter mutter as she passed under the archway with the mewling child cuddled against her. Gervase, riding alongside, sucked in his cheeks and burst into a fit of coughing.

He reached over and took hold of her horse's bridle as they reined in at the stables. "I think your porter has decided the matter of whether we lay together, lady," he chuckled, with a grin at Father Gilbert.

"I might well take issue with you for such levity, my son, save that tonight you proved a hero."

In equal dilemma, Johanna sighed. Gervase might find the servant's jape amusing, but clearly her reputation had become as fragile as eggshells. Best leave the issue until the morning, her tired mind advised.

Someone cheered, and around them the puddled ground of the bailey reflecting the moving torches was rather like she imagined Hell without the torment; the shadows of the horses, knights and raggle-taggle villagers monstrously huge upon the speckled walls, while poor Sir Geoffrey strove to bring some order to the confusion.

Her mother was waiting for them on the steps of the new hall, solemn above the hurly-burly, like a niched saint over a cathedral porch. Had she not been a noble lady, she might have whistled at their dishevelled state. "All are accounted for! I congratulate you!" she exclaimed above the tumult. Though as she herded them up to the steamy hall which smelt as though a pack of dogs had been drying off before the hearth, she added cheerfully, "Mind, if you were both under five, I should smack you each soundly and send you to bed supperless."

Johanna dripped into the rushes before a fire in the great chamber, shoeless and muddyfooted, but extremely cheerful as she wrung out her hair to the annoyance of her mother's monkey which was competing for the heat. Did a dog feel like this, she wondered as Agnes towelled her head, when it slunk home after a night of sport? The sense of achievement was there in full measure; yet guilt, too, that her pleasure in being useful had come at the expense of others. Oh, she had a fine bedchamber to return to, whereas who knew what possessions would be left to many of the villagers by dawn. Gratefully, she sipped the hot mulled wine that her mother had summoned and cradled the beaker in her hands as she felt the gorgeous warmth seep outwards to her toes and fingertips.

"Oh, my lady, 'tis a fine sight you are," clucked Agnes.

As terrible as Gervase? His fair hair hung in hanks, dirt streaked his cheeks, the hanging sleeves were no longer in existence and his cote-hardie and steaming hose looked as though they had been used to wipe down the flanks of a mud-spattered horse. Jonah emerging from the whale's belly would have looked more respectable, but Johanna was able to gaze on him with admiration. She doubted even her own father could have done so well in ordering the villagers to safety. Perhaps being a schoolmaster, her stranger had merely treated the commoners like schoolboys, sending them hither and thither for their own good.

Catching her stare, he grinned at her over his beaker, though as usual there was that hard intelligent shadow behind the charm. Of a sudden, she wondered if he had deliberately seized the opportunity to make himself a hero, but she dismissed the sinful notion, cursing herself as unworthy for even letting it enter her thoughts.

"You are looking like an old-world goddess, my lady."

"Yes, of the privies and sewers, no doubt."

A roguish smile lit his scratched face. "Bedaubed enough to lure a discerning river god." The beaker was raised to her teasingly in a toast before he downed the heated wine in a few gulps. For an instant she felt beautiful, her damaged face forgotten, then she put up exploring fingers and found the tenderness in her hair where Edgar had hit her. Remembering the lechery in the ribald's eyes, she raised her face to the scholar, certain of discovering the signs of betrayal there also. The humour had gone from him and there was a sudden stillness about his expression that made her catch her breath.

Geraint had the foolish desire to frame her face within his hands and celebrate their survival with a kiss that would tell her he needed a woman and he wanted her. Such folly was prevented. Her mother came between them with her usual briskness and handed him a cloth to mop the moisture from his tangled hair. "I have had a bath prepared for you in your bedchamber," she told Johanna. "Do not tarry! Agnes is waiting to disrobe you."

"Large enough for both of us, I trust." Geraint threw the remark to her like a ball behind her mother's back. Lady Constance's jaw fell in astonishment at his presumption and Johanna, with a little gasp, stepped back as if the air between them burned her. "I shall keep my drawers on," he assured her.

His pretend wife was looking at him speechless. She recovered herself, aware that Sir Geoffrey and Lady Edyth had followed her mother in. "Of course, sir," she said demurely for their benefit and removed herself from the great chamber.

He bade the others goodnight and caught up with her in the hall. Her frown of displeasure was edged with nervousness. Her agreement had been mere lip service. Only a fool could think otherwise.

"You can go in first or have it to yourself, I care not," she snarled.

"Afraid of me?" He squared up to her; his smile would have entertained babes.

"No!"

"But you agree it is customary for lovers to share a tub."

"Sir Gervase, this is not . . ." Lady Constance had followed him out and was evidently searching for words to match her thoughts.

He shook his head, laughing. "No, I was gulling you, mesdames. In truth, I am so weary that were a whole pack of dragons to attack tonight, I doubt the hubbub would arouse me. Watkyn's good offices will be sufficient, I assure you. Goodnight to you both."

"No wait, Gervase." Lady Constance's fingers brushed his arm. "Did Sir Geoffrey remember to tell you? We have had tidings that the archdeacon's officer for the hearing is held up by the floods, but fortunately the proctor has arrived in good time and I have summoned him to come and speak with us tomorrow."

Geraint groaned. If the court officials would not arrive until after the river level had dropped sufficiently to make the nearest ford viable, he was going to be stranded in this disguising even longer. That was unless they chose to ride miles out of the way to a bridge that had held.

Mind, to look on the bright side, Sir Fulk and Sir Ralph were beyond the swollen river so neither could lay hands on him and he could leave the castle at will—come and go as he pleased—until the water could be crossed. It seemed an eternity since he had not been hunted. Perhaps he should neglect the matters of the kingdom for a few days and play at manorial master. Come morning, he would ride down like a dutiful lord should to inspect the damage. And he must speak with the proctor too.

Lady Constance set a hand on his sullied sleeve. "I must not tarry. Father Gilbert tells me one of the weaver women is having birthpains. Oh God give me patience, here comes Edyth again, but no matter." With great show and care not to dirty her kirtle, she kissed Gervase on the cheek as if he was indeed an acquired son and did the same for her daughter. "Sleep well and thank you both. I am coming, Edyth!"

Johanna definitely tarried.

"Go, lady, to the delights of rosewater."

"I want to thank you as well," she said softly.

Geraint raised his head from ruefully inspecting the ruined embroidery of his shirt sleeves, so admired by Edmund.

"I suppose it would be useless to say, my lady, that by leaving the castle you put your life at considerable risk from Fulk."

"Yes." She looked adorably soggy, like a lapdog that had been in the puddles.

"Here, let me." He made a gesture in the air above her head with both hands.

"What are you doing?" It was satisfying that he had her concerned, uncertain of his mood.

"Adjusting your halo. You were an angel of mercy, brave and

uncomplaining. I salute your courage." He carried her damp fingers to his lips.

She laughed, clearly relieved that he was not going to lecture her. "Your reputation will have fared well too," she answered huskily. It was the first time that he had heard her laugh or seen her hair loosened about her shoulders. As if unable to meet his intense gaze, she bit her lip and looked away. "I have to apologise for being so ungrateful this morning."

So the man-shy doe was coming to his hand. Given time he could heal the injuries inside her. He sensed the growing friendship between them, but to let the burgeoning trust ripen into intimacy, no, that could not be. He must be free to walk away from Conisthorpe and, unlike Orpheus, not look back. To do otherwise would hurt this young woman beyond measure and greater matters than hers needed his swordarm.

"Sir?"

He could not help enjoy looking at her, this dishevelled Johanna who had partnered him tonight, lady to his lord, without questioning. He had to end this conversation before he did something foolish. "Your bath is waiting."

She untangled a leaf from the hair curling over her breasts. "I . . . do understand how much effort you are making and that it is not easy to play a role to which you are unaccustomed." Now was that a slap or a compliment?

"Are we talking about prancing around as a knight or playing your lord?" He watched the little chin rise defiantly, but she could not find the words. "No matter, lady, I am sure you will behave better or I will slip my collar like the disobedient cur I am."

"I never called you that," she protested and the dark, lustrous lashes curled down hiding the hurt.

He waited until he had her silvery-green gaze again upon his face.

"Oh, believe it for both our sakes. That is exactly what I am."

Fourteen

HE BOWED AND LEFT THE HALL. THE LADY WAS growing softer. By all the Saints, he might have got away with sharing the bathtub but he did not want an interrogation on his shoulder wound and it was hurting damnably, curse it! Something jagged had torn at him beneath the bridge, or was it when Fulk's man had charged at him? In the candlelight of the chamber adjoining Sir Geoffrey's quarters, after Jankyn had helped him off with the tunic, he paled at the dark stain spreading into the surrounding damp of his shirt.

"I would Dame Christiana were here, great one. I have filched a clean dressing, but what healing skills I have are made of words."

"No matter, Jankyn, patch me as best you can."

He was too tired to seek out the brawny Yolonya's help tonight; besides, the tiring woman had her hands full—the wailing of the woman in childbirth rose above the other noises outside the keep walls. Bandaged and with clean towels bound above the wound to staunch the bleeding and a hot brick for his feet, he lay down thankfully but sent Jankyn out again to fetch him more mulled wine.

The jester stretched out on the palliasse at his feet. "You did much good, friend, and the lady too. She was happy tonight."

"Aye, until I offered to sponge her back. I suppose it would be foolish to ask what worm cankered your brain to allow her into danger."

"Hayforks."

"Numbskull! If no one takes an ague from this day's work, Jankyn, I shall light candles of thanks, I tell you."

"We made excellent horses in harness, the lady, you and I."

"I could not want a better esquire and I will pat you on the head again in the morning. Sleep like the blessed, Jankyn!"

He was still awake when Sir Geoffrey tiptoed through later like an incompetent ghost trying to find his way to a grave before sunrise.

"Is all well?"

"Aye, lad, all settled. A pity you are not staying longer."

Geraint smiled wryly and closed his eyes again. As an antidote to the woman's birthpang shrieks and the pain that made it impossible to find comfort for his arm, he foolishly pictured Johanna naked in her bath. But the wound tormented him more than his imaginings. He felt the heat and palpitations visit him again as they had the night before and knew that the abscess must be dealt with lest the infection eat into the rest of him. Sleep only absolved him after the cry of a newborn baby rang out across the yard. It reminded him of heirs and expectations. His earlier instincts were right; he must be out of here within the week.

THE KNOCK ON HER BEDCHAMBER HALFWAY THROUGH THE MORNING was urgent, but before Johanna could answer the ring handle twisted and the large scholar suddenly filled her small realm. The Devil take the great lout! She glared pointedly at the fresh mud on the sides of his riding boots and twitched the uncut velvet to safety.

He looked as though he had slept ill; the shadows beneath the blue eyes were excessive and the gold of his hair seemed unusually diminished. But even if he was last night's hero, it was no excuse for today's churlish invasion. And she was definitely at a disadvantage—on all fours in the middle of the flagstone floor with a large piece of blue fabric puddled out in front of her and a mouthful of pins. Well, something had to be said to force this Sir Galahad back into line. Sitting up on her knees with squirrelish alertness, Johanna blew the pins into the palm of her hand and drew breath to berate him for invading her privacy.

"I have just been down to inspect the damage," he informed her loftily without being asked, as if he had gone without her mother or Sir Geoffrey. "One of the old fishers says the Wharfe is higher than in the sixth year of our king's reign when half of Christendom starved."

That corresponded with her own observation; after showing the little maid her own image in a silver mirror, Johanna had inspected the damage from the battlements with Yolonya and Amice.

"From what we can see from the ramparts and the river bank, the weavers' homes are flattened," he continued.

"Then we shall have work in plenty." She did not tell Gervase that she had already been down in the hall with Father Gilbert and the villagers to discuss repairs. "Thank you for keeping me informed but now that you have played the town crier perhaps you would be kind enough to march off and ring your bell somewhere else. I am quite busy as you see and this needs concentration—"

The man flung up an imperious hand to silence her. "I need your help," he snapped, and glowered down at her as if he expected her to spring to attention.

Johanna tipped the pins into a tiny alabaster box with sluglike tardiness while she announced with a tone which would have rivalled the north wind in January for iciness: "If you think you can just stride in . . ."

But his mind had moved on. She no longer rated attention; he was viewing the bedchamber as if he was its lord determined on repossession. Johanna watched him note the wall-hangings, the empty cage, the pieces of weld yellow taffeta and scarlet samite folded upon her bed, the maid's mattress trundled beneath it, a discarded mud-caked ball that was probably yesterday's stocking which had escaped removal for laundering and the detachable sleeve that Agnes was placidly darning in the comfort of the windowseat, before his lapis gaze found her again and widened at the scissors, rule, selection of glass buttons, charcoal stick and fabric before her.

He had been short with her. It was not that Geraint did not feel like observing niceties, but his shoulder was throbbing. He just wanted it attended to without Johanna behaving like an officious coroner and it was annoying him that apart from her bruises, she looked not only sweetly industrious but as though she should belong to someone. This spacious, comfortable bower with its softhued tapestries and femininity exuded a serenity he lacked in his life. It was an affront, a criticism. It made him discontent; by now he should have had land and sufficient fortune to command a haven like this.

This industrious lady, he was learning, was dangerous to him in a subtle, unselfconscious way and he had no intention of letting the wench worm her way under his skin like she had last night. Squaring his shoulders with a wince, he dismissed his yearning for his own hearth and a woman legally obliged to be dutiful.

"Stride in? Of course I can. I am married to you, remember. I said I need your help and I am here, my lady, because where else can I have some privacy in this damnable castle? Agnes, leave that and fetch me up some hot water—without inviting curiosity, if you please!"

The maid tumbled the mending from her lap, all dimples and compliance.

"Stay where you are!" Johanna grabbed the skirt of the girl's plain surcote. How dare he march into her small kingdom and order her servant! "Is Watkyn sick then? You expect us to shave you?"

For an instant, he blinked down at her in utter surprise and then his expression shed some of its hardness. "No, he is not, and you think that I would let you near me with a freshly stropped blade?" His voice was ripe with irony. "Heaven forbid, lady!" The attempt at humour fell on stony ground and his tone gentled a little. "No, I require a tender cleansing hand . . ." He hesitated and addressed Agnes, "Napkins too, and fresh clean moss, but pray fetch the water first. Discretion, Agnes, hmm?"

The maidservant, still tethered, was diplomatically waiting for her lady's permission. Clearly, the scholar did not trust *her* nursely qualities, thought Johanna, kicking her foot free of her kirtle so she might stand up. Moss! She let go of Agnes. "Oh, do as he says!"

The maid beamed at Gervase, curtsied and scampered off.

"What are you doing?" He peered down at the fabric.

Johanna regarded him suspiciously. Was this a lick of words to put her in sweeter temper? If anyone needed sweetening, it was him.

"Making you a cote-hardie since you ruined yesterday's apparel."

His jaw slackened. "Me!"

Ha, that was a blow that winded him below the belt.

"Yes, master scholar, your grandeur at the hearing is deemed important. We thought you would like the colour. Do you?"

He suddenly remembered his manners and offered her his hand to help her up. "Yes, I do, very much."

The courteous, firm touch of his fingers inflicted a return blow on her. For an inexplicable reason, she felt deprived of breath again.

"We-we have not cut it for you yet but there is a tawny or a honey-suckle if you . . ." Why was she babbling like this?

The irritation above her had utterly vanished to be replaced by a charm of expression that could unseat the less wary. "I suspect I was not to be allowed a choice."

"The . . . the blue will become you well with your fairness." There was an intensity about his gaze that suddenly had her foolishly tongue-tied. Swiftly she looked down at the velvet at her feet. What was the matter with her? Was it the sudden intimacy of having this stranger in her bedchamber? Reorganising her wits, she lifted her face to his. "W-why do you need the hot water?"

"You may see for yourself if you will help me off with this." He started to unbelt his tunic. The gesture was familiar enough to make her flee but she staunched the rising panic Fulk had always invoked in her.

"Sit down on the bed. Let me move these." As she stacked the material neatly on the windowseat, her practical compassion—enforced by curiosity—regained mastery, and with a demure expression of wifely compliance, she managed to help him remove his tunic. The crumpled shirt beneath was stained and bloody. So he had been injured last night.

One arm free, he was trying to ease down the other sleeve. She took over and slowly inched it back, gasping as she recognised the purulent fluid beneath the surface of his skin and beheld the jagged meshing below it in horror. However had he done this? She hardly heard his words.

"Not for the fainthearted, eh? Can you and Agnes manage? If not, perhaps your mother could send for the healer in the woods. My lady . . . are you listening? You are not going to swoon, are you?"

"No. Yes, I can manage."

Something had ripped into his shoulder and opened up some of his back as well. The lower part was healing, but it would have taken several days for this mustering of pus close to his collarbone. "Upon my soul, master scholar! This was not done last night!"

He had paled beneath the tan. "Nor with ink and a sheath of goose quills. Have you not worked out the riddle yet? I met an outlaw with better qualifications."

"Wait a trice, Sir Ralph said . . . Dear God, are you one of the Boroughbridge rebels?"

"Boroughbridge, my lady! Your imagination has sprouted fairy wings. Do you imagine if I had managed to reach here from Boroughbridge, I should indulge in this outrageous scheme of your mother's? Better to stay hidden, for God's sake! Would a rebel be sitting here meekly like a lambkin?"

Johanna raised her gaze from his wound in mild curiosity. "What *would* a rebel be doing?"

"Why, threatening to strangle you if you breathed a word of your daft suspicions and, as you see, I am not. Although I have no doubt I shall feel like throttling you very soon. I have come close to it several times already."

"You could be pretending about not being a rebel," she countered, wishing Agnes would not take so long. "Why else did you come to me privily with this?"

For a moment he regarded her with admiration. "Because, madam wife, you are supposed to minister to my needs. Who else should a husband turn to?" She felt like smacking him for his wicked smile but the seriousness of the wound concerned her. It had been made with two different weapons, she was sure of that, and she doubted that one assailant . . . With an oath, she sprang back from him, crossing herself. "Jesus save us, you *were* at Borough—"

He was on his feet, grabbing her fingers away from her lips. "One word of this to anyone save your mother and I will . . ."

The lack of trust stung her more than the painful manacle of flesh around her wrist. He was hurting her and, dear God, he was strong! Stronger than Fulk. The old fear came rushing back with a vengeance and with it the reflex to quickly mollify.

"W-what do you imagine I will do, b-bid a pair of coopers nail you in a barrel and d-dump you on the sheriff's doorstep as a gratuity?" She struggled to free herself. "You are s-supposed to be my husband . . ." The full implications struck her. "God ha' mercy, if anyone takes you for a rebel—"

"Yes, you will suffer for it," he answered grimly, releasing her at last, "but not as much as I. You will be carried back to Enderby in a litter for private chastisement, but I will be dragged on a hurdle through the streets of York to finish on a scaffold."

Johanna gazed at him appalled, imagining such torture. "Then . . . then you were in great peril yesterday if Sir Ralph had believed Edyth . . ." And to think she had thought the skittishness was because he must play the knight amongst his betters.

Agnes, calling to be let in, broke the antler-lock between them and Gervase sat down heavily on the coverlet. "It is your decision," he said with a sigh, jerking his head towards the door. "Admit her. If we are to trust her as a marriage witness, I shall trust her in this."

Johanna nodded, tight-lipped, and let her tiring woman in. Agnes set down the ewer of steaming water, unloaded the napkins draped across her arm and inspected the wound without surprise as if she was a barber-surgeon.

"Agnes, this must not be spoken of," Johanna whispered.

"Aye, I know, the battle. 'Tis why Father Gilbert bested you, is't not, Sir Gervase?"

"Aye, little nurse, you are no fool." He sighed, "I thought it would have healed by now." Easing himself free of his shirt completely, he tossed it at his feet.

"Well, pardon me for saying so, sir, but what do you expect if you will go frisking at the quintain showing off to my lady and then rescuing Peter? Was it a sword or a lance, sir?"

"A pitchfork did that one." He ran his fingers over his gashed arm carelessly. "Or was it a pike?" he wondered nonchalantly. "A pike, I think. I was too busy parrying blows to my right." They gazed at him in horror. "But this? A flail. From one of my own side," he added with bitterness. "He wanted my horse. I remember—it was in the field by one of those great Devil stones and there was a priest trying to clamber up upon it like some ancient prophet. He was haranguing us, telling us to go back, the fool."

Agnes examined his inflamed shoulder and glanced across him at her mistress. "Shall I go down and heat a knife then?"

"Use this." Gervase unsheathed his own. "I have whetted it."

Johanna took it with quiet authority and tested the blade. "It will suffice. If you prefer, sirrah, I could first try a poultice to draw out the poison. I have known it to work." She plunged the steel into the steaming jug and raised grave eyes to him, awaiting his decision.

"No, lance it!" Geraint answered fiercely. If Christiana had recommended it, it must be done. His vehemence startled her and he gentled his tone. "Who taught you such matters, the healer in the woods?"

"Yes, Christiana. A grumpy old harridan she is too, but very skilled. Be assured I shall send for her if . . . if need be."

So she did not know he had come from the holy widow's. Her mother at least was no blabmouth. "Harridans make excellent teachers when they have a mind to it." He was trying to make light of it, but it was going to hurt damnably. His so-called wife had the haft in her hand now.

"Gervase, this could kill you if we do not rid it of the poison. You should have come to me yesterday. Keep still!"

He stared up at the wall opposite. "You, you hostile wench! You would have hurled a burning hot cockatrice at me for my impudence. That is why I went to the wild wood. To try and find the healer. *Oh, Christ* . . . keep me!"

"Go quickly, Agnes! Fetch moss from my mother, and see that it be clean and wholesome."

The poison oozed out. Again and again Johanna applied the napkin, pressing it over the outside of the skin to make the abscess suppurate. His lower lip curled in distaste. It was as well he could not watch her ministration.

"My lady, I am sorry that you must do this labour for me," he apologised, gritting his teeth. By Heaven, how much more would she squeeze out of him? She merely shook her head in answer, her cheeks sucked in with concentration.

Agnes brought the moss in a clean towel and her mistress with admirable foresight sent her off to fetch mulled wine.

"I think that is an end to it," Johanna murmured, satisfied that the purulent fluid had given way to a watery blood, and began to pack the hollow with the moss. "You will need rest."

Geraint shook his head despairingly. He had not even a decent bed to call his own. The stark chamber in the keep depressed him whereas here above the new hall was sun-dappled. "And to think Mother let you sleep in the hall that first night."

"That was my choice and you had your door stoutly barred," he goaded, but she refused to rise to that challenge. She was studying her handiwork, frowning.

"Well, you must have good bedding and quiet. Perhaps Yolonya should sleep within call."

"It must be high tide and my laden ship is in," he retorted witheringly, and rose stiffly, gently flexing his shoulder.

"Sit down. I have not finished yet."

"In a moment, I beg you." Gervase drew a sharp breath, his face still ashen. His blemished side half-turned from her, his left hand palming the cavity of his shoulder, the man's warrior body jolted Johanna's senses. Did Psyche feel like this seeing her lord Cupid for the first time? No, Psyche would have longed to brush her fingers across the broad triangle of golden hairs which lay between his nipples and plunged downwards over his belly but . . . but Gervase's bared flesh reawoke her revulsion; she saw again Fulk lowering himself onto her and she started to her feet, almost knocking the bowl over in her haste, trying to quell her shaking. Oh, she could tend Gervase's wounds without a qualm but . . .

"What is the matter?"

Miserably, she searched for an answer that would satisfy him, but she could not tell him the truth—that she was tainted. Not rusted like a neglected sword blade but bent, distorted, hammered into an ugliness she shuddered to accept. "Nothing," she lied, not looking at him, hastily stooping to gather up his discarded shirt. "I will ask Agnes to soak this before we give it to be laundered."

"Destroy any evidence, yes? What is it, my lady?"

She kept her face averted, conscious of his bare flesh, like a wall filling her vision. Why could he not move away, cover himself?

"I . . ." Dear God, let him take her confusion as a surfeit of modesty, but an honest answer to satisfy him rose at last unbidden. "I-I have just realised you cannot p-possibly be a schoolmaster."

A grim laugh reinforced her self-chastisement at her blindness. "No, my lady, I am not a schoolmaster."

She felt the heat in her cheeks. Oh, God forgive her, she had used that so unkindly as a weapon to goad him.

"Will it please you sit again so I may finish this?" Dressing his wound, she would forget Fulk and the torments of the sexual act. Mercifully the man sat down once more. "You must be a knight." She busied herself, pressing more moss firmly into the cavity. "It . . . it comes so easily to you." Now she was able to look at his body, to worry about the scar that would mar those proud, fine shoulders after—God willing—the wound had dried and sealed again.

Geraint was thinking fast, weighing honesty against discretion. "No," he lied softly, "I am too poor to be a knight."

"Ah, an esquire then. You fought with your lord at Borough—"

"I wish Agnes would hurry," he muttered. "This is throbbing like . . ." He bit back the scurrilous tourney language and fell silent. He did not want more questions coming at him like crossbolts and mercifully she made no comment. "This will keep, my lady. Another time I will tell you the why and the how." It was his turn to look at her because she bestowed no answer.

"You will have to believe it will work—the moss, I mean." The words came finally as she stared down at him with the tormented look that usually clouded her face whenever Fulk's name was spoken and made Geraint feel compassion anew for her. She had suffered, was suffering. Save for the bruising, there was no colour in her face. Too wan, too thin, too frightened but capable and bravehearted. What had Christiana said? *I had lief have her on my side in trouble than the rest at Conisthorpe?* So would I, he decided. Poor wench, she deserved better from Fortune. Physician, heal thyself.

"You have to believe it too," he said softly, transfixing her with the sharpness of his gaze.

His words clearly confused her and mayhap she would have coaxed the meaning out of him had not Agnes breezed cheerfully back.

"Yolonya says this will be better than wine, sir."

"The stink is diabolical," he growled, pushing the cup the girl was proffering back towards her. "What is it? Infusion of toadskin?"

"It will dull the pain, sir."

Wrinkling his nose, he took a gulp and nearly spewed it out. "Heaven forgive you, Agnes. It is abominable." But he downed it.

"Yolonya also says 'twould be of benefit, my lady, if Sir Gervase could rest where we can keep an eye on him, and keep the wound exposed at least an hour," whispered Agnes, as if the medicine had rendered him deaf.

"Then you had better lie down here, sir." Johanna, not waiting for an answer, began to spread clean towels across the pillow.

Geraint dragged off one boot, wincing at the effort, and Agnes knelt and removed the other. He lay down first on his undamaged side, trying to ease his body into greater comfort, but his arm ached to the elbow, the flesh around the abscess was throbbing and he felt tired beyond belief. Soft fingers helped him turn and rearrange his arm. It was bliss to surrender to their ministrations. He closed his eyes and the women's voices became a murmur like lapping water as they spread the blue velvet again and returned to their cutting out.

THE SERENITY OF THE SUNLIT BEDCHAMBER MOCKED JOHANNA AS SHE sat in the casement seat an hour later, a half-sewn seam neglected on her lap. She envied Agnes who was happily humming as she worked. One day the girl would have a hearth and a husband while she . . . It was hard to staunch the tears, to confront yet again her damaged soul and admit her loss. Watching the stranger's breast rise and fall beneath the coverlet and listening to his peaceful breathing, she knew this intimacy might have been her destiny had God decided differently. Now ugly self-pity clawed at her for attention. Two husbands, but no future save the cloister and a lonely bed. No children. It would be so! She would never let another man do to her what she had suffered nightly in Fulk's bed. The thrusting, the undignified invasion of her body's orifice. Not for her, never, never again!

"Johanna, is Agnes—" Coming from her bedchamber which adjoined this room above the hall, Lady Constance breezed in unbidden like a windchange and halted, taking in Gervase sprawled fast asleep upon her daughter's bed.

"Hush, he needs the sleep," Johanna admonished.

Her mother raised an eyebrow at the domesticity of the scene. "I expected you to follow my advice, Johanna, but not quite so thoroughly."

She ignored the sarcasm. "I am exceedingly angry with you,

Maman. Why did you not tell me he was fleeing from Borough-bridge?"

Unabashed at the accusation, her mother waved a hand dismissively. "We can talk later. Rouse him, the proctor has arrived. Come with me, Agnes, I need your help." She sailed down the staircase which led to the pantry. Agnes shrugged and followed, leaving Johanna unanswered and fuming.

"She probably thinks I was swything you," murmured a sleepy male voice as the door closed behind them. Geraint lifted his head and yawned. "Your pardon, my lady, I had no intention of dozing off."

"But that was exactly what you needed," replied Johanna briskly. "Here is a clean shirt for you. How is the wound? No more throbbing?"

He stretched slowly like a great cat, swung his stockinged feet to the floor and cautiously flexed his shoulder. "Should I be getting a throbbing?"

She was getting to recognise the teasing in his voice. "No, definitely not," she answered as innocently as she could, busying herself with tidying up the blue scraps from the floor and deliberately leaving him to put the shirt on by himself.

"My thanks for your labours." Standing up, he reached for his tunic.

"Oh, I have some skills," she answered caustically.

"I never said you did not. I intend to try out most of them." At least that was what it sounded like he said as he pulled the garment over his head.

"What in the name of Heaven do you mean by that?" She helped him tug it into position. An unfriendly dog would have empathised with her risen hackles.

He had the grace to emerge looking sheepish. "I mean that if you can heal me then perhaps I can . . ." He caught up his belt and located its ends. ". . . heal you, and when I leave Conisthorpe some more worthy man may come along . . ."

And to think she had felt in harmony with him, even let him use her pillow. "Do you think there is nothing better in the world than sharing a man's bed?" Her voice sank to a dangerous growl. "Get out of my bedchamber, sir!"

Having buckled up, he raised his head and studied her.

"Do you think me blind, Johanna?" he retaliated. "I am beginning to realise the entirety of what that devil Fulk has done to you."

Oh, now she caught his meaning. This arrogant, conceited man had glimpsed her earlier repugnance and thought he could exorcise her demons, did he?

"I tended you, did I not?"

"Oh yes, my lady, pity on a poor wounded creature. But what about the rest of me? It is evident my wholesome flesh makes you feel like puking."

Brushing off the meandering blue threads clinging to her surcote, she did not need to look at him. "I regret that you noticed. Please understand. It . . . it works both ways. Do you want to kiss my bruised cheek?" She gazed up and caught the faint revulsion in the tightening of his mouth. "No, I see you do not. It is the same thing."

"Your face will mend."

"And my repugnance will not, will it?" The ensuing silence was raw with pain on her side. She walked to the window, away from the blue eyes mirroring her image.

"Heal yourself, my lady. If you do not, you will have let Fulk crush you like a flowerbud beneath his heel."

Her fingers twisted frantically. "What happens here after you leave Conisthorpe is not your business, sir. All you are paid to do is perjure yourself and then return to whatever safety you may find."

She heard the rustle of his clothing as he stepped up behind her and sensed the hesitation. His words when he spoke were too close for her peace. "So you despise me," he snarled and she felt his angry breath upon her temple. "I see, I am a mercenary whore, paid to perform but not permitted to give an opinion."

Turning, she flung herself past him to the door and wrenched it open.

"Sir," she said coldly, waiting for him to leave, not daring to glance up as he came towards her and stopped within kissing distance. Her heart was beating frantically.

His fingers came gently round her face as if it were a rose. "Perhaps if we both close our eyes."

She squeezed her eyelids shut, not to obey him but so she could not look. She felt the soft touch of his lips on her bruised cheek then his mouth came down on hers and she fought instinctively against the iron arms that held her.

"Ah well, it was worth the try."

As she opened her eyes, his face filled her entire vision. If he felt her heart pounding, the blue gaze did not taunt her for her vulnerability. It was cruel but needful for Johanna to deliberately draw the back of her hand across her mouth.

Geraint let her go. Humiliated at his failure, ashamed at forcing her, he nevertheless felt the tug of desire and the tantalisation of the hunt. He would not apologise and he would try not to care.

"I will await you downstairs," he told her. "Wear the scarlet."

Fifteen

"I PROMISE TO BEHAVE, JOHANNA," GERAINT MURMURED later as they coincided in punctuality at the threshold of the hall.

"Ha!"

"Be advised, lady, if you hurl the nearest tankard at me, I will have nothing respectable left to wear."

The lady's hand settled upon his wrist like a reluctant hawk on the glove. His attempt at humour seemed to mollify her somewhat albeit she was chewing her lower lip, a telltale sign of inner nerves at meeting the proctor. He had only himself to blame for compounding the wretched wench's problems. But, after all, one did not throw away a good shoe if the outer casing was still sturdy; if merely the lining was torn, you tried mending it.

And one half of her face was very kissable.

She had draped her veil generously at the sides of her face and the laps of her hair were tugged forward. Although the puffiness around her eye had cleared, only her mirror or a brave man would have told her she had acquired a very noticeable graze from the last day's adventure.

"You look as sweet as a cherry," he was able to tell her sincerely from her undamaged side, his gaze sweeping admiringly down the red kirtle. And edible, he added to himself, his gaze dwelling unashamedly on the rise of her breasts.

"A fruit with a stone at its heart," she replied charmingly. "Are we going in or are you going to stand here lying all morning?"

"Let us do it this way for the proctor, darling dear." Dropping his wrist away from hers, he caught her fingers instead and led her playfully into the hall.

The brown-robed stranger conversing with Lady Constance and Father Gilbert as they warmed themselves by the dais hearth had a large girth which betokened well.

Geraint's hand drew Johanna close and he bent his head and whispered, "You can judge a proctor's eloquence by his waistline," so that she would still be smiling when they reached the man of law.

Stephen de Norwood might have taken holy orders, but the man's demeanour was more hearty than holy. Friar Tuck would have recognised a kindred soul.

"Sir Gervase." He shook Geraint's hand vigorously and respectfully bobbed his head. "And the beauteous hub of this matter, madam, your humble servant." Johanna's skeptical reaction to the man's impolitic attempt to fascinate was predictable. She swiftly withdrew her hand; given encouragement, the fellow would have carried it to his lips.

"You managed to reach here safely, I see, Brother Stephen," Geraint commented politely. "I understand that your colleagues were less fortunate."

"Ah yes, these things happen, sir, but I am certain they will only be delayed by a few days, and I assure you that the curse of the weather may be a blessing in disguise. We may all prepare ourselves more fully, and, immodest though it may seem of me to suggest it, I shall be able to offer you,"—here the proctor nodded to him rather than the ladies—"valuable advice that may stand you in good stead considering the new circumstances."

"*New?*" Johanna shook the word as though it were a bone. "What do you mean, master proctor?"

"Perhaps not new, but as you are not experienced in these matters, my lady, you may not have anticipated that . . ." He waved his hands in the air. "Forgive me, I ramble. To put it in a nutshell, madam, your hus—Sir Fulk has also filed a petition." He turned to Gervase, "You and Sir Fulk are now what is termed *competitiores*, you are each bringing a petition against this charming lady."

Geraint noticed the flicker of distaste Johanna's lips betrayed. Even expected, the delivery of the news must chill her. It was to be a tournament of words with her as the prize, assuming, of course, that her real husband would play an honourable game.

"I should do the same thing in his shoes," Geraint observed, bestowing an ostentatiously generous smile on his beloved.

"I have just informed Brother Stephen of the unfortunate circumstances that have caused this unhappy business," Lady Constance said briskly. She must have caught the fraction of alarm in Johanna's eyes and unease in his own, for she added swiftly: "You can both give him your side of the matter, of course, but I have explained that in essence it is all due to your covert marriage and my lord's later refusal to listen to Johanna's protests." She turned her attention to the proctor. "My husband sadly cannot provide an account of his part in this. I tell you in confidence that God has smitten him."

The proctor nodded, clicking his tongue sympathetically. "Most unfortunate for Lord Alan, although of course the Lord God may have incapacitated him for an entirely different reason." Here, he glanced cautiously at Father Gilbert, adding, "However, it seems that the Almighty has intervened to bring about Sir Gervase's safe return." He received a thoughtful nod from the chaplain and, emboldened, swivelled round to direct his attention to Geraint. "*Dominus litis*, Sir Gervase. You shall be well served. Some proctors, like myself, are bachelors of canon law."

"Perhaps you would like to explain your position, Brother Stephen," Geraint suggested.

"For the noble ladies' better understanding, of course. As you are no doubt aware, Sir Gervase, a proctor is an official of the archdeacon's court—the consistory court. It is our task to introduce the facts to the court and organise the evidence. We argue to the judge the strength of our party's legal position. An advocate, on the other hand, is paid to present legal points and questions. A proctor, however, may also act as an advocate in cases of a complicated and . . ." here he coughed, "delicate nature.

"I am available to advise you, sir, but, naturally, I must request payment for my extra services if I am to act as your advocate as well. My fees are most reasonable, I assure you."

Geraint received a faint signal of acceptance from Lady Constance, but having never seen the nobility enthusiastic to spend their money, he played his role to the letter. "I will give due thought to your suggestion," he said as if only mildly interested.

"Indeed, Sir Gervase, to show my honesty and value, I will give you a morsel of advice for free this very instant."

Schooling his expression to indifference, Geraint waited.

Enthused, the proctor delivered. "The court may request you to provide the name of your parish priest." Was this tidbit calculated to impress?

"Ah." Father Gilbert, at least, nodded.

Geraint glanced at the chaplain. "Why?"

The proctor beamed and elaborated. "So that the court may write to your priest to verify who you are, whether you are a bachelor or widower and eligible to be married to this lady, and so he may avow your sincerity as a virtuous knight."

Johanna's mother swayed. Fortunately Stephen de Norwood was beside her and did not notice.

"Of course," agreed Geraint suavely as if he had known it all along. The proctor waited respectfully for more of a response and if he was disappointed that his potential client was neither astonished nor grateful, he did not show it.

Johanna, perhaps irritated by her knight's coolness, was busy evaluating the advice. "Why should that procedure be necessary, Brother Stephen? Even a village idiot can perceive that Sir Gervase is a knight and gently bred." She ignored the covert smirk from her so-called husband.

The proctor obviously preferred to avoid any business dealings with women, but he was reasonably polite. "Lady Johanna, this verification should have been acquired by the priest who married you. I assume that because of the hasty nature of your troth plighting this was never done." He bestowed a stern, myopic look upon her.

Johanna bit her lip and directed a reproachful glance at Geraint before she shook her head with less shame than was appropriate.

The proctor smugly continued. "Because Sir Gervase was not known in these parts, the priest who joined you—Father Benedict, did you say earlier, Lady Constance?—should have sent to Sir Gervase's parish for confirmation that he was not a trickster out to cozen a young demoiselle into his bed."

Distracted by the tiny twitch at the corners of his mouth, Johanna knew that Gervase was suppressing a grin. Caught out, he sent her a chastising glance and enthusiastically directed his attention to the proctor.

"Had Father Benedict behaved in a correct manner, he would have read the banns on three consecutive Sundays," Stephen de Norwood was saying.

Frowning, Johanna interrupted hastily, looking to Father Gilbert. "I do not understand the importance of 'banns.' If Father Benedict called them at our marriage, is that not sufficient?"

"The whole idea of the banns, my daughter, is for everyone in the vicinity to give thought to a forthcoming marriage," the chaplain answered.

"Permit me to demonstrate, my lady." Stephen held up the forefinger of each hand. "Supposing, let us say, that Joan de Mickleford," he wriggled his left finger, "wishes to wed Thomas de Ilkley." Here he waggled his right finger—its nail could have been cleaner, thought Johanna and tried to listen more carefully as the man continued. "The banns are called for the first time and, of a sudden, ancient Mary, who is the oldest surviving creature in the village of Mickleford, remembers that Joan's grandsire once begat a child out of wedlock on a woman from Ilkley. Everyone else in the village now begins to remember bits and pieces. Together they work out that the woman from Ilkley was actually Thomas's grandmother. The young couple, Joan and Thomas, are therefore in prohibited consanguinity. They would have to get a papal dispensation to marry. If they were to wed and have a babe, there would be good odds that their child might be cursed. Besides, supposing their marriage was not fully lawful, Thomas might decide to set Joan aside at some future day if his roving glance found a wealthier woman or one who pleased him better. Do you wish to add anything, Father?"

"It seems clear to me so far," Father Gilbert answered. "I fear Father Benedict, God rest his soul, was not always as diligent as he should have been."

Lady Constance's foot tapped irritably. "But this procedure of writing to Sir Gervase's parish will create all manner of problems. He spent the last few years in Gascony, for Heaven's sake."

"Gascony?" Stephen de Norwood looked apologetic. "But it still would be wise to send there. To have everything moving forward, preplanned, anticipated, is essential. Do you not see, mesdames," he deigned to include Johanna, "that it is still conceivable—pardon my unfortunate choice of words—that one of Sir Gervase's ancestors might have married one of your family or Lord Alan's kin. Or it could be that Sir Gervase is—pardon me, sir—an adventurer. This knight may have been married already or he might have been excommunicated at the time he wed you, Lady Johanna, and so be denied the sacraments of the church."

"Which, of course, is not so," Johanna's so-called husband declared calmly, deciding to run a finger down her good cheek to show his supposed affection. She caught the sparkle of controlled annoyance in his glance and tried to suppress the pessimism brewing up inside her. She had feared that the hearing would be a quagmire for the treading but if this was a taste of what was to come, they might already be doomed to failure. Even this simple procedure had been unknown to them.

"This is extremely complicated, not to mention tiresome," muttered Lady Constance. "It could take months to send to Gascony and receive an answer."

"I did suggest a bishop's court would have been quicker," Gervase reminded her mother. He kept his tone quiet and devoid of irony but Johanna knew the rebuke was there.

The proctor nodded. "Yes, it surprises me that you have not sought an audience with the Archbishop of York. It is somewhat unusual to have a case brought before the archdeacon's court by persons of noble birth." He smiled obsequiously at Gervase before adding: "Indeed, the court usually hears matters brought by the common people."

Lady Constance gave an angry sigh. "We are proceeding with the matter in the hopes of justice, proctor. Archbishop Melton is in debt to Sir Fulk for some favours and we cannot rely on his lordship's objectivity."

Stephen de Norwood glanced questioningly at Father Gilbert, but the chaplain was suddenly showing more interest in a mark on his sleeve. A politic man, Johanna observed.

"To wit, certain parts of the cathedral would be devoid of embellishment had it not been for my hus—Sir Fulk," she announced.

The brief silence that followed was inconveniently uncomfortable. Geraint watched Johanna's face and neck flame at the predictable unspoken male condemnation of her forwardness in making such remarks. The proctor, however, still had a veritable warehouse of words and a determination for business.

"I do not say that the court will definitely request that a letter be sent to Gascony. It is a request that you should anticipate. Well, Sir Gervase," he bobbed once more deferentially, "I trust I have demonstrated my worth. I will be happy to act as your advocate as well as proctor and present your argument. As I said, my fees are extremely reasonable, but a man must live and, as you will appreciate, the archdeacon does not pay me a particularly generous wage. I would not wish to offer further advice without some arrangement. Perhaps you would like time to think it over. With your leave, sir, gracious madam, I will seek some air."

Lady Constance inclined her head graciously and he withdrew.

"Jesu!" exclaimed Geraint. He looked as if he wanted to drive his fist into the nearest door.

"We can forge the letter from your priest," Johanna suggested swiftly.

"Oh, yes, we can do a great deal. And if the court demands such a letter, am I supposed to cool my heels here while this imaginary letter sails off to Gascony and back? You know my circumstances, Lady Constance. Even one week here is too much. This matter is becoming more like a hornet's nest with every day that passes." His angry glance particularly included Johanna.

"You will remain until this is settled," Lady Constance snapped and then added more consolingly, "Besides, Gervase, if you are seen to abandon Johanna again, there will be a hue and cry after you with Sir Fulk and Sir Ralph leading it."

He did not like that truth and cursed, turning his back on them.

"So are we to engage this man's services, madam?" Johanna sounded hopeful that her mother still would be willing to bear the cost. Trying to manage without Stephen de Norwood's advice would mean crossing the hazardous marsh of canon law without a guide.

Geraint jerked his head round at them. "I certainly do not intend to proceed without legal advice," he declared curtly.

"I think you should engage him, madam," Father Gilbert murmured.

"I suppose so," Lady Constance agreed with a sigh, doubtless disappointed that the matter was not so straightforward as she had imagined. "Call the man in again and let us negotiate his extra fee."

"I will fetch him in myself. I need some fresh air to keep my wits straight," muttered Geraint. Three weeks at least while the letter business was settled! He felt as though he had spent a wretched month with them already.

The proctor was sunning himself on the wall flanking the steps. He stopped humming as Geraint approached and rose respectfully.

"I have decided to engage your services, proctor. We can negotiate your fees in a moment and I should like to consult you straightway, but . . . but seeing this is the lady of Conisthorpe's demesne, she will wish to be present at any discussions and I shall not be able to exclude her or my wife without causing offence. However, if we could manage to speak privily . . ."

"Of course, that is understood, Sir Gervase. After all, the lady Johanna is the defendant and women are notorious weathervanes. Even if you are . . ." He broke off and coughed politely.

Geraint, distracted by the return of Sir Geoffrey across the drawbridge with an empty cart being driven in behind him, apologised for not listening and Stephen de Norwood, a trifle put out, pursed his lips briefly. "I was saying, sir, that no matter how devoted you are to the lady Johanna and her mother, it would be best to confide in no one but myself until this case is over."

If only I could, thought Geraint, nodding. Mayhap this man of law could find him a swift way out of the hellish impasse.

"Say no more, sir. Perhaps I can meet you this afternoon? Do you know the alehouse hard by Bainham Priory down the dale?"

"No, but I shall find it," Geraint muttered doggedly as they mounted the steps. Oh yes, he needed to take a breath of freedom and discover exactly where he stood.

THE SCHOOLMASTER—NO, SHE MUST CEASE CALLING HIM THAT— was looking mighty pleased with himself as he sat down to dine, Johanna decided. Perhaps his wound had stilled its aching. He astonished her further by telling the table a jest about the Scots which no one had heard before and he did not pick at the stockfish as he had the previous day. Her mother, on his right, was looking very pleased with his performance.

When Sir Geoffrey and Brother Stephen, sitting beyond Lady Constance, fell into a discussion of hare coursing with mutual enthusiasm, Gervase leant back in her father's chair. She sensed his sideways glance.

"What happened to Lady Edyth? I cannot say I have missed her."

Johanna drew breath hesitantly before she answered, but the seat on the other side of her was safely empty. Her brother had been sent back to his lessons before the fruit and wafers.

"Mother has locked her in the keep for the morning, but we did give her the two most comely men in the garrison to guard her."

"Fortunate Edyth," he nodded, adding, "Remind me to give you the letter I wrote to you before our wedding so you can wear it against your skin for the next few days. You will appreciate it needs to acquire a perfumed, wept-over appearance."

"In such a few days? Perhaps I should drop it in my bathwater, or I could use one of mother's onions again."

"But then it might acquire a mixed aroma."

"I hope you wrote nothing there that would bring blushes to my cheeks in court," she answered primly.

"Well, it might certainly turn the left one into a rainbow." He swiftly shifted his leg nearest to her out of kicking range. Staring down the table, he added, "Shall we try a good helping of ostentatious flirting? Pity you added to your hurts last night." Before she could move her head back, he took her chin in his fingers with a husbandly freedom that she resented. He seemed to be making a habit of it.

"Let me go!" Clenched teeth behind a honeyed smile.

Inspecting her skin, he ran a calloused thumb over the unkind marks. "Calm yourself, beloved. It is fading fast like . . . Help me, Johanna, I am trying to look a besotted, spangled lover. Like a . . ."

"Like a puddle drying up," she offered, trying to put out any fires.

"No!" He let go of her, laughing. "Have you no soul? I was trying to find more courtly words."

She licked a flick of gravy from the side of her mouth and saw the blue merriment metamorphose into a deep ocean that she could not fathom. In Fulk's gaze she had read only calculation, cruelty, condemnation in abundance—but this man's eyes, like the shining surface of water, changed constantly. She wanted to gain his trust. *You want to wear him on your finger like a lodesterre,* her conscience warned her, and, she admitted honestly to herself, she was beginning to relish the pretending. Mayhap her thoughts showed for Gervase of a sudden looked away, his forehead creasing as if he had suddenly bitten into something he disliked.

Swiftly, Johanna sought to re-establish the rapport but it was like mending a spider's web; the silken threads that briefly bound them had been carried away. She was forced to rely on practicalities instead.

"I have been thinking," she cast down a plank of conversation for him to step on. "Could Father Gilbert suddenly remember that he had some papers belonging to Father Benedict? He might even find a reply from an imaginary priest in Gascony or Laval."

"Forge *another* letter, you mean?" Gervase asked softly and shook his head, his lip curling. "I think Father Gilbert has probably tested the limit of his friend at the priory's goodwill, but we can ask him—if your mother has not already done so. Seeing the way this shire runs, Heaven knows how many of the priory documents have had their ends snipped off over the years."

"You can manage three weeks, can you not?" Her tone was humble, from her heart, and she looked down modestly as she spoke. His silence alarmed her. *Please be kind to me,* she prayed. She did not want to have to beg.

It was disappointing. The rogue did not deign to look at her. He was staring arrogantly at the arras on the end wall.

"I do not want to speak of it further."

It was a silencing device that both Fulk and her father had used, and now this man was employing it too. His refusal to reassure her was like a spur to her side.

"Heaven curse you! You are going to raise your price."

Geraint jerked his head round, lips drawn back to snarl at the insult, but he remembered their circumstances in time and checked swiftly to see if anyone had observed them.

"Christ Almighty, woman!" he muttered. "Do you really want to pick a quarrel with me here?"

"I am sorry, Gervase." She spoke his name insolently, sounding bitter as she added, "The trouble is that when a man says he does not want to discuss something with me, I become rather angry, even though, being a mere woman I should used to such dismissiveness. I doubt, sir, you would close the lid on a conversation with Father Gilbert or Sir Geoffrey in such a manner. Answer me. If my mother does not raise your fee, will you leave?"

While two of the menservants stripped away the cloth with its spatters of gravy and set a fresh one before them, she was forced to wait impatiently for his answer. When it came, it was clear the reins of his temper were held again. He tossed his long hair back in the lordly way he had. "I will leave this place as soon as I can, my lady."

The honesty of the answer chilled her. Somewhere inside her a spark of idealism had still burned like a tiny light in the appalling darkness, a belief that he actually wanted to help—that it was not golden coins and a gift of shiny armour that lured him like a greedy adventurer.

"I knew you were lily-livered," she hissed. "Arrows such as you always fall short."

Not looking at her, he idly rubbed a finger across an ancient, puckered stain on the cloth. "I can see now why Father Gilbert is encouraging you to hide yourself in a cloister. You have a tongue like a scourge and a mind like a miser's. But how does the proverb go? 'Better a shrew than a sheep.' "

It was unforgivable. She rose abruptly, needing to flee the truth. But where could she hide from herself?

"Johanna, is something wrong?" her mother called out at the scrape of the stool legs on the flagstones.

"My lady." Gervase managed to catch Johanna by the arm with one large hand and keep the seat behind her knees with the other so that she could not withdraw. She tried to free herself from the knave without calling attention to the struggle, but with little exertion because of his great strength, he pulled her back down. "I fear I have been teasing her, Lady Constance," he called along the table.

Her back straight as a measuring rod, Johanna clasped her hands in front of her on the board and took a deep breath, chastising herself inwardly that she had allowed the months of ill-treatment by Fulk to leave her so vulnerable, so foolish that she always raised her hackles without thinking.

With a sigh, the man beside her set his large powerful right hand over hers. "I swear to you it is not the money, Johanna, that keeps me here." Her glance flew up, searching whether his face was open for her to read, but she found him ready, offering compassion instead of enlightenment. "Believe me, it is not the money."

She would have played at bellows, fanned more words from him, but her mother was knocking on the board for everyone's attention.

"We may as well stay comfortable here." Lady Constance dabbled her fingers in the ewer being taken round to each person at the high table. "Now that you are acting on Sir Gervase's behalf, Brother Stephen, pray tell us the procedure."

Johanna, with an inward sigh, forced herself to pay attention. She wanted to be alone with Gervase and exact his motives; instead she had to watch Stephen de Norwood wriggle self-importantly on his seat as if he were easing himself onto a clutch of eggs before he began.

"On the first day of the hearing the proctors of the court take their oaths and the plaintiff, that is you, Sir Gervase, will bring your libel against Lady Johanna here, the defendant. And, of course, Sir Fulk will do likewise. On the second day, Lady Johanna will answer the libels from each husband."

Gervase's hand had found its way around her shoulders and was idly fingering the embroidery of her surcote.

Johanna, trying to ease forward, away from that distracting caress, gestured the proctor to halt. "But what exactly is this libel that Sir Gervase is to bring against me?"

"It is a petition, madam. Sometimes unlettered plaintiffs submit it orally, but generally it is a short document. In this case, Sir Gervase will allege that you have unlawfully married Sir Fulk when you are already married to him. It usually ends with a plea. Sir Gervase will be requesting that you honour your contract with him."

As if to give emphasis to the proctor's words, Gervase's fingers slid onto her bare flesh. She tried hard to listen as Stephen de

Norwood continued, but the possessive touch was playing unfair games.

"Sir Fulk, in his petition, will no doubt allege that your precontract with Sir Gervase is either unlawful or that it never took place, and his plea will request that the court recognise his marriage with you as binding and order you to rejoin him."

Johanna received a comforting smile from Gervase that was designed to impress the proctor, while his fingers moved to the side of her neck, carrying out some strategy of their own that both confused and angered her. It was necessary, of course, to present a semblance of intimacy, although she was tempted to insert her elbow into his ribs the moment they were unobserved.

Stephen de Norwood pressed on. "As I said, my lady, you will make answer to both libels. On the third day, I will introduce the questions that are to be set to the witnesses called on behalf of the plaintiff, Sir Gervase. Sir Fulk will also name witnesses to attest to the validity of your second marriage and may employ an advocate to question them. I will be stating your 'positions,' sir—here I use the word to mean arguments in your favour. As the case proceeds there will be interrogatories from both the judge and the examiner."

"Examiner?" Gervase shifted irritably, mercifully letting go of her, his glance meeting her anxious eyes. The name alone boded ill.

"Part of the usual procedure, sir. The examiner is an officer of the court who will pose the written questions to the plaintiffs, the defendant and the witnesses. It is his task to test the veracity and credibility of the parties and witnesses. He will ask them the day your marriage took place, the time, the place, whether the sun was shining and so forth. He will also ensure that the witnesses have no hidden interests, that they have not been bribed, for instance."

Johanna, biting her lip, received a further sideways glance from Gervase before he asked, "Does the examiner ask these questions in the common hearing?"

"In the court, you mean? No, sir, this is all done privily outside the hearing." Johanna heaved an inward sigh of relief. "The depositions are written down, however, and will be read out later in court. When all this has been done, the judge will determine the verdict.

"Do you have any further questions on the procedure, sir, mesdames? If you have not, forgive me, but the Prior of Bainham has asked me to give an opinion this afternoon on some pressing ecclesiastical matters."

"Will it take long, proctor?" Gervase asked, frowning at the inconvenience. "I require further discussion with you. After all, who knows how soon the archdeacon's officers may arrive. I am willing to come and consult you at the priory this afternoon as soon as the prior's matters are settled."

"Of course, Sir Gervase."

"May I come?" Johanna asked later as they left the hall together for the sake of appearances.

There was a pause before he replied, clearly trying not to give her further offence. "I think Stephen de Norwood may be more open with me if I am alone."

That was probably true. "But I need advice too."

"That is understood," Geraint answered gently, halting at the foot of the stairs which led to her quarters. "Tell me your questions, my lady, and I shall put them to him."

"I only have one for the nonce." He was not prepared for the sharp simplicity of it but it cut to the quick of the matter.

"Ask him," said Johanna, "who I am married to while the case is being heard."

Sixteen

WAS THAT NOT THE HEART OF THE MATTER? GEraint pondered as he rode out of the castle with Jankyn and two of the castle men-at-arms as escort, but he set aside the issue, giving his mind release and enjoying the sheer pleasure of being in the saddle.

The town, sunlit and puddled on the eve of Lady Day, was making ready for the new year and there was a joyful cheer about the place, despite the roofs that needed mending, or maybe it reflected the fleeting freedom he was feeling in himself at being saluted and smiled upon.

At a gallop, save where a fallen tree forced them off the track, it took little time before Bainham, about two miles up the dale from Conisthorpe, lay within their view. The flooded river, curled in a wide sweep around the priory, now lapped hungrily at its foundations, and the meadows, flooded, shone in the sunlight like a rich lady's mirror.

An anthem rose from the hidden chancel of the abbey, disconcerting Geraint, stirring the past up from a deep pool of loathsome memories yet thrilling him too with its perfection. The harmony, the interweaving of gorgeous cadences, rose against the perverse bleat of the priory's ewes and the rhythmless descant from the March lambs as they scampered out of the path of the visitors' horses.

Like many an Augustine house, Bainham Priory lay cheek by jowl with a village that had matured beside it like a fungus, feeding on the respectability and employment that was offered. The canons provided board and bed to travellers, but the tavern keeper in the village was nevertheless prosperous. Geraint, entering its taproom, found it spacious. Although the windows were but wicker lattice, there was little draught. Clean rushes carpeted the flagstones and a generous fire burned hot as lust in a hooded grate beneath a stone chimney so that the rafters were not grimed with soot nor was the air unbreathable with smoke. One wall was painted with the story of St. Robert the hermit and his persecution by Sir William de Stuteville, while the other depicted the cowherd Caedmon, albeit looking too lackwit to herd a hen let alone wax lyrical. The benches were all manned and gusty with conversation though it lessened somewhat as Geraint found himself observed.

Stephen de Norwood rose respectfully from the scrubbed board, wiped his fingers on his haunches and offered his hand in greeting. Two drinkers at the proctor's trestle swiftly stood up to make space and Geraint sat down graciously, enjoying the fact that the others at the board had shuffled along respectfully to leave him elbow room.

His escort was easily housed. A glower from Sir Geoffrey's men freed them another table as two journeymen and a lanky apprentice sluggishly gave them precedence and slunk back to their trades. One of the Conisthorpe men produced a dice and they happily settled into a game with Jankyn who raised his eyebrows to Geraint with a wicked gleam.

"A jack of ale, sir?" The ale-maid's fingers meaningfully resettled the low neck of her kirtle as her pretty almond-shaped eyes swiftly rated Geraint's capacity to appreciate her other services. Some other man's blue ribbon already suppressed her abundant golden hair and a glass lozenge rose and fell on a leather thong between her generous breasts.

Oh, it was very fine to be in the world again with money in his purse.

"Aye, my darling." He grinned, adding loudly to the proctor to make himself heard, "We shall need to discuss our business somewhere more peaceful."

The proctor nodded and both men admired the waggle of the girl's hips as she departed for the taps.

"She is clean and consequently expensive," Stephen leaned across to shout in his ear, "and I do not advise you to indulge yourself while your case is being heard." The warning was presumptuous but the proctor would have been slack in his duty to leave it unspoken.

"Of course not," Geraint agreed smoothly, stretching his long legs out, his affability only checked when another horseman, known to the Conisthorpe men, entered and joined the dicers. The newcomer exclaimed that he had been stranded in the town earlier with a lame horse—a cursed old creature that should be put out to graze—and had naught to amuse him until the river fell and he could join Sir Ralph's company again. An ass would swallow such a bag of lies but . . . Jankyn, meeting his master's narrowing glance, was safely primed like a crossbow against indiscretion.

"Sir," chirruped a cheerful voice. The maidservant set the leather jack before him and made pretence of stumbling delightfully over his feet so that she fell frothily upon his lap.

"Not now, sweetheart." He lifted her off him and gave her a gentle pat. She left them with a pout that would have burst the seams of many a man's hose and it was an effort to redirect his thoughts to the service of the female bundle of contradictions who was stabbing her needle in and out of his velvet jupon back at Conisthorpe. "I want this hearing settled as fast as I may, proctor. How long is it likely to take?"

"We have allotted you six months. Now that Sir Fulk is bringing a countercase, it may take longer. I know of one which took three years."

"Six months!" Geraint's hand slammed down so hard that the men at the other end of the board went silent at the judder and a slumbering shepherd dog beneath sprang out barking. Jankyn's die flew halfway across the floor where they had to be coaxed, spittle-covered, from a hound's mouth.

Geraint swiftly thrust himself forward, doubling with laughter as if his companion had told a princely joke. The hubbub rapidly resumed around him and, with a silent prayer, he straightened up and pretended to wipe his eyes. Across at the other table, he sensed that Jankyn's mind was not on the game.

"I see it bothers you," observed the proctor dryly. He would have won prizes if making understatements had been a popular pastime.

"Oh not at all," muttered Geraint caustically and took a deep draught of ale. How many more marvels were hidden away in the legal head opposite, to be brought out, one by one, each costly and custom made? "But I came for the counsel not the ale."

"Is everything to your liking, sir?" The alehouse owner, with judicious timing, must have counted several heartbeats before he came across to investigate.

"Yes, landlord, most excellent, but I have to go." With feigned nonchalance Geraint downed the contents of his alecup and made payment into the waiting palm. *To his liking?* It was a lie; the earth beneath his feet was trying to toss him down on his knees again. *Yes, I must be going,* he decided.

"Sir." Jankyn half-rose from the bench with a shade too much alacrity for an esquire and came across at his master's beckoning. Outside Geraint pressed a coin into his hand. "We are leaving Conisthorpe," he declared decisively and met Jankyn's astonishment. "Get your friends soused as pickled herrings and be up behind yonder parish church with the horses in half an hour. Can you do it?"

"Trust me, I have more drinking games in my repertorium than Holy Church has saints' days. But we shall talk of this further, friend, be sure of that!"

"Go to it then."

He must dissemble a little longer but he was impatient to leave. There had been occasions before in his life when it had been necessary to cut loose swiftly, to yell "Enough!" at Heaven. Six months playing a lovesick bridegroom! He needed to be away from here— he and Edmund. Better to seize this afternoon's opportunity and make a run for it. If he could reach Ludlow, he could send word to Edmund's wife and maybe seek advice from his mentor, Bishop Adam Orleton of Hereford, the man who had placed him in the Mortimer household. Assuming, of course, that the king had not hauled the bishop to the Tower as well.

A few paces behind his client in the sunlit doorway, Stephen de Norwood put his hands on his belt and stretched his back like a lazy cat waking. "A true caress of spring in the air, sir."

"You reckon so?" If there was, it was competing with the sea-coal smoke issuing from the priory's cooking fires or the dead dog's carcase that was lying in the ditch.

The two men picked their way across the balding sward of grass with its worm knots, avoiding the miry cart tracks that ribboned it on either side, and made their way up the road.

"A pox on it!" muttered Geraint. "Is there nothing can be done to make this cursed millstone grind faster? Six months!"

"You could outbid Sir Fulk with the archbishop. A rose window for the west transept perhaps?" the proctor jabbed good humouredly, adding, "Of course, you and your lady do not have to be present at the hearing except for the first two days, and possibly when your depositions are being examined, but given the circumstances and the nature of Sir Fulk, you would be ill-advised to do otherwise."

Geraint chewed the cud of that, striding on in silence as the road took an angle like a joiner's set square at a stone cross and ascended towards the church. The village had seen as much damage as Conisthorpe and not a few dwellings needed roof repairs. The churchyard had suffered; the gale had seized the lychgate roof and raided the trees to strew a plethora of twigs and branches untidily across the graves. The proctor sauntered to a standstill in a patch of weakening sunlight, avoiding the shadows cast by the yew trees hemming the graveyard, and leaned his elbows back upon the thickly mossed wall. They were alone save for two sextons whistling cheerfully as they tossed spadefuls of earth out of a fresh grave over on the far side.

"Tell me, sir, are you and the lady Johanna living together as man and wife?"

Geraint paused in his attempt to dislodge a fist-sized boulder from its nest of grass with his bootcap, and lifted his face in surprise. Mayhap Johanna's question would be answered without the asking, save he would not be the one to share it with her.

"We are living together under my lady's mother's roof."

"Not quite the same is it, Sir Gervase? Let me rephrase the question. Are you and the lady indulging *in delectatio*?"

"Your pardon?"

"Carnal knowledge! Are you sharing a bed? Is the lady willing and dutiful? You must be prepared for such questions, Sir Gervase. They will come at you like heavy bolts from bombards."

"All right," snarled Geraint. "No!"

"Now that, sir, is a mistake. Is there any logic behind your decision?"

"I, my lady . . . well, we thought it best to stay celibate while we await the court's judgment. If Lady Johanna were to . . . if we . . . were to share a bed . . . and . . ." he sensed the proctor's amusement at his stumbling, "and if the court was to declare our marriage invalid then living with me would compound her sin. I . . . well . . . she is a virtuous woman. She does not wish the world to condemn her for living in adultery."

Stephen de Norwood clucked disapprovingly. "That is no way to talk, sir, as if you are ready to surrender." He paced away and turned, thrusting his fist into the air. "Unfurl your banner! Point your lance! Make your marriage as sound as a saint's honour. To put it in a nutshell, I think you should take your wife to bed as soon as possible."

Geraint gulped, sure that he was blushing like a virgin. Take Johanna to bed! Oh yes and he would be given a coronation in Westminster Abbey next morning.

"Sir Gervase," prompted Stephen sympathetically. "Think of your wife as a house."

"A house?" A loose and battered cannon running amok perhaps, but . . .

"Yes, a pretty, covetable house. If it stands empty and the owner is away, any passerby can move in and say, 'This is my house now.' If, however, you, sir, are living in the house, no one will be able to evict you easily. Your enemies will have to prove ownership to remove you. Possession, Sir Gervase!"

They were in shadow now. The plump lawyer moved, following the sunlight.

"Wait, proctor, are you saying the court might see our case in a better light if we were . . . *in delectatio?*"

"*Yes*, sir, well done!" Stephen turned and beamed at him like a tutor. "Holy Church wishes merely to give its blessing to the intimate relations between a man and a woman. When a couple wishes to bind themselves eternally to each other and consummate their relationship, the church is there to help them give their vows public utterance and to sanctify that relationship."

"But Johanna publically married Sir Fulk whereas she and I . . ."

"If you have witnesses, said the right words and consummated the match, then all will be well. And if you live in intimacy for the duration of the hearing and beget a child on your lady, there should be no problem at all about the verdict. These matters lie within the hands of God ... but an able man like yourself, sir, should be able to set a babe within her womb in a minimum of six months."

His head was spinning. Geraint clapped his hands to his temples and leaned back against the wall.

"Did Lady Johanna conceive at all while living with Sir Fulk?" Geraint must have looked at him blankly for the lawyer pursed his lips at such ignorance. "Hmm, so the lady could be barren. Has this Fulk children by any earlier marriages?"

"I cannot say. Not that I know of." He watched Stephen steeple his fingers and pensively tread out a circle as if he was chanting a spell.

"The circumstances of conception are still much debated. One school of thought holds that a woman only conceives if she derives pleasure from the coupling which is one of the reasons, I suppose, why our stewhouses are full of barren women. If the Lady Johanna loves and honours you ..." He chuckled and shrugged. "You can only try."

Geraint wondered if the moon was affecting him. He wanted to roar with mirth at the folly of it all. He could imagine returning to Conisthorpe. The expressions on the noble ladies' faces would be worth all the gold in Christendom. Laughter welled out of him unbidden, pure exhausting laughter which opened the windows of his soul and cleared his heart and head.

"But what if ... What I am trying to say is that Lady Johanna is virtuous and she has been ill-treated by Fulk."

The proctor grabbed his meaning. "And is a trifle wary, is she?" Bless the man for his intelligence. It was a relief to discuss the matter openly. "Come, Sir Gervase, I do not need to tell a handsome knight like you how to proceed. Woo her or command her, what you will. Virtue is highly commendable in any wife, but the essence of the argument is surely that if she prefers you to Sir Fulk, then she must do her duty by you. She is definitely married to one of you. The lady must choose."

"SO WHO PUT A BRAND WHERE HE SHOULD NOT?" JANKYN JIBED AS Geraint set his foot in the stirrup at their meeting place later than he intended. Receiving a stony look, the jester continued unabashed, "And more fuel was added. I will wager all my winnings that yonder priest asked you for a new roof for the lychgate."

"Yes!" fumed Geraint, with a backward scowl at the importuning churchman who had materialised, as welcome as a cockroach on a pie, after Stephen de Norwood had left him. "I have just lit a candle to St. Jude. Now in that saint's name, let us get out of here!"

If the angels used celestial carrier pigeons to wing the prayers up, the patron saint of hopeless causes must be covered in feathers and the busiest in Heaven, Geraint thought, as he gave spur up the laneway.

"I take it you have given this decision your usual hayload of thought."

"Later, Jankyn!"

"Clever proctor, eh, to set fire to your conscience. Do you know where we are going?"

"No. Yes, to Dame Christiana's, I hope. There should be a bridle path north of Conisthorpe linking to the packhorse track which leads to the park. Are you sure you left those fellows useless, Jankyn?"

"Our escorts? Aye, as teats on my grandsire."

Geraint spurred his horse to a gallop, thinking about the third man who had diced with Jankyn. If the deputy sheriff had set the man as watch on him, he needed to leave Conisthorpe while the river was high and before the hearing began. It was not pleasant feeling guilty at leaving. The thought of abandoning Johanna's cause tore at him as if he truly wore her favours.

"Do not take it so hard, great one!" muttered Jankyn, absolving him for his impatience when, having been lost, they finally nosed out the paling and ditch of the park and followed it round to the gate.

"If we cannot take Edmund with us, I will call the bitch's bluff," thundered Geraint, as he slid the bolt home behind them.

"So sits the wind in that quarter, eh? I think you owe me an explanation. What said the merry proctor? Why must my lusty dicers lie snoring under the table?"

"Lawyers! The knave reckoned the hearing would take at least six months—if not years—and urged me to beget a child on Lady

Johanna as soon as possible. If you laugh, I will unhorse you into the dirtiest stream I can find."

Jankyn kept so sober a face that Geraint, in slightly better humour, clouted him lightly anyway as they reached Dame Christiana's dwelling and dismounted at a wary distance.

An unpleasant herbal sort of stink that would have thrilled the nearest coven of witches infected the air. Jankyn gave the usual signal whistle and from behind the brushwood wall came the answering clang as Dame Christiana whammed the small shovel against an iron pot.

"They have taken him, lad," she exclaimed, hurrying forth, waving her arms like wind-buffeted streamers.

Geraint ran past her into the hovel. "Who have?" he demanded. Edmund's pallet was indeed unoccupied.

"I was out gathering, but see, lad, naught has been thieved or o'er-turned. Like as not, it is the Lady Constance meddling again for there has not been a whiff of the high sheriff's men nor any other strangers."

"There are cart tracks," Jankyn joined them. "If it had been an arrest, they would have flung him over a horse heedless of his wounds."

"Sir Geoffrey, I will wager," growled Geraint, remembering the empty cart trundling back across the drawbridge. "May they rot in Hell for this! If he should die . . ."

"Any notion where they may have carried him?" Jankyn asked.

The old woman shook her head. "If my lady discovers what a misery your friend is, she will be right loath to send him to annoy God afore his time. Shall you take the risk and go? I will have ale and bread ready for you in a trice and there is a bag of fodder you can take for the horses." She hastened indoors at Geraint's grim nod.

"And I suppose you expect me to go with you like a faithful dog?" Jankyn glared glumly at the lengthening shadows.

"Unless you prefer to end up spiked on one of the local swords," retorted Geraint, checking the stallion's girths. "Do what you will but I am going to seek out Edmund's wife, Elizabeth Baddlesmere. Mayhap she can offer a ransom for him."

"Mayhap she will not want him back." Jankyn made no move

to accompany him even when old Christiana came back out with a leather bottle and a large kerchief of provisions.

"Well?" demanded Geraint.

"I think you are running away, friend."

Geraint's knuckles whitened as he clenched the reins. "I am not going to be manipulated by a pack of women. If they think I am going to kick my heels in Conisthorpe for God knows how long, they judge me ill."

It had been the same as a lad at the monastery, this sense of being prodded down the wrong path. Straightening, he faced the smaller man. "I cannot stay here, Jankyn." He had an audience of two now for Christiana had ranged herself beside the fool. He struggled to find words that would make them understand. "All my life people have tried to take control of me, force me into a mould and the only way out is to cut loose. I will be master of my own affairs. I only stayed with the Mortimer affinity because I chose to do so and, clearly, I can do more for Edmund now by leaving here. I have taken an oath to set Sir Roger at liberty and I can hardly keep it while leashed to Lady Constance's wrist."

Jankyn stuck his thumbs in his belt and took a turn about. "Is it just that, friend?" he asked eventually. "I really wonder if you have thought the matter through sufficiently."

"Humph, best stay here tonight and sleep on it." Christiana's stare picked at him, as if she was looking for a hidden explanation. She reserved the provisions against her scrawny chest.

And be escorted back to Conisthorpe by Sir Geoffrey and his men? Knowing they both meant well, Geraint stared helplessly down at the pair, his mind a maelstrom of confusion. Did they think him a coward? He could not explain that Conisthorpe was poking feeders into him like poison ivy, enmeshing him, or that, even setting aside the danger of being arrested for a rebel, someone else here threatened his independent spirit. "I am sorry," he told them, his mouth tightening. "I must go."

AT CONISTHORPE, JOHANNA WAITED, ASHEN AND TIGHT-LIPPED. TWO of the garrison, pickled as walnuts, had been retrieved from the town mayor, to be locked into cells next to the well below the keep until Sir Geoffrey was in a more merciful humour. The stranger styling himself Sir Gervase de Laval and his unusual esquire had not returned, and so a messenger had been dispatched to summon the proctor.

Johanna toiled up the straight staircase of the keep and stood, glad of the miserable wind to dry the droplets on her cheeks, watching into the half-light. It was neither the treason of his spirit nor that the stranger had begun to expect more than she could give; these things Johanna forgave him, that was the way men were. No, what irked her was that she had felt the sunlight on her fingers, fleeting, unable to be caught within two cupped palms like a pretty insect. Knowing hurt. The loneliness was back, together with a dreadful destiny and now she could only wish she had not learned to smile again.

"Johanna?" Father Gilbert had climbed the stairs, but she did not want to be found, not yet. "I know you are here, my daughter."

"Are you afraid I will cast myself down?"

"No." He waited until his breath was even again. "Young men do not think, forgive him that. The quintain, fetching your father down to watch, rescuing young Peter from the torrent . . . he acts impulsively but out of goodness of soul, and there are other reasons, I suspect, that cannot be laid at the door of anyone here."

"You mean that he deserves to be hanged." The priest might sift the ambiguity of her words for her real meaning, but she had spoken without gall. She added with a puzzled sadness, "Gervase was adamant he was not helping us just for payment. Do you think we were merely a cave to shelter in until the wolves slunk off to hunt elsewhere? I know he felt himself part of the greater matters being played out in the kingdom."

"I honestly do not know the answer, my daughter, but trust in prayer. We shall find the means for you to give yourself to Christ and find peace of spirit. As I told you before there are abbeys in the south that will receive you. Come to the chapel now and forgive your enemies."

He drew a cross of blessing in the air and left her to follow, but lingering, she leaned back against the unfeeling wall and stared at a pincushion-size patch of distant stars. At the back of her throat tears queued up begging to be shed and she swallowed them with difficulty, trying not to wallow in self-misery. She had been an undutiful child, a barren wife, and now she had made no effort to bind the man who might have been her salvation. God probably

did not want her either. The cloister? Plentiful prayers and starving
herself had neither brought her closer to Heaven nor freed her of
earthly torment.

But while the cold wind might complement her heaviness of
spirit, there was a limit to self-chastisement and gooseflesh. Eventually mundane physical discomfort overcame her.

As she descended past one of the open embrasures, the glimmer
of a light moving behind her father's tower window made her
pause. Surely Aidan would be fetching my lord's dinner from the
kitchen? He usually lingered a little in the noisy warmth, ribbing
the young scullions and loading up with fresh gossip.

Her curiosity alerted, Johanna hastened across the darkening
bailey and stealthfully climbed the short staircase to her father's
chamber. She took a deep breath, placed both hands on the ring
and flung open the door.

"*Merde!*" exclaimed Edyth, springing to her feet and shrieking
as she overturned a candle onto the rushes. The matting flared up
easily around her skirts, but it was Johanna who grabbed the fur
cover from the bed and threw it down, stamping out the flames.
She glared at Edyth's now pious composure. *Why was she hiding
her hands?*

"By the Rood, what are you doing here?"

"Reading to this poor neglected soul," replied her sister-in-law
in the sanctimonious tone she usually dusted off for visiting bishops.

"Reading!" scoffed Johanna, discovering the tumbled inkwell as
she pulled back the singed covering. Edyth made a run for the
door but Johanna caught her and wrenched a parchment from her
hand.

"What in God's Name . . ." She cast an appalled glance at her
father, watching her from the pillows, his breathing heavy. "But
this is . . ." Her little knowledge of letters armed her sufficiently to
decipher a word or two, but the numerals she understood. Her
gaze fell in horror to the jagged cross above her father's name.
"You fiend! So that is why Fulk left you here. Not only to spy but
to trick my father into signing away—"

Edyth flounced across the room to the corner hearth.

"—dowry money that is rightfully my brother's. This miser,"
she tossed a contemptuous look at the broken man, "cozened Fulk

into taking you when no one else would and for what?" She swooped at the fire and faced Johanna. "Look at you—a barren, disobedient whore. My brother deserves every penny, and have it, he shall! Give that to me!"

Johanna stared in horror at the brand smoking in the other woman's hand; the shadow on the wall behind her was predatory.

"Kill me for it then!"

"Jezebel!" hissed Edyth, her face as malevolent as a sorceress's. "Give it to me or I will scar you."

Johanna edged along the bed, the document behind her back. She had to reach the stairs or—

"Aggh!" The strangled sound from the bed was sufficient to distract Edyth. In that instant, Johanna flung herself across the bed and thrust the parchment into the candleflame in the wall bracket.

"You interfering shrew!" Edyth made a snatch to save it but Johanna grabbed it away, waving it both in defence and to speed the burning. Then she tossed it through the half-opened shutter into the moat.

Edyth shoved the brand at her face.

The scream must have come from her as she grabbed her veil out of the path of the licking flame and suddenly a metal bowl came hurtling between them like Greek fire, its contents exploding over their kirtles.

"My lady!" Aidan, no longer bearing a covered dish in his hands, stood on the threshold, his eyes bulging at Edyth.

"Thank you, Aidan," Johanna's breath returned to normal. Mercifully she was unscathed. Not taking her gaze from Edyth, she backed across the room until she was next to the servant.

Edyth, with a shrug, briskly thrust the faggot back on the fire as if she had been coaxing more heat. "Have you looked at yourself in a mirror today, sister-in-law?"

"Get out!" snarled Johanna. She turned to the servant. "Escort this . . . this spawn of Satan back to the hall, Aidan, and then you had better bring my father some more broth. From this day forward, he must be guarded."

"Oh, you will rue this, never fear. Where is he, your swaggering bully? Gone, hasn't he? Could not satisfy his lust, could you? Fulk saw to that." Edyth picked up her skirts and, head held high despite the spills upon her bosom, she left the room like an outraged princess.

Her father made a grunting sound and Johanna turned. "So I finally have something to thank you for, my lord father," she said, drawing the covers back up beneath his arms. "For once you have acted charitably towards me. I wonder if you really understood what she was at." The face on the pillow stared at her without emotion and with a sigh, she bent and gently kissed his brow before she set the stool back beside the bed.

"LEASTWAYS, THANKS TO THE LOVELY CHRISTIANA, WE DO NOT HAVE to buy or pilfer," muttered Jankyn, as they drew rein briefly at dusk to assuage their hunger. It was tempting to dismount, but Geraint was as jumpy as a warren rabbit that has had its burrow blocked.

Jankyn wiped the crumbs from his mouth and scanned the road. "Pardon me, but I cannot help worrying that ere long we shall see the ladies Johanna and Constance on the horizon brandishing broomsticks. Lady Edyth might even manage to fly here."

Geraint snorted. "More likely some local bailiff will challenge us in a sudden belch of officiousness."

"This wife of Sir Edmund's that you seek, would she be the daughter of Sir Bartholomew of Blean, hard by Canterbury?"

"Aye, the very same. He was Constable of Leeds Castle until his wife denied Queen Isabella entry and the king made war on him."

"But will there be help from that quarter, my friend? I heard Sir Bartholomew was in prison."

"What are you implying, Jankyn? That I am a fool and we should go back and seek Edmund out?"

"What if Lady Elizabeth is not at Ludlow?"

Geraint sighed. He was not prepared to mention his acquaintance with the rebellious Bishop Orleton. "Then I will go to Kent and seek her. I have to be free of Conisthorpe." He was repeating it so much it was like a litany but Jankyn merely raised an eyebrow and said no more.

From the shelter of the trees, they could see the road they had journeyed. Apart from a man driving his laden donkey up the hill, his curses loud upon the wind, and a pair of mendicant friars, armed with staves, marching stalwartly in the opposite direction, there was no peril—yet.

They crossed the sturdy Wharfe bridge at Ilkley by night and rode across Rombalds Moor. Weary, they exchanged the horses just past cock crow next day at a horse dealer's. Such establishments extracted any news carried past them like tentacled sea creatures but Geraint, negotiating with the garrulous horse dealer, was anxious to keep his business brisk. Weary and mud-encrusted, he managed to be cheerful but concise and hoped that Jankyn, gossiping outside in the yard with a travelling chapman, would not let himself be hindered.

The jester was unusually silent as they rode away and Geraint studied him with concern. Shadows of fatigue as large as scallop shells underlay the smaller man's eyes, while the dark bristles burgeoning on his cheeks lent him a villainous mien. Geraint, rubbing his own itching chin and knowing he was rank with sweat—his own and the horse's—supposed Jankyn was as tired of the muddy furrowed road as he was. They dismounted by a rill and broke their fast with the remains of Christiana's saddlebag food, alone with the sad cry of the curlews and the distant caws of nesting rooks.

Used to words tumbling and twisting from Jankyn as fast as acrobats, Geraint found the silence disturbing. The fool was sitting with his arms clasped tightly around his knees, his gaze downcast and gloomy as a paid mourner's.

"What is it, man? Have I offended you?" A splash of water plopped upon the jester's wrist. Geraint questioned the grey indecisive sky. There was no rain. "For God's sake, Jankyn, what ails you?"

"Such ill tidings and the year not a day old. Think you my Lady Constance knew of it and did not tell us?" muttered his companion, blinking tearfully at the clouds. "I should have been there at Pomfret, not sitting on my hands at Conisthorpe. My master now is headless. As I am, him being so."

His current master for an instant was thrown off course and then his jaw slackened. "What! Has the king executed Thomas of Lancaster?" He crossed himself, despite his incredulity. "Come, are you sure it is not a foolish rumour?"

The jester shook his head, sniffling back his tears. "The chapman was at Pomfret and saw it all. They brought my lord there with the filth that the honourable citizens of York had thrown at him still clinging to his beard. The king refused him clean garments or water to cleanse himself, and imprisoned him in the tower he himself had newly built. Ah, he was so proud of that castle."

"So the king was there?"

"Aye, he was and appointed my lords of Pembroke, Kent and Brittany together with Sir Robert de Malmethorpe and Sir Hugh Despenser to sit in judgment."

"Which Despenser?" Geraint's voice was sharp.

"What of it? The older Hugh, I think the fellow said.

"Anyhow, my lord was chained and clad in only a shirt and hose when they brought him down into his own hall to hear the charges. It was packed so tight that a woman was crushed to death as they surged forwards. Sir Robert proclaimed my lord must die even though he was the King Edward's cousin and the most esteemed of all the lords. They were like pack dogs, the chapman said, baying and snarling at a noble courser. And it was no true trial, for the king," Jankyn spat, "would not allow him any defence, so when they had delivered the verdict my lord faced them and spoke scathingly to them, saying that it was a powerful court and great in authority where no answer might be made."

"But how soon was Lancaster executed? They must have acted mighty swiftly."

"Immediately. Some Gascon, a friend of Gaveston's, the chapman supposed, hung a tattered, dirty cap on my lord's head, and they set him on a sorry white nag without a saddle, and led him to the little hill which lies south of the castle wall. I know it well. It is where they hang the thieves and murderers."

"But surely he was allowed a confessor?"

"Aye, they summoned a preaching friar and my lord prayed all the while as they led him out, but then . . ." he wiped the moisture from his lip, "the townspeople—his own people, damn them— hurled pellets of dung at him. He knelt down and made his peace, but just as the executioner, some villein of London, raised his axe to take off my lord's head, one of Sir Andrew de Harcla's men, a fellow from Muston who had been one of his keepers, cried, 'No, make the traitor face towards Scotland!' and so he was forced to shift before they headed him. I should have been there." Jankyn hid his face against his knees and howled.

"And what could you have done, my friend?" argued Geraint. "Be thankful his end was swift and merciful. They could have given him the death for traitors."

But the fool shook away his hand and refused to be comforted. Geraint gave him privacy and stood forth a distance, his arms folded, and sternly stared at the scatter of sheep grazing their way across the tussocks. He could not mourn Thomas of Lancaster even though he had fought on his side. The earl had been no saint, despite his jester's adoration, and his desperate attempt to bring King Edward finally to heel by calling on England's enemy, the Scots, to help him had been a sign of weakness. It was also because of Thomas, who had failed to come to the aid of the Marcher lords when they needed him, that Sir Roger Mortimer was in the Tower.

Geraint was sure he was not the only one on the eve of the debacle at Boroughbridge who had doubted the purity of Lancaster's mouthings against his royal kinsman. On the road up from the Trent, Geraint had heard for himself how envious the earl had become, reminding them all constantly that he had Plantagenet blood and could rule England better. Rule better! King Edward had slithered away from his counsel at every turn. In a sense it had been inevitable, save that no one thought King Edward would actually execute his own cousin. Everyone in the kingdom knew the king blamed Lancaster for the execution of the gorgeous Gaveston. And Geraint guessed who had stiffened King Edward's resolve and put fire once more into his belly—the younger Hugh Despenser who was hated by nobles and commoners alike. Mind, it would not have taken many carefully delivered calumnies to feed the royal rage.

And so within the space of a little week, the flat earth had tilted. With a shiver, Geraint wound the liripipe of his hood more tightly round his neck. The abscess cavity needed repacking by a skilled hand and both his shoulder and his soul were aching.

With Lancaster gone, the rebels were not only scattered but headless in truth, seeing that the only other man capable of rallying them, Roger Mortimer, was immured in the Tower. The news was ill. The vengeful king might sweep all his enemies from the board. Certes, Edmund Mortimer's future was not worth a farthing for the nonce. And if Sir Roger was executed, what should he do then? Seek a new lord? Or abandon principles and grip hold of the wheel of fortune that had thrown Hugh up to glory?

A greedy world now for any to survive in. Was it worth struggling through to the Marches? Somehow he doubted that Edmund's young wife would be able to find the ransom to buy her husband's life from Lady Constance. Oh, he would wager a very earldom that Despenser's notaries were already knocking at her door and Bishop Orleton's to make their inventories. And Wales would lie like a dog at Hugh Despenser's bidding now. No question of that. The Despensers would punish all who had opposed them—lords, bishops and women.

What had he told Johanna? There was no chivalry. To further his prospects he needed a powerful patron—and a wealthy heiress. And contrary, bruised Johanna, her dowry in dispute, could not compete but at least he might free her. He had been wrong to leave.

"Let us return to Conisthorpe, Jankyn!" he shouted, whipping round, his conscience pricking sharp as demons' forks, but Jankyn was huddled miserably in his cloak, on his side like a babe, his breath regular not ragged as it had been before. Sleep on a little longer, thought Geraint wryly, displeased at being left alone with his fears. Sleep on.

SILENCE RODE WITH THEM LIKE A THIRD COMPANION AS THEY STRUCK north back across the moor towards Conisthorpe and the greyness closed around them filling their breathing. Without the sun for a signpost, the thin, stony road they eventually found looked unfamiliar. Lured by an alewife's candle lighting the gloomy morning, they stopped in the next village to learn direction. What they heard between gulps of mulled ale blunted their thirst—the village was Enderby. They had stumbled into Fulk's demesne.

The news that Sir Fulk's men were visiting all the villages asking questions about travellers of their mien and stature was given freely; but it took another coin beside the payment for the meal to buy the alewife's silence. They did not speak of their blunder afterwards but grimly left the road, fording the ditches from field to field where the ivy and tangle of thicket permitted, skirting the undergrowth until the towers of Fulk's keep were beyond their sight. The wind rolled the clouds away like tumbled corn bales and they journeyed with a tearful sun behind their left shoulders, trusting that they should come to the River Wharfe eventually. They would need to follow it along to find a crossing.

"A most excellent strategy this—returning," remarked Jankyn dryly. "At least the Mallet will not have posted scouts to watch the bridges if he thinks we are running away. They will be making inquiries further south."

"Please God!" Geraint crossed himself. "Unless the alewife betrays us."

The bridle track delivered them onto a churned but broader road and a steep rise. About a furlong on they came upon a forge. Jankyn spun a story that they were seeking service with Sir Ralph de Middlesbrough. The smith shrugged at the name, shook his head then stared fishlike at the road they had toiled up. Beyond a cooper's wain, men-at-arms in yellow and black were whipping their steeds up the hill.

Geraint drew his sword, spurred down and hacked the rope that held the wain's barrels. Thundering down the hill, the rotund missiles drove panic into the oncoming horses, dispersing the riders in all directions, and giving the fugitives the chance to outpace them for a further mile across the open country. But the horses were tiring.

"We need sanctuary," panted Geraint, wincing with pain. "Some abbey altar to crouch behind and, please God, a healer."

"Mayhap a crowd will do instead. It's a river crossing we're coming down to and a town besides. Be cheerful, sir, see!"

With a prayer on his lips, Geraint spurred his horse onto a bridge already perilously jammed with carts.

The town with its dark grey stone clearly owed its existence to the bridge and some of its prosperity to the exorbitant toll they paid to cross it. The market square was jaunty with pennons, its air redolent with the tantalising aroma of sucking pig. They dismounted and tugged their horses with them past the stalls. The itinerant vendors were there—the usual basket stalls, piemen, conjurers and sellers of elixirs and pastes for boils and pustules.

Goosed, Geraint swung round with haughty demeanour to see only a thin little bawd, not long past childhood judging by her small breasts. She gave him a smile that was somewhat toothless and, rebuffed, spat at their heels.

"She might have found us a hiding place for the afternoon."

"Against a wall?" snapped Geraint. "You go after her then."

"I wish I could but—"

Geraint followed his gaze and swiftly ducked down to hide his height, feigning to check a spur fastening.

"Dear God in Heaven! Jankyn, save yourself! It is me they want."

Eight or so knights were forcing their horses through the crowd. The people, surly until they felt the leather thongs bite against their faces, fell back, the flow of their curses turned off to a dribble of mumbles. A child whimpered and was hushed.

"Sirs!" Presumably it was the mayor who stepped bravely into the space that had grown about Geraint and confronted the cordon of horsemen. "Sir Edgar, I pray you, do not break the king's peace."

At a sign from their leader the men dismounted and the knight, still astride, pushed up his visor. The gingery beard and narrow eyes meant nothing to Geraint but the mocking tilt of the head reminded him of Fulk's man who had attacked him by the flooding river. Oh, by the Saints, they had been tracked like wayward lambs and here were the dogs slavering to rip out their bellies.

"Master mayor, we have been seeking these traitors for the past day. They are rebels from Boroughbridge."

The crowd muttered. "Where's that?" asked someone.

Geraint surveyed the sea of faces with a cheerfulness he did not feel. "Do I look like a rebel to you?" he asked, grinning as he took an apple pie from the stall behind him and bit into it with gusto.

"You look like a stout joist that needs laying!" chortled a female voice and Geraint kissed his hand to his unseen admirer.

"Do I?" asked Jankyn saucily, flicking his wrist behind his cap.

One of the armed men stepped up to the stall and with a violent heave sent it onto its side. The crowd gasped and drew back, leaving the scattered pies untouched. The mayor swallowed, rubbing his thumbs against his fingers uncertainly. Sir Edgar swung himself out of the saddle and his men flanked him and moved forward one at a time as if with some premeditated strategy.

Geraint seemed unperturbed by the menacing enemy ring as if

they were merely flies buzzing around him. Then he aimed his pie straight at their captain. It hit Edgar's breast, leaving a trickle of apple upon the hauberk. Sticking his thumbs in his belt, Geraint laughed and addressed the townsfolk. "He misleads you, good people. Ignore them, mayor. 'Tis but a quarrel over a woman."

"Told you," said someone.

"I will prove myself by trial of arms but not against a host of cowards who think themselves above the laws of Holy Church." He plucked his glove off and tossed it disdainfully at Edgar.

"Aye, here's sport," shouted someone. "My purse on the young braggart."

Edgar de Laverton ground it into the dust with his heel and then he clicked his fingers. The first clash of the men's drawn swords against their shields was out of unison but by the third beat they had it perfectly.

"St Jude, help us!" muttered Jankyn, as the people fell back and the men in armour, drumming malevolently, closed in.

There were angry growls from the back of the crowd directed at Edgar, as though the besieged strangers shared with them a common enemy—the beleaguered against the privileged. But the swashing of the blades against the bucklers had not faltered.

The mayor gave a stifled twitter of protest, his hands in the air, as two of the men-at-arms ceased drumming and turned their swordpoints towards him.

"*Ignore them?*" spluttered Jankyn, with a dry laugh, "Oh surely not." But they were coming too close for humour. "You might at least take two to the Devil with us." The jester's voice was sharp with fear. "Oh, God save me, who comes here?"

The villagers' eyes goggled at the menacing armoured figure who calmly rode his horse through the crowd, the visor glaring straight at Geraint. The people parted as swiftly as the sea before Moses. The knight reached the space and slowly, with the timing of a skilled interlude player, removed his helm. It was Sir Fulk de Enderby himself.

Someone hissed and a glob of spit was heard landing.

"At least the town is on our side." Geraint folded his arms tightly and stood back-to-back with Jankyn, still not drawing his sword.

"Aye, and about as useful as a basket of whelks. Shall we walk crablike across to the potter's stall and shy jugs at them?"

The drumming was finding its mark; Geraint felt his nerves wearing as thin as a beggar's breechclout but still he did not unfold his arms and suddenly the pattern of noise stopped. The silence was worse. His heart was doing the drumming now. The crowd had fallen back further, pressing against the stalls.

Fulk's horse daintily danced about them. "I will be merciful. I will give you a safe escort out of the riding now and we will forget the whole matter." Aye, and no doubt they would slit his throat before they heaved him into the county palatine of Lancaster.

"But I have swyvved *my* wife right lustily, Sir Fulk."

The cold metallic eyes met his enemy's cheerfulness without blinking. "I doubt it. That is not the arrangement, is it?"

The assumption shook Geraint unaccountably. The calculated cruelty that Johanna had spoken of was now believable. This man was a reptile—an amphisbaena beyond the reach of God.

"You wish to risk rearing my bastard for your heir? Rather foolhardy, Sir Fulk. I now see they do not call you 'the Mallet' for naught. Blunt and stupid withal. Let the archdeacon's court decide or else let us fight it out man to man."

For answer, Sir Fulk signalled to the leader of his men and they surged forward. Geraint had barely time to draw his sword. He sent one fellow crashing to the ground and another stumbling back before they fell upon him. Jankyn was easily down but rolled and went somersaulting, kicking one jaw before he sprang on another man's back and clung like a hump. Outnumbered, it was hopeless. Two of the men set on Geraint from behind and hung on to him with their full weight. His wound protested. Biting back the pain, he swung around trying to shake them off, but two more came at him.

Sir Fulk dismounted. Geraint braced himself as the knight's fist drove into his belly. At the second blow, he doubled up, tears of pain blinding his vision as the men hauled him up again for their master's gloved fist to send his lower jaw upwards, jarring his head back.

"Hold!" There were suddenly horses everywhere.

"Hell's teeth, man!" roared a voice that was miraculously familiar. Sir Ralph de Middlesbrough reined his horse in beside Sir Fulk. "What are you at?"

Hands let Geraint go and he crashed face first on the ground.

"To Hell with you!" growled Sir Fulk. "I will cut off his manhood and send my lady the thing she prizes."

"Lay a further fist into this man and you can cool your heels in my dungeon for 'writ of trespass,' sir. I will have justice in this shire. You have broken the king's peace with force and arms, and on a holy day too."

"Justice?" Sir Fulk spat. "Then none of our wives and daughters are safe. Any knave may ride in and lay claim to them. Take him!" He drove a mailed foot into Geraint's ribs. "I will soon have him by the balls whether he kisses the archdeacon's arse or not."

Geraint struggled back to consciousness as strong hands turned him onto his back.

"Is his neck snapped?" asked someone.

A hand felt for a pulse. "Nah, don't be a daffe. He's alive."

Wishing he was not, Geraint opened his eyes to see a half-dozen faces bent over him, including the deputy sheriff's.

"I thank you," he gasped and struggled to sit up, his head ringing, and felt his jaw. His lip was cut and bruised, his mouth awash with blood. "Where is my esquire?"

Jankyn, his face bloody, dropped to his knees beside him. "Oh Lordy, that was close. They are going to trundle you back to Lady Johanna like a sack of horsedung." He understood. Not a traitor's hurdle then—yet.

Another pair of legs stopped and stooped and Geraint blinked dazedly into the face of the stranger who had diced at Bainham alehouse.

"Sheriff's man, you, wasn't it?" He tried to jab a finger belligerently into the man's boot.

"Aye, and Agnes's brother besides. But 'tweren't you I and another were bidden to track. It was Edgar de Laverton. Been stirrin' up trouble, evictin' FitzHenry's serfs, pillagin' 'n burnin'. Followed you t' Bainham, he did, wi' his Enderby brigands not far off, skulkin', so I sent the other fellar back to warn Sir Ralph. Led us all a fair chase you did. Lucky though, eh?"

Which happy saint was the patron of numbskulls and harpies? They must have had half of Yorkshire on his tail. At least the Lady

Edyth had not manifested herself, but in this infernal shire anything was possible. Geraint groaned. His problems were queuing
up like soldiers outside a harlot's tent.

Agnes's large brother grinned with a fiendish glee that Lucifer
himself could not have emulated. "I tell you this, Sir Gervase," he
chortled, setting his gauntleted hands beneath Geraint's armpits
and levering him to his feet. "Upon my soul, I'd not like to be in
your shoes when you get back to Conisthorpe."

Seventeen

JOHANNA, THE CRACK IN HER SELF-ESTEEM AT GERVASE'S leaving plastered over to withstand common viewing, finally found the courage to see if he had awoken. Her mother had dosed him the previous night with enough syrup of scarlet corn-roses, mixed with honey, to put a carthorse to sleep. Horizontal and with his eyes shut, he looked reasonably manageable if she kept about four paces from her bed and put a fence around it.

She was expecting hostility—a temper sheathed in a scabbard of aloofness; he would be waiting for a tongue-lashing from her mother and tears on her part. Instead she found him dozing beneath the fur coverlet like a great . . . no, not a bear . . . a proud, battered destrier exhausted by battle.

"Well, I am back, my lady," he spoke drowsily, opening one dangerous eye, and before she could draw breath, added, "The king has executed my lord of Lancaster, did you hear?" It was as if he was asking her opinion, and for an instant she was deceived until he spoilt it by adding, "I should be grateful to know if there are other tidings."

Arrogant whoreson! That told her what little importance her feelings rated. No contrition, not a word of apology, no plumping up his features into a sheepish grin, no flash of charming teeth and softening of gaze. The only shred of his character that she could salvage was honesty. At least he was not making a show of something he did not feel.

Or—a new suspicion occurred to her—was this a device to suffocate her recriminations? Well, two could play this nonchalant game; she had her anger safely folded away for a later airing.

"Yes, a messenger did ride in with a proclamation from my lord high sheriff yesterday. The king has given orders that the leading rebels be . . . be dispatched in their home shires."

She watched him lift out a hand from beneath the sheet and rub the corners of his eyes with his thumb and forefinger. The languorous movement belied his sharp interrogatory tone.

"Did you hear it?"

"Who did not?" she retorted. "It was proclaimed by the mayor in the square and then Mother had it read out to the entire castle."

"Were there any names given?" He was employing the impatient tone that her father and Fulk always used but she stifled her resentment; maybe he was acquainted with some of those sentenced.

"Henry de Montford and two other Henries. De Wilingford and—"

"Wilington. Those two were with the force from Bristol." He was gravely silent as if he were praying for them. "You are doing well, my lady. Any other names?"

"Henry de Tyeysat and John de Gifford. One I had heard of, Bartholomew Badles—"

"God ha' mercy! Badlesmere!" Geraint sat up, wincing. Edmund's father-in-law!

"Yes, he was to be dragged by horses out of Canterbury—"

"But he was nowhere near . . ." His hand masked his face from her. "I need to see your mother," he said darkly.

"I should like to understand," she answered gently.

"I have promised you I will explain why we committed treason, my lady, but not today while the news is raw. Forgive me that, at least."

Fulk's chaplain had told her that women could not feel the same depth of spiritual suffering as men. A nonsense, but she kept silent as Gervase stared unseeing at the coverlet, running his fingers absent-mindedly through the fur as if the touching must be balm to his imagining, and then shook his head in disbelief.

"And Rome abandoned its republic and created an emperor. The fools!"

"What do you mean?"

"I mean, my lady, we can be ruled by a donkey if he wears a crown." Forehead creased, he shook his head further, staring at the ceiling beams. Then as if he suddenly remembered her presence, he turned his face to her.

Her hands plucked at the gris edging of her surcote beneath his hard scrutiny. Greater matters had been dealt with; now it was her turn on the list. "Are you not going to ask me how I am feeling?" He was going to squeeze the bitterness out of her as if she were a pustule.

"No." She inspected a loose thread on the tippet of her sleeve, hiding her face from the blue gaze. "I am trying not to be predictable."

"Then you have succeeded. I expected . . ." He looked away, like a wicked but adorably sinful rogue, ". . . well, what I deserve. But if it please you to stopper it until later when I no longer feel . . ."

"Feel what?"

"As stiff as a cloth soaked in glue, then I will quiver beneath the blasts of your rage. I knew I had to do something to lie between your sheets." He tried to laugh at her frosted face, grimaced at the effort and groaned instead. "There is more choice of injuries now. Inspect them—*please*."

He was observing her face as she came forward diffidently and leaned down to peer at his flesh. The wholesome skin had become a macabre rainbow of hues. From what she could see of the old wound, it had reopened, but amazingly there was no yellowness around the edge that betokened foulness though the abscess cavity needed fresh dressing. She pushed him back onto the pillow and gently probed about his ribcage. His bones were astonishingly sound considering the beating.

He swore concisely in peasant English. "I hope you are getting some satisfaction out of this," he muttered. "Playing physician, I mean." At least he was not accusing her of revelling in his bruises. "I have been trying to breathe normally like they said, but it is always—*careful!*—painful."

So being kicked in the ribs was not a new experience. Johanna shook her head at the male way of settling differences. She felt his chest and listened as he breathed in and out. "You do not seem to have flail chest, God be praised."

He watched the pelt of his chest rising and falling for the telltale signs of abnormality and tried to sigh in relief, but it hurt too much.

"The ache is further down." For a second he had her gulled, and then she turned scarlet and dropped the sheet down on him. "I met your husband," he added swiftly.

"Yes, I know." She looked around, trying to find labour to stop her hands betraying her. Fulk would win. It was a miracle that he had been prevented from sticking a dagger between this great oaf's ribs.

"Gormless, I know. But if the man had a mind between his ears instead of a peapod, he would have let me go with a blessing instead of a beating. I cannot say I would have enjoyed sharing a bed with him."

Johanna stared at him suspiciously. Was he actually trying to make her laugh or was he behaving like a crass idiot?

She sighed and fell back on practicalities. "You look abominable. Shall I send someone to shave you?"

"Slit my throat, eh?" He slowly swung his legs to the floor, managing to keep himself modestly covered from knees to ribs. "You would not care to order a bath and dribble rosewater over me like a delectable handmaiden? No, I thought not."

She realised, the heat rising in her cheeks, that he was unclothed and the only items she could see belonging to him were a pair of metal poleyns, semi-spheres of steel, unaccountably left beside his saddlepack. One of them might have hidden his gender instead of his kneecaps, she thought, and surprised herself at wanting to giggle. What ailed her? Why should she be feeling absurdly light-headed when her real husband wanted to beat her to pancake consistency and her pretend husband had run away from her?

"Where did you sleep?" His glance fell on a palliasse shoved to the side of the chamber. "Oh." He seemed to be having trouble continuing the conversation.

"Yolonya kept vigil, not me."

His eyebrows rose as if he was disappointed. "Two matters we must discuss, my lady," he muttered, glancing around for the remnants of his clothing. He noticed the poleyns and seemed to be suppressing harsh language.

Only two? His manner had knocked all levity out of her; she delivered him a glare which would have frozen the moat.

"Yes, two things. What is your mother telling people about my . . . my absence?"

"You went carousing—again."

"Hmm. Feeble. Did the proctor tell you the nature of our conversation?"

"Oh yes, very forthcoming when it finally dawned on him that it was Mother who was paying for his services."

He ignored her sarcasm. "So you now know his advice."

"Yes. Is that why you ran away?"

"I do not belong here, my lady. There are matters elsewhere that need my attention." He wanted to stitch together the tear in her confidence. "One of the reasons is that I thought Sir Ralph had plans to arrest me, and not only did that thought not delight me to the core of my being but also the possibility that you and your mother could be fined or imprisoned for helping me crossed my mind. I suppose that sounds rehearsed."

"Yes, very." Johanna's tone was testy. "Really, Sir Gervase. You do underestimate our capacity for cunning. Women are supposed to have the intellect of fleas. Mother would have merely pleaded stupidity at being gulled and I would have admitted paying you to fool the archdeacon."

"And then have been sent back to Fulk?"

"Only in a coffin." He did not know whether she was in earnest.

"We need to talk properly about . . . about us. A pox on it! Where in Hell are my clothes? This is your mother meddling again. Am I supposed to attend the court hearing in a fur coverlet?"

Folding her arms in a deliberate imitation of him, Johanna smiled coldly. "Talk properly about whom? Us or the two people who fell in love two years ago?"

"Both, I suppose." His expression was starting to become exceedingly sulky. Perhaps he needed to relieve himself, or did he feel at a disadvantage if he could not loom over her like a giant? "Which brings me to the second matter. How soon is the poxy hearing?"

"Tomorrow."

"*Tomorrow!* For God's sake! That does not give us much time and we have not finalised the details with Ja—with Watkyn and Agnes yet. Tomorrow!" He suddenly slapped the bed impatiently, making her start. "Upon my soul, Johanna, I wish you would be angry and have done. I cannot bear surly women who only grumble behind a man's back, and I will swear you and your mother have had a feasting of that."

"Oh, I will be angry with you," she promised.

"Well, do not be too long about it, my lady," he snorted and looked about him. She made no move to go, enjoying pinioning him for once.

He noticed the untouched food from yesterday's supper and, scowling, looked at the palliasse once more. "Not eating again? My fault, I suppose." Johanna did not answer him. It was none of his business. His blue eyes were examining her almost with the objectivity of an honest physician. "What will the court think? You need to look as plump and happy as a sheep with cloverbloat."

She turned away to the window. "I do not think you would begin to understand."

"Try me, lady. Talking to a stranger may be easier than you imagine."

Talking? Did he think he could lick her into a normal state of enduring womanhood like she-bears tongued their unformed babes into cubs? "I am sorry," she said softly after a while, raising her eyes to the stone carving round the window.

"Johanna." He knew that she was not talking about confidences and she felt like crying because he had said her name with gentleness. "Johanna, I cannot pretend that I am glad to be back and yet . . . There were times on the road when my conscience pricked me so painfully because of what you would feel, and I hoped you would understand it was nothing to do with you."

"No? Ha, what kind of addlepate do you think I am, sir? Do not lie to me. The proctor tells you to get me with child and you flee as if—"

"Will you not interrupt! I am perfectly happy to do whatever is necessary . . ." His gaze deliberately slid over her body with such lusty roguishness that she felt the tips of her breasts hardening. Her lips parted in protest at his teasing but he forestalled her with a less harmful, almost bashful, grin. "Well, enough said . . . we know what is necessary . . . but *six months*, my lady! I feared for my life and Jank—"

"Who on earth is Jank?" she spoke breathlessly, quickly, glad to have a question to hold on to, words to anchor her mind since her body was caught by a fearful wave beyond her control.

"Oh," he sighed, having turned away his magician's stare, "what harm is there in only you knowing? Watkyn—that is, Jankyn—was Thomas of Lancaster's fool."

That morsel hit her like fast poison to the belly. "Christ preserve us!" She turned away, biting her lip. How much more was there unrevealed? And who in God's name was this man sitting on her bed? She inadvertently swung round at the thud of the coverlet on the floor. Save us, what now?

He had managed to stand, and was knotting the sheet about his loins in the fashion worn by the holy prophets. His smile was wry. "See, I am here with you, manacled with silken embroideries."

"Hardly," she retorted, wondering how she could find him so exhilaratingly dangerous and yet worthwhile company. With swift modesty, she lowered her gaze only to find she was staring at strong muscular legs sheened with golden hair but not overly. With an inward curse she lowered her study further; feet were not sinful and his were quite different to Fulk's—comfortably fleshed with a scattering of glint above the instep. "They will be holding auditions soon in York and the Salome wagon might have a vacancy for St. John the Baptist. Mind, you would have to apply very—"

"My lady." His voice compelled her to meet his glance. Oh, that feigned sheepish smile would make her insides melt if her mind had not been damaged beyond repair. "I cannot give you my promise that I will stay until the hearing is completely over, but I will stand with you for the next week. You might have to prop me up but I doubt it." He took a step towards her, his draperies precarious, and Johanna gave a squeak and fled to fetch the moss for his shoulder.

LADY CONSTANCE DID NOT LOOK UP AS HE ENTERED THE KEEP ROOM where the muniments and manor rolls were kept. The atmosphere was cold despite the stand of hot coals—frosty with unspoken grievances. Geraint did not care that she was busy checking a ledger with Sir Geoffrey nor that there was a trio of reeves waiting outside the door with their weekly tidings.

"Can this not wait, sir?" She did not deign to look up.

"I can make my point rather loudly and jettison your plans for tomorrow if you prefer, madam."

His employer gave a sigh. "The impatience of youth. He has come to apologise, Sir Geoffrey, so let us have it over and done with. Do you intend to grovel for long, Sir Gervase?"

Staunching an oath that would have brought a blush even to the seneschal, Geraint growled and turned his back, angrily folding his arms.

Sir Geoffrey cleared his throat unnecessarily and rose. "Do not be too hard on the lad, madam," he advised, with a chuckle calculated to inflame further.

Geraint turned as the door latched. Lady Constance had folded her hands on the board and waited.

"Where is he?"

"Your peevish friend? Safe."

"Curse you, madam, where?"

"Remember Aesop's tale of the sun and the moon. Strong language does not move me, Gervase, so perhaps you should sheath that tongue of yours. I have arranged for the lad to be moved, in comfortable stages, I might add, further south. You will be pleased to know he makes good recovery."

"You should have consulted me." He glared at her. *Manipulative, interfering . . .*

"I have decided not to raise the matter of your desertion. I shall not mention the terms 'cowardice' or 'treachery' because I have observed it is still in your nature to be impulsive. Presumably the wisdom that comes with age and experience will smooth out these wrinkles in your character."

She rose, tidying the quills as she spoke, taking care not to look at him. "I can sympathise with your reaction to the possibility that the hearing may take longer than any of us had anticipated. I do not share the proctor's prognosis, nor should you." Her gaze rose to inspect him chillingly as if he was a villein before his manor lord. "I think we are agreed now—and even. Take up where you left off."

He unknotted his arms and paced away to the brazier, his shoulders heaving. He should have had a whole quiver of arrows to spend on her but what was the use, and, yes, he was as guilty as

Judas. Johanna's forbearance had made him feel worse. But there was more.

"This matter of living in wedlock and begetting a child. How may we remedy this without causing my daughter further grief?"

He glared at her. "Upon my soul, madam, what had you in mind? Shall I ask the archangel Gabriel to make representations on my behalf? I am afraid my influence does not carry that far." He watched the thin mouth twitch admiringly at the blasphemy. "What would you have me do? Seduce her? Is that what you are saying? Make a whore of your own daughter?" At least she looked affronted at that. "Or is there another motive behind this? A happy ending? You dream, madam."

"No, there is something else. It needs to be resolved," she answered cryptically. "See to it!"

THE MEN STOOD AS JOHANNA, ACCOMPANIED BY AGNES, ENTERED Father Gilbert's cell. Gervase raised his eyebrows in surprise as the maidservant placed the cushion on the bench for her ease. Well, let him think she was a milksop. Someone coughed and she realised that Father Gilbert was waiting for her attention and dutifully closed her eyes while the chaplain prayed that God would guide and keep them in His wisdom.

He drew a cross over them in the air and gave Johanna a small bow. "I shall be with madam your mother, my lady, should you require my advice." Johanna rejoiced he was absenting himself for he seemed to watch over her with the disapproving air of a mistress of novices, waiting for either her or Gervase to err. Besides, Stephen de Norwood was expected later to help them practise their testimony and present the written libel for Gervase to sign.

"Be seated." The rebel, taking charge now, preferred to pace around as if he was delivering a lecture. "First of all, Agnes, you must understand what may be required of you. There will be questioning about your lady by an examiner. It is his duty to discover whether all of us are telling him the truth. He will ask you what you remember of our marriage two years ago and questions about how my lady and I deal with one another now. What we each tell him must be our individual version of the same truth."

"I understand, sir."

"It will be perjury, Agnes. We are all doing it to free your mistress from a cruel marriage, but if we are found out, we shall all be excommunicated and denied the sacraments of Holy Church."

"You are frightening her," protested Johanna.

"No, I am telling her the facts, my lady. If she feels uncomfortable with this, then she must withdraw now."

Agnes shook her head. "No, 'tis for a very good reason and anyhow, sir, I couldn't refuse to help my lady. 'Twould be on my conscience to send her back to such a heartless devil and I am sure the lord God will know that on Judgment Day. 'Sides who else will do the office, sir? You need at least two witnesses to prove a marriage contract."

"Agnes, thank you. We are in your debt. Now before we go into the wheres and whens of our handfasting, let me tell you what we have agreed upon so far. I met my lady when the king's court was at Bristol."

"Oh yes, sir, we accompanied my lord Alan down because of the Lady Alicia's wedding."

"My second sister," Johanna explained to Gervase, giving him a chance to gather the reins again.

"I later followed Lady Johanna to Yorkshire and met her secretly twice here in the wild wood. Both times she left the castle disguised in your hooded tunic, Agnes. I persuaded my lady to agree to become contracted to me and I sent her a letter saying so. Father Benedict read it to her and agreed to marry us. My lady met me for our trothplight.

"Agnes and Watkyn, you witnessed the vows. You will both have to remember the words of the oaths that my lady and I spoke to one another—we will rehearse them in a moment—as I am assured that it is extremely important that I am reported as saying, 'I will *have* thee as my wife' rather than, 'I will *take* thee as my wife.' Apparently the latter is less binding. Where was I? Ah, then we went to the dwelling where Dame Christiana now lives. It was unoccupied at the time. My lady and I consummated our marriage." He spoke swiftly and without emotion as though he were discussing repairs to the walls. "Yes, Agnes?"

"Please you, sir, where were Watkyn and I while you were pleasuring my lady?"

Gervase's cool gaze moved to Johanna's face. Choose a commoner word and the nuance became erotic. His lips tightened slightly, sinfully. She felt the telltale blush rise to shame her cheeks. Why was it this man could quicken her blood just with a different way of looking at her?

For his part, Jankyn looked askance. "Dear me, Agnes, sweet damsel, I imagine we stayed below like good and faithful servants."

"No." Johanna, embarrassed that they would have heard every sound even if it was just a story, shook her head. "No, you . . . you sat outside, yes, there is a tumbled tree."

The esquire ran with the notion. "Where I, dearest Agnes, told you tales of ladies wooed and won, with my thoughts on nothing but—"

"Oh, go your ways, Watkyn," Agnes swatted him and turned a smile upon the knight. "Now, how long would you have taken, sir? My lady would have had to be back by sundown, leastways I would have."

Johanna bristled at the girl's impudence and the fact that the maidservant's eyelashes seemed to acquire amazing speed whenever she spoke to Gervase.

He seemed hard put to staunch his laughter as he dragged his gaze away from Agnes's coy posturing to regard Johanna with a disturbing speculation. If he dares ask me, Johanna fumed, I shall leave the room this instant. As he drew breath, she answered hastily, "There would have been a short dalliance, no more."

Her supposed husband was having difficulty controlling his pride. "Speaking for myself, *I* do not dally," he retorted. "Where in this dwelling did you *dally*, my lady?"

"What is that to the point?"

"Let me tell you. There is, as is common in such hovels, a simple ladder, one piece of timber, the rungs nailed to its center, that takes you to a narrow upper floor beneath the beams. There is no room to stand, in case you are unaware of it, madam. What did we lie on, my lady?"

"Straw?"

"No, Watkyn had gathered some bracken the day before and I spread my tunic over that. It was no featherbed, but we had our minds on less mundane matters. What were you wearing?"

"I-I, why my—"

"Oh no, my lady," Agnes corrected, enjoying a rare superiority, "you would have been wearing *my* best gown. It is blue, sir, with quite a low neckline and—"

"Thank you, Agnes," Gervase cut in, although he was tempted to let her continue just to annoy her mistress. "And how was I clothed?"

"As God made you, I imagine, sir," quipped the fool. "In nothing at all."

Gervase must have seen Johanna clench her jaw, for he swooped a hand down upon his esquire's shoulder and half-hauled him from the bench. "Jest not! If aught goes wrong, you will feel Holy Church's lash as fierce as I."

Johanna fidgeted, trying to retrieve the story. "Green, sir, you would have worn a hunting green so that you could not be seen easily in the woods, and brown hose."

"The weather—" began Gervase but she interrupted.

"I hardly imagine the weather was—"

"We need to remember the details together. I might not have had my mind on the weather, but Watkyn and Agnes sitting on the log may have noted it. We have decided on St. John's eve but we need to know whether the sun shone. If it rained all day, we may all be liars and proven to be in collaboration."

"It might be better to have a day when the weather was memorable," Johanna pointed out. "Then everyone who hears will say, 'Ah yes, I remember that.' "

"I know, I know," Agnes fanned the air enthusiastically with her fists. "What about after the storm that summer's day when the tower at Bainham Priory was struck by a fiery bolt?"

"But which day was it, Agnes?"

"In June. The eve of the Feast of St. Mary Magdalene."

"My lady?" Gervase was waiting for Johanna to decide.

"Yes," she said slowly. "That might suffice. I oversaw some dyeing," she caught his astonished expression, "—no, cloth dyeing, sir—in the morning and the violent rainstorm washed the colour out because the quantity of mordant was not sufficient. Petronella was not pleased."

Gervase was regarding her with polite astonishment. "Petronella is my oldest married sister," she explained, adding, "No, I know dyeing is not a respectable pursuit and I probably should have been the daughter of a mercer or dyer, but the Conisthorpe retinue colours are some of the finest—"

"Can we keep to the track, my lady, if you please."

"*Bridal* path," punned the jester, slapping the table, more of his old cheerfulness returning. Gervase silenced him with a frown and continued to cross-examine her.

"Why did you not order the cloth to be brought in?"

"Oh, let me see, I fell asleep in my bedchamber. It was a very moist day, sufficient to turn the milk." It had been so hot that all the dogs had lain panting in the shade and the menservants had worn dampened apparel to keep sane.

"Did no one else think to bring the cloth in or rouse you? Your mother—"

"My mother was most displeased later but she also took to her bed and my lord father was away attending parliament. He returned the following week for Petronella's wedding. I would have been more likely to commit a folly if he was absent."

"The Lord take me if such a noteworthy day does not have its dangers," the esquire interrupted. "You would do better, sir, to choose a mundane day. Where was the priest on this day? That is the nub. We may concoct stories to our heart's content, but if there are a half-dozen villeins who will swear that Father Benedict was drunk as a lord—beg pardon, sir—and snoring like a pig throughout the storm, what then?"

"True. Did the priest keep a servant?"

"Servant?" Agnes sniffed disgustedly. "Leman, more like, sir, a fierce old besom she was too. Passed away soon after him, she did. The new priest turned her out and they found her dead in a ditch atwixt the Studleys up Ripon way a few weeks later."

"That is to the good, though God forgive me for saying so," Johanna rose and paced, "but what if Father Benedict was called to a shriving or some such?"

"Sir, sir, we could ask Father Gilbert, or Aidan would be sure to know—pull a wing off a fly and it will be all over the town by curfew."

"Heaven forbid, Agnes, castle gossips are the last we should ask. The good chaplain will suffice. Now, let us sit and think out what we are going to say very carefully and then later I am going to ask the proctor to examine us on our stories in turn and discuss any errors."

"MY BRAIN FEELS AS THOUGH IT HAS BEEN DRAINED," JOHANNA MUR-mured later after morning mass, rubbing her fingers across her eyelids.

"The rest of you does not sound it. I have been trying to ignore your belly's gurglings for the last hour." Gervase paused on the steps to the new hall as he spoke. The lady was a riddle; if she was hungry, why did she never assuage it? He had never known a woman eat so little and he disliked the results he saw in her pallor. "I can hear horses. That must be your men escorting the proctor in for dinner. I know it is a chore going over the story again with him, but practice makes perfect."

"Yes, I am sorry. It must be very irksome for you," she replied gravely and found he was laughing at her.

"Describing where and how I consummated my marriage with you? No, not so." He gestured for her to enter before him.

"Well, it would have been," Johanna assured him. "Now tell me what questions the proctor is setting for . . . for Fulk?"

"The articles, you mean," he said loftily, with that male habit of insisting on precision; a woman would have given the answer knowing exactly what was meant. "I want him to demonstrate to the court that your lack of obedience to Fulk was due to the fact that you were beaten and starved into the match when you knew yourself to be contracted to me." He held up a hand and tapped his fingers one at a time. "I have suggested he ask: whether Fulk was aware that you had been coerced into the marriage; and whether it is true that he felt compelled to beat you into submis-sion several times a week?"

Johanna paused before the hearth and raised her skirts a little to dry the hem. "Does this need to be aired? *Sir?*" He looked con-fused for a moment, as if the view of woolly-stockinged ankles had disconcerted him. "I am not talking about this," she continued, shaking the hem.

"It is not just a matter of the truth," he muttered, looking back up at her face, "but whether the court perceives we are worthy characters. Since we are not as white as snow, blackening Fulk may help. Given time, about eight years or so, you could bring a libel for divorce *a mensa et thoro*—that is, a judicial separation on the grounds of cruelty because of continual and undeserved physical force."

"I think I would be extremely dead. Eight years!"

"Fortunate I came along." His tone was dry and he fell silent, as if he was thinking more on the morrow's hearing. There were voices behind them as her mother led the proctor in and Gervase turned with a sigh.

Johanna knew he shared her apprehension. "I wish tomorrow was over," she whispered softly.

"Tomorrow is the easy part."

Eighteen

ER HEAD ACHED SO AFTER THE LONG SESSION FIN-
alising their testimony with Stephen de Norwood
in the great chamber before dinner that Johanna
fled to her bedchamber. Her mother found her sitting in the early
afternoon sun, a line of split-stitching embroidery neglected across
her lap. She had tried to nap but her thoughts were too anxious.

"Why did you not come down to dine?" exclaimed her mother,
a little breathless from the stairs and a heavy repast.

"I-I am not hungry."

A derisive snort came from the stairwell. So the upstart esquire
still thought he had the right to walk in, lording it.

"Ha!" Johanna rose, tossing her needlework onto the bed. "Anyone else coming to disturb me in my bed-chamber? The lord chan-
cellor, the king's favourite hunting dog or are we limited for
choice?" She glared pointedly at Gervase.

"Johanna." Her mother looked as though she was about to make
a proclamation. Undeterred by her offspring's suspicious scowl,
Lady Constance announced, "Johanna, Gervase and I have been
talking. Since the world expects you to live as man and wife, we
should follow the proctor's advice without delay."

"We!" Johanna threw her mother a look of furious reproach.

"Gervase has made an extremely practical suggestion."

"Have you, Gervase, dear heart? What a treasure you are."

"May I remind you, Johanna," exclaimed her mother, her fingers
tapping folded arms, "that we are dependent on Gervase's performance in court."

"Yes, Mother dearest, and he is being paid for *that*, not for performing in my bedchamber."

"I suppose hunger is making you peevish." Gervase looked damnably contrary himself.

"Peevish!"

"Yes, womanish, perverse, lacking in common sense. You are wasting time, my lady. We have to shift your belongings out of here." He turned an angry shoulder on her and picking up a fallen bodkin, placed it back in her wooden needlebox.

"Shift my belongings!" She swished her skirts and fronted her mother waspishly. "Oh, I thought my lord Gervase was moving in here with me, considering he has slept in my bed more than I have recently."

Her mother slapped her palms together. "Be quiet, Johanna! I insist that you do as he suggests."

"I can imagine what he suggests!" hissed Johanna, "No! You cannot expect me to lie with this arrogant upstart. He could have the crabs for aught I know."

Gervase took an angry breath and wheeled round on her with the fury of a robbed miser.

"Oh, for Heaven's sake, Johanna!" exclaimed her mother, stepping in between them. "Will you not hear this matter out! You do not have to actually lie with Gervase, dearest."

Johanna's glare told her differently. "What *are* you expecting me to do, Mother? Close the hayloft off for an hour each afternoon and set up a crier to proclaim we are fornicating?"

"Very inventive," snarled Gervase venomously, closing in on her, flaunting his height and strength. "And how do I know *you* do not have crabs?"

Lady Constance held up her hands as if keeping them from throttling the other. "Hush, the pair of you! I am sure we can settle this amicably."

"Amicably! Oh yes, and Fulk will turn into a sugarplum tomorrow and withdraw his petition. Any other impossible solutions, Mother?"

"We have to resolve this today, Johanna. I have agreed that the south tower is to be refurbished for your use. You may take the upper chamber and Gervase shall have the lower. It may not be as comfortable—"

"No!"

"Then I will refuse to appear in court." Johanna did not miss the cold, wicked glint in his eyes as he stood before the hearth. "Let us have an end to this, my lady. I have discussed with your steward how this may be managed as soon as possible and he merely awaits your mother's assent." He tossed his head back like a haughty stallion, his glance challenging her. Arranged it, had he? Well, if he thought she was going to give him an intimate pat and a piece of apple, he would be disappointed.

"Get out of my sight, you braggart! You and Stephen de Norwood may go hang."

"Johanna, keep your voice down."

"If he thinks he is going to beget a child on me . . ." She grabbed off her shoe and hurled it at his loins. It hit him lightly in the belly but he caught the second before it met his head.

He folded his arms. "Pah, lie with a wench who only attracts pigs." The sewing box broke its hinge against his breast, exploding spools of thread all over him. He kicked his legs free of the coloured cobweb catching upon the cuffs of his kneeboots and strode to the window, thrusting open the shutters. "You wish to shout abuse. Do so. They will say that Fulk de Enderby is well rid of you."

"I thought you were honourable!" Her voice shrank to a whisper.

"Me, oh no, how can I be? I am willing to perjure myself for your mother's gold."

"I will not be your whore."

He cocked his head. "No, nor my wife either, it seems. We agreed to provide the semblance of two cooing turtle-doves, yes or no?"

"You Hellspawn!" He was smiling like the Devil welcoming another sinner.

"We have to believe our vows, Johanna, if we are to convince the world and his wife. So, how are we to do that, if the world knows you deny me your bed?"

"Oh you are enjoying this!"

"You think so? Have done!" He sighed, and let the fight go out of him. Turning to Lady Constance, his tone was stern. "Rest assured, I have no intention of becoming embroiled with this Fury between the sheets. A viper would be more friendly." With a curt bow to her mother, he left them staring at one another.

Lady Constance had her lips glued together, but her eyes were brimming with laughter.

"Ohhhh!" The sewing box made another flight, this time through the open window. "A pox on it!" Johanna rushed to the casement and hiked herself out. Jankyn was staring at the landed box in amazement. Her supposed husband, entering the courtyard down the steps, was hailed and invited to examine the missile. He looked up, blew her a kiss and took charge of the box.

"I will kill him before this is through!" Johanna ducked back in. "I warned you he was more trouble than he was worth."

Lady Constance gave a little sigh but it was not at the mess of silken threads scattering the floor.

"Oh I will do that." Johanna set her aside and knelt to sort out the tangle. She sent a covert glance up at her mother and caught the wistfulness in the older woman's face. "Would you contemplate him as a lover?"

"Gervase? In your shoes, probably." Then realising that Johanna was not amused, she abandoned her smile and added gravely, "No, my darling, no one is expecting that of you, least of all me, not after what you have suffered. And Gervase is not either." She looked around at Johanna's chamber. "This is a beautiful room and I can understand that you are loath to leave here, but you can be private in the south tower and no one will know that you are not lying together."

Johanna was still imagining what it might be like to know Gervase as a lover. Once she would have had her mother's courage.

"I wish I could—but I cannot, *Maman*." Her eyes misted and she sniffed. "Fulk has—" She broke off, tears choking her voice. "This morning crossing the courtyard I saw the fair-haired groom you sent to me at Enderby lathering himself in one of the troughs. Had I let her, Agnes would have lingered to enjoy watching him but I looked away—nearly ran away—because I could not bear the sight of him naked."

Her mother crouched down before her. "Time will heal you, my love." Fingers gently, reassuringly, clasped her shoulders.

"I-I do not think so." Johanna averted her glance from the pity in her mother's face. "Besides, that upstart is the same under the skin as every other man."

"The weavers and the fishers might not agree with you. There is more to a man than a crowing cock."

"Mother!" But Johanna found she could laugh.

Constance sighed and let go of her. "Do agree to moving your belongings, my love. You need pay lipservice only to Brother Stephen's advice, and you must remember Gervase is suggesting you share the tower, not his bed."

"He will expect more than is his due. Come, madam, you know men think only with their pricks when their lust is upon them. Even priests. No, truly. I have gone along with this outrageous notion of yours but now you ask too much."

Her mother nodded with seeming resignation and rose. In her face, Johanna guiltily glimpsed the shadow of aging and recognised the weight of cares she struggled to carry.

"Did you remember to send the parliament writ back?" she asked her.

"Oh yes, I did that. Father Gilbert couched it beautifully. An unspecific excuse about your father being temporarily indisposed. Of course, they will not swallow it for long. The king is out to strengthen his hold over the north and will want an active, vigilant constable here at Conisthorpe to hold the dale against raids. He will soon send another man to fill the post. Oh, my darling, if only we can hold them off until the hearing is through." She sat down on the windowseat that Johanna had vacated and rested her head wearily against the side of the recess. "I did not tell you that there was a fire in one of our barns up near the Franciscans' fishponds and Fulk's reeve has been trying to force rents from one of my villeins on your dowry land."

"It is costing too much, is it not?"

The older woman passed a hand across her eyes. "It will if it takes more than a few weeks. There is rumour too that the Scots will come down again before the autumn and harry us. If Hal had lived . . ."

Her mother still grieved. To bear a son and see him grow to manhood, handsome and blithe, blessed by God with intelligence and courage, only to have him slain by the Scots at Bannockburn. Had he lived still, he would have been scarcely older than Gervase.

Johanna knelt before her and carried her mother's hand to her cheek. "You should have been a warrior princess, *Maman*. My lord father did not deserve you and nor do I. When I used to hear the other demoiselles at Richmond talk about their parents, I realised that you were uncommon rare."

"What is to be done? I am tired, Johanna, and you, look at you, you urchin. Such wan cheeks. You should go and sit in the sunshine to gain a milkmaid countenance for tomorrow." She stroked the lap of hair above Johanna's temple and tugged at one of her plaits with a watery smile. "Your father loved you just as much as I, you know, in his own way."

"So much that he finally said, 'The next man who asks for her shall have her!' and gave me to his good old friend Fulk."

"Forgive him," whispered her mother softly. "I know you despise him, but . . . Do you remember when he rode off to the Scots war when you were a little maid? There was such splendour in him. I was so proud and he came back after Bannockburn so ashamed at the defeat and poor Hal's death. He laid his head upon my lap and wept."

"But we do not need him. It is unjust that we must be turned out. For God's sake, *Maman*, you have shown you can run Conisthorpe better than any man."

"But I cannot lead the knights to war. That is what this whole kingdom depends upon. Supplying men when the king snaps his fingers."

"Mother," Johanna took her hand. "Do-do you ever miss my father as a, you know . . ."

"There are times, my darling, when only a man's arms around you will suffice."

"But women are strong if they care to be. Look at you, Mother, you have fought for me like a tigress."

"And shall do as long as I have breath, my darling, but this is a world that is ruled by the sword for all Holy Church would have it otherwise, and besides, it is more complex than that. I . . . I needed your father and I miss him, even if he could be unreasonable at times, and I like to think he needed me."

Johanna put her arms about her. "I will move to the south tower," she whispered upon a sigh. "To please you, to make the hearing move faster and to sweeten the verdict, whatever you want, save I will not let him lie with me."

"No, I never expected that of you," sniffed her mother, searching in the silken purse on her girdle for a kerchief.

"No, I know that, *Maman*, but if you set a drink in a man's hand, have you ever found one who will not try it?"

SHE SAT OBEDIENTLY IN THE CASTLE GARDEN LATER WITH A CUSHION and a fur rug beneath her on the stone seat, her toes perched on a footstool above the wet grass. A pelisson of coney furs kept her upper body warm for the wind was still fresh even in the shelter of her mother's herber. Unused to being idle, she had a shirt for Gervase across her lap, but only the first row of the collar embroidery was finished and she neglected it now. It was at times like this she missed her little dog. He would have been on her lap. The tears came but she smudged them away and tried hard not to be afraid.

Her mother's minstrel arrived to sit on a stool at her feet, and with his bow drew forth sweet sad notes from the psaltery, while Agnes busied herself unbidden tucking daisies into her mistress's unpinned braids.

For a small space, Johanna managed not to think about the morrow's hearing, her own discomfort or the two husbands who plagued her peace, but put her mind into a state of grace and delighted in the loveliness of the moment. The white daisies and yellow primroses sprinkled the tiny mede and there were shy violets and periwinkles beneath the opening leaves of the hawthorn hedge. Surely a God who had made such beauty could not return her to Fulk's cruelty! But she knew that tomorrow he could demolish all her lies. She supposed she should forewarn her mother and Gervase, but there was nothing they could do. Fulk would win. Perhaps the Lord Saviour who had been scourged and tormented by his enemies would aid her. But although above the bailey the flock of castle doves exuberantly wheeled in a whirr of snowy wings, the cock robin in the hedge piped a warning. Johanna blinked back the tears again, feeling vulnerable and alone. Even the poor robin knew tranquillity could not last; there were cats in the flowerbeds and goshawks in the sky.

Gervase's shadow fell across her and before she could forbid them to go, the servants obeyed his flick of dismissal. Oblivious of her scowl, the arrogant upstart put his hands upon his belt, stretched his back and stood deciphering the clouds. There was a large smudge of whitewash upon his right sleeve and a lettering of cobwebs on his left stocking, which together with the bruise on the edge of his jaw made her wonder whether either of them could be taken as respectable.

"Go away!" she said sternly.

Geraint ignored her words and let his gaze loose to wander over her. He had rarely seen his supposed wife without her hair braided tightly beneath a caul and veil, but today she wore it in two loose plaits with flowers threaded through them. Merely a thin band tethered the fine lawn veil for the sake of propriety and the chrysoprase green of her outer kirtle where it showed against her breast beneath the tawny fur drew forth the green of her eyes. No artist could have imagined a sweeter scene and she could easily have played the model for a saint or holy maiden from the scriptures.

"Will you stop humming?" Johanna ordered, but not unkindly.

"Was I? It is nearly done, you know. You should come and say where you want your wall-hangings placed if you feel up to it." He meant if her bad temper had dissipated, so she scowled and made no answer. The smile about his handsome mouth remained amiable, but his tone was less friendly: "Lady Edyth's broomstick has been saddled. Want to kiss her farewell?"

"No, I leave kissing to you along with ordering my servants. I thought my mother was paying you to be a noble not a cobweb broom."

He looked down and brushed off the dusty spider-threads and, moving the shirt and mended needlebox, sat down uninvited beside her. In silence they watched one of the villeins downwind barrowing dung onto a distant herb bed.

Geraint had a list of matters to raise before the morrow. One was uppermost in his mind but he forbore to ask her straightway, choosing instead to edge his way slowly along that hazardous cliff top.

"A short dalliance, indeed," he scoffed, reminding her of the morning's labours. "You lack imagination, you know that?" He rang the nearest dark plait, like a bellpull. One of the daisies fell out.

"How long *do* you take?"

He kept his profile to her but his lips twisted in good humour. "Wait and find out."

She parried the remark. "You mean you would keep me waiting?"

He scratched at a chalky patch on his knee. "I mean it academically, of course. You see, I may have to testify how long we were in the hovel. Let us agree upon two hours."

He watched her eyes widen as she swallowed her surprise. "Two! Two hours, sir? Impossible! Oh, I suppose you might do it several times to be sure—but two hours!"

He roared with laughter. "Dear God, Johanna, you are a goosehead," he exclaimed, slapping his hands on his hose.

"I am not!" she hissed and lowered her voice. "What happened the rest of the time when we were on the bracken? If we talked, we must decide what we talked about."

"We did not do very much talking."

"Then we must have slept for most of it."

"Waste that precious time sleeping! You have no inkling, have you, Johanna?" She could only blink at him in puzzlement. "If the examiner asks, my lady, can you tell him how we spent the time? He may ask, you know. You need to give it some thought."

"True but it might save a great deal of bother if you tell me what you will tell him. *He may ask, you know,*" she mimicked.

"You want me to tell you what I did to you that afternoon?" he asked incredulously.

"Why not? If you can narrate it in a sensible manner. After all, we are two mature beings and . . ."

"Oh, lady, this is foolish."

"Please, Gervase, as you point out, I need to know."

"I am not sure your motives are honourable," he muttered suspiciously.

"Of course, my reasons are honourable," she protested, gazing at him innocuously and then looking away. The limpid blue depths were swirling, unreadable.

If she was gulling him and up to mischief, it was impressive, but Geraint conveniently found her innocence believable. Knowing Johanna's past, it was possible she was truly ignorant, and it might

help heal her as well as clarify matters, should the examiner in-
terrogate them.

"So, begin, sir!"

"We went up into the loft. I went first and then helped pull you
up. There is no room to stand so you would have crawled across
to the bracken."

"It must have been dark."

"Yes, but there were cracks of daylight."

"If the light was from the roof, then it would have leaked during
the storm." It was an apt but annoying observation.

"No, the light came through cracks in the walls."

"It would have been very hot then."

"Yes, but the rain cooled the air. I . . ." He ran his glance over
her surcote where the fur cloak had parted. "Since you were
garbed simply, like Agnes, I loosened your hair from your coif and
pushed you gently down on your back and then I began to kiss
you and slide your gown down over your shoulders to free your
breasts." He tried not to look at them now.

The lady seemed unimpressed. Dear Heaven, perhaps he had
better not go on with this; he was becoming moved by the imagining.

"Well, that does not take very long. I still do not understand
how it would all take two hours and you surely would not undress
me thrice."

"I removed your shoes, I very slowly untied each garter with
my teeth and kissed my way up your thighs as I unrolled your
stockings. Oh, Christ Almighty, Johanna, stop looking at me like
that!" The little wretch was working out whether he could do both
at the same time. His words were having no effect on her whatsoever but they were arousing him.

"Then I pushed your skirts right up over your head to stop you
making foolish conversation for the rest of the time," he snorted,
and lapsed into sulky silence, one thumb stroking a graze upon
his knuckles.

"I do not believe you," she said crossly.

"I wonder why not. Well, if you must know, Johanna, I would
have stroked and kissed and caressed you until you were pleading
with me."

"I knew it," she sighed. "Pleading with you to stop. I always do it."

"No, pleading with me to *continue*."

"Ha! Most unlikely."

"You were hot and wet with desire and you were arching your hips towards me wanting more."

She frowned. "Do some women do that?"

"All the women I sleep with."

She shook her head. "I am sure you are not boasting but truly I do not think it would have happened like that. Not with me."

"No doubt you would have tried talking me out of an arousal," he muttered.

"I was a different person then," the words were spoken softly, "but we shall pretend it was as you say."

"By all the Saints, woman, I cannot believe this absurd conversation is taking place." Unable to withstand the challenge, Geraint clenched his jaw and continued swiftly, "You were groaning and sighing, desperate for me to enter you."

"Ha!" Johanna tried to stand up but he caught her arm and pulled her back down.

"I swear if you say 'ha' one more time, I shall toss you over into the moat. You were hot, wet and sweet as I brought you to your fulfilment."

"What do you mean?"

"Oh, Johanna, do you know nothing?" he exclaimed, taking her by the forearms. "Have you never . . . Oh, it is the woman's equivalent of a man's pleasure, a letting go, a sweet surrender."

"Ha!" She closed her lips with a snap as he released her. "The words, the words are all wrong. It is always conquest and surrender." She reached across him to gather up the shirt.

He caught her wrist, staying her. "It can be the other way round."

"How, if the man must barge into the woman, violating her?"

His gaze met hers with honesty. "I have never barged in nor have I ever violated."

She swallowed and gathered the shirt to her as if it would protect her. "I am sorry." Her tone grew wistful as she added, "You probably were chivalrous and gentle."

He swivelled to face her and took hold of her braids. "And that afternoon you were kind and generous and loving. You welcomed me between your thighs and it was Paradise to find release inside you."

Visibly, she was shaking. "I-I wish I could believe such ecstasy was possible."

Geraint could not help saying it, his voice husky. "Let me prove it to you. I could." He doubled her plaits around his hands shortening the distance between them.

"No," Johanna whispered practically, setting a hand preventatively against the velvet jupon that clothed him. "I doubt you could and, in any case, it would do us both harm. You will be leaving and I want to take my vows. This perjury is evil enough without sinning fur—"

His mouth came down upon hers and he pulled her into his body. She struggled but he held her tightly. His tongue and lips were coaxing her into submission. Her body thrilled at his hands upon her; her mind shrank back warily. As if he could feel the confusion in her, he raised his head.

"This is not sensible," she whispered without rancour.

"No." His voice was a dreamy murmur but his blue, intense gaze willed her to accept his lordship over her. "Do you know how much you make me want to touch you?"

This then was seduction, the sinful temptation of the flesh warned against in sermons. For a moment Johanna permitted herself to enjoy the sensations that were weakening her body. For a breath in time, this large stranger made her feel desirable, but it was the false, warm sense of feeling safe and protected within that embrace that was the danger. His kindness was purely transitory, a surrender to his body's temptations. Within the month she would be just a memory and she could not endure to be hurt and then discarded. Johanna pushed her hands up between them and tried to break his hold. "I want to be able to trust you, sir. I wish you will not say such things."

"Trust me, I will heal you, every single sinful—"

A loud "ahem" set them apart with a jerk. Jankyn, his hands on his hips, stood before them. Gervase sent him a fierce look but Johanna, back in the saddle of her feelings, smoothed her skirts, amused.

"Well, Jankyn?" her wooer asked tersely, reddening somewhat.

"There is a package arrived for my lady at the gate."

"Package!" Jankyn had her attention now. No one sent her packages, except that time at Enderby when Fulk . . . She sprang to her feet in horror, snatching up her skirts.

Knowing the obstacles, she was fleet-footed, dodging the children and the brewer's cart. Gervase almost caught her before she reached the barbican. Sir Geoffrey was standing in the gateway with the porter and two of the garrison beside him.

"In God's Name, keep her back!" he bawled at Gervase.

Strong hands seized her around the ribs but she fought, screaming like a madwoman. She did not have to investigate the maggot-covered contents that had tumbled from the canvas sack, she could smell the repulsive stink of flesh.

Fulk had sent her back her little dog.

Nineteen

ETCHING, JOHANNA STAGGERED BACK AGAINST THE cart. Then, thrusting her knuckles hard against her mouth, sobbing as though her heart was broken, she ran to God.

Unwanted, Geraint paused later at the chapel door. His lady lay prostrate on the tiled floor, her face cradled in her arms. Although her body no longer shook, her fingers were spread like claws as if she had been trying to burrow into Hell. Father Gilbert, hearing the creak of leather that betrayed an eavesdropper, drew him out into the fading daylight.

"I feel as useless as a scabbard without a sword."

"She is fearful, my son, that Barnabas will be the next."

"Barnabas? Who is Barnabas?"

"The little pageboy she favoured at Enderby. Did you not know that Sir Fulk used the child as a scapegoat to force her compliance?"

"By Christ, I hope that whoreson roasts for eternity!" He wanted to carry Johanna into the sunlight and put his arms about her, but any promises he might make in haste, he could not keep. "By your leave, Father, Lady Constance bid me see my lady Johanna to her chamber to rest before dinner." Not exactly a lie, but he could not in conscience leave her on the cold flagstones. The household would expect him to offer her tender comfort.

The chaplain looked dubious. "Very well, my son, but I suggest you ask Yolonya for something to make her sleep deeply tonight. Go to her."

Expecting harsh words, Geraint dropped cautiously on one knee and, gently clasping the frail shoulders, turned her warily.

Amazingly she let him guide her to her feet and compel her out of the dim, candlelit chapel into the courtyard bustle and through the garden postern, past the lenten sprouts and the spinach rows. Geraint scooped up the discarded fur, forgotten by Agnes, tossed it over his good shoulder and led Johanna down to where they could watch the river, still brown and turbulent, frothing as it buffeted the boulders. He settled the fur about her shoulders and angled her before him so his body might protect her from the east wind that had sprung up.

"I have always held that dogs have souls. And pigs," he added as an afterthought.

Johanna, peeping sideways, saw him shift his stare from the unclothed branches reflected in the sluggish water on the opposite bank to pensively study her as if evaluating the devastation left by her tears upon a face that was already sunken-eyed. Impossible to share the burden, she thought miserably. I wish I could tell him what else Fulk has done to me, but he can either do nothing or else something foolishly impulsive. And he is still a stranger for all that we have been tossed together.

"You are trying to humour me. There is a fine line between triteness and goodwill," she answered finally. Was it only a few days that she had known this man? It seemed like . . . she tried not to think but for this very moment. Thinking hurt.

"Yes, I apologise, but my motives presently are as pure as gold. I suppose you will argue with that too, the quality of gold, I mean." He heard her little sigh and observed, "You realise people will probably give you lapdogs from all directions now out of sympathy." He slid his arm protectively around her shoulders. "You can have a fleet of them in your wake." Then he asked her, "Are you with child?"

It was premeditated, like jabbing a pin deliberately into her. Johanna blinked at him in appalled anger. But he was ready for her furious effort to run away.

"You!" she almost spat in her indignation, but he remained unruffled. Ha! His consideration had all been calculated; a pretty view to soothe her grief, the little dabs of humour, and now he was using his iron strength to cower her just as Fulk had. *He* used to shake her.

"It is not just your little dog, is it, Johanna? You were weeping earlier. I need to know why."

"Let me go!"

"I am your husband, lady, or so the world thinks. Answer me! Why will you not eat?"

"Because I choose not."

"Answer me!" He turned her, trapping her upward glance in the shaft of his gaze. The eyes that watched her were not red-flecked, old and angry like Fulk's, but fathomless as deep water. There was no cruelty about his lips, only a fierce determination, but his assumption that, like Fulk, he could force compliance from her made her tremble. *"Are you with child?"*

She swallowed, and shook her head.

The mouth above her curved into a self-satisfied smile at having wrung that drop of truth from her and then, unpredictably, he suddenly relented, freed her and stepped back. Was this a tactic too?

"I suppose, sir, you will tell me next you are berating me out of loving kindness. Do you think I shall forget to mourn if you make me angry?"

"Believe me, I am sorry for your grief, my lady, but I will not have you appearing at the hearing tomorrow as if you lack love from me." His glance slid from her leather slippers slowly up over her body as if trying to make her realise how the archdeacon's officer would see her. "Johanna, I have to know this. If you are not carrying a child, then why the secret tears this morning? Are you sick? Or is this some kind of regular melancholy you indulge in when the moon is old?"

"How dare you!"

"A religious vow then," he cut in swiftly, his tone derisive. "No food for Lent. You seek to dry up all bodily fluids and become a creature entirely of spirit." Then his voice dropped, "Do not staunch the woman in you, lady. It makes you what you are, what God wanted you to be."

"Do not preach to me." She watched the sinfulness dance in his eyes, but already it was chosen, another weapon selected from his arsenal.

"Ah, I have it!" He paced and turned, now with an indignant mien. "Admit it, you have fallen in love with that winsome groom."

For an instant Johanna stared at him as if he had announced the earth had started encircling the sun and then she astonished both of them by laughing at the absurdity, joyful of his clemency and that his mercurial nature could so easily provide an antidote to the poison working in her. "You are too clever. I languish for him nightly."

"Ah." He held out his hand, his fingers curling with the delicately angled balance of enticement and insistence. "That excuse will satisfy me for the time being. Come and approve the arrangement of your bedchamber."

She took the gift of his hand. But it was not over; nothing was over yet.

THE TWO STEPS UP TO THE TOWER DOOR WERE GLISTENING WITH moisture and the entire floor had been swabbed to remove the splashes of whitewash.

"Watch out for your sleeves." He tested the wall with his fingerpads.

His esquire turned from supervising the setting up of a bed by two of the servants and bowed politely to her. "I am sorry about your poor little dog," he said gravely, straightening up. On receipt of a reproving look from his master at resurrecting her sorrow, Jankyn retaliated with a second bow. "Sir Gervase snores, my lady."

She permitted Gervase to draw her out of the lower room and up to the lighter chamber. Already her bed had been set up, but its hangings were missing and the walls around it were bare as yet. Agnes rose from laying the fire in the hearth and withdrew. At least there was some warmth to dry the floor. While this chamber was not so modern and luxurious as her bedchamber over the hall, it was more intimate in its smallness and Gervase filled it, unnerving her with his presence.

This arrangement must endure until the hearing was over or the king evicted them. It would be transitory. She would be lying in a nun's simple cell soon.

Gervase, her new self-appointed tower sentry, was waiting for her reaction; his smile would have bridged their river. But what gave her pause was that he had deliberately engineered this control of her privacy. He would, she realised, know every coming and going to her bedchamber.

Her glance flew to the door. There was no lock, merely a wooden bar propped against the corner angle.

The blue stare spoke volumes. Oh, he had read her thoughts.

"I trust I have your compliance in this, madam wife."

"And if you have not?"

"The dice is thrown, but I can have your possessions moved back above the hall if you insist." And I will have you eating from my hand, his expression told her.

"In case you have forgotten, master esquire, I am quite capable of organising my servants." Frowning, she opened the door for him. "God speed."

SUPPER WAS A CHILLED AFFAIR. THE FOOD WAS HOT CONSIDERING IT was hurried through draughty passageways from the kitchen; it was the conversation that was tepid. Geraint made a helpless face at Miles but unfortunately the boy lacked discretion.

"Why do you not tell jests like you used to, Johanna? Remember that one about the two chickens?"

"No," snapped Johanna.

Her brother pouted. "Everyone sits around with pokey long faces since you came back from Enderby." He had turned his bread into a siege-tower and was trundling it into attack on the great salt, a castle of silver.

"Be quiet, Miles, and behave!" Lady Constance smacked the manpower and demolished the assault, tossing the trencher to a lurking hound. "Show some sensitivity! Your sister is grieving for her dog."

"I will croak you a song, Miles," announced Gervase. "It will bore you so much that you will be happy to go and occupy yourself elsewhere."

"Oh my," muttered Johanna.

Lady Constance snapped her fingers at the resident minstrel.

"Sir Gervase would like some music to ease Lady Johanna's sorrow."

Alacrity personified, the minstrel grabbed his lute and came to know their pleasure.

"No, no, I insist on providing the entertainment."

"When do you not," muttered Johanna under her breath.

"This song," Geraint persisted—perhaps he had drunk too much—"was written originally by a poet named Vogelweide who lived in the realm of the Holy Roman Emperor. It has suffered many translations. This version I heard from a Gascon troubadour."

The minstrel beamed and his fingers rippled out a cascade of sweet notes. "Permit me to accompany you."

"Excellent," drawled Gervase. "I dedicate this song to my dear wife. Appreciate it, my darling dear, this is a rare event."

He just hoped he could remember the words. He sang the first two lines, smiling as his audience hushed and listened. Surprised at his skill, the minstrel joined in and even improvised a counterpoint at the chorus.

> *Beneath the leaves*
> *Of the lime tree*
> *I built a bower for two,*
> *As love oft weaves.*
> *"Come, pluck with me,*
> *Flowers of each hue."*
> *At the edge of a wild wood in a vale,*
> *Tandaraday! sang the nightingale.*
>
> *Away I stole*
> *To see my love.*
> *"Fair knight," she said.*
> *I made her whole,*
> *Sweet as a dove,*
> *Upon that bed.*
> *Did I kiss her? Yes, with a thousand sips.*
> *Tandaraday! See, the redness of her lips.*
>
> *That she lay with me,*
> *No one must know,*
> *No wight must tell.*

So blithe and free,
God keep from woe
And the fire of Hell.
It is 'twixt us two and that little bird,
Tandaraday! who will keep his word.

Meeting Gervase's provocative smile as he ended, Johanna felt an uncertain yearning stirring within her at the lure of so seductive a lyric sung with such feeling, and she was truly angry with Miles for kicking his stool all through Gervase's singing. So was everyone else; consequently the applause was somewhat excessive.

"It was tedious," the boy muttered. "Why are all the songs about love? Who cares about such trifling matters? You used to like the song about the frogs, Johanna."

"That was when I was thirteen."

Gervase laughed and set his arm about her shoulders with sufficient husbandly kindness.

Johanna realised belatedly that the song had been merely part of the mummery. For an infinitesimal moment, the length of a sigh, she had fallen under the spell of the singer. Perhaps Master Vogelweide might have been worth the knowing.

She leaned her chin upon her hand and stared glumly at the untouched wafer on the cloth before her. If a man could write so, surely love must be something wondrously beautiful. And yet, her cynical nature asserted, words might be a palliative for something that was merely as brief and brutal as the coupling of wildfowl. She had seen drakes land on top of females, pushing them underwater. They would surface, the drake holding the lady-duck's nape fiercely in his beak. He would penetrate her and it was over. No, chivalry was just a surcote that hid the ugly steel beneath and clothed rape, robbery and bloody slaughter in meaningless mouthings of honour. And courtly love hid the sordid couplings. A queen might have a lovesick knight at her feet by day creating lyrics to her eyes and lips, but at night he would go home to cuff his wife and the queen would return to her empty, loveless bed. Or if her husband was King of England, he would hang her jewels around the neck of Hugh Despenser. Poor French Isabella, with only babes to comfort her.

"You did not like it."

She who had never experienced any delights in tandaradaying made an effort to be courteous. He had been brave to sing with sore ribs.

"You sing with great . . . feeling, sir."

He smiled and raised his cup to her. "For you, my sweet lady, a little courtly love." Oh Jesu, did the man have to have a smile that scooped her heart up and held it gently as though it were a fragile, fluffed-up fledgling? It was all so overwhelming after Fulk's regime.

"Courtly love," mused her mother, "I wonder if Eleanor of Aquitaine used it as a mirror to her own vanity. I have always admired her but do you imagine she actually enjoyed going on the crusade? All that sand," she continued prosaically. "I am sure Richard Coeur-de-Lion must have regarded it as a great inconvenience having his mother along. But what courage she had to travel to the Holy Land."

Geraint did not answer Lady Constance. He had observed with concern that Johanna had eaten almost nothing during supper, and while he sympathised with her grief and her fear of facing her heartless husband at the hearing, he was becoming certain that there was concealment in her abstinence. She was hollow-eyed and growing gaunter by the day. If this was indeed some vow for Lent, then Father Gilbert must answer to him. Godsakes, she was drooping now, almost faint with hunger.

"Madam, your daughter!" Rising, he stepped behind her and, hands about her shoulders, lifted her to her feet.

Lady Constance cast a concerned look at her daughter's ashen face and urged her through to the great chamber.

"Has she eaten anything at all this last week?" Geraint snapped at the two tiring women as he followed them in.

Yolonya shook her head, hands on her huge hips as she swivelled to face her mistress. "I warned you, my lady, that the mite was starving herself. You must take her in hand, my lord."

"Fetch some of the broth they served earlier, Agnes!"

Restored somewhat by the nourishment, Johanna tried to best him as he spooned more food between her lips.

"Stop it. I will feed myself, thank you." She grabbed the spoon and finished the bowlful, knowing that he would stand over her until she did. It did reinvigorate her until her upstart companion began his tirade.

"What in God's Name is the matter with you, my lady? I took you for having common sense, not for being as featherheaded as a pillow."

"Go away, all of you!" Johanna buried her face in her hands.

"Gervase!" Lady Constance held open the door for him.

"No, I will not leave. Are you all blind, you geese?" Agnes and Yolonya unfortunately met the full weight of his anger, but it was her mother he was aiming at. "Can you not see that something ails her, madam?"

Her mother closed the door again with a sigh and came to look down at her. "Johanna, what is going on, dearest?"

"That first time!" Pacing the room, Geraint suddenly flung his hands in the air, and whirled round on the women. "That first time when I arrived. The swoon was real."

"Yes," whispered Johanna. "Now leave me be."

"It is this hearing hanging over us," declared Lady Constance.

"Is it indeed? She needs exercise, fresh air and food actually inside her, not merely on her plate." He paused in mid-stride to snarl down at her, "You only exercise your fingers, my lady, plying a needle in and out. Pah, no wonder you lack an appetite." He halted his pacing and crouched before her. "Listen, Johanna, if we take all the garrison as escort to render us modest and keep off predators, will you come hawking with me tomorrow afternoon if the judge lets us out to play?" She shook her head, knuckling her tears away. "Why ever not? It is springtime, lady, a new year. You need roses in your cheeks and . . ." He floundered, frowning at her as he tried further coaxing. "And do not tell me that I am not yet mended to manage it. I am and I do not issue invitations lightly. Flying the birds with me is a privilege."

Johanna smiled, close to tears again because she must refuse. His company gave her courage. If only she might confide in him— but the matter was too shameful, too intimate.

He shook his clenched hands in furious frustration. "Then you must rest, my lady."

"Leave me to try to sleep a little here, sir, and thank you. I appreciate you trying to cheer me earlier and for your care," she added, tucking her feet up. "The broth has restored me."

But it did not bode well for tomorrow.

Twenty

THE PARISH CHURCH BESIDE THE MARKETPLACE NEXT morning was more crammed than a looter's bag during a rebellion and the retainers of Conisthorpe and Enderby eyed each other between the Norman pillars like leashed, snarling dogs. With their master not come in to abuse them, Fulk's men enjoyed jeering at Gervase.

"This is a house of God and if anyone makes another 'cuckoo' noise, I will have them removed from here straightway," bellowed the glowering sergeant-at-law at the Enderby men.

The cuckoo in question pressed Johanna's shoulder reassuringly. He stood behind the bench that had been set for the noble ladies, looking every inch a lord. The cuckold, Fulk, on the other hand, clanked into the church in sabatons and full armour, making play on his renown as a man whose reputation had not been dimmed by the disgraceful losses at Bannockburn.

"Do you receive the impression that we are beholding a hero?" muttered Gervase. "Perhaps I should have worn my matching six and eightpenny gauntlets and a ten-shilling bascinet." Johanna was too tense to appreciate his humor. Fulk, clearly horn-mad at Gervase's arm about her, was eyeing her as malevolently as a cruel-beaked bird of prey.

"Who is that?" On Johanna's other side, her mother was glancing back at a richly clad woman with a pleated wimple beneath her chin.

"Sir Maurice's widow, Maud de Roos," whispered Father Gilbert. "They say she is already seeking a second husband."

"Well, it is rude of her to stare," growled Johanna, wondering whether the whole of Yorkshire had come to gape. A horn sounded and they rose for the judge's entrance.

A magistrate's board with quills, ink and parchment stood before the rood screen, but above it the great statue of Christ, his arms outspread in pain, stared bleakly Heavenwards, reminding them that whatever the outcome, God's judgment alone prevailed.

William de Bedford, the archdeacon's officer judging the case, proved to be a small, lean man of tidy appearance, who sternly scrutinised them as he sat down upon the bench, his expression proclaiming that they sat in God's house and that their purpose must not be to trivialise the law.

The constitution of the proctors was carried out first and then the plaintiffs' libels were called for. Johanna, hiding behind her veil, was shocked when the judge required her to set it back so that the two men claiming possession of her could each assert that she was indeed the woman concerned. Fulk's petition against her was then presented in writing, but he chose to add an oral endorsement, striding into the space between the bench and the congregation with the confidence of a Pericles or Cicero, but only steel authority rattled forth.

Geraint knew his kind—the sort who enjoyed cracking out brief, precise orders. A disobedient conscripted villein under Fulk's command might end with a noose around his neck or be flogged within an inch of his life. Poor Johanna. She would have had to be disciplined too.

"Most of the people gathered here today," Fulk thundered, "witnessed me wed this woman before the chapel door and our union was blessed by the cleric standing there!" Father Gilbert's expression tightened and there were murmurs of approval from the assembly. "There is no question that the marriage was consummated and I will avow on yon Holy Bible that this adulterous woman," he thrust a long malicious finger at her, "was a virgin when I first lay with her."

Johanna blanched. Somewhere a woman tittered, and Gervase coolly raised mocking eyebrows at Fulk.

"Lucky maid!" sneered someone derisively.

"Did you take your armour off first?" another voice yelled from

the back. It could have been the brewer's wife for Jankyn had a fit
of coughing.

William de Bedford stared dispassionately at the congregation.
"I will clear this court if there are any further interruptions. Have
you anything more to say, Sir Fulk?"

"Yes." He leaned upon the board, so close his spittle might have
fallen upon the judge as he snarled, "An audience with my lord
archbishop could resolve this matter right swiftly. This hearing is
a waste of this court's time and mine." He gave the cloth a fistblow
that startled the inkpots and made the notary blot the parchment,
then he strode back to his place, his haubergeon rattling.

It was a wonder the archdeacon's officer did not bristle at the
insult, for it was known that my lord archbishop had disputed his
right to hear cases in half of the shire. He ignored the criticism.

"Sir Gervase."

Stephen de Norwood set the ribboned and sealed petition before
the judge with a bow. It was unrolled and scanned.

"Do you have anything to add, Sir Gervase?"

Gervase bowed to the judge. Johanna was proud of him. Her
mother had indeed chosen him well and the blue velvet tunic with
its neck and sleeves bordered with yellow silk circles like inter-
locking suns emphasised his fair hair and handsome face, as if he
brought the goodness of the open sky into the church.

"Only this, my lord judge and worthies all, I pray you do not
call into question the honour of this my noble and gracious lady.
Let her rather receive your pity and compassion. It is I who must
bear the full guilt for this unfortunate tangle. Circumstances compelled me to leave this place before I could inform Lord Alan that
I had married his daughter, but before God I swear that the lady
Johanna and I exchanged our vows lawfully before a priest and
witnesses and straightway consummated our handfast. I understand Sir Fulk's anger at the shame brought upon him, but I affirm
most solemnly that in God's sight the lady was married to me first
and . . ." he swung round to face Johanna, "I honour her."

A sob broke from Agnes, Johanna's vision misted and Yolonya
was dabbing her eyes with her apron but the judge, even if he
sensed the accusation levelled at Fulk, nodded to Geraint to resume his place, requested Johanna to answer the petition in two

days time on Wednesday, the feast of St. Benjamin, and moved on
to the next case.

Veiling her face, Johanna rose and with her mother on one side
and Gervase on the other started down the nave, but Fulk blocked
her path, an ominous wall of metal.

Johanna shook. She had forgotten how much he could terrify
her but reassuring hands came from either side to steady her. Remembering Cob, she spat at Fulk's feet and would have passed
by, but he reached out a gauntleted hand to grab her painfully by
the shoulder.

"How now, wife! You hardly look like a woman suffering from
Cupid's bolts. What are you paying the boy here to lie for you?
Certes, the coward can never lie *with* you."

Johanna's cheeks flamed.

Setting her to one side, Gervase was mocking as he looked eye
to eye with him. "Now why do you say that, Fulk de Enderby,
when all of Conisthorpe knows differently? I suppose you want to
set your men on me again? Win this case and you will have a
cuckoo's egg in your nest for sure."

"Why you—"

"On your way! All of you!" Sir Ralph thrust himself between
them. "I will not have the king's peace broken!"

Fulk's gaze crawled over Johanna, making her skin feel goose-
fleshed. "The examiner will break you, wife, you and the boy. As
for your witnesses," he eyed Agnes with icy malevolence, "if they
are found to be lying, they will be flogged in the market square."

"You are intimidating the witnesses," exclaimed Lady Constance.

"Yes, I certainly am," growled Fulk.

"WHAT HAPPENS NEXT?" GERAINT ASKED STEPHEN DE NORWOOD
outside the churchyard, once they were within the safety of a cordon of Conisthorpe's garrison. The ladies were already seated in
the litter and the entourage was waiting for his signal to return to
the castle. The proctor drew him aside.

"Well, after St. Benjamin's Day, Sir Fulk's proctor will present
positions and I surmise he will allege a case of *glossa ordinaria*."

"Does it sound as dull in the vernacular?"

"It means adultery, sir. That you misled the lady and your pur-

pose was merely fornication. He will probably also plead that any
abuse of the lady by himself was done for the purpose of 'reducing
her from errors.' "

"Hmm, and am I right in thinking you will not see the questions
that are going to be put to Sir Fulk's witnesses by his proctor?"

"Correct, sir. Sir Fulk's advocate will not see the questions I
have set either. Only the examiner does. As for yourself, you will
not hear the cross-examination until the depositions are read out
in court."

Remembering Johanna's fears, he muttered, "Well, I hope the
examiner is an honest man and no craven."

"Just tell your esquire to be sparing with his wit in case it an-
noys the examiner. The women are always more of a liability in
cases like this. Clever questioning can tie their tongues in knots.
There is one further matter that you must broach with your lady.
How will she answer Fulk's assertion touching her virginity when
he lay with her on their marriage night?"

"I have not discussed it."

Stephen de Norwood patted his arm. "Chicken blood. Since you
had already had her maidenhead, I expect her mother or that huge
tiring woman who gave me the pimpernel mixture for my diges-
tion the other day told her how to keep a bridegroom feeling secure. Yes?"

"My thanks." Geraint inclined his head courteously. "I will tell
her and warn Lady Constance."

Stephen de Norwood nodded. "By the way, I have informed the
officers of the court and Sir Ralph about the violent demise of my
lady's dog. Take care, sir. All of you."

"You also, Stephen," answered Geraint grimly.

THAT IS NOT THE ARRANGEMENT, IS IT? AS HE RODE BACK BESIDE SIR
Geoffrey at the head of their company, Fulk's words jangled in
Geraint's head like folly bells. Somehow he did not think it was
bluster on Fulk's part; the man seemed damnably sure that he had
committed no indiscretions with Johanna. Why was that? Even if
Lady Edyth had assumed that there was no intimacy between
them, she could not swear to her brother that she was certain. After
all, Geraint had been seen to sleep in Johanna's bedchamber on
two occasions albeit he had been alone in her bed. Why was Fulk

so sure? Was he certain of Johanna's character—that she was over-virtuous or frigid? *He can never lie with you.* It was time, Geraint decided as he rode behind the swaying litter, that he got through to the skin of the matter.

"I want to talk to you," he murmured, assisting Johanna out after they arrived at Conisthorpe. She flinched when he would have put his arm about her.

"No, please. I thank you for what you said this morning, sir, but I need to have some solitude. I will take my meal in my bed-chamber alone." So he would not be able to make her eat, thought Geraint glumly.

"If answering the libel on Wednesday bothers you, could you not plead you are indisposed? I gather that women can become, well . . . irregular at such times of stress."

"No, I will be there." So she was not suffering from cramps or any of the ills that might afflict women at the time of their courses.

Agnes made a sympathetic face at him behind her mistress's back. Surely she must know what was going on?

He followed the two young women across to the south tower and waited in his bedchamber for Agnes to descend the stairs alone, then immediately caught her hand and hauled her up to the small landing outside Johanna's door. Caught off guard with no time to bar the door, his pretend wife stiffened her shoulders and faced him with a dignified control that a princess might have envied.

"What do you want?"

He stepped behind the maidservant, sternly setting her before Johanna like a mirror. "On your mother's soul, Agnes. Tell me if your lady here still has her monthly courses."

"Yes, sir, but the way she is starving herself, 'twon't be for much longer. Tell him, my lady. Or would you have him find out for himself?"

"You have gone too far, Agnes!"

"I mean no mischief, my lady," the girl answered stoutly. "But I can't bear to see you starving yourself to death."

It was Gervase who found a voice first. "Leave us, Agnes," he said hoarsely, as if the words found trouble seeking life.

His gaze did not waver from Johanna as Agnes, with a sob, her fingers to her mouth, ran out past him. The girl's presumption that

Johanna must inevitably surrender her body to him hung in the air between them.

He used the weapons that men had ever used, standing there feet apart in his costly clothes, every inch of him proclaiming greater strength and male authority, affirming in his arrogant study of her that he had the right to bend her to his will and that his wisdom was for her good, but he kept his anger in its scabbard.

She was not going to enlighten him. He was still the outsider. With dignity, she gestured to the open door.

Geraint raised his arms, his hands open-palmed, and then despairingly dropped them to his sides with an angry breath. "I thank you for your trust, lady," he told her cuttingly and left her standing forlorn and alone.

"IT WEREN'T NO USE, I SUPPOSE," AGNES MUTTERED, WHEN HE planted himself in her path as she brought her mistress's meal from the kitchens. "An' she'll treat this as though it's poisoned."

"She thinks Fulk is trying to poison her?"

Agnes giggled at his shocked tone as though he had the intelligence of a wart on a dog's nose. "No, sir, 'course not, she isn't that daft."

"So you will not tell me." He stubbornly folded his arms. "Well, I shall not wave a white clout yet. Ensure your mistress has a good night's slumber. Ask Yolonya for some potion to settle her tonight and if she is to take her meals in her bedchamber, it will be in my presence. I intend to make sure she eats properly from now on."

"Aye, you can say so, sir, but lourin' over her like old Fulk did won't solve matters. But I tell you this, I have had enough, sir. If my lady won't help herself nor tell you or madam her mother, maybe chaplain can advise. I'll be off to him when I've given her this." She bobbed him a curtsey and continued on her way.

Geraint's arms unknotted themselves. "In God's Name, Agnes, tell me what is amiss with her. Upon my honour, I shall do what is needful." He grabbed the platter. "You doubt my word? Look at me, Agnes!"

The wench avoided his eyes, fumbling with her linen coif, straightening it needlessly. "My lips are sealed, sir. My lady made me take an oath."

"Agnes," he coaxed softly, "there are ways to help a man guess.

I will walk barefoot in the desert and surrender myself to the Sar-acens if your mistress desires it of me so long as she does not carry Fulk de Enderby's seed within her womb."

"Oh no, sir, nothing like that."

Said easily, it had him as confused as a mouse in a cheese larder. He thrust the platter back at her. "Think, Agnes. How may I guess?"

"Have you . . ." She blushed, pursing her lips, "Have you not put your hand lower, sir? You being her husband like."

"*Lower?* She *wants* me to lower my hand?" he asked in genuine innocence, not only wondering what Agnes was actually implying but whether any woman ever managed to make sense. Never tell me my lady icicle is weeping because I have played the chivalrous knight, he thought. No, God would present him with a halo and a pair of fluffy, feathery wings before that ever happened. Johanna had given him no encouragement whatsoever and he knew the wretched woman was set on becoming a nun.

Agnes sniffed and he could not tell if the waggle of her head was a nod or a denial. "I promised not to say, sir, but them knaves in Florence have a lot to answer for," she bleated, and bolted like a panicked ewe, her eyes saltwatery.

Geraint was left standing alone, convinced he would never un-derstand women. Where was their rational thinking? Knaves? Flor-ence?

Jankyn materialised at his elbow. "If I tie ribbons on you we could use you as a maypole as well as a husband. I merely inquire because you have been standing here stock still and such idleness is to be despised. Did the fair Agnes glue your feet to the flag-stones?"

"What do you want, Jankyn?"

"I have been sifting through some of the exquisite movables that were stored in the tower and now risk the weather. Do you want to come and tell me if you want to salvage any of them?"

"No!"

Jankyn followed him up into his bedchamber. "So now you and the lady are shoved in the same bag, shall you claim the spoils? You might get the constableship."

"Who me?" Geraint sighed, inwardly wary at how much the jester read in him. He closed the door. "Lady Constance does not want me hanging around her castle like a stinking moat. The moment the verdict is given, she will forget she ever met me."

"And you might do better, eh? You still have not told me who you really are. The King of Elfland preparing to make love to the lady between the toadstools? One of Edward Longshank's bastards—oh, wash my mouth out! I have it! You are a spy for Robert the Bruce and pray to the patron saint of sporrans."

The fool received a reassuring hand on his shoulder. "Aye, you may ask the Scots the next time they come raiding. I have a test for you, man. Tell me, what is Florence known for?"

"Making barn lofts vibrate. Ouch!" he danced back at the friendly clout. "Oh, foolish of me, you mean the city-state. Glass, artists, girdles, although the latter is a false assertion."

"Perhaps we should hold this conversation in English. The words are shorter and I am obviously stupid. What are you blathering about?"

"Florentine girdles, my friend. Why are you looking at me as though I have managed to change cowpats into gold?"

His master triumphantly slapped his palms together, feeling like the conqueror Alexander must have when he sliced through the Gordian knot. Johanna was wearing a chastity belt.

GERAINT DELIBERATED ON PUTTING AGNES'S ADVICE TO THE TEST, but the way Johanna was behaving he would be lucky to handle her fingers let alone the lady's more alluring parts. Any touching other than in merest courtesy seemed now an anathema to her.

Agnes was a different matter. He delayed her easily with a hand on her elbow. "I have solved your riddle, but it is a pity for my lady's health that you did not hint at it sooner."

"So you may say, but my lady forbade me to tell anyone, least of all a man and a newcomer at that. It is chafing her right sorely. That is why she will not ride with you and she is trying to starve herself so she may be able to wriggle out of it."

Geraint cursed. Fulk of Enderby needed to be gelded. "How long has she been wearing it?"

"Since we left Enderby, but 'tis not the first time. That monster," she spat, "made her wear it whenever he was away."

"And you say her mother knows nothing of this?"

"No, sir, Lady Johanna has been very discreet and she will allow no one else to bathe or robe her. Anyhow, sir, I am right glad you know now. We have tried filing it but she can hardly call in one of the carpenters or Bart the smith. It really is a matter for you, sir, as her husband."

By all the Saints! Geraint cast his gaze heavenwards. Was there no end to what was expected of him? But he had to do something.

That is not the arrangement, is it? Fulk had sneered at him. As matters stood, the proctor's advice was useless. His supposed marriage with Johanna would not stand. Fulk, damn him to Hell, knew he could not have carnal knowledge of Johanna even were he to stay a twelve month. But what could he do to help her? Nothing unless he knew the lie of the land, so to speak. He turned his head to the south tower, took a deep breath and braced himself to confront the little female dragon.

AGNES LET HIM IN, A FINGER ON HER LIPS.

"Maman?" Johanna stretched and yawned delightfully like a kitten, until she opened her eyes and saw him. "What do you want here?" Despite her ill pleasure, he was relieved to see she had the crinkled, pillowed look of having slept deeply.

"Nothing that you are not prepared to give," he answered, signalling to Agnes to remain. "But you cannot, even if you want to. Supposing I want to touch you as a husband should? What should I find if I slide my hand up to explore your secrets, Johanna?"

She was off the bed in a trice and had her hand on the doorhandle. "Lay hands on me and I will scar your face with these nails, I swear it!"

"Let me set you a hypothesis, my lady." He gave a tight smile at her irritated puzzlement. "Just supposing, Johanna, that we had met before you were wed to Fulk and fallen in love." He watched the wariness creep into her eyes. "If you were in love with me, you would surrender to me sweetly now, would you not?"

She swallowed. "I . . . I have no understanding of these matters but yes, I suppose I would."

"But you cannot, can you, Johanna? You are locked into perpetual chastity."

She flinched. "You are saying that I have a crippled mind concerning fornication. Yes, you are right. I have no wish to have carnal knowledge of you or any other man. It offers no pleasure."

Well, he would see about that.

"Lady," he answered gently. "Time will heal your scars, I promise you. However, it was not the chastity of your thoughts I meant, it was the chastity that is enforced upon you."

Johanna's gaze met his squarely and then her eyes widened in anger. "The Devil take you!"

"I imagine he will, lady. You and I both."

"Did you tell him, Agnes? If you did, I shall—"

"No," he cut in, "Agnes has not betrayed you. If anyone, it was Fulk." He warmed to his purpose. "A Florentine girdle, Johanna? Is that what that incubus forced you to wear?"

Johanna tore her gaze away from his stern perusal, tears glistening. "I cannot get it off and it is hurting me."

He wanted to hold her, to draw her against his shoulder, but he knew that she was like a wild creature. If the twig cracked beneath the foot of the hunter, she would run.

"Can I help?" It was offered with the most profound gentleness.

Johanna saw him through a blur of tears. His presence shimmered as if he were an angel rather than a man and the change of image lessened her shame and added comfort. She closed her eyes, trying to staunch her weeping, and shook her head in despair.

"Sir, the device is hardfast. If it was easy for a man to break the lock, there would be no point in forcing wives to wear this torture. He did not have to do this." Her eyes were brimming afresh with bitter tears. "After what he has done to me, I would crawl to Jerusalem on my knees rather than lie down with any man."

Geraint's mouth tightened. "Be that as it may. You cannot wear a chastity belt for the rest of your life, my dear. You will become very sick indeed if you cannot remove it. I have seen what manacles can do to flesh and . . ." He directed his gaze towards her nether regions. "Women's flesh, especially those intimate . . . parts . . . is especially tender."

Agnes smothered a giggle and Johanna raised an eyebrow. Despite her dire predicament, with a little push she would become hysterical with laughter. This upstart rogue of hers was getting himself truly into the deepest water.

"You have had a great deal of experience in those areas?" she countered gravely, not daring to look at Agnes.

"Yes," he growled, scowling at her. "You . . . you have to resolve this matter, lady."

Johanna bit her lip. "We have been trying to do so but it seems to me, sir, that it is my problem and I beg you to mind your own affairs."

"I see, my lady," he retorted loftily. "You plan to starve yourself so you can step out of it in a year's time? Is that why you have the appetite of a . . . a sick sparrow?" Pampered lapdog had been on his lips, but fortunately he had not said it. "Or had you some other solution in mind? Is the blacksmith due after noon? A tasty morsel of gossip that will be."

"I will think of something," muttered Johanna.

"*We* will think of something and right swiftly, lady, for it is my business." His fingers framed her cheeks, forcing her to look at him. "You have not thought this through, Johanna. If Fulk tells the judge you are wearing a chastity belt, it will be clear that we have not consummated our reunion. Remember that Stephen de Norwood advised that my possession of you, lady, was a strong argument for our marriage to prevail."

His possession of her. For an instant, something beyond her control flickered in her, lighting sufficient flame to heat her pale cheeks.

Geraint felt her quiver delightfully and saw the frail beauty that had been growing back steadily with cherishing and time's repair. There was only a faint purple now where Fulk had hit her. Did she feel what she might not want to name? Had she ever experienced desire for a man? He wanted to taste the innocence in her and lead her to a pavilion of earthly pleasure.

"May the Devil roast Fulk!" she cursed and flung away from him, shoulders that were becoming more enticing to him by the instant shaking with fury.

"Agnes, I will inspect my lady before you robe her for supper and we will see if something may be done to put you out of your misery, Johanna."

"Inspect me!" exclaimed Johanna, whirling round on him, her fists clenched. "You will not . . ." She lowered her voice from a shriek as she realised the whole castle would be twitching their antennae towards the courtyard. ". . . inspect me. You will not come near me, you rogue."

"Since I am risking excommunication and my honour to rescue you, you little shrew, you will obey me. I am the lord of this castle for the present and if you gainsay me, I will toss you back to Fulk and good riddance."

"Ohhh!" She grabbed up a stool to hurl at him and Geraint wisely fled.

Johanna shut herself up in her tower room for the rest of the day and bade Agnes try once more the file and wires. By the time the waning sun sent rich, golden light tumbling across the furnishings, both women were feeling as inadequate as eunuchs in a harem.

"He is coming," exclaimed Agnes, her bosom thrust out of the turret sill. "Proper dour he looks. By my troth, madam, I rather think he is as afeared of this meeting as you."

GERAINT PAUSED IN MIDSTRIDE ON THE THRESHOLD. "WHAT IN HELL is this!"

His so-called wife lay upon her half-curtained bed with a sheet covering her from toe to waist, the rest of her was hidden behind a second sheet suspended vertically over the bed from a beam. Agnes was standing to attention beside her mistress's draped feet.

"I see," muttered Geraint. "I am now become a physician, am I? Would you like me to examine you for flat feet or some interesting blemishes as well while the mood is on me?"

The shape beneath the sheet twitched.

"My lady will permit you to look at the device but she will not speak to you while you make the examination."

Cunning! So he was to be inspecting merely an item, not a person.

"Very well, it seems a fair enough bargain," he exclaimed briskly. "Shall we begin?" He jerked his head at Agnes to peel the bedsheet back, but even he was not sufficiently braced for the brutality of what he saw.

Disembodied between a curtain of white and the sheet that hid her legs, the garment that encircled Johanna's slender body was simple and cruel. There was a metal band about her waist and welded into it at centre front and back was a second strip of metal, half a span wide, which looped between her legs. The side panels were of leather which presumably partially lined the metal bands.

A thin ribbon of chafed skin was beginning to show. Heaven knows how sore she must be further down.

"Set the sheet back further," he ordered and noted the responding tremble of unease from the bed. "Agnes, let us consult together on this. You have tried wire in the lock and I can see where you have filed. How tight is this?" He slid his fingers under it to test the tightness of the waist band. Johanna squealed. "I beg your pardon, I should have breathed on my fingers first. Aye, there is no purchase here." The skin around her waist was reddened, but with her jerking the curtain had slid back to reveal a delightful navel and pearly skin. Geraint said a prayer to St. Cuthbert who was known to have stood in the cold North Sea for hours as penance for even speaking to a woman, and tried to concentrate.

The lock was cunningly wrought and its making would have cost a great deal. He ran a finger down the metal that descended tightly across Johanna's belly and noticed another place where the women had cut the leather and tried to file.

"How loose is it beneath?" He pointed to between her legs where the band disappeared out of sight. The thighs beneath the metal quivered and the covering sheet slid lower. A few dark curling hairs were escaping into sight.

"Not loose at all, sir, as you would expect. There is a hole jagged with sharp teeth so that—excuse me, sir, but I must needs be frank—so that a man's prick or finger could progress further but not withdraw undamaged, and there is an opening for my lady's other business."

Behind the hanging sheet, a fist pounded the mattress and the curtain threatened to descend. Geraint caught the back of his hand to his mouth, but seeing the soreness where the leather chafed Johanna's inner thigh, his laughter fled, and he dropped the sheet fully over her again. The form beneath lost its tenseness.

"Tell your mistress that she shall be free of this even if I have to take the keys from Fulk at swordpoint. Have you been putting ointment on her to ease the rubbing?"

"I am not a halfwit, sir," Agnes answered primly, "but last time it happened, it eventually broke the skin."

"How long ago was that?"

"Three weeks before Yuletide. He was away in London. Even the ointment could not stop the chafing."

"God ha' mercy!"

Johanna heard the latch close violently. She sat up and snatched up her wrap, muttering curses on every man living, including Gervase because he had insisted on seeing her in her shame. She sniffed unhappily but she had had her fill of crying. Anyway, weeping was merely taking the lid off a pan over the fire; some of the steamy anger escaped but it never stopped the seething inside.

"You did the right thing, my lady." Agnes was hard put not to laugh. "Oh, you should have seen his face when he saw the sheets."

Johanna tried to look grim and then she could not help herself. "*My lady's other business*! By all the Saints, you wretch, Agnes. I could have strangled you. I should have loved to see his expression when you said that."

"Oh, truly, my lady, it was beyond price."

"Help me with my kirtle. Oh, Heaven, Agnes, you do not suppose he will do anything foolhardy? What if the poor man thinks he must ride off to Enderby and demand the key?"

"Surely not in the dark, my lady."

"I doubt that would deter him. Oh, Agnes, I am not sure I can face him over supper."

"Courage, madam. If he was your real husband, he would have seen everything of you by now anyway. I would not mind, in your shoes. Honest, my lady, any woman would be pleased to have such a comely man on the leash."

The rare laughter left Johanna. "It is different for me."

Agnes laced her kirtle up the back with more vigour than usual. "Well, 'tis not for me to say, but I would make hay before it rains again."

AWAITING HER IN THE COURTYARD TO ESCORT HER TO THE HALL, Gervase de Laval was wearing a grin that would have made a cathedral door look narrow.

"If you splutter, I shall not accompany you."

"No, come back, I agree it is no laughing matter, but I promise you we shall resolve it."

"*We!*"

"And I shall warm my hands next time. No, Johanna, come back!"

At the board, he insisted that she eat a full meal, softly pointing out to her that she would be dead before she would be thin enough to slither from her torment.

"How fare you now?" he asked later as he led her to the great chamber where they stood before the fire together. The minstrel was playing at her mother's feet and Sir Geoffrey and Father Gilbert were reminiscing about pilgrimages.

"Not as comfortable as I should like, sir. My belly is complaining after such idleness." She gave a deep sigh, sliding her palm along the invisible steel encircling her. "I hope you do not see this as a challenge."

"Perish the thought!" he muttered. "I am certainly not pounding across the Enderby drawbridge on a destrier with my lance lowered. If we had the time, we could sit you in a horse trough for the summer until it rusted away."

At least it brought a smile to her lips but he continued, graver now. "If the vengeful Fulk insists you be examined, and proves you and I liars, my lady, the court may believe we have lied about everything. Do not forget that these men who sit in judgment have mostly denied themselves the company of women."

"Ah yes, women contaminate the pure air of the spirit. I fear the men who become examiners, Gervase. They are the sort who would be pleased to burn women as witches or make them do penance as whores."

"Men who take an infinite delight in thumbscrews, hmm." Frowning, he leaned his forearm against the mantel, his chin sunk on his chest, his thumb rubbing at the quillon of his dagger. "I could try abducting the Enderby locksmith."

"The man died of lung rot during Advent."

He straightened, catching her fingers in his. "What did you do, my darling dear, stick pins in the wretch's image?"

"That is not amusing," she snarled, snatching away her hand.

He deliberately snared it again and carried her fingers to his lips. "I think I can break the lock." His words were warm breath against her skin.

The green-grey eyes widened and her lips parted delightfully. "By all the Saints! How?"

Another woman might have hung about his neck like a May garland. He sensed Johanna wanted to do so but fear still shackled

her soul. She was bereft of all but words to offer him; even promises were beyond her yet but he was filled with a sinful hope.

"How?" he echoed, and his blue gaze, fierce with mischief and
the joy of challenge, became transfigured with sternness. "My lady,
how brave are you?"

Twenty-one

"HOW BRAVE?"

Geraint saw the hope rush into her eyes like a spring tide, and masked his own apprehension.

"Are you fully primed for the examiner?" Lady Constance called out, only to be perturbed by her daughter's unexpected ebullience.

"Like crossbows, mother? Yes."

Father Gilbert, having bested the seneschal, received a concerned message. He was being whistled up by his owner to save the lamb from the wolf.

Geraint showed a sudden interest in the fire irons. He received a bright smile from Johanna, so he could not have been looking too predatory.

"May I have a word with you, my daughter?" called Father Gilbert.

"You have not explained, Gervase," Johanna muttered, reluctant to leave her knight even if he resembled St. George having second thoughts about fighting dragons.

"Later," Gervase answered casually. "After all we no longer have to be chaperoned." A virginal blush pinkened cheeks already rosy from the fire's warmth. "You will be quite safe." His glance slid lazily down her surcote. He did not add "for now."

Johanna found herself breathing shallowly. "I . . . I suppose so."

If Father Gilbert noticed her unnatural colour, he made no comment but moved to make room for her on the windowseat. "You look happier tonight, my daughter."

"I am not sure why," she answered, watching Gervase join the minstrel. "None of my problems are solved as yet."

"He grows more malleable, but such young men build up much energy. It needs to be let like blood. Perhaps Sir Geoffrey should arrange a hunt tomorrow to exhaust him."

Johanna observed the priest shrewdly. "You are worried about my virtue?"

"You must be careful, my daughter. The proximity of your bedchamber to this young man's is foolhardy."

"There is no cause to worry, Father. I am the last woman on earth to be seduced, and we are only carrying out Stephen de Norwood's advice."

"Yes, but, despite his holy vows, the proctor is a worldly man with no other target than to win the case. Sir Gervase is pleasing to the eye, my lady, and charming withal. It is my observation you are slowly falling beneath his spell."

"Nonsense, Father, we are becoming friends, that is all." The priest's piercing gaze was trying to pinion her soul.

"Sin—temptation—wears a smile of friendship. His blood will be hot, Johanna. Give him a shoe nail and he will take the entire horse. You know nothing of his history."

"Do you?" His silence spoke. As a priest, he could not deny the truth. "Is he married then?"

"Why that question, my daughter? Why not ask whether I know his true name? You see, you fall into the trap of lust quite innocently."

"Oh, fie. Well, who is he then?"

"I do not know that."

"Ah, but you know some of his friends. Well, so do I." She lowered her voice even more. "He fought at Boroughbridge. He needed me to put a fresh dressing on his wound. Well, I am his wife, after all." Closing her mouth with a snap, she looked away from the chaplain's omniscient stare. "Nothing has changed, Father, and I promise you I still intend to be a nun. The pleasures of the flesh—if they exist—hold no enticement."

He smiled sadly, "You speak bravely, but I do not want to see you hurt again, my child. You know that because he is hunted, this young man cannot stay and care for you as you deserve. We are all risking the wrath of Holy Church because we wish to see a golden crown for you in Heaven after all your suffering."

One could not say "ha" to one's chaplain. She was grateful for his counsel but he did not understand how much Gervase's friendship meant to her. "Hmm." Johanna wriggled the scarlet toes of her shoes. "I think that I shall be at the back of the heavenly diadem queue somehow. I do not feel purified by affliction, in fact, quite the reverse. I have no humility whatsoever and why should I forgive such a beast as Fulk? My sufferings were not deserved."

"Child, you must never doubt God's love for you. You have prayed for divine help and your prayers have been answered."

"Yes," she said softly, but her feet had begun to tap. The minstrel was beating out a rhythm on the naker while Gervase, borrowing the viol, struck up a merry pace with the bow. They were laughing and talking to each other as they played and here she was, a grown woman, being chastised.

"Johanna, look at me." The priest's expression was grave. "Women are frail and easily tempted as you are now. I think you should spend tonight in prayer."

"No, Father," she answered, wondering if he would also lead Gervase aside and offer him a golden heavenly helm. "Forgive me, but I do not think that would be wise. I was unwell this morning."

"And you did not come to mass."

"I needed rest. Perhaps tomorrow night I will come to the chapel." She set her hand upon his rigid arm in an attempt to reassure him. "Please, do not abandon me. I will not be foolish, I swear, but I . . . I have to present to the archdeacon's court as a woman who two years ago let her heart lead her head and there is another reason which I will explain as well, but I am not infatuated with him. There is nothing for you to fear." She glanced once more at the two young men and caught Gervase watching her consideringly. He gave her a swift, understanding smile before lowering his gaze to the fingerboard of the viol. "He will leave as soon as he can, I promise you."

"I have supported you in this deception, my daughter, but I am warning you that Satan will be heating irons for both of you if you give in to pleasure."

"Pleasure!" Her rebellious soul protested. "Father, no one knows better than I that there is little pleasure in procreation. Upon my soul, I am in more danger from Fulk than from Gervase de Laval and I shall never be at liberty to become a nun if I do not have his trust and support at the hearing. The last thing I am going to do is treat him as though he were lust personified."

"The young are ambitious. This one was ragged when I found him. What if he refuses to leave?"

"First, he would have to dispute my dower land with Fulk—though at least most of the arrangement was in coin and movable goods which my lord father has not yet parted with—and Gervase would certainly not receive Conisthorpe which is only within the king's gift, and then the rest of the inheritance goes to Miles, which reminds me . . ." she was desperate to drive the conversation into a safe fold, ". . . I wish my mother or you, Father, would discipline the little scoundrel. He is running amok."

The priest would not be distracted. "Meditate upon my warning. This life is fleeting and worldly delights will carry you to the Devil. I think you are walking in great moral danger and I will pray for you."

OUTSIDE THE HALL SHE CAME TO GERAINT'S ARM LIKE A FALCON dangled its bait. He wagered she would have skipped at his side had she not been a lady or sorely chafed.

"If you do not explain this instant . . ." she warned him, quickening her steps to his stride. He noted she was not afraid to follow him into his chamber; her mind, it seemed, was soaring larklike with all manner of possibilities.

"It might come with a price, Johanna." Would she be able to comprehend how much it would demand of them both?

That quelled her optimism. "I-I see," she stiffened, her little chin rising coldly. Now what hazardous ground was her agile mind springing onto? To let him enjoy her? He thought as much. So the chaplain had been reminding her of the sins of the flesh.

"Oh, not that, you goose. Dear God, Johanna, must you think every man is out to lay you on your back? Even if it is a worthwhile thought." He sent her a heated glance that had her panicking again. By all the Saints, he could play her like the viol. Did she not realise how predictable she was?

"I suppose you are going to explain eventually." She twitched her skirts, a sure sign of her skittishness.

He leaned against the wall and sternly folded his arms. "Are you prepared to trust me with your life?"

"My life!" The delicate head jerked up, eyes wide. She was beautiful, did she know that? "My life," she echoed bleakly. "As I told you on our first meeting, my life is not worth a bruised flowerpetal. What are you proposing?"

"You are being evasive with your answer, lady." He unfolded his arms and came across to stare down at her. "Do you think you could stable your rebellious soul and grant me an hour of your total obedience?"

"What are you going to do?"

"Hurt you." He reached out and without touching her framed her throat within his large hands. "Have you the courage to trust and obey me to the letter? I cannot help you otherwise."

"It sounds as though we are being made handfast. Yes, I trust you, whoever you are." He felt her condemnation that he demanded her trust and yet would not vouchsafe his. But this was his bargain, not hers.

"Be certain! I do not make this offer lightly. It will be as hard for me, harder perhaps."

She scowled. "You are demanding my trust without explaining what you intend."

"Yes. I could draw blasphemous comparisons. I have always sympathised with Doubting Thomas but sometimes you have to make a decision."

Why was he expecting so much, he wondered. Why was it suddenly important that he test her so, that she demonstrate her faith in him? Because he could kill her? But . . .

"Very well," she was saying, interrupting his pensiveness. "Do what is needful."

"Excellent." He gave her forearms a brotherly squeeze of congratulation. "Such good sense. You should have been born a camel." And let go of her, his grin turning roguish. "Of course, if it only takes a thrice, you will have sworn to be obedient to me for the rest of the hour." He pulled at Johanna's sensitive tail, teasing her again. This time she did not change colour.

"I-I have said I trust you," Johanna declared bravely, gravely ignoring his lightheartedness. "Now will you tell me, *please*."

"Tomorrow, lady." If he told her now, she might well swoon.

*   *   *

LATER, HE LAY AWAKE INTO THE EARLY HOURS, FRETFUL ABOUT what he must attempt, cursing that he could smell the scent of Johanna in his bedchamber. It was too long since he had had a woman and the only one his body had began to lust for could not bear his hand upon her.

If he succeeded in freeing her from the Florentine girdle, what then? Would he be able to stay in this bedchamber, knowing she lay above? Could he in all conscience take advantage of her, telling her it was for her own good when it was because he wanted her? He wanted to tangle his fingers in her hair and tease her body until she writhed and arched beneath him, begging him to enter. What had Stephen de Norwood called her? A house. This pretty dwelling was waiting for a caring hand and he would take possession.

He turned over with a groan, hating himself that his lusty desire should so dilute his honour, and if he prayed that God smite him a smashing blow on the skull and send him into oblivion, Heaven was not answering.

GERVASE EXPLAINED HIS PLAN CAREFULLY TO HIS NOBLE LADY NEXT morning. Short of invading Enderby and getting himself and others killed, there was no other solution.

Johanna, rebinding his shoulder, faltered and the bandage leapt from her fingers and unravelled half of its length across his bed. She had not expected the truth to be so hard.

"Dear Jesu," she whispered. "You would attempt this for me? I care not for myself, but if aught goes wrong they will hang you for murder."

"It is your choice, my lady. We are damned if we do, and damned if we lack the courage, but if we are agreed, it must be attempted this very day. Who knows when Fulk will demand the court examine you."

She grimaced and walked across to the window. He finished the binding awkwardly himself, allowing her time to think.

"Then let us do it," she declared, bringing the palms of her hands together. "I will make sure Agnes and my mother fulfil their parts."

"And bid them do no more than that, Johanna. This is like a

bridal bed, I want no audience for my performance, especially not
your mother. Now," his voice was brisk with an edge of sadness,
"I will set all in motion and meet you in the chapel. We must both
be in a state of grace, you understand?"

She nodded and gave him a curtsey before she quit his presence
as if he were her true lord.

"Pray hard," he commanded her grimly, when he joined her
later in the chapel. "We need all the help God can offer."

Kneeling beside her, like a bridegroom at the church door, he
watched the lozenges of sunlight delivered by the expensive windows quivering upon her face—a tough little lioness for all her
fragility—before he looked beseechingly at Christ hanging in
agony upon the Rood. *Help me, my most just Lord.* This would not
be Boroughbridge, but it would test his mental reserves to the uttermost. It would need a steady hand. He felt he could supply that,
providing Johanna had the courage to play her part. Dear God,
the thought of the ordeal made him sweat already, for if he killed
Johanna, Hell would not be hereafter, it would be every instant of
the rest of his brief life.

THEY WALKED INTO THE FORGE, HAND IN HAND—LIKE CHILDREN EN-
tering the darkness of a wood from which there might be no return. For Geraint, any smithy was familiar. He had spent too many
hours over the last years waiting for horses to be shod not to know
the implements which littered Bart's demesne—the swageblock,
the mandrels used for shaping hoops and rings, the fullers and
flatters of various sizes, the cold sett hammer and others of its ilk,
the various tongs, the iron lazy stand for trimming the hooves, the
chains, and the huge bellows. But for the lady at his side it was
another matter. He sensed her panic and squeezed her hand to
give her comfort.

In truth Johanna was a little unsteady on her feet. On Gervase's
bidding, she had drunk sufficient wine to put her at ease but now
the regular clanging of the hammer upon iron set her quaking. She
would have clapped her hands to her ears and fled had she not
been so desperate.

As a child, she had loathed the smithy, sensitive to the possible
pain of the coursers as the iron was hammered onto their hooves,

detesting the noise, the furnace, and the heavy stink of horse odour, sweltering skin and scorching metal.

The smokiness resurrected another unwelcome memory. Of the day Fulk and his physician had compelled her to kneel naked in a small chamber, her thighs straddling a trivet of smoking herbs. It was to tether her restless womb, the physician said, and cure her barrenness. They kept her there shamefully and immodestly for nigh on two hours, her elbows propped on joiners' stalls, the doctor replenishing the burning leaves so vigorously that the stench nearly suffocated her. Beyond a curtain, innocent of her suffering, the Enderby chaplain had read to her from the scriptures how Abraham's wife, Sarah, had eventually conceived. When Fulk had finally permitted the physician to release her, she had been feeble from exhaustion and witless from the vapours. Suffumigation, they had called it.

She must have reeled a little at the hideousness of the recall, for Gervase patted her arm, drawn through his, reassuringly. Dear God, what was she putting him through? Swiftly she set aside self-pity and saw in dismay the strain in his expression. Droplets already shone upon his brow and, with a tight smile, he let go of her and ran a finger along the inside of his shirt collar.

It was going to plan so far. Bart the smith was working alone. Gervase had already sent Jankyn to lure the man's apprentice away.

Bestowing upon the pair of them the disdainful glance of a menial who knows his professional value, the blacksmith set the hammer down and grabbed a rag from a hook on the wall. He mopped his face and naked breast before he was ready to inspect the broken bracelet that Johanna produced from the purse on her girdle.

As Gervase apprised the man of their trivial errand, Johanna watched the drops of sweat trickling down the blacksmith's brawny back into the fabric of the clout about his waist to save his hose and shuddered at the horror of labouring for hours on end at the mercy of the glowing furnace. After just a few hideous moments in this smoky heat, perspiration had sapped into the pads beneath her arms and was oozing down the small of her back. The moisture of her palm was replenished by the equal wetness of Gervase's but he still held her like a loving husband.

The hour bell sounded and Agnes appeared, wrinkling her nose as she set foot in the smoky interior. "My lady wants you this instant, Bart."

The smith looked fit to curse heartily at this second invasion of his time. Then he was caught in a servant's dilemma; if he hastened to Lady Constance, he might offend her son-in-law.

Gervase nonchalantly gave him leave. "Make speed to my lady. Ours is a trivial matter. Go, I will watch your fire."

"You can put horseshoes on my feet, sir," Johanna flounced her skirts coquettishly at her knight. Inside she was almost molten with fear.

"That is mighty kind, my lord." Bart pulled his forelock to him and thrust his massive arms swiftly into his worn leather jupon. They waited, as if counting to ten after the man left, before Jankyn stuck his head around the door. "Now?"

"*Now!*"

Agnes fastened the shutters and Jankyn disappeared to perform sentry duty.

"Out with you, Agnes. Stay within call." Gervase swiftly barred the door behind her, took an ugly spiked bolt from his purse and thrust it into the embers.

"I hope this holds," he muttered, turning to test the strength of the long poles bearing the smith's straw-stuffed mattress. With a wry face, he unclipped the leather flask upon his belt. Johanna took a deep draught from it as they had agreed. "Lie down." He gave the glowing wood a blast with the bellows to intensify the heat.

She obeyed him. To be submissively horizontal, belly up like a cowardly dog, was against her nature. It brought back the dread of watching Fulk descend upon her naked.

"I know it is not comfortable but I will be as swift as I can. And I have been thinking it would be sensible to tie your feet. If you flinch at the wrong moment . . ."

"I suppose so." He swiftly tied her ankles together and bound the leather thong securely around the poles.

"God ha' mercy!"

"I am going to tether your wrists beneath the bedframe."

Her alarm was a reflex she tried hard to fight. "I can hold on to the bedframe."

"It is safer this way," he answered tersely, taking her wrists. "You promised to trust me."

Her breathing grew short. "I-I cannot bear it—b-being tied."

"Johanna, have faith. There is not time for argument. Now, you will need to bite on something." He had a piece of thick leather ready. "Are you going to hinder me, lady?" he asked.

Unthinking, she parted her lips, "N—ohh!."

Gervase pushed the leather into her mouth. She railed curses against him in her head while her common sense fought to calm her. This is not Fulk. He is not going to rape me. A lesser man might have exulted at her helplessness, at the tears of fear and fury running down her face, but Gervase had other business. She watched him moving around methodically, heard the clink of the heating iron as he checked its colour and the blast of the bellows encouraging the fire before he came back to her again.

"You have the sheepskin in place?" The woollen pad was already tucked beneath the waistband of the chastity belt to protect her skin from the vicious heat. She nodded with a furious groan and he began to ease up her skirts. Sweet heaven, it was bad enough being unexpectedly tethered like a goat for dragon fodder, but it was the incongruous intimacy which now mortified her even though she knew that he must peel back her clothing.

With the estimation of a journeyman, Geraint wriggled his fingers beneath the belt's lock, testing the space between the metal band and the sheepskin that lay fleece side down over his lady's belly. Then he drew out a thin piece of wood a span wide and two spans long from the breast of his cote and inserted it beneath the steel. The fit was extremely tight, but it was needful to protect her belly and lowermost ribs.

"Not long," he whispered, stroking her face with his knuckles. "Perhaps I should have given you more fortified liquor, my darling dear."

Joanna groaned again as he leaned the frightening hammer against the palliasse's wooden supports, and shifted uncomfortably on the straw. "Remember, you will have to lie still when the time comes," he warned. "If you flinch, I could kill you." He glanced at the embers. "Almost there." Then he crouched down beside her. "I think it best that I blindfold you. If you move, you understand . . ."

She shook her head frantically but he already had a black cloth in his hand. With a calm smile that belied the urgency of his fingers, he tied it about her face.

Johanna heard him mutter a swift prayer to St. Eligius, the patron saint of locksmiths, and then the sound of pincers as he seized the spike—it must be white-hot now—and plunged it into the barrel of water. She heard the scream of the water and the hiss of steam.

"Brace yourself, Johanna. Breathe deeply."

Geraint positioned himself, his face straining with concentration to stop his left hand shaking as he pointed the burning red spike down into the hole of the lock.

"Hold your breath when I say 'now!' NOW!"

He brought the hammer down.

"SWEET CHRIST!" EXCLAIMED GERAINT, SHAKING FROM HEAD TO TOE as he cast the hammer aside and flung the bolt and pincers into the water. The lock had given. But had he killed her?

"*Johanna!*" He hurriedly tugged out the gag. Searching for a pulse of life in her neck with one hand, he pulled the charred wood and burnt wool away to estimate her injury. The fleece had saved her skin from burning.

Shaking her by the shoulder, he ran his right hand probingly across her belly, searching for protrusions beneath the flesh. Mercifully there seemed to be nothing unusual. With a prayer of relief, he hastily flung her skirts across the shattered mess of metal and rushing to the door, unbarred it.

"She's in a faint," he exclaimed, dragging Agnes swiftly to the bed. "Do something!" As Agnes slapped frantically at her lady's cheeks, he cut the bonds which held her and removed the blindfold.

"Try blowing into her mouth," suggested Jankyn from the door.

Gervase thrust Agnes aside and set his lips to Johanna's. He tasted the dryness of the leather upon her parched mouth as he took a deep breath and blew.

"Put the cloth over her nose or the breath will come out again," urged Jankyn, now at his elbow. "That's it. Keep going."

"I can feel her heart," cried Agnes, withdrawing her hand from beneath Johanna's kirtle.

Geraint stood up and put a hand to the wall to steady himself.

Relief seemed to leech all power from him. Did women feel so
after childbirth?

Jankyn, severing the remains of the leather trusses from the mattress and tossing them into the fire, eyed him with concern. "Master!" He pointed to the drawstring bag still tucked beneath
Geraint's belt. There were voices across the courtyard and the
jester hastened to the door.

Geraint rallied. He grabbed at the bag and threw it to Agnes.
"Hold this open!" Then he put his hands up Johanna's skirts, dragging the splintered metal girdle swiftly over her hips and down
her legs. Agnes held out the bag to receive it and drew the string
tight.

Johanna stirred and he gathered her up into his arms triumphantly.

"Easy, brave heart. Your mother is come."

Lady Constance paused on the threshold, blinking at the sudden
darkness. Agnes thrust the shutters open.

"My lady swooned with the heat," she explained, bobbing a
curtsey.

Johanna's mother stepped forward. "Gervase?" Her voice was
uneven, serrated by her fear.

"All is well, I think," he answered calmly. He must be smiling
foolishly but there was a simple joy in him that spread from the
knowing in his head down his entire being to touch the inside of
his soles. If he died tomorrow, God's judgment roll would have
one entry on the right side of his ledger.

Twenty-two

SLIDING HER ARMS AROUND THE BROAD SHOULDERS, Johanna snuggled into Gervase's chest. Inebriated by the relief and the strong wine, she did not know whether to laugh or weep, but she had never felt so safe in all her life and she wanted to hug that sensation close for all eternity. The shackle that Fulk had placed upon her was shattered and it was as if his evil sorcery was broken. Did the princess feel so after St. George had saved her from the dragon? Or did the devastating hero ride away to rescue more virgins and beat all other unsuspecting dragons into scaly pulp? She gave a gurgle of laughter and burrowed her face further into Gervase's clothing. For an instant she sensed him falter in his stride and then he readjusted his grip and hoisted her higher.

He did not mount to her chamber for the staircase was narrow and hazardous, but tipped her out onto his bed. She opened her eyes to find her mother and Agnes hovering anxiously.

Gervase had subsided onto a stool, his fingers to his temples. "God forbid I ever have to do anything like that ever again," he muttered as Jankyn pushed a winecup into his hands.

"Is all well then?" Lady Constance sank in a billow of skirts onto the bed and rocked her tearful daughter against her fur-edged bodice, but Johanna freed herself—it was not where she wanted to be.

As if sensing more than she understood, her mother rose complaining. "And you need not starve yourself any longer. Why did you not tell me sooner, you foolish girl?"

Johanna turned her face away into Gervase's pillow. "I thought I could manage."

Unperturbed at the subtle dismissal, her mother nodded. "Rest then. I know you have still some preparation for tomorrow. Gervase . . ." He stood up as she turned to face him. "Thank you for what you did." She kissed his cheek and then included the others in her smile. "If you can do as well with words tomorrow . . ."

"We will do our best," he murmured, walking with her to the door. "I think yon lady might be better for a sleep before we go over matters a final time."

"No, stay sir." Even though he looked exhausted, Johanna could not let him go with the others.

"Would you like me to help you up to your chamber?" Geraint asked huskily, no longer daring to look at her—the black hair enmeshing his pillow, her red lips parted, one pretty arm flung up behind her head in wanton innocence. It would be a triumph indeed to thieve what he should not.

"I should not take more, but I would like a drink please."

"Of course, what a churl I am. I should have—" How could his hand that held the burning spike tremble as he filled the beaker? Her availability tantalised him unbearably. He came across and held the wine out to her, watching her slowly stretch and turn to lean on her elbow. "I-Is there any discomfort?"

She ran a hand over her belly, unaware that she was arousing him further. "Sore," she whispered. "Oh, but it is like being liberated after a siege—the pleasure of eating again and knowing there is a tomorrow. Do not stand there so afraid, Gervase. I wager you are more embarrassed now than I."

"I am not embarrassed," he answered in a choked voice, turning away. He had known the temptation would come, but not so soon. But he would do nothing. It could take months to accustom her to a man's hand again and he had another life. "Johanna, no!"

Slim feminine arms girdled themselves around his waist, the whole sweet length of her was against his body.

"I wanted to say thank you. What you did today was the bravest thing I ever saw. And," she leaned her forehead against his spine, "I apologise for being so . . . so difficult. I did trust you deep down, believe me. It was when you tied me up, it was so much like . . ." Gervase nodded but made no move to turn or hold her. "Were you afraid?" She was trying to fill the air with words to keep him as if she feared he might vanish like vapour through her fingers.

"Yes." The word was a breath. He turned abruptly and caught her by the wrists, his thumbs against her palms.

"Do you understand what you are doing to me?" His face was a visor of self-restraint, his voice ragged. She hung within his grasp, her lips parting unhappily. The last thing she wanted now was to give him sorrow. "You are beautiful, you know that, Johanna? Seeing you lying there just now, I wanted you."

He must have seen the astonishment mingled with fear in her eyes for he let go of her and stared up miserably at the arras.

Johanna had thought that friendship with him was possible. "Oh, I wish that Hell would take me *now!*" she exclaimed, sitting down heavily upon his bed.

Courteous amazement replaced the anguish in his face. Glad that he could bear to look on her again, she flung her hands in the air. "Why does life have to be so . . . oh . . . so difficult? Where are you, Gervase?"

"What do you mean, where am I?" he asked bewildered.

"The man who is always trying to make me laugh. Is this the real you, the stranger I have never met, the man with the other name?" Tears sparkled on her lashes, veiling him from her. She paced to the door, not to leave but to hide her face from him.

"Johanna. We . . . we went through a great deal this morning. Forget what I said just now. It is a reaction, nothing more. You do not have to fear me. I would not harm you."

"Do you not think," said Johanna through clenched teeth, "that I would reward you if I could? Do you think I like being unwhole, different?"

"You are not different. I could heal you." Geraint had not meant to offer a false promise. Even were he to stay, it might be beyond him. He paced to the open embrasure, staring out at the thickening grey clouds, angry at his own weakness. Vanity or sinfulness? He was entangled in a mess of emotion, losing his common sense.

"Then . . . then try."

"What!" He whirled round to stare at her.

She was breathing wildly, her mind, raped and pillaged, desperate for order. She must be lunatic, she thought. Where had the words come from? But she had held him just now of her own volition. It was a beginning. And when he had carried her from the forge—dear Heaven, her body was warring with her mind.

The man before her, colossus-like, was gazing down at her in disbelief. "Goosehead, do you know what you are saying?"

"No," she muttered testily, sitting down heavily again. "I feel hysterical. Forget what I said. Maybe my brains were all safely locked up in that . . ." She could not go on, there were no words for her to describe the monstrosity that had bound her.

Glaring at him through her curling hair, she discovered him in as much a confusion as she was. "Well, I shall try." He drove his fist resolutely against his thigh.

"W-what?"

He sat down decisively beside her. It was not the wobble of the bedstead at his weight that set her insides trembling. "Aye, why not?"

"W-w-why not! Because you shall not." With him close to her, large, male and predatory, her old fear returned.

"Johanna, I have other names. Gervase de Laval is an illusion, but for a little space I shall be whatever you please. If I can restore you, you will thank me for it. After I leave Conisthorpe, you should be able to find someone to cherish you as you deserve. Think about this when you are calmer and then give me your answer."

She rested her chin glumly in her hands, her elbows on her knees. It was friendship she wanted; someone who could make her laugh again, not a creature clothed in steel mesh who ignored her by day only to enter her bed and pump his seed into her for a few grunting minutes by night. But was she in error—were all men the same? Did Gervase tease and laugh as he enjoyed a woman?

She studied his profile through her lashes. A golden-maned stallion of fable. Noble and brave? Or was he in truth a gorgeous, opportunist rascal? "Who *are* you?" Johanna pleaded again.

"No one very important, lady." Geraint reached out and set his large hand over hers reassuringly, "But I have ambitions and am not without friends." Even if most of them are manacled to walls.

"I knew it." Something in her fizzled into darkness like a sodden firecracker. "You need to marry an heiress to improve your fortunes." His lack of denial hurt. And I have no great estates, she thought. But why am I thinking like this? I can become an abbess in time. It is his companionship that I find valuable.

"It is the way of the world." The blue eyes were intense. He had covered the distance before she suspected. His right hand moulded the back of her head, preventing her drawing back from him, and his mouth came down on hers. Soft, insistent, playful, then he drew back from her.

"You did not fight me."

"Hmm, do you have a range of kisses or is that it?"

Geraint laughed, his white teeth grinning at her. "Johanna, you cat! I will make you purr, lady, I swear it."

"Purr?" she frowned, unable to manage this weather-cock, this man spinning as his words tossed, first reassuring then alarming her. And now, he was definitely smiling in a quite unprincipled manner. Whatever did a man do to make a woman purr—tickle her behind the ears or just stroke her gently?

She pinkened and rose, running a palm down her kirtle. "You certainly will not. I beg you as a knight—well, I mean, as if you were a true knight, to forget this conversation. We really should go across to Father Gilbert and make sure everyone's depositions will corroborate ours."

"Very well," he answered in a somewhat sulky tone as he got up. "But you will have to understand that the proximity I am forced into with you is going to be a strain."

"Nonsense," she said briskly. "You just need to pray for strength of spirit, that is all."

"My lady," he opened the door with a sigh. "Believe me, I wish it was so simple."

Twenty-three

GERAINT HEARD HER SCREAMING IN THE NIGHT AND flung himself up the moonlit stairs to find Agnes bending over the bed with a candlestick in her hand, crooning reassurance.

"A nightmare, sir. My lady dreams she is still at Enderby."

Johanna was sitting up, the fingers of her left hand clutched across her mouth. But it was her tousled dark ringlets wild upon her naked shoulders that caused Geraint agony. Seeing him, she clutched the bedsheet tightly to her bare breasts with virginal shyness, but the expression she offered him was too trusting for his peace of mind.

"I must have woken you, sir. Forgive me, it was knowing I have to answer that foul devil's libels again tomorrow."

Agnes set down the candle. "Oh sir, you return to your bed. I will settle my lady."

But the dark-haired witch who haunted his wakefulness was not prepared to be merciful. "No, do not go, sir," she pleaded, raising eyes that were devastatingly innocent. "Talk to me a little, anything that will take my mind off tomorrow. That is, if it pleases you."

It was dangerous letting him stay. Did she realise that? But the tiring wench was there to keep him sane—or was she? Agnes's smiles were becoming rather warm and she was dimpling at him now.

"I do think that might be a good idea, sir," the wench told him conspiratorially and, without waiting for an answer, she padded back to her palliasse.

Geraint shivered. Picking up one of Johanna's gowns, he draped it ridiculously in the style of a gorget over his hastily donned tunic and sat down on the clothing chest at a decorous distance. *Once upon a time*, he thought, *there was a man who could not take much more temptation.* He wriggled his toes and stared at them morosely. Which would send him back to bed first—the cold or his lust?

"So." He cleared his throat. "Would you like me to whistle a lullaby and set the dogs howling? Or I can tell you a scurrilous tale of the three tailor mice of Hinckley Ridge who lost their tails and whiskers."

"Heaven forbid!" Johanna spluttered. "But you did promise to tell me why King Edward has had Thomas of Lancaster beheaded."

"Now?" He gawked at her as if the moonlight had rendered her witless.

"Yes."

He sucked in his cheeks and gave her a resentful glare as if she had spoilt his mood. "Women!" With a groan, he pushed his hair back from his forehead and wondered where to begin.

"You could try it in epic verse," she pointed out dryly and received in retaliation a hot yet reproachful look that hinted he might have had other, lustier thoughts in mind.

"I will only give you the bare bones, nothing more." Huffily he rearranged her gown around his throat. "Before the old king, Edward Longshanks, died, he exiled his son's friend, Piers Gaveston. When Prince Edward inherited the crown, the first thing he did was summon Gaveston back and load him with titles and gifts. He made him Earl of Cornwall which is a title usually reserved for royal blood and that offended many of the prince's kinsmen, especially his cousin, Thomas of Lancaster. As king, young Edward began to rely very heavily on Gaveston's advice and forswore the counsel of the other lords, including Thomas. This infuriated them even more and after some years of civil strife several of the leading barons—"

"Warwick!"

"Yes," Gervase answered with a sigh, "he was one of them. Try not to interrupt, my lady. I am not exactly at my intellectual zenith at this hour in the morning. Where was I? Ah yes, as you know, the barons managed to capture Gaveston and execute him. Lancaster was one of those responsible and the king never forgave him."

"But there was peace for a little while?"

"Yes, some good came of it. The lords forced the king to accept certain ordinances for the well-being of the kingdom. He did so albeit with an ill grace. Then he found another favourite."

"Hugh Despenser the younger."

He frowned as if uneasy. "You have met him, my lady?"

"No, only his father, remember?" Johanna wriggled onto her side. "I am told Hugh has eyes like a cat."

"A cat!" Gervase's lip curled. "I suppose you might say that."

"Then you have seen him?" She leaned her chin upon her elbow. "Is he as devastatingly handsome as Gaveston was?"

"I never saw Gaveston. Hugh Despenser is of average height, has a small beard and—"

"How boring you make him sound. They say that all the Despensers are charming. They sit at table with you and smile in your face while their servants saw the legs off the bench you are sitting on."

His face tightened, close to anger. "Am I doing the telling or you? Just like Gaveston, Hugh"—again that flash of a sneer—"was brought up in the royal household as a companion to the prince. At first he belonged to the faction supporting Thomas of Lancaster but he sought to rise high in the king's favour together with his father, old Hugh, who was then well respected. Once Gaveston was dead, Hugh the younger seized the opportunity to make himself invaluable to King Edward."

"Ha! *In many ways!* The king had an unnatural affection for Gaveston, so I am told. Is it the same for Sir Hugh?"

Gervase stiffened his shoulders haughtily. "These matters should not be discussed."

Oh, he was touchy tonight. She supposed he despised the younger Despenser for pleasuring the king. Was Hugh an affront to the brotherhood of knights or did Gervase seek to hide some personal grievance? "Why are you of a sudden so pompous, sir? Everyone says the king is a sodomite."

"But it is not *wise* to say so."

"But to you."

"Not even to me! I am going to bed."

"What of his wife? Give me the distaff details before you retire in a sulk or I might just have a nightmare in an hour's time and wake you up again."

"I am not in a sulk." Gervase scowled at her as she folded her hands in demure supplication. "I shall catch an ague and be too sick to appear at the hearing."

"Ha! Tell me about Despenser's wife."

"Nell—Eleanor de Clare is the Earl of Gloucester's sister. When Gilbert de Clare died at the battle of Bannockburn, his demesne was divided between his three sisters. Hugh Despenser was already married to Eleanor, the eldest, so he did very well."

"Gaveston's widow was also one of the sisters, was she not?" Johanna chirped, but her storyteller had gone pensive again. "I have heard that Hugh Despenser's father is as greedy and ruthless as his . . . Sir?"

Gervase, deep in his own thoughts, raised his head and returned reluctantly to his story, ignoring her question. "What many people do not realise is that there is a bloody feud between the Despensers and the house of Mortimer over the slaying of the Despensers' grandsire. It continues still."

"Is that why the Mortimers do not like to see the Despensers grown so thick with the king?"

"Aye, and over manors too. Hugh the younger was set on acquiring more holdings in the Welsh Marches, and so he soon came into enmity not only with the Earl of Hereford and the Mortimers, who are—were—great in those parts, but also most of the other Marcher lords. Together these lords forced the king to send Hugh and his father into exile, saying they estranged King Edward from his people and usurped his powers. Early this year, however, the king managed to arrest Sir Roger Mortimer and has him in the Tower of London—alive still, I hope." He sighed morosely, staring unseeing at the wall above her head. "That is why he was not at Boroughbridge."

"Mortimer. He is supposed to be a demi-god to look upon." She critically studied him sitting there bare-legged, comparing him with her imagination of the handsome Roger.

"I suppose so," muttered Gervase, "if you like hair the colour of earwax and eyes that cannot stop roving."

"Earwax! Such a marvellously envious description. I cannot wait to meet him." She hurtled a provocative smile at him and watched her storyteller squirm as if he had given away some secret. She must stop teasing him, but tonight it was so easy.

"I jest," he muttered as if it was her fault she had mistaken him. "Mortimer is a worthy and valiant man. Do not keep interrupting!

"Anyway, after his arrest the king routed the Marcher lords and Thomas of Lancaster down at the Trent, and harried them north. Earl Thomas was trying to escape to his castle at Dunstanburgh in Northumberland. The rest you have heard already—the king's officers managed to block the Great North Road at Boroughbridge. And now Lancaster has been beheaded."

"Sir Ralph reckoned Lancaster was trying to make a pact with the Scots." She shifted, leaning once more upon her elbow, the sheet straining somewhat over one breast.

"Yes, and there was truth in that," he answered rapidly, studying his feet again. "He had been having some truck with them for a while, and to my way of thinking it was not honourable. Now," he slapped the chest he was sitting on angrily, "he is suddenly a martyr and a saint to the common people. Did your mother not tell us yesterday there is some talk of miracles occurring at his tomb at Pomfret? Observe that there were no wondrous cures claimed at Gaveston's tomb. Mind, the king did have him privily buried at Langley where he might mourn him without the world gaping." Gervase seemed to be babbling like a flooded beck, but his glance kept sliding sideways to her. "No, Lancaster was no saint, definitely not, although Jankyn would have it otherwise. Why, Thomas's wife ran off with an esquire, for Heaven's sake."

"Perhaps he was being too holy for her taste," interrupted Johanna.

Her supposed husband looked surprised at such a worldly remark. "Too holy! What, inadequate for her purpose?" His cheeks reddened unbelievably. "No, not him." He redirected the conversation. "If you want my opinion, I would say Thomas coveted the crown."

"And yet you fought for him." *Did Gervase want to lie with her?* she wondered. After all, he had been trying not to look at her.

"No, my lady, I was there in the service of another lord whose name I do not propose to tell you, so do not pry further."

Smiling to herself, she lay back on the pillow and gazed enigmatically at the arched ceiling. "So both the Despensers are back from exile."

Gervase rose and paced like a schoolmaster. "The king is not of the same ilk as his father. He dislikes the cares of kingship. He had much rather ride with the hunt, or indulge himself with rowing upon the river or gossiping with common workmen. Hugh Despenser the younger, for all his many faults, is very capable. That is why he is—pardon the humour—indispensable. He is content to handle the day-to-day running of the kingdom while the king frolics."

"So we are back to Hugh. If he is capable, Gervase, why will the lords not be content for him to help King Edward?"

"My lady, the king is the type of man who bestows all his attention on one favourite at a time to the exclusion of all other lords. He did it with Piers Gaveston and he is doing it with Hugh. The other lords resent it. Instead of consulting a council and sharing the duties out or carrying some responsibility himself, the king lets everything fall on Hugh's shoulders."

She turned again. This time most of her back was bared and she plucked the sheet up to keep her warm.

Gervase glared at her. "My feet are freezing, my lady, have I your permission to retire?"

Well, thought Johanna mischievously. *This has been your punishment for running away last week.* She was feeling merciless and unaccountably skittish, as if she wanted to test this man to his limits.

"What has suddenly stung you?" She lowered her voice huskily, watching him unwind the kirtle from his neck. Wriggling down, she nestled her head into her pillow. "You belong to it, that world of factions and patronage but it seems to me very hazardous. I suppose if you were to find service with the Despensers, you might rise very swiftly."

His lips twisted derisively at the notion, and the innocent innuendo. Rise! Tormented by her lying there, he bit back the unlicensed comment that came readily to his lips and instead answered politically. "I might." What ailed the woman? Was she teasing him, keeping him talking in her bedchamber, or was this done out of innocence? If freeing her from the chastity belt had loosened her morals, how far dare he push his luck? Best leave her now.

"You put your wager on the wrong cock, did you not?"

Her vocabulary, innocuously uttered, was unfortunate.

"Yes, Johanna," he answered wearily. "Now be quiet or I will kiss you goodnight," and headed for the sanity of the stairs.

"Perhaps you should."

He swung round abruptly. She had extended a white arm, the wrist angled for his courtesy, her eyes feline in the candlelight. The air was silent between them; Geraint was aware that Agnes's breathing had grown rhythmic.

"You have been playing me like a fish, madam," he declared softly, his tone as chilled as the whitewashed wall at his back. "Well, I have spines and teeth."

"Spines and teeth and talk," she countered haughtily.

He stepped forward. "I am in your pay. What service may I do for you?" If his voice sounded brutal, it was because he felt used.

"I do not know," Johanna whispered, seeming to ignore his callousness as if she could not take his feelings seriously. "Please do not be difficult. I . . . have a question. I-I want to know so I can make up my mind whether I should take holy vows. *Is* it possible for a woman to enjoy the act of procreation?"

"The Devil take you, Johanna!" He buried his face in his hands with a groan and sat down heavily on the bed beside her. "I am not going to procreate with you to . . . to order. My feet are freezing, you have kept me here lullabying you about Hugh Despenser for quite false reasons, and what is more you have been deliberately flaunting your nakedness."

He raised his head to glare at her for her silence, only to find she was studying him in amazement, her eyes wide and candid. "But I have not done a thing. I was listening to every word you said."

"Yes, and you even managed one intelligent question, but you were undeniably flaunting yourself before me." He knew he should return to his room, but he could not move. Her lips were parted, moist. Her breasts were within a stretch and curl of his fingers.

"Am I doing it now?"

"What?"

"This . . . this flaunting."

"Yes!"

"But I am not doing anything."

"God ha' mercy, woman, you do not need to. You only have to lie there in bed without anything on."

"Oh."

"However . . ." he refused to look at her, clasping his hands in front of him, his knuckles white. "However, the fact that you are doing so and that you have just asked me to kiss your hand rather implies that you are experiencing what is commonplace in such circumstances."

"I am?"

"Yes, you are interested."

"In what?"

"The fact that I am sitting here in your bedchamber with no breechclout. Your act of encouraging me to be here definitely shows that you are healing."

Plucking at a glinting loose thread in the crimson coverlet, Johanna murmured, "You still haven't answered my question."

She turned upon her elbows and he could not help staring his fill at the shadowy valley between her breasts. "How can you be so sure whether a woman is enjoying whatever you do to her?"

Heaven put him out of his misery! Which saint should he pray to? St. Valentine or St. Cuthbert?

"She makes a noise."

"Your pardon?" She jerked her head round at him, her hair brushing his arm. "A *noise*? That is all? What sort of noise?"

"A groany-gaspy sort of—yes, a gasp, a sigh of pleasure." He drew his shoulders back with vanity as St. Valentine and St. Cuthbert answered his prayer simultaneously. "I could actually prove it to you without the . . . the act of procreation taking place. That is, if you are not too chafed and sore."

Johanna held his gaze, wondering how much she might trust him. Dear God, if he could prove to her that there was kindness! "Could you? What, now?"

He nodded proudly, without a smile. If this would save her from the cloister, mend her and render her marriageable again for a better man than him, what harm was there, providing he could keep himself in control. Easy, Geraint told himself. Do not show enthusiasm. Step on a creaking stair and she will arm herself again.

"Prove it!"

"*Johanna.*"

"Yes, now, without carnal knowledge or whatever."

"But it would be sinful."

"Gervase." She caught his hand within her slender fingers. "I want to know. Please, as a friend . . ."

He looked as if he was having pain in swallowing. "Very well," he answered gruffly, glancing at Agnes's back. Loosening the bed coverings, he slid in beside her.

"She is asleep. Pull the bed curtain. What do you do first?"

"I am not teaching swordplay. You cannot do it by instructions. It is more subtle than that." He pushed her down. "I have to kiss you first."

"But we have tried that and it does not work."

"Johanna, do you think you could just lie there, keep silent and leave it to me?"

"But we should discu—"

His mouth came down on hers, stifling further conversation and he eased himself into lying full length beside her, resting on his left elbow. It was not ideal but what was the twingeing of a wound compared with restoring a lady?

Johanna supposed she might get used to it. It was remarkable the emotions a man could put into kissing. Gervase's mouth upon hers was tender yet forceful, demanding yet generous. Her lips parted beneath his and he eventually laughed and raised his head. Then he kissed her neck and throat, brushing his lips over her skin as he slid down to her shoulders. It was an interesting sensation.

"Do you want me to snuff out the candle?" His voice was like the newly invented velvet, rich, silky and deep.

"Please," she whispered.

His lips came back down on her.

"Ohhhh!"

"What is it?"

"I—your hand is like ice."

"Warm it for me. Breathe on it." He held his palm to her lips. She complied. His mouth curled in a smile. He bent his face to hers again, his lips urging hers to part for him while his hand had moved to touch the tip of her right breast. He did not grab like Fulk had done. This man's touch was gentle, tantalising, teasing.

Johanna began to feel the magic. Sensations swirled within the casing of her hips. She was trying to fathom how it was possible that by caressing her nipple to a peak, he could unleash a sense of softness between her thighs. Then she gave up the labour of thought and surrendered to the feelings flowing through her.

"That is wondrous," she murmured.

"You like it? Welcome news. We may progress further."

He stroked a finger down over her belly and drew battle plans across her skin; sorties and forays took place.

"Hmmm." She would have purred, had she been a cat. "I shall go to sleep if you do that much longer." His fingers tormented her breast again and she wriggled.

"This next part is important. It could take a while but you will enjoy it, I promise. Lie still." His fingers slid over the nest of hair between her legs. She tensed. He stroked the hair, soothing her and then slid his whole hand between her legs to palm her. Surprisingly the feeling that he was setting a hand of ownership upon her stirred her pleasurably and Johanna, who had sworn never to let a man's hand near her thighs again, was astonished at her own reaction. Then he parted her and began to gently caress her.

She tightened her defences instantly against him.

"No, you are becoming too intimate," she protested, pulling at his wrist to stay him.

The remark was somewhat late but he complied. "Then you will never know. It is your decision."

"Very well, a little longer then."

"Just try to feel drowsy and unafraid. All I shall do is touch you with my fingers, softly, caressingly. There is no danger, nothing to fear. Close your eyes and feel the tiny waves of pleasure begin to grow."

Gervase's experience was evident. Taking her own hand, he placed it where he had been touching her. "Feel that you are wet and slick with moisture."

"This is so strange. Why is it so?"

"Your body is lighting beacons and balefires." He set his mouth upon hers again while his sensual fingers stirred her further.

"That Master Vogelweide," she whispered against his lips.

"Hmmm?"

"I suppose he was a journeyman in the art of love."

"I doubt it."

"Ohhh!"

"There, eh?" He bent his head to her breast and teased her nipple with his tongue while his finger laboured vigorously further down. Fulk had tried licking her breast and it had left her feeling nauseous, but this man . . . she buried her fingers in the long golden hair and he laughed. Her body grew hot and she wanted to arch towards him, gasping as his fingers played between her thighs relentlessly.

"I want . . ." she gasped.

"What do you want?"

"*You!*" A further wave of heat rushed through her and a second wave, indescribable, drove her up onto a nameless shore and she subsided, gasping.

The man kissed her on the forehead and stood up. "Good night, Johanna." His own loins were on fire. Outside her door, he leaned his forehead against the cold stone, his breath uneven.

"Ho," chortled Jankyn some minutes later as Geraint tripped over a boot and cursed ribaldly before he reached his chilly bed.

"Not exactly *ho*, Jankyn. My lady wanted a bedtime story about Hugh Despenser."

"How he fell in love with a beautiful prince?" The jester's tone was a sigh. "Who are you, Gervase?"

For answer the chamber blew into darkness. It was his secret.

Twenty-four

IF CATS HAD SOULS, MIGHT A WILD MOUSER WHO HAD feasted on a stolen bowl of cream remember that delicious taste next morning? Johanna tried hard to recall exactly how the magical sensation had felt, but mere words were useless. The enchantment had been fleeting but proof that she was not broken beyond repair.

And now here was her bowl of cream, large and available, standing behind her at the hearing next day. But bowls of cream lacked souls. This soul was looking decidedly pleased with himself—a stallion that had found his way into the next field.

"How fare you?" He bent his head and in full gaze of Fulk kissed her on the neck. She turned and caught his hand, bringing it to her cheek, and saw Fulk's lizard visage metamorphose to ugly red. He looked primed to charge across the nave and smash his mailed fist into her face. With a prayer to Our Lady, Johanna crossed her fingers guiltily within the folds of her skirts. No, she was not out of the wood into safe pasture yet. It was needful to be vigilant and in a state of grace; last night she had behaved as badly as any recalcitrant sinner.

Fewer people were gathered in the church this second day. The hearing's notoriety had dimmed—after all, there were goods to be sold and crops to be tended. Even Fulk's men were more subdued. Yawns and the creak and rasp of armoured limbs frequently rearranging themselves showed they were bored and disgruntled. Only Edgar de Laverton, who was ogling Johanna unashamedly from behind his lord's back, showed any enthusiasm for being there.

Called to answer the libels, Johanna presented her answer through the proctor. A little of her old courage returning, she had been tempted to make an oral answer as well as present the written counter-libel, but her mother and the proctor had advised her against it; she was a lady. It was sufficiently damaging to her honour having her affairs aired in the common hearing—better to play the meek sheep than the assertive shrew.

The rumble of comment after she sat down dismayed her. Opinion rarely sided with an abused wife. Few women in unhappy marriages had the generous spirit to applaud another regaining her freedom; if they suffered, why should not she!

"Yon hoary scoundrel is going to trundle a whole arsenal of weapons against us," muttered Gervase, leaning forward and breaking into her wretched fears. "Look to Agnes, mesdames. Watkyn was offered a very fat purse yesterday."

"Pah, Agnes is as loyal as a flea on a healthy dog," whispered her mother. "No, Gervase, what I am waiting to discover is which venal wretches that whoreson has bribed for tomorrow. You mark my words, there will be a half-dozen eager to swear that Father Benedict was elsewhere on the day he made you handfast."

"My life on it," agreed Gervase softly, "and if he can prove me a rascal, he will. I could still hang."

"Then it is as well you are now much loved in this town. It is not forgotten what you did for the weavers and the fisherfolk. I saw the judge note the cheers from the townspeople when you entered the court on Monday."

JOHANNA AND GERVASE SPENT THE AFTERNOON IN A MOCK QUES-tioning of Jankyn and Agnes. Had it been merely a game, it would have been amusing, but after supper Aidan found Johanna's pig refusing to touch his trough and several rats lying dead close by. The obvious evidence of hellebore poison sent them to their beds early, stunned and unhappy.

The third day, the celebration of the Conversion of St. Mary Magdalene but also the Feast of Fools, began with the naming of witnesses: her mother, Agnes and Watkyn on Gervase's behalf; and Edyth, Father Gilbert and several others were named by Fulk as witnesses to her real marriage. Johanna idly noticed with relief that Edgar was absent and that there were fewer of Fulk's retainers present. What she was not expecting was the judge announcing that the examiner would take her deposition at the castle after dinner that afternoon.

"Oh, God protect me, Gervase. My wits are so addled."

"Courage, Johanna, you will manage. Just remember the chicken blood."

The examiner, Martin de Scruton, was waiting for her in Conisthorpe's great chamber, dark-robed and wearing the grave face that was the stamp of his profession. This man did not torture people, she reminded herself; this was a church court that derived its bread and butter mostly from small issues. As she entered, he rose from behind the small linened board set up for his convenience, and indicated the stool before it.

At the end of the table, the notary, his balding head bonneted, his sheaf of quills sharpened, rubbed at the outside of his nose, watching her unsmiling. The huge calloused side of his third finger threatened to snare her attention but she forced herself to chastely lower her gaze, sensing the man's gritty eyes feeding on her body as if he was hoping shortly for some salacious tidbits to enliven his routine.

In the long, inscrutable face of her interrogator, however, was frozen the cold asceticism of years of celibacy. "Put your hand on the Holy Gospels, my lady, and swear to tell the truth."

She set her palm flat upon the embossed cover and repeated the oath after him. The leather felt comfortable against her fingers. God was not angry with her yet. Well, Heavenly Lord, she told Him inwardly, it will be as close to the truth as I possibly dare.

Stephen of Norwood's skilfully worded articles were known to her so she had her answers ready, but eventually they arrived at Fulk's advocate's questions and these were a different matter.

"Would you say you were an obedient wife to Sir Fulk?"

"No, sir, he expected me to obey his orders precisely. I could never please him."

"But were you not wilful?"

"I suppose I defended myself for my shortcomings. He beat me daily."

"For being a poor housewife?"

"No, for not bearing him a son."

"You were not free with your favours to him?"

"It is true that I found the act of procreation unpleasant. Despite his efforts, I remained barren. That was why he beat me—every day."

"Was he sober when he beat you?"

"Always."

"Men are allowed to correct their wives. The law allows it."

"Where it is deserved."

"Did you use a sponge soaked in vinegar, or take any potions that would prevent conception?"

"No, sir."

"Did you wish to bear him a child?"

She hesitated. "If it would stop the beatings, yes." She was tempted to add that she abided by God's will, but it may have been seen as presumptuous.

"Would you say you did your uttermost to disobey his commands?"

"No, sir. He delighted in humiliating me in our bedchamber. Last time he hit me, I could not see properly out of my left eye for a week. There were plenty of witnesses."

"Is Gervase de Laval your lover?"

"He is my lawful husband, but after he had consummated our marriage I never saw him until last week when he came to Conisthorpe and claimed me."

"What was he doing during his absence?"

"That is for him to tell you, sir. To speak otherwise would be hearsay."

The examiner took a heavy breath as if he considered it too cunning an answer, but made no comment.

"Did you have carnal knowledge with any man before your marriage with Sir Fulk was consummated? You are under oath, remember."

"Only with my lawful husband, Gervase, on the day Father Benedict wed us."

"Surely it occurred to you that Sir Fulk would be angered to find you already spoiled?"

"Yes. I had a phial of chicken blood. I deceived him." She felt like adding wryly that Fulk had neglected to take the necessary

precaution of passing her through St. Wilfred's Needle at Ripon—
the hole in the wall that was reputed to trap the deflowered. "I . . .
I was also advised by a wise woman of a recipe mentioned in one
of the treatises of Trotula that would constrict the passage to my
womb, but I did not take any potion because I had only experienced carnal knowledge once and that had been at the handfasting
with Sir Gervase at least a year before. Indeed, sir, I was very naive
in such matters."

"It did not occur to you to be honest with Sir Fulk?"

"I was frightened of him."

"Sir Fulk has deposed under oath that he found you *intacta* and
that the blood on the bedsheet was yours."

"No."

"What bothers me, my lady, is that if you lied to Sir Fulk, you
are quite capable of lying to this court."

"If I deceived him then, it was to save my life and on my
mother's advice. I pray you ask her. I believe Sir Fulk would have
whipped me almost to death had he suspected."

"But surely when the banns were called, you had leisure to fur-
nish proof to your father that there were reasons for not proceeding with the marriage?"

"Sir, first, I had had no word from Sir Gervase since he departed
following our marriage. Second, not wanting to dishonour my
family's name with scandal, I made my protest to my father privily, saying I was wed and could not lawfully be plighted to Sir
Fulk, but my father scoffed. He chastised me saying that Sir Gervase had made a whore of me. I protested, arguing that Father
Benedict and I had agreed to the handfasting in good faith. 'The
priest is dead,' replied my father, 'and this Gervase has sent you
no further word and must be a false fellow, and as far as I am
concerned, you will obey me.' He had me locked up, beaten with
the rod and fed me naught but dry trenchers and water until I
submitted."

"You are living with Sir Gervase as his wife in all senses of the
word?"

"I understand your meaning, sir. Yes, Sir Gervase has . . .
has . . ."

". . . had carnal knowledge of you."

She nodded, her fingers twisting upon her lap.

"Sir Fulk alleges that this is not possible. He states that he locked you into a device that would prevent any wanton behaviour while you were away from him. Is this true?"

"Yes."

"Then how can you be a true wife to Sir Gervase?"

"Sir Gervase broke the lock, sir."

The notary's pen spluttered, sending a line of blots, like a skimmed stone, across the parchment. His interest overt, the examiner leaned forwards across the board, hands clasped, his smile of manly authority patronising and sceptical.

"And how did he do that?" His eyes slid sideways at the notary, sharing the jest.

"My lord inserted a burning hot spike into the lock and smote it with a hammer." She watched Martin de Scruton's jaw slacken. Even the notary had set down the goose quill and was staring at her as if she had sprouted fairy wings. "I do not wish this to be read out in court," she added softly, pressing her advantage. "It has been a humiliation that I wish to be kept private."

Like deep water, the examiner's expression gave no indication of the thoughts that swam beneath until he continued, "How often were you placed in this device?"

"Every time Sir Fulk was absent from Enderby."

"Does that not imply he considered you untrustworthy and of a lascivious character?"

"Sir, at Enderby I was right glad of the device, as God is my witness. When Sir Fulk was away, I was always afeared. There were many knights and men-at-arms there whose looks made me uncomfortable."

"Sir Fulk knew this?"

"He understood his men. He rationed their ale when he was present, but sometimes in his absence they took advantage of the steward."

"I congratulate you for arguing most cunningly in your defence on this matter, my lady, but the veracity of Sir Fulk's allegation must still be determined. He requires you to be thoroughly examined. Let it be done presently." Without waiting for her answer, he loudly rang the small handbell set before him.

Horrified, Johanna rose to her feet.

"I protest! This is not necessary. *Sir Fulk requires!*" she sneered.

"What does the judge require? I presume he is in charge of this hearing. No, do not write that down!" she snapped at the scribe, slamming the board with the flat of her hand, making his quill leap.

Martin de Scruton stood up to stare her down. "Calm yourself, my lady! Let me clarify this, namely, the plaintiff's advocate requires you be physically examined."

"Do you want to look for scars of beatings too?"

Not a merciful muscle moved in the face opposite her. "No, that will not be required," he responded dispassionately.

I wager it will not, thought Johanna furiously and nearly said so.

It was the mayor's wife, Adela Mercer, who entered white-faced, clearly as reluctant as Johanna to take part in this ordeal—a small, ancient lady of impeccable grace. She was accompanied by the wife of one of the aldermen, Margery Fuller, and Lady Constance.

The examiner rose and inclined his head in greeting to the ladies before addressing Johanna again. "I think all that is necessary is that you draw your kirtle up over one hip, my lady."

"Then you must turn your backs," she replied icily.

His answering smile was tight. "No, it is understood that we shall leave the room." The condescending tone underscored the masculine reproof, implying that her improper conclusion that he and the notary would remain reeked of lewdness and ill-breeding.

The alderman's wife tumbled into a lavish curtsey.

"Oh, my lady, so distressing. We are most aggrieved that we must put you to this shameful ordeal, are we not, Mistress Mercer?" The older woman, fragile as a tiny treecreeper, nodded with more refinement.

"It is no fault of yours, Mistress Fuller." Lady Constance swept between them. "You can see my daughter has been under much strain so let us have this done without any fuss and bother." She retired to the side of the chamber with the grandeur of a tournament marshal.

Sighing, Johanna steadied her weight on her left foot and, bending, grasped the hem of her kirtle through the thickness of the blue surcote. Raising her right heel, she gracefully drew the fabric up her side to thigh height, exposing her stockinged leg with its simple garter. The chafing of the Florentine girdle was still evident at the top of her leg.

Adela Mercer peered forward myopically. "I think it had better be to your waist, my lady." Her aged voice was laced with apology.

Johanna was seething at the indignity, but with outward patience hoicked her clothing the necessary distance, keeping her gender modestly covered. "To my underarm, Mistress Mercer, if it be required."

"Enough, my lady."

"Thank you, good dames." Letting drop her skirts, Johanna reached across and rang the bell fiercely.

The examiner strode back in with the notary scurrying ratlike after him, and frowning, surveyed the women expectantly.

Mistress Fuller moistened her lips and walked across to the table, positioning her fingers carefully upon the cover of the Holy Book. "My lady wears no garments beneath her skirts save her stockings and garters."

Adela, her fingers stiffened and twisted cruelly by time, did likewise and added a codicil: "There is no truth in the allegation that Lady Johanna FitzHenry is restricted carnally by any device, but there is evidence of marking on my lady's flesh to show that such a garment may have been worn recently."

Martin de Scruton nodded and raised his brow at Lady Constance. "My lady, will you affirm that this examination has been made with diligence and without prejudice?" He received a silent nod. "Then the court thanks you, good women, and will declare your findings at the hearing." He opened the door for them and jerked his head at Johanna to resume her seat. So there was to be more interrogation.

Pedestrian, outwardly innocuous questions came at her now: What had Gervase been wearing at their trothplight? Had he any distinguishing marks on his body that might be known only to her? Thanking a miscellany of saints that she had dressed his wounds, she was able to blush and answer competently.

Martin de Scruton moved on to dig further holes and set a half-score of traps before he finally dismissed her, fatigued and confused as to whether she had outwitted him. If she had found it hard, how would poor Agnes fare?

Leaving the two men to the wafers and ale which her mother sent in when the interrogation finished, Johanna summoned Agnes, anxious to quickly advise her of what to expect. But as the servants returned one by one alone, having briefly searched keep, kitchens, gardens, new hall and each of the towers, Johanna realised with sinking heart that Agnes was unaccountably missing.

Her mother swiftly substituted Father Gilbert to placate the examiner's growing curiosity and to attest to Johanna's character and piety, while outside a muffled version of hue and cry ensued.

Geraint, interrupted in a session of putting the garrison through combat practice, carried out his own meticulous search within the castle precinct although he guessed the futile outcome. Fulk had seized their chiefwitness. The cruel killing of Johanna's lapdog, the attempt to poison her pet pig, and now Agnes's likely abduction, let alone the bruises he himself carried from the beating by Fulk's men, had Geraint mouthing obscenities beneath his breath as he scoured the keep. He was burning to run the whoreson through, but that would send him to the gallows for sure.

"Oh Gervase, this is a terrible business," Lady Constance called to him. She was in the gateway of the barbican giving orders to an extremely flustered Sir Geoffrey. It was needful to discreetly search the town, but finding the girl was as likely as persuading Hugh Despenser to give away one of his fifty-nine manors. "But at least that dreadful Martin has left for today, thank God," she continued, tucking her arm into his as they walked back to the hall, "else we should have had to send you in next and that would be unfortunate if Johanna has had no time to tell you what she was asked."

"So how fares she? Is she distraught?" He moderated his pace to Lady Constance's slower step.

"Dyeing," answered Lady Constance, "it is a wonder she did not do it when Cob died—" and realised she had left him behind her stock still. Observing he had changed colour, she added hastily, "No, next to the kitchens," as if that explained everything.

He found Johanna in an old surcote that had been used for the task before, judging by a mess of colourful drips and splashes that Joseph of Egypt's brothers might have envied, furiously poking a wooden pole into a breast-high tub of water. The tippets of her ancient sleeves were tied in a loose knot behind her back and a heathenish cloth swathed her head. Tiny droplets of moisture clung to the coils of hair that were straggling across her damp, reddened cheeks.

One shirted manservant, sweaty and scarlet, was standing by to work the bellows which kept the fire below the vat healthily glowing, while a second man waited alert beside her, armed with a large flagon of water. A shallow, cloth-lined pannier, hedgehogged full of rusty nails, and two earthenware pots of whitish powder, presumably precious alum of Yemen and common salt, flanked her heels.

Since she was wearing an expression of martyred housewifely zeal and was clearly engaged in a furious effort to banish thinking, Geraint wisely said nothing and sauntered in. Deliberating how best to manage Johanna, he idly reached out and unstoppered one of the jars standing to attention on a shelf. It proved to be mature urine and he set it back and turned to frown at his lady through the steam, wondering if this excessive industry was doing either of them much good.

If she wanted distraction, he would concur. "Not a very ladylike occupation, madam wife. Do you always see to this personally?"

Johanna drove the pole into the skeins with vicious hands.

"The colour must be precisely to my liking. More water, Dickon!"

He waited as she supervised the specific amount and then issued his own orders, towering menacingly above them all. "Leave us. I wish to speak to my lady privily. Unless," he relented, gesturing to the evil red brew bubbling between them, "the moment is critical."

Glaring at each other through the vapour, they could be taken for a couple of frustrated alchemists trying to make gold.

Johanna gave his request some consideration, and then felinely pawing an itch on the tip of her nose with the back of her hand, she answered doubtfully, "Only if you are willing to hoist an occasional pail instead, sir."

"Over you, my lady?" It was spoken with a wry kindness that the menservants found amusing as they withdrew. His so-called wife viewed him with a baleful twist of her lips, and he wondered if left to marinate in this chymical marvel she would turn cherry red or onion hued.

"Has anyone found her?" Her dispirited tone smacked of defeat.

"There is no news," he announced. He could see that she had been weeping—and what better place? The servants might think the vapours affected her. "I am sorry that you carry this added suffering."

"If Agnes was taken in the castle, someone might have . . ." Her lip trembled.

"I lowered a man into both wells, aye, and had the earthworks and ditches 'twixt the town walls and our curtain walls perused. My money is on Edgar. I'll hazard it was as we left the church this morning."

"You would have thought that someone would have noticed. Oh, now do not look disapprovingly at me like that. She is pure gold. She would not leave me now."

"No lover at Enderby to lure her back?"

"No! It is over, is it not?" she exclaimed, biting her lip and wielding the pole with both hands to move the fabric round. "Upon my life, if that whoreson allows a hair of Agnes's head to be harmed, I will poison him, I swear I will. Has the town been thoroughly combed?"

"Aye," Geraint answered wearily, "so thoroughly even the lice have been interrogated. I have asked your mother to inform the archdeacon's court that our main witness has been abducted."

"Much good that will do. Even if William de Bedford believes us, we cannot prove that Fulk is responsible. God rot him, he will try every filthy trick he can think of. I would swear he is dining with the judge at this very moment and trying to bribe him." She mopped her forehead with her sleeve then drew breath as if she was about to deliver a proclamation. "Gervase, I cannot expect you to stay here any longer. For one thing it would be asking too much and for another I do not wish to put your life in jeopardy." She blinked hard as if her tears were close to flowing again.

His smile was wistful as he scolded, "You cannot show a white tailfeather now, my fighting bird. Will you kick off your spurs after coming this far? What of that vow of yours never to return to Fulk?"

For a moment, she stared at the wall above his head before she regained control and replied with an excess of briskness. "There was always a contingency line of action." She ran her tongue nervously along her lips. "I must tell you it is settled that Mother will give me an armed escort down to Shaftesbury Abbey. I will leave at first light. Father Gilbert can accompany me, if he wishes." She was eyeing him warily. Did she think he would ignite of a sudden? Well, he might! "Come with us, please you," she added swiftly, "I should be glad of your sword arm."

The secrecy and dismissal hurt, but it was her decision to seek the cloister that displeased him most. Or was she to be coerced into taking the veil? "Shaftesbury! Godsakes, lady, that is in . . . in Dorset. It will take days, and you are too sore for hard riding yet. Shaftesbury, why?"

"Mother knows the abbess so I am sure they will take me in until somewhere permanent is found for me . . . and it makes sense, sir. It is an extremely wealthy abbey so they will not be cowed by Fulk's threats."

His sorrowful little witch looked as though she was about to cry into the great cauldron. "It-it seems to be the only solution. But if you will not escort me, then I think you and Jankyn should leave as soon as you can. Fulk will have men watching the drawbridge so you could go over the walls after dusk." A foolish female suggestion barely thought out; it sounded too suspiciously easy and either plan would give Fulk the opportunity to pursue them like adulterous lovers and destroy them, alleging their flight was proof of guilt.

Johanna sniffed miserably and groped for more mordant, peeping up at him guiltily through her dark lashes as she scattered it in.

His chin was haughty. "Thank you for your trust, madam wife. So I am to be paid and plumblined from the wall and there's an end to it. No, my darling dear, it will not wash!" His gaze skimmed the urine jar. "I am not a flux that you can eject from your castle bowels when it suits you."

"Dear God, I do not want to lose your company but your safety is—"

"My safety! What about the hostage for my good behaviour?"

She lost the pole. It bobbed unpiloted on the ugly sea between them until she grabbed it again defiantly. "I do not know what you are babbling about, sir."

He leaned forward, facing her across the vat. "The third man, my dear sweet ignoramus. Jesu, Johanna, leave the dyeing be, will you! The wounded youth your mother has used to earn my compliance." He spoke slowly, insultingly, as if she was a child. "Even a dullard can see, of course, I cannot leave without him."

"Third?" An owlet could not have looked more round-eyed with astonishment.

"You mean your conniving mother has not confided in you, Johanna?" She had the nestling's hunger on her now and, satisfied, he shrugged and walked to the door only to find her blocking his passing, the pole brandished like a quarterstaff before her.

"Tell me!" she demanded fiercely.

"But I should not like to distract you, saint of the dyeing. Your priority is for the bubbling colours of Conisthorpe—if your men have time to wear them. See me as but a passing cloud, Johanna, that lit upon your hills." With a fast movement, he jerked the staff from her before she could whack the end into his toecap, and holding it horizontally beneath her breasts, pushed her firmly against the door.

"Cloud!" retaliated Johanna with a bitter laugh. She watched that mobile mouth curl menacingly.

"Very well, a foolish conceit. How about *clown*, since you and your mother want to make a jape of me? How admirable you are! You will turn lily-livered and leave poor little Agnes to her fate."

"No, no, Gervase! Believe me, I seek to save her life by this." She tried to push the pole away but it pleased him to keep it between them. God curse him! She was being honest. What other way was there to save poor Agnes? She swallowed at the anger still flickering in his eyes. "Who is this other hostage?" she whispered.

"A companion-in-arms."

"But . . ." She hated the chill in his face. Tomb effigies stared at church ceilings with more feeling.

"We escaped the battle together. Jankyn fell in with us later."

"By Heaven, sir," she exclaimed evasively. "Why did you not tell me before? Where is he?"

"Lady, how should I know?" His voice was a snarl. "Your mother will not tell me. I am just a poor minion paid to mind my manners. But no matter," he muttered scathingly and scowled down at her, "go your ways to Shaftesbury, Lady Johanna, and hide these playthings out of men's temptation." His gaze slid pro-vocatively over her breasts. It was as if he touched her and her body flamed of its own volition to his summons. She felt the pole slide and swayed involuntarily. "Think on the pleasures you are missing when you lie alone in your cold, bare cell." He raised his hand imperiously to touch her lips, but his words belittled her. "And, siren of the cloister, do keep your sandals on in bed. It will save you fumbling for them when you rise at two for matins and lauds."

Johanna, bereft of experience, grazed by his sarcasm, could only shield herself with sincerity. "Please listen. If I could hold back the sea of time, I would. Do you not see I have to end this? Not just for Agnes's sake, but for all of us. I am falling in too deep, Gervase. Your friendship has been the best, the most beautiful thing that has ever happened to me and whether it is tonight or within a month, I have to let you go back to your own life before it is too late."

"What do you mean?"

He knew perfectly well, curse him! He was too clever not to understand, but the reckoning had come and she had to make him see that it had to be finished as cleanly as possible.

"Because, to be frank, sir, if we do not part . . . Oh, Devil take it!" She hammered her fists against the door. "Dickon!" The latch against her shoulder blade shifted in a thrice and the door inched open.

Businesslike, Johanna grabbed the pole from her disconcerted husband and thrust it at her servant. "I cannot keep my mind on this, Dickon. Give it a little longer. You know what to do."

Hastening out into the day, she tried not to think about the confusion bubbling up within her or the rejection she must endure. Her costly truth was out now like spilt perfume. An instant more and she would have been babbling incoherently of love. And love hurt. Fulk would take everything she loved. And in any case, her paltry love would be the last thing this stranger wanted. Belatedly the hard truth hit her and she halted, her lips parting, her breath short. What a fool she was! Gervase de Laval had only stayed because her mother had forced him.

"I begin to understand," she exclaimed angrily, unwrapping the headclout and shaking out her hair. Curse *Maman*! Why had she not been honest!

"Understand what?"

Geraint watched as Johanna pulled one shoulder of the spattered surcote over her head and wriggled it down over her hips with innocuous allure. Then she thrust the garment into his hands, treating him like a servant, and charged off towards the stairs up to the ramparts as though a horsefly had bitten her.

In a few bounds, he had planted himself beside her. Both deprived of breath, they stared at one another. She was worth a kingdom, this thorny briar rose; thought Geraint.

"Go away!" Jabbing her elbows on the wall, Johanna glared ferociously across the valley at the knot of villeins busily repairing the banks. Realising he was not going to give her privacy, she smote her palm fiercely upon her forehead. "What a jape! All along I thought you were here for the wages but then you said no, it was not so, and I hoped . . ." The words fluttered unspoken into the void between them. He watched her face harden. "How foolish of me. It is because of him, this other man. You cannot leave without him and he is too ill to ride."

"Not anymore." He turned her to face him, taking her hands in his.

"You must go," she affirmed, her voice brittle, hating her vulnerability. He had almost had her soul and if she stayed . . . The vital flesh, the golden haze of hair, was sensuous beneath her fingertips.

Geraint heard her breathing grow more ragged as she refused to meet his gaze, and guessed the turmoil seething in her. His body was giving him answers to questions he could not frame. He knew the urge to plunder and protect, to torment yet to treasure. And she, unready, was trying to tidy up the unravelled ends between them, as if it was that simple.

"I will make all right, sir, I promise you. Mother shall surrender your friend to you and you must carry him to safety."

"My lady." Why was it this brave, bedraggled urchin with her large beseeching eyes could reach unfathomed depths in him? She was right; it should be over.

Her fingers struggled now for freedom. "Be merciful, Gervase. Please let me run away and hide."

"Johanna. Look at me!"

She noted him now, adorably perplexed.

"Johanna, if I flee now, with or without Edmund, all the world will know me for a rebel and a fornicator, and you for a liar and an adulteress, and I will not have that so. Can you not see this is what Fulk wants, to panic us?"

"But—"

His arms fastened about her in full view of the castle and he pressed her head against his breast, his thumb stroking her neck. His clothing, clean and new, smelt fresh against her face. She wanted to keep those strong arms about her and imagine herself treasured and loved.

I am wading in too deep, she thought. Warlock! Manipulator! But was there no way to snare the magician himself without the gift of her body and soul?

"Can you not see the other dangers?" she whispered into his velvet jupon. Could he not guess she was trying not to love him?

For Geraint, last night was unfinished and he was unsatiated, desirous of punishing her for bewitching him. The wench was right; if he stayed much longer, she would have him as besotted for her as the king was for Hugh Despenser. Siren, indeed! He needed to tie himself to the mast like Ulysses and block his ears.

"Brace yourself, Johanna." He plundered her mouth but with subtle gentleness, his lips telling her he wanted nothing but submission, that he could perform miracles if she would let him. He sensed the softening in her and laughed quietly at his power.

"Why?"

"Because I want to," he said against the corner of her mouth, and then to finish the embrace and bring them back to earth, he deliberately provoked her. "And for appearances. You need reassurance."

"Reassurance!"

He anticipated her furious struggle but she might just as well have tried to overturn a rooted oak.

"I tell you this!" she swore defiantly, when he finally gave her air. "I am leaving tonight and will welcome the cloister!"

"No, lady, enough! You and your meddling mother will do as I—"

"Sir! Sir!" Jankyn's bawl reached them from the yard below.

Geraint set his armful aside and tore down the steps. The bell of Conisthorpe began to ring a warning and suddenly there was shouting everywhere.

"Have they found Agnes, Jankyn?"

"No," he managed to gasp.

"Dear God protect us, a Scots raid!" Johanna exclaimed in horror, hastening down.

"No." The jester's eyes were on her companion; the news was for him. "My Lord Despenser is arriving at Conisthorpe within the hour."

Twenty-five

JOHANNA WATCHED GERVASE GO ASHEN.

"God ha'mercy!" she whispered. Grabbing his hand, she dragged him like a blind man to the hall. He seemed distracted, and well he might. Despenser must be nosing out the rebels.

Within the hall, her mother was issuing orders. "Into the great chamber!" she exclaimed on seeing them. Gervase ignored her, his whole stance a proclamation of rebelliousness, until Sir Geoffrey urged him through and he threw himself upon the windowseat in a sprawl of limbs that challenged her mother's authority.

Her mother closed the door on the hall, a half-dozen oaths spending beneath her breath. "Poking his nose in. God curse the man! Lent too!"

Johanna bestowed a cautious look on Gervase and tried to throw some common sense into the situation. "Well, Mother, there are plenty of sweetwater fish but we could make the illustrious Hugh eat stockfish and mock eggs like the rest of us. What does the wretched man expect if he arrives at short warning?"

"Oh, do you not see, Johanna! I need to convince him that Conisthorpe is managed well and that your father is but briefly incapacitated. Oh, a pox on Despenser, and with the wretched hearing going on, as if I have not enough to suffer. Poor Agnes missing. Oh, there is so much to do, the bed linen needing airing—and your pig. Who knows what else may have been poisoned in the last hour?"

Johanna halted her in mid-pace. "We shall manage, madam. But there are more important worries. What about Gervase's safety and this other man you have been hiding? And I cannot understand why you never told me. Where is he?"

"Oh, do not worry about him now."

Sir Geoffrey intervened. "My lady, I must protest. This is treason we are discussing."

Father Gilbert stepped forward beside him. "Madam, we are harbouring rebels and King Edward's right hand is bearing down on us. The man has been hanging traitors all over the kingdom and you tell us not to worry."

"No, chaplain, I sent the other lad out of the shire to Sir John before the hearing started."

"Godssakes!" seethed Gervase, thrusting himself to his feet. "Who in poxy Hell is drawn in now?"

Johanna pushed between them. "My sister Petronella's husband in Lincolnshire. No, your friend will be safe, I promise you. Have you received word, Maman?"

"Yes, yes, it is taken care of. He is mending well, though Petronella says he never stops complaining."

At her words, a little of the fight seemed to leave Gervase but he flung himself away from them and leaned upon the mantel of the fireplace, his back heaving.

"We have to hide you." Johanna set her hand upon his hanging sleeve.

He shook his head. "Too late. Despenser will have heard about the hearing and your father's illness from his agents."

"From Fulk even," Sir Geoffrey suggested. "They have met enough times."

Johanna whirled round to face the older man. "You think Fulk has summoned him to influence the verdict?"

"Do not be ridiculous!" exclaimed her mother. "Despenser is far mightier than Fulk. No one can summon him save King Edward. He is coming for Conisthorpe."

"My lady!" The steward's voice sounded urgently outside the door.

"Agnes?" whispered Johanna, letting him through.

"No, my lady, but another messenger from my lord Despenser has just arrived at the postern."

"I will go and see," snarled Gervase. "Come with me, Sir Geoffrey."

"How dare he give orders!" snapped Lady Constance, whirling round upon Johanna. "He needs slapping down to size again. Who does he think he is!"

"Yes, mother, who *does* he think he is? So you forced Gervase to act as my husband. Dear God, it explains everything. And this other man, who is he?"

"Insignificant."

"Really?" she sneered, looking to Father Gilbert for support. "And Hugh Despenser is coming here to admire the view! What a coincidence! I do not understand what is going on but I mislike the whole stink of it."

Her mother shrugged and refused to answer.

Johanna was still glowering by the window when the two men returned.

"Sir Geoffrey?" Her mother disregarded Gervase.

"Well, my lady, it is thus: my lord Despenser has changed his plans and travels directly to my lord of Brittany's at Richmond and we are bidden to meet with him there. All the local lords have been sent for."

"Wondrous news!" exclaimed Johanna. "You may remain here, sir."

The men exchanged looks.

"My lady Johanna, Sir Gervase is ordered by name to Richmond."

Johanna sank down upon the stool beside the fire, cursing. "This is unbelievable. Hugh Despenser *knows* I have two husbands?"

"Yes, and that," warned her younger husband, "is only the beginning!"

THICKLY MANTLED IN TUNICS AND CLOAKS LINED WITH CONEY FUR, for the wind was mean enough to threaten snow even though it was April, they rode north at dawn. Their breath formed vapour and they spoke little, their throats and lips scarved. Although Sir Ralph de Middlebrough's party had joined with theirs, the Conisthorpe men-at-arms were in half-armour, on guard lest the Enderby men made an assault. Without litters, and with the ground hard in the dales and the moor roads still passable, they rode swifter than sumpter pace and made good progress.

At Thornleigh, the Priory of White Canons gave them a night's lodging, but the fare was meagre since the prior was away at Easeby Abbey, the hosteller was bedridden with a disease of the joints and a Scots raid had deprived the good brothers of their plate. Next day the going was easier but it was not a journey for revelations; a questionable future hung over all their heads like the sword of Damocles.

Johanna found the riding painful. The saddle chafed her bruises and Gervase was too deep in his own thoughts to cheer her. She feared for Agnes and for him. The lonely wastes, unlit by the gorgeous sun, were in harmony with her sadness. The touch of his hand as he silently brought her a cup of gill water whenever they drew rein to rest the horses was both bitter and sweet to her bruised spirits.

Geraint was keeping his distance. Better so. He did not want to hurt her any more than was unavoidable and his lifespan might be merely a hand of days.

Only one person was cheerful. Miles came with them. Lady Constance had received word he might return to Helmsley, but it was hazardous to let him from their sight with Fulk so vengeful and mayhap the Lord of Helmsley would be at Richmond and could take him back with him.

Johanna was thankful to sight the candlelit windows of Richmond Castle beaconing the grey hillside and she felt a sense of coming home as they crossed the Swale and passed through the Bar. The Honour of Richmond was a prosperous one, its ancient holding coveted. She knew its history well, that the land had been granted by William the Conqueror to his companion-in-arms, Alan the Red, and here she had spent some happy years of service. She would have shared that confidence with Gervase but he rode gloomily at her side, his chin sunk into the folds of his mantle. He had barely exchanged a brace of words with anyone for the last hour and Johanna's courage began to falter. Of a sudden the castle's familiar keep seemed ominous, the persistent stallkeepers at their stirrups were a plague and she shivered in the bitter wind as it whined around the market cross.

There was only one Despenser flag fluttering from the castle walls, its black diagonal bar cutting through the argent and gules quarters. Geraint noted it with a cynical lift of eyebrow.

"Are we likely to forget who owns this holding?" he muttered at last, tersely eyeing my lord of Richmond's coat of arms. The blue and yellow chequerboard flanked by prancing golden lions, and the argent powdered with miniver adorned the fluttering pennons and decorated the gatehouse.

Johanna gave a tight smile. Perhaps John de Dreux, Duke of Brittany and Constable of Richmond, was subtly reminding the royal favourite which of them was veined with princely blood.

"I see you are still with us in spirit after all, sir. I know you fear to encounter so many noble lords and ladies, but try to feign some cheer from now on." She found herself wincing beneath the disgusted look he gave her.

"We are the objects of scandal, not to mention fornicators and traitors, and you are worried I might be gauche?"

"I did not mean that. And I am sure I can find somewhere to hide you if there is any danger. I lived here from my eighth until my seventeenth year." Dear God, she did not mean to sound so trite.

"How reassuring. Perhaps you should have given me a charcoal sketch showing the secret passages. Blocked? Then, thank you, Johanna, you are worth the entire crusader force put together. No wonder they never regained Jerusalem."

"At least I might manage to find out who you really are," she retaliated, and lapsed into a silence punctuated by tiny sniffs.

He curbed his foul temper and became more conciliatory as a boy of no more than ten years ambushed Miles in the outer bailey. It was one of the Helmsley pages.

Her mother wistfully watched the two boys scamper away into the keep. "I will miss him sadly when he returns to Helmsley. Still, he will make useful friends and they will give him discipline."

"So long as it is deserved," growled Geraint. His painful memories had kept pace with him across the moors, regurgitating in his mind like bile.

If he expected to be shown the dungeons as a welcome, his relief when he reached Scolland's hall unfettered was hidden beneath the irritable shock of facing a garrulous throng of Yorkshire nobility. The tumult was oppressive; the air was stifling; most of the shutters were fastened; smoke misted the rafters; and, at chin level, the odour of lavender, musk and ambergris vied ineffectually with finery that had been coffered too long and the stink of those who had preferred not to wash during winter. Added to which he could see that the flagons were moving in the opposite direction and that Sir Fulk had already gained the guest of honour's attention.

"It seems we shall be sleeping with our boots on," he growled testily.

"Aye, sir," quipped a nearby knight in samite, wearing a disgusting excess of peacock feathers in his hat, "but the good news is that my lord of Richmond is two hours tardy with supper so at least we shall be fed first."

The man would have been friendly had his wife not dug him in the ribs and whispered behind her hand. She was not the only noble lady who drew her skirts pointedly aside as if he and the Conisthorpe ladies carried the pox, but when the courteous Lord of Richmond greeted Johanna with a kiss on each cheek, and shook him by the hand, the Yorkshire worthies began to thaw rapidly, oozing almost.

Johanna noted the coquettish smiles that were darted across the hall at her hireling husband—lips bitten to appear more red, here the judicious adjustment of a neckline, there the silky glance beneath the lashes, but Gervase, thank the Saints, was far more interested in the lords. As if stalked, he was giving little away and listening much.

It was uncomfortable being the centre of attention. She never discovered which aging baron goosed her, but she did manage to foil the gossipmongers and meddlers who tried to manoeuvre her so that she was face to face with Fulk. She was not providing a spectacle.

Nor it seemed was Gervase. No armed retainers came to haul him forth, no one greeted him as a long-lost bastard, and when Sir Ralph was pleased to introduce him to the lord High Sheriff, Sir Roger de Somerville, it was merely to cajole him to tell his jest about the Irishman, the Welshman and the Scotsman.

She was ravenous by the time they were finally seated at the board, knights along one side and the ladies on the opposite side of the hall, congratulating herself that she had a satisfactory view of the high table and especially of Hugh Despenser the younger.

Knowing his reputation clouded her perception. She had always felt sympathy for the poor queen, said to be the loveliest woman in England yet yoked to a king who shunned her for a man in his mid-thirties who did not look, well, particularly remarkable.

Oh he wore his light brown hair fashionably parted at the centre and it was still plentiful as it curled at chin length but she did not like the cut of his small beard; together with his almond eyes, it gave him a fey look. Otherwise he appeared rather ordinary in stature—slight compared to the tall, thin Lord of Richmond on his right. He inclined his head charmingly as he listened to Lord John, but his looks went everywhere. For an instant he mirrored Johanna's stare. In panic, she coloured and busied herself with her trencher, before she dared peep up again and observe his sanguine splendour. Half of her wished she could manage a close look at the motifs on his sleeve and note the seams and type of stitches. The other half of her wondered how the man could sleep sound o' nights; it was common gossip that he had had a young widow tortured into yielding up her lands, and there were many such tales.

Her burgeoning fears were mercifully halted when one of the de Scriven ladies from Knaresborough leaned across her mother. "Is that a Sicilian brocade you are wearing, Lady Johanna? Such an exquisite blue . . ." The talk of fashion unfrosted her mother's tense demeanour and by the time Gervase strode across and set his hands upon Johanna's shoulders, the older ladies had settled into comparing flood damage. Soon they would alarm each other as to whether the Scots would raid their demesnes during the summer.

Her temporary lord was at ease and smiling.

"No hudder-mudder?" she asked as he escorted her from the board.

"No secrets, but much conference. Fulk has been trying to bend *le beau* Despenser's ear all evening, that is whenever he has been able to escape the attentions of Maud de Roos. She is taking an uncommon interest in the progress of our little matter. Ah yes, and Sybilla de Wysham wants to know where you purchased these buttons." He flicked one of the cobalt glass buttons that peapodded the openings of his perse jupon. "Aye, and Alice de Raby loves the oak-leafed edging to my gorget. She examined it extremely

closely. Tall demoiselle, is she not? The one with the brooch between her—ouch! You will ruin the rose windows on my shoes."

"But no one has challenged you?"

Geraint did not share his conclusions with her, instead he carried her fingers to his lips reassuringly, watching the gems of her
caul catching the candlelight. Her soul was glowing in her eyes
tonight. Her loveliness drew out the rusty poet in him. The patterned brocade moulded her sweet breasts and her sleek hips were
enhanced by a glistening girdle of samite embossed, orphrey-like,
with little horses prancing in cusped leaves. God ha' mercy, he
was beginning to sound like a needlewoman in full prattle. He
gave up at that point, content to just enjoy feasting his eyes on
her, but her fingers fluttered restlessly on his wrist.

"You will dance with me? *Please.*"

"It will cost you extra," he replied with mock gravity. The musicians could scarcely be heard yet for the servants were noisily
propping the trestle boards and reversing the forms against the
side of the hall.

"I have not trod any measure since I was last at Skipton when
we were bidden to a feasting," Johanna exclaimed happily, pushing the danger away for a beautiful moment. Her golden husband
turned heads even if he was rented. If all else went awry, she
would keep this memory fresh until they ordered her shroud. He
was hers, just hers, for a little space.

Geraint, his instincts sensing that whatever danger threatened
him was covert and subtle, surrendered to the moment. He knew
that her vivacity was drawing attention but he wanted to indulge
her. She had lost her hollow-eyed mien and was tantalising him
with her mischievious green eyes as they linked hands and whirled
down the clapping set. He desired nothing better than to unfetter
those braids and rope that sweet lithe body hard against him and
caress her until she was aflame with passion for him. And where
were they? Cursed Richmond and the only sleeping space was on
a dog if you were lucky enough to be a flea.

Johanna was startled as the music stopped when he curved one
of his large calloused palms against her cheek.

"I want you."

The hubbub of conversation receded and time drew breath.

"It is the danger," she explained breathlessly. "It changes people. You start to think this might be your last night on earth and—"

"It might be." He led her gently by the wrist into a shadowy recess. There he took her fingers and drew her across the very air. His arms fastened about her and he pressed his body hard against hers, as if he was Adam straining to absorb Eve's flesh back into his. "If it was not snowing," he murmured against the gilded net of her hair, "I would take you out into the castle garden and make love to you."

"Well, it is and this is foolish. The coin you offer is too dear. I cannot afford it."

"Shrew! A bucket of words to defuse a wet squib, hmm?" In the dim light, there was a bitter lining to his bashful grin as if for an infinitesimal instant he had been in earnest, but he did not set her free. "Should we not make the best of every precious moment? I know there is unfulfilled desire in you." But even as he spoke with teasing lightness, he knew that beneath the exhilaration she was afraid, for him and for Agnes. Talk must suffice, it was hazardous to venture further.

"And I know naught save you are an onion, sir."

"Onion!"

She felt the rumble of laughter. "Yes, truly, the real man is layers deep."

"I am not so sure. Perhaps Gervase de Laval should kill off all his other persona and live for the moment."

"Dear God! How many have you got?"

Hiding behind her shield of words, Johanna had seen how much he wanted her. Whenever Fulk had looked at her like that, she had trembled at what she must be expected to perform, but this man made her feel precious, like a jewel that he wanted to take alone to his bedchamber and uncover.

"If I promise not to rearrange your embroideries, will you walk with me? I need sweeter air."

Somehow they found her cloak among the many and he arranged her furred hood around her face and followed her out to the neat garden.

"Here is one way of withstanding the weather." He took her in his arms but turned her so he could watch who entered the garden.

The duke would not want him bleeding over the rose bushes and breaking the lavender.

She laughed, unafraid of him, clasping her tight-cuffed wrists behind his neck and he burrowed his arms into her perfumed hanging sleeves and felt her, fragrant and desirable, within his hands.

"Was disguising yourself as a student only to throw off pursuit or is that also one of your faces?" *Tonight he might tell me who he is.*

"I was not that kind of scholar. Come, you know what happens to younger sons, lady mine, the poor asses are branded as church fodder the moment they draw their first breath. My father sent me to the Benedictines but there was one monk who made my life . . . unendurable, so I ran away, dishonouring my family. I have earned my own pay as an esquire ever since."

"Ha, so that is how you came to be lettered. But why were you dressed like a poor student when Father Gilbert found you—to evade the bounty hunters?"

"It is a bloody tale."

She shook him. "Nevertheless, tell me."

"Here? Are you not freezing?"

It was worth the cold seeping up through her thin soles to hear some truths. For an instant she thought he would baulk at the telling but instead he tugged his fur collar closer and searched for a beginning.

"My company," he began finally, "some half-dozen of us, escaped from Boroughbridge the night before Thomas of Lancaster surrendered and we happened across a man lying dead beside his meagre fire, a poor scholar by his garb. His purse was cut and so was his throat, poor wretch. It was agreed that I should put on his apparel, such as it was. No, do not look askance, it was not bloodstained. It was decided I was to go to the nearest village at dawn— I am not quite sure where we were—near Markington, perhaps— to seek news. I was on the road when a dozen horsemen passed me. They did not give me a second glance, thank Heaven, but it was evident they were following our tracks. I turned back running, but it was all over by the time I reached them. The bounty hunters, God rot them, were stripping the bodies like carrion. I thought to hide, but the whoresons heard me and dragged me forth and took my purse. I knew it was the end of the road for me, I can tell you, but they actually believed I was waiting to see what pickings they might leave, and that I must be a scholar even though my hair was not cropped."

"Why did they not take your boots?"

"You would make a worthy examiner, my lady. The jest of it was that they found my boots with my armour. 'Here,' they said, in a fit of generosity, 'these would fit you. We would be hard put to find a man with feet as big as yours to buy them. Have them!' Then they loaded our horses with the booty and left me with the bodies. I had no spade to bury my friends, God rest their souls, nothing. It was like some imagining of Hell. They were all dead save . . ."

"Your friend Edmund."

"Aye, they had thieved every piece of his armour and he was lying there, his shirt bloodied, but he was still alive. I had my cloak still so I wrapped him in that and carried him on my good shoulder out along the king's highway. A carter took us up an hour later, thinking us poor scholars who had drunk too much, and so I came to the woods near Conisthorpe."

She slid down her palms to nestle against his velvet breast, not in defence, but giving instead. "And then two women forced you to play a husband. My problems must have seemed so trite to you."

"No, never trite, Johanna, but I wanted no part. You may have cursed me for a coward when I fled from you, but I was trying to escape to Edmund's kin so that they could ransom him from your mother and send him to Ireland or France. His safety was more important than mine."

She neither passed judgment nor questioned him on Edmund. "And is that where you will go?"

"France, if God wills it." But he sighed, and looked towards the hall windows as if the lights were luring him like wreckers' beacons.

Her fingers touched his cheek and she smiled mistily at the snowflakes spangling his beaked hat.

"By the Saints, lady, your fingers are like icicles! We must return." At the steps, he hesitated. "Johanna, if aught perilous befalls me tonight, you must take no care for me. I am not afraid."

Before she could find an answer, drunken and belching roister-
ers with flaming torches stumbled out from the hall to relieve
themselves on the pathway.

There were still too many hours until morning.

ALL THE BEDCHAMBERS WERE SO CRAMMED WITH DESPENSER'S
courtiers that the rest of the visiting entourages slept in the passageways and recesses, or in the hall if they were fortunate. Rolled
in her cloak, Johanna lay with her fears, between her mother and
Gervase, but when his arm scooped her into the curve of his body,
she made no protest but set her feet against his warm body in
wifely fashion and fell asleep.

It was past midnight when she heard the soft creak of expensive
leather and, looking up, found two pairs of legs within a hand's
grasp. They were pulling Geraint to his feet, taking him from her.
Johanna drew breath to scream but he dropped on his haunches
and swiftly set his fingers across her lips.

"I will be back, I swear it. Go to sleep."

It could have been a false promise.

HUGH DESPENSER THE YOUNGER OPENED HIS EYES AND LOOKED UP
lazily from his bath. A spatter of dried rose petals bobbed languidly in front of him, nudging the wet hairs plastered to his chest.

"So, twice the size and beefier, but still with that honest wholesome gleam I always liked in you. And no beard, my dear. How
many years is it?" He raised a dripping hand and with the flick of
a glistening forefinger dismissed all the servants save for his
comely varlet. "More hot!"

Wordlessly, Geraint lifted his palms, only three of his fingers
curled down.

"Seven years! Was I nigh thirty when we last met? This conversation begins to age me already." The hot water cascaded from
the jug into the miniature sea between Despenser's knees and
belly. The rose petals disappeared beneath the waterfall and vapour rose. "Be seated."

"I prefer to stand. Will this take long?" Geraint was careless
with his tone. This silky scrutiny, the batting of words with catlike
glee, reminded him too much of facing the novicemaster for the

first time and suffering the slimy appraisal that had made his flesh crawl.

"That rather depends on you, my dear *Gervase de Laval*."

"Do you mind?" Geraint indicated the jug of wine. It was a mere courtesy, something to say, but given permission, he poured himself a generous goblet and was grateful for it. Something to hold, something to fortify him against this unwelcome audience.

"The wench in blue with the horses stitched on her girdle?"

"Yes, the lady's own work. Johanna, Fulk de Enderby's wife."

"But your wife too, I believe."

Geraint picked up Despenser's crimson and gold coat and ran a thumb across the stiff threads. "She gave me orders to inspect your dragons," he lied.

"Be plain with me, Geraint. What is this woman to you? She has no lands save those which are in dispute and her fecundity is questionable."

Geraint began to enjoy himself. He tossed aside the tunic and taking up his winecup again, watched Despenser over the rim. "It is a temporary arrangement."

Hugh squeezed the expensive soap so it shot up into the air and fell into the water again. "I am relieved to hear it. You need to improve your prospects . . . and maybe I want you back where I can, shall we say, use your talents."

Raising the goblet, Geraint savoured his wine. "I see," he said slowly. "I noticed the Mallet of the English managed to speak with you. Putting you right about Bannockburn, was he?" The verbal jab produced an angry hiss.

"I cannot bear people who revel in telling me they have drunk horse's piss. Did you hear that I am now become a pirate?"

"You always were, Hugh."

"I think I like this brawnier version of you, Geraint. The leather is tougher but everyone has their price and I know yours. Pour me another, my dear." Hugh held out the chased goblet.

His ill will unconcealed, Geraint took up the elegant waisted jug and stepped across. Hugh grabbed his wrist as he poured. "He will withdraw his petition."

The Bordeaux streamed and missed the cup, reddening the water for an instant. Forced by the surprising strength to bend his knee, Geraint smelt Hugh's wine-perfumed breath upon his face.

The derisive smile that always assaulted him with its mockery was there now, curling the corners of the other man's mouth. Like a candle, it could lure foolish moths to destruction.

This had to be a trap. Why would the old veteran Fulk suddenly be asking for terms when he held Agnes as hostage?

The wet fingers unmanacled themselves from his cuff.

"I can always read you, Geraint. You were not expecting this?"

"But?" the younger man prompted icily, retreating as honourably as he could and rising to his feet.

"Quite so." Hugh savoured his wine, teasing him with the wait. *"But,"* he conceded eventually, "the old warhorse wants Conisburgh—no, that is further south."

"Conisthorpe." Geraint tried not to move, to betray any hint of emotion other than surprise. "Sir Fulk wants Conisthorpe?"

"He desires to be made the constable." Hugh handed the goblet to his varlet, and at some unseen understanding between them, leaned forward so the youth could sponge his shoulders. "Enlighten me as to why Lord Alan is not here to kiss hands—and keep to the truth, Geraint, for you know I like to find out if people are lying."

As if bewitched, Geraint dragged his gaze away with an effort and stared at the tasselled tapestry on the opposite wall. The truth would steal in under Hugh's door eventually.

"The old lord is stricken down one side and cannot speak. His lady, Constance, has been hiding the fact because she does not want to be evicted and I suspect she believes there is some chance of her lord's recovery, but it was a visitation from God. I doubt FitzHenry will make it through the summer, the lack of exercise will weaken him." He shrugged. "The castle, however, is presently well maintained, no question of that. Our lord king would find no fault with Lady Constance's management nor her loyalty."

"Except she gave shelter to a rebel. Is that how you have concealed yourself, playing the returned lover?"

"You have been listening to the Mallet. What else does he want—my head on the tip of your sword?"

Hugh's lower lip curled down indifferently. He began to shake his head and then smiled. "Oh, I forgot," he raised his forefinger, "he wants his sister Edyth given a place in the queen's household."

Geraint's sudden cynical laughter rang out. "I would have thought that even you—"

With annoyance, Hugh Despenser lifted a finger to his lips, hushing him. "Oh yes, I can arrange even that."

Slow mocking applause from Geraint broke the silence between them. "You have grown mighty," he sneered, his disgust at the older man's prostitution of himself for royal power scarcely concealed. "Can you manipulate canon law too, my lord? But I suppose you can, a lucrative benefice here, a bishopric there, a carrier pigeon to his Holiness. *Everyone has their price.*"

"I intend you no harm, Geraint. Can we not set the past differences aside and begin again?"

Geraint rested his hands against the mantel of the hearth, staring morosely at the glowing embers.

"So where have we arrived?" pursued that clear, rich voice that he knew so well. "This Fulk pledges the withdrawal of his petition, and your witness—the old dun was smug about that—shall be returned, and that leaves you, my dear, and I have plans for you."

So all was resolved. And the price? Nothing was free. He guessed now he would be leaving Conisthorpe within days. And what would befall Johanna? Must she accept the cloister and abandon the secular world? But he had a dice of his own to roll.

"Since you can order the queen's household, my lord, arrange for the lady Johanna to be given a place as well. Let word be sent to her once the hearing is over." He jerked his head round for an answer.

He watched Hugh whistle and waggle his fingers as if he had burnt them. "Ouch! Two placements, my dear? A little delicate. Our beauteous Isabella will baulk at that, especially since we have been advising her to economise. More hot!"

"But I thought you ruled England now, Hugh," Geraint taunted, observing the obedient servant's face, but it registered nothing as if its owner was not at home. "What is more, Lady Johanna's dower land is to be returned." He watched Hugh make a distasteful rosebud of his mouth, and added, to provoke him further, "And the boy Barnabas at Enderby is to be freed, alive and hale, to join the FitzHenry household."

"What is the boy to you?" The acute interest appalled Geraint. It made him wish he had not spoken.

"I never saw him. It is but a sop to please the lady. Be thankful that I am not asking you for pigs and lapdogs."

"I hate to inquire further." With a delicate shrug, as if he sensed he had been baited, Hugh lapsed into a brief sulky silence. "No doubt all this may be accomplished," he declared eventually, as if the matter now bored him, adding as a caution, "Provided I get you back."

"Are you sure you want that?" Geraint's expression was not friendly. "I do not approve of your methods. I never have."

"But regard me now, Geraint. I am ruling England. The King needs me. I have my uses although men such as you are mighty swift to curse me, all muscle and chivalrous integrity you are, and what good is that to the economy of this realm? Despise me, if you will, for feathering my nest, but I have done England great service and I defy you to best me on that score, dear heart. Because of my counsel, the king still acts within the spirit of the ordinances although it irks him. I intend to check the power of the barons by ensuring that parliament must discuss all legislation before it becomes law, and what is more I have set in motion a complete revision of the entire exchequer system. Walter Stapledon is going to carry out a survey of all government practices within the next three years."

"If the Scots do not manage to sink a crossbolt in you."

"Ah, war, the bottomless grave into which we hurl coins and bodies. I could not give a mouse's turd on which side of the border Berwick ends up. We need a truce not a poxy summer campaign but, no, my lord the king still scratches at the scars from Bannockburn. Fiery people the English, always have to be fighting someone. War is what ruins the economy."

"Unless you are on the winning side. But you always are, my lord, even when you are banished. *Daemon ut antefuit*. What rates are your Italian bankers charging to store your funds off the shores of England?"

"Plenty, my dear, and, yes, I know the adage. I have always been a demon." Hugh answered smoothly, shooting the soap straight into the fire's heart. His visitor's face tightened at the waste; a peasant could have fed his family for a month by selling that soft, eroded sliver. "Now, dear lad, about our little arrangement . . ."

He stood up and, taking his servant's hand, stepped over the edge to stand dripping before the fire. Geraint moved aside as if a brush of flesh might give him leprosy, and yet his gaze was drawn mothlike to the beauty of the older man as it had been in the past. The firelight danced upon Hugh's shimmering unblemished skin as the water pearled off him onto my lord of Richmond's expensive imported carpet. The young manservant knelt, patting the moisture from his master's legs.

"You do agree?" The blue eyes, hard as sapphires, evaluated him.

"What choice have I?"

"None." The wet hand came down upon his shoulder. "I should not want to hear of you being hanged in some small town square like a common felon. You must be with me in time for the late summer campaign. Is the bargain made?"

Geraint nodded, surly at the manipulation.

"Then go—freely. And Geraint?" At the door, he turned reluctantly. "Does this woman Johanna know the truth? Of what we once were to each other and may be again?"

His lower lip curling into a sneer, Geraint shook his head.

"Then you cannot take her a kerchief with a dragon?"

"No." With a careful smile, he managed an unshared joke at Hugh's expense. "As you have observed, she prefers horses."

He said nothing to either of the Conisthorpe ladies on his return, though Johanna's curiosity would have had her dragging him for an interrogation in the garderobe had he let her and he might have ended up with his head stuck down the latrine. He merely said he had answered questions from some of my lord of Richmond's officers, and fell asleep.

Lady Constance received the expected summons to Hugh Despenser next morning. Johanna, philosophically accepting the inevitable, that her father was about to be removed from office, observed from her place at the women's table that Miles had abandoned his fellow pages and was taking his meal beside a cheerful Gervase. Perhaps her brother imagined some of the large knight's experience and manliness might rub off on him like pollen. The other Helmsley boys sidled over as well. The sight of Gervase surrounded like an uncle both delighted and saddened Johanna, especially when he looked across and gave her a heart-warming grimace. Thus encouraged, she rose and circumnavigated the hall to stand behind him.

He was ruffling her brother's hair to a state that would annoy her mother. "No doubt we shall be gone before dinnertime, Miles."

"Aye, I know. I wish you well with the hearing, sister. I am right glad that Gervase is pleased your haunches are broad enough. I think I should like a nephew before next spring. Isobel Clifford's are pretty narrow at the moment, but I think Mother may be calling that arrangement off if she can since the Cliffords are in—Ouch!"

"Oh pardon, Miles, was that your toe?" Gervase lifted himself off the bench, his eyes upon the ceiling bosses. "Would you like to show me the combat yard before we leave?"

"Haunches?" Johanna pounced on the word.

"Aye," exclaimed her brother, disentangling himself from the form and moving round behind her, as if he was demonstrating some new breed to the other boys. "It is of paramount importance that a prospective wife's haunches are of sufficient width to foal easily. Now see, with my sister here—What are you doing, sir . . ."

Gervase turned him upside down and set him down behind him out of range of Johanna. "Removing you and I from trouble, Miles."

"Foal easily!" she hissed. "Women are half of Christendom. Without us, none of you would exist and yet we are barred from the priesthood, from schooling, from high government. I tell you this, if it was your haunches, Miles, that did the foaling, our mother should be the constable at Conisthorpe and I should be next." Actually to argue a point of law, her sister Petronella would be as she was the eldest.

"My lady—" Her so-called husband looked as though he would hurry her away at any moment.

"But, madam," one of the pages suggested thoughtfully, "your sex has not the strength to wear armour and protect these northern shires against the Scots."

"Protect! Ha, how many times have the Scots harried us since Bannockburn?" She was straying onto miry ground and caught Gervase's warning frown. There were a few older heads tilted in her direction. "I-I will say this. Beating the enemy does not ensure victory but only nourishes the feud. There is no loss of face, no damage to honour, to sit down and talk the matter out around a board whether it is between two kingdoms, a father and sons or a husband and wife who are at odds."

There was an embarrassed hush and then a single clapping came from a few paces away; it was the Sheriff of Carlisle, Sir Andrew de Harcla, who applauded and saluted her from where he sat.

"You have made the sun shine this day, raven-haired darlin'," he exclaimed. The compliment to her hair had rather tainted the praise but no matter.

"And," said Johanna, quick-wittedly grabbing Miles by the shoulders and addressing the three interested little faces, her voice carrying to anyone who dared argue, "a sister with a small brother is allowed to wallop *his* haunches on any saint's day."

"That is any day!" yelled one of the other pages, thumping Miles on the back, and the hall resumed eating.

"Your pardon," she muttered to Gervase. "I should not have drawn attention to us."

"No matter, but here is further meat for the chewing. Your mother comes with ill tidings, I fear. What say you to some privacy?" He grabbed Miles, dismissed the others and led the way to the garden.

Lady Constance's perfumed skin was tougher than he had anticipated as she appraised her children of the news in a secluded corner of the herber. A gardener followed them in and set about weeding beneath the trellised roses and sweetbriar with a hook and fork.

Forewarned, Geraint bucklered himself for female tears and boyish tantrums, but there was a certain amount of acceptance there already. After all, it had been inevitable that they must leave Conisthorpe and Johanna's mother, as always, had a retreat strategy. She had dower lands and Lord Alan held manors in Yorkshire and a castle in Herefordshire. It was Johanna Geraint pitied. She sat bleak-faced, fearful of what else her mother had to say.

"Is it already decided who is to have Conisthorpe, then?" Her voice was weary.

Lady Constance's normally stalwart lip trembled. "Lord Despenser and my lord of Richmond have agreed that Fulk should be appointed constable in your father's place."

"God rot them!" exclaimed Johanna, springing up. "This is intolerable!"

"Sit down, my lady!" Geraint ordered, noting the gardener was observing her behaviour with uncommon interest. She drew her fur cloak tightly about her and subsided sullenly onto the stone seat.

"In return," continued Lady Constance, "Fulk will restore Agnes to you and withdraw his counter-petition from the hearing. *Johanna?*"

The younger woman looked as though she could have spat arrows. "You mean, madam, that although Fulk admits he has abducted Agnes, he is to go unpunished, and my lord Despenser will ensure the verdict will be manipulated in our favour. Is this the king's justice?" She threw off the restraining hand that Geraint settled warningly upon her shoulder.

"The king does not enter into this, madam wife, since it is a matter for canon law."

"Do not quell me with your male pedantry, sir. King's bench, archdeacon's court, does it matter which?"

Lady Constance was more pragmatic. "For Christ's blessed sake, Johanna, shall you run with the hare and hunt with the hounds? All it means is that Fulk is not disputing your marriage to Gervase. But the court will still expect you to prove that your earlier marriage to Gervase was lawful."

"I see. So you are telling me it is not cut and dried after all. Fie, I was not born yesterday. To be sure they will dance to a certain great lord's piping."

"One lord or another's." Lady Constance nonchalantly played with a loose thread where the coney fur trim was stitched to the bodice of her surcote.

"God preserve us, madam," whispered Johanna. "And so is this kingdom foully run by favours. Well, I would I had its ruling, I should appoint men of honour, not venal lily-livered weasels." She paced away and wheeled round, her anger icy. "What else did you negotiate, Mother? A different heiress for Miles now that Clifford's niece is no longer acceptable to know?"

"Yes, as a matter of fact, Johanna. Do not scowl so. One must make the best of these opportunities. My lord of Richmond mentioned Margaret de Beaumont."

"I knew it!"

"Then make sure she is not the daughter with the squint, ma-dam," Geraint threw in dryly. "And if you mention haunches, Miles . . ." he stroked his gloves menacingly betwixt his thumb and forefinger.

The boy was glum. "You may jest, sir. It is not your father who has lost his office."

"The greater the man, the bigger the drop," Geraint answered cryptically. His skin crawled; were they being observed behind the closed shutters of the solar? He slapped his gloves against his palm. "Miles, I am sorry for it, but I suggest we should depart right soon. Be diligent at Helmsley."

"I am not going to Helmsley. My lord Despenser asked if I should like to go to his household at Caerphilly."

"*No!*" The exclamation exploded from the three adults in uni-son; the gardener decided to shape the ends of the hedge nearest to them.

Geraint recovered first. "If you agreed to that, I shall—"

"No, sir, if you will let me finish . . ." Miles protested. "I ex-plained to my lord Despenser that I had already asked my lord of Richmond to request my wardship from the king, and my lord Despenser was not displeased to hear that, I assure you." The boy drew himself up with a swagger and added, "Now my father is incapacitated, I need to look after my interests." Johanna saw her mother draw a deep breath and glare suspiciously at her hireling as if he had been the inspiration.

In relief, Geraint threw an avuncular arm about the child's shoulders. "You have done well, Miles, and acted wisely. My lord of Richmond is a most honourable man."

An embarrassing pink heated the boy's face and he kicked at the stone edging. "Well, Johanna always said this was a fine house-hold to serve in and my lord is well thought of by our lord the king."

So too was Hugh Despenser, thought Geraint, wondering to what lengths he would need to have gone as a brother-in-law to protect the boy's innocence. He grinned at Miles afresh, and then regretted there was no time to take the brat aside and make him aware of the human dangers that still might confront him before he reached full manhood.

Johanna's thoughts were hurtling down a different path. She rose, her tone freezing. "So, in summary, Fulk de Enderby is rewarded with Conisthorpe, our father's horseshoes are removed and he is put out to pasture, Miles's interests are to be managed providing he grows up to doff his cap to the Despensers, and you get pai—" Remembering Miles's presence, she snapped her lips together, meeting his quizzical smile.

"And I get you," Geraint finished.

Twenty-six

THERE WAS MUCH SHE DID NOT UNDERSTAND ABOUT God's method of doing things or Gervase's, Johanna reflected three days later, as she sat in her father's chamber frowning over the new motif she had just sketched out in charcoal. With one hand, the Almighty was freeing her from Fulk; but with the other, He was rewarding that cruel devil with Conisthorpe.

As for Gervase, the wretched man had divulged nothing concerning the midnight interrogation at Richmond and had barely spoken on the journey back, as if he was already withdrawing in mind from Conisthorpe. And within days, he would be free to leave unless . . .

Win all or lose all! She drew in pine needles behind the great seed cone and understood what she must do. The Johanna, who through Gervase's help, had crawled up from an inferno to glimpse Paradise—well, not exactly Paradise, for he had his faults—was resolute. Even though her mind rebelled at surrendering to a wifely duty, it was the only weapon she had left. If her body could endure Fulk's nightly assault, the gift to Gervase of what he desired was scant recompense for his kindness to her. And there would be no humiliation in it. It would be on her terms. And, yes, she must ask him once more about Richmond.

"DO YOU MIND IF I STAND?" GERAINT ROSE WITHOUT PERMISSION, purposely dwarfing the examiner and the scribe. He was wearing half-armour to coerce them. The former scowled and staunched any comment. "Begin," ordered their witness, spreading his hands openly. "Commence the articles."

The examiner shook his notes, the only sign of his annoyance. "Sir Gervase, why was it you took so long to return and claim your wife?"

"I saw service in Gascony. I warned my lady Johanna that I might not be able to return for some time, not until I had acquired land and might claim her from her father."

"Is there anyone who would verify this under oath?"

"Here in Yorkshire, no. But I can arrange for letters to be sent to obtain confirmation. I apologise, what with the flood, and then the coming of my lord Despenser, and the enmity of this other husband whose presence I had not anticipated, there has been no time to organise such evidence. You must take my word under oath for the nonce."

"When you plighted your troth, what words did Father Benedict advise you to use?"

"*Ego volo habere te pro uxore mea quantum vita mea durare poterit.*" He spoke it so fluently that the notary pursed his lips in surprise.

"You speak Latin?"

"Yes, and write it too. Lady Johanna does not, of course, but she can read and write a little. You saw the letter I sent her."

The examiner nodded.

"I was going to be a priest," Geraint observed. "There is no need to write this down, man," he told the notary irritably and challenged Martin de Scruton to disagree, but instead the man was curious.

"Then what made you change your mind, sir? The temptations of the flesh?"

"No," Geraint paced. "I felt confined. As you see, God has bestowed on me physical strength. I could have laboured in an abbey vineyard but there are other ways to serve God."

"Would you take the Cross if it was offered you?"

Geraint threw the man a pensive look. "Rescue Jerusalem? If there was a good leader, yes, perhaps, and if I thought the enterprise would succeed. Master examiner, I should not be persevering in this suit had I not thought my arguments just and true. I need an heir."

The examiner shifted. The natural river of words had been diverted and the initiative temporarily lost.

"You had every intention of returning for Lady Johanna?"

"My presence is evidence surely?"

"Was it not unfair to the lady to seduce her into consummating the handfast with you when you dared not confront her father and were unable to claim her?"

"It seemed sensible at the time. In retrospect, yes, it was a cruel decision and most unfair to my lady Johanna as time has proved."

"Were you in love with the lady and she with you?"

"I was besotted with her. As for her affections, I cannot answer for her. If I did not love and honour her, would I have returned?"

"You first met in the forest?"

"No, in Bristol at the Earl of Winchester's house and I became so infatuated, I journeyed after her."

Oh he was enjoying this. For the next half-hour, Geraint made play of his status, his confidence, his height, his knowledge that Hugh Despenser had already jabbed a finger through the pastry crust, and when the examiner ran out of articles and would have dismissed him, he set his great hands upon the table.

"When I returned to Conisthorpe last week, I found my beautiful Johanna bruised and beaten by this Fulk. The scoundrel has attempted my life, abducted my wife's servant who was one of our witnesses and killed a creature near to my lady's heart. Now he has withdrawn his petition contesting his right to her. That is mighty fortunate for if there be any who imagine I would let her return to a life of humiliation and beating, they are mistaken."

"I take your point, sir. The verdict will be just."

HER HUSBAND WAS DEEP IN THOUGHT DURING SUPPER, CHEWING IN silence, not that the topics—curing bacon and whether they would order the town lorimer in on the morrow to check all the horse bits and other metalwork in the harnesses—were thrilling in any case. Since they had returned to the castle, Gervase's conversation had been about as stimulating as dinner time in a silent religious order.

"A silver penny!"

Johanna blinked in relief at the silver moonlet on the cloth. The old Gervase was there still. She gazed anew at the clean, golden hair maning the intelligent brow, the clever mouth, the straight, patrician nose that hinted at him being some noble's bastard and made her own eyes wide, her lips inviting. She wanted this man beside her forever. The world without him would lack all hue and flavour.

"Is this a bribe?" she asked. "Or a yearly peppercorn rent?"

"No, a silver penny for your thoughts."

"Losing you." Strike while the iron was accessible let alone hot. She had to brand her name upon his heart.

"No frowns, sweetheart. Your toes have scarce touched the water. By my father's soul, you cannot yet have waded in so deep." So he was warning her off with light words. Desire but not love; friendship but not commitment; and kindness but not passion.

"Gervase, it can only take a moment. A child can drown in a thrice when no one is looking, and as for me, I cannot swim."

His blue eyes, deep but wary, still were an ocean of compassion to drown in. "Must I teach you that as well, Johanna?"

God knows how she might have answered him had the steward not run up the hall, his dignity forgotten.

"Madam! Sir! The Enderby men have returned Agnes."

WHILE THE HOUSEHOLD CELEBRATED IN THE HALL, JOHANNA ROCKED the weeping girl in the south tower. The women would be counting the weeks.

Told to go away, Gervase perversely let himself into Johanna's bedchamber later with Jankyn and the minstrel at his heels. She glared at the trio in futile fury, but her tearful Agnes roused from her arms and she let them stay. Jankyn had been the poor songbird that Martin de Scruton had fixed his talons into after dinner, but he looked like a dog that had stolen a bone and was boasting that even Stephen de Norwood could not have given better answers.

A look from Johanna quelled him and he sat down goodnaturedly at the maidservant's feet. Together the three men drove the conversation along as if life had returned to normal and the room became a tavern to be filled with music, sending the women's feet tapping or bringing them to tears. They sang for Agnes until Father Gilbert marched across from his cell and shouted that this was the holy day on which the Blessed Saviour had driven the moneylenders from the temple.

"Is there anything in the Gospels about our Lord Saviour driving out musicians?" Gervase asked his companions, but the music ceased.

IT TOOK HOURS OF GATHERING COURAGE TO KNOCK LATER ON GERvase's door. The mumbled answer scarce gave permission, but she lifted the latch quietly. The stealthy entrance was ruined; she fell over a pair of boots.

English words, blunt and concise, assaulted her noble ears and put paid to the trembling she felt. A wooden platter skimmed the top of her head and she squealed.

"Johanna? Hell's fire!"

Strong hands fumbled for her forearms and pulled her to her feet, but her hem was trapped beneath her heel and Gervase had to keep hold of her.

"Could you strike a candle, please?"

"If you wish. Perhaps you would care to explain why you are here?"

He freed her, and holding a wick into the fire, he illuminated more than she expected.

"Ohhh!"

He was completely unclothed. The river of dark blond hair flowed down his broad chest—oh, that she had seen before—but her glance could not help following down the ripple to where it disappeared between his narrow thighs. Try to forget Fulk, she fiercely warned herself, or you will never be healed. Abandoning the natural modesty in her nature, she tried to behave like a worldly lady.

Save for the ribbon of scarring, his was not the milk-hued skin of ancient Fulk or the fair-headed groom, but shone golden and lustrous. Think as an artist. Yes, that helped. He could have commanded a fee as a model for the depiction of David at King Saul's court in Holy Jerusalem. No, David must have been slighter. Her mind turned secular—a naked Lancelot? Now there was a thought.

"Would you like me to move slowly round for you?" Geraint was trying not to laugh. Thoughts were tossing across her face like reflections on a wind-scuffed pool. Surprise and panic had given way to scientific study. Was she planning to stitch him an embroidered loincloth?

"I-I . . . your pardon." Blushing enchantingly, she averted her eyes to the empty palliasse. Her excuse surfaced huskily. "I-I did not know you were already abed."

Geraint shrugged, unabashed by his nudity. "Jankyn is carousing with the pantler—he never sleeps soundly." His tone was sardonic, challenging her to look at him again.

"Could you cov—do return to your bed. I am sure you must be cold. I came to ask you something—out of friendship, I might add—so please do not be alarmed."

He made no move to obey her. "Why will the matter not wait until morning?" he asked arrogantly and stood at ease before the dying fire.

Damn him, Johanna fumed, the pose was calculated, giving her a shameless chance to stare sinfully at the broad shoulders tapering to the perfect buttocks and the wonderful gilt-hazed limbs that supported him.

"You are being vain," she whispered.

"No, I have other reasons, but I can fetch you a ewer if you feel like being sick."

"I am not going to—oh, for Heaven's sake, Gervase."

"It is cold, my lady. Is there a long preamble or would you care to come to the peroration of your midnight visit?"

"P-please will you stop being so . . . so brittle."

"I can guess what you have come to say. Would you like to get it over with?"

Yes, she did have her speech ready and there was not an alternative version for contingencies like this. A pox on him! "You will be leaving soon and we will probably never meet again."

"You run before me to market, my sweet. I was not thinking of going without breaking my fast."

"Just be quiet, please. I should like to have a child."

That wiped the smile off his—well, off his back. Every bit of him tightened and an angry oath shook him but then he laughed.

"Now I have heard everything. The planets must be in strange alliance for this is out of character for you."

Geraint's words belied his inner turmoil. Gazing up unseeing at the dark crevasses of mortar, he fought the desire to take her in his arms and lead her into a false paradise. He had dreaded this, watching her day by day unfurl her courage and learn to trust again. And having freed her from the girdle and shown her kindness, it was inevitable that this fledgeling love should seek some bond with him.

A child? Oh no, this was but the outer, rational form of her argument; the woman inside her was trying to bind him with desire, to cast a net of love over him and tether him to Conisthorpe. And it would be so easy to love her with his mind and body.

He glanced over his shoulder at her dark head, bowed by his unkindness, and pitied them both. He needed time to think.

"I gave the matter much thought on the journey from Richmond." She looked up from her twisting fingers to find he had turned and was scowling.

"I see." Gervase strode across to the bed and grabbed up the coverlet, flinging it over his shoulder so that its dark brown folds gave him some modesty while he faced her like some ancient Druid god. "You want me to lie with you."

"Well, yes, if you please."

"But, Johanna, is it not written that women only conceive if they feel pleasure? Did you not tell me on several occasions that you find the carnal act repulsive?" Was he laughing at her or hiding his scorn in practicalities?

"Well, I thought if I tried not to think or . . ." His jaw clenched at her clumsy words. "This is not easy for me, Gervase, but I-I want to have something left to love. I know we are barely acquainted but . . ."

"Depending on the phase of the moon and your fecundity"—it was as if he found the word poisonous—"not to mention your admission of indifference, the process may need to be repeated several times and even then may not be successful."

He was marshalling his arguments like a lawyer and Johanna, who had taken all day to come to this resolution and all darkness to force herself to ask him, could only stand there close to tears, feeling as though she was a tiny beetle and he was about to crush her beneath the heel of his boot.

Stand firm, she told herself, *do not let him rile you.*

"Sir, I came to ask you out of friendship."

"Friendship?" He weighed the word with wry tenderness. "What you desire goes by other names."

She trembled beneath his shadowy gaze but not with fear. "It would be easy for you."

"No," his voice was a tired whisper as he turned away but the denial was not over, "I do not have command of my emotions like you do."

"But I—"

She did not see the quiver of his hand as he pressed the heel of his palm against his closed eyes. "My lady," he held his voice steady as if words might spill unbidden, "Johanna, you offer me a gift I cannot accept."

"But you will think about it," she said as he strode to the door and set it open for her to leave, his face unreadable.

"How can I not?" he answered darkly and closed the door behind her.

Twenty-seven

IT WAS SAFER TO STAY IN HER BEDCHAMBER NEXT MORN-
ing and lick her wounds. He had been right to reject
her.

"My lady!" The whistle on the other side of the door came from
Jankyn. Johanna smiled at the still sleeping Agnes and unbarred
the door herself.

"My master says that since the day is fine you are to go hawking
with him."

"Tell him to go hang, Jankyn!"

"My sweet lady, the primroses have unfurled their skirts these
last three weeks and lack admiration before they wither, the sky-
larks are singing an anthem to the risen sun and you are sulking—
your pardon—skulking here like last night's wine bibbler with a
headache wasting the precious hours."

"Go to, Jankyn. I am displeased with your master."

"But your master he is, or so the world must see, and he says
that if you come not, he will set you across his saddle upon your
belly and bear you hence."

Agnes stirred and blinked. "He is your husband, my lady, and
it be a lovely day."

"You will please do as I say." Gervase halted outside her door,
his saddlebag over his shoulder. For answer, he received a hum-
phy jerk of her shoulders. "Very well, madam. I am not ordering,
I am begging you for your company and I will take it very ill if
you respond to my short-lived humility with less than feminine
courtesy."

*   *   *

APRIL HAD GROWN GENTLE, THE WIND HAD CHANGED TO A KINDLY westerly and although the sky was lacy with clouds, none of them clustered defiantly. A knight and his lady, they rode out with Sir Geoffrey and a full escort through the fields and along the stony lanes into higher country where flocks rambled. It was too perfect. Even the lilting reed pipe of a shepherd boy coincided with their passing and the thanks of a silver penny arced, glinting, through the air from Gervase's gloved hand.

But the spring weather could not be mocked and Johanna, who delighted in the dales whatever the season, was proud of the valley's beauty. The slight white flowers of the blackthorn lit the edges of the ploughed fields and the hawthorn and bramble thickets fell back giving way to the yew that ribboned the skirt of the hill. The edge of the moor was fringed with gorse and bracken, flattened and dried by the winter snows. To the south, sheep pasture velveted the hillside, descending to a church and a scattering of dwellings, folds and byres.

Gervase flew her mother's merlin and Sir Geoffrey tried out his young long-winged hawk for the first time. Then, as the sun moved close to its zenith, the men unpacked leather bottles, soft white bread and ripe cheeses from the saddle panniers. Johanna, happy and exhilarated, was invited to be seated upon an unstrapped packsaddle. The rest of the company sat on their cloaks about her and the sated birds dozed within their tufted hoods upon their stand. Beneath her feet, the moss was tinted with dried grass and wondrously softer than any carpet. Lured by its texture, she took off her glove and stroked it, wondering at the dry surrender beneath her fingerpads and how this curious turf mede welcomed her.

Gervase sprawled upon his back at her feet, one arm flung across his face, and Johanna, looking upon him, despite last night's irresolution, felt such overwhelming love that she was hard put not to weep, not only for the day's joy but also in sadness that her pleasure in his company must be so fleeting. This hawk would fly and she had no lands to lure him nor jesses strong enough to tether him.

He was sitting up now, speaking to Sir Geoffrey, the wind playing with his fair hair. "My lady and I will find our way down from here. Meet us as we arranged."

Sir Geoffrey raised his hand in kindly salute, his expression indulgent but with an edge of wariness. There had been more instructions, Johanna suspected, as the men scrambled to their feet and grabbed their horses' bridles.

"Come." Gervase's shadow fell across her face but it was Sir Geoffrey who drew her to her feet and, like a father sensing matters to be spoken, left her alone with him. The company dispersed tactfully out of sight.

Johanna, exasperated, manipulated, her wishes not consulted, wondered if an apology was forthcoming and resolved to make him suffer a little. He held out his fingers to take her gloved hand in his but she refused and began walking. What was he at now? He must know that for several reasons she was no longer comfortable in his presence. Did he believe the haunting loveliness of the hills would cleanse away the humiliation of his refusal and so bring about a mutual absolution? Was this the beginning of his leaving?

He was not following, but gathering up the horses' reins. It halted her momentum and she waited, biting her lip, for him to join her. Taking the palfrey's reins from him, she asked, "Is this a sop dipped in honey to sweeten your imminent departure?"

He smiled and held his free hand up, away from his sword in surrender. "No, we are looking for curlews and every time you hear one, I shall kiss you."

She wished she had managed to kick him at midnight. "Perhaps rabbits might be a safer choice. I have gone quite deaf with the altitude."

The mournful cry reached them and a black and white bird floppily took off from the breast of the hill. "That was a peewit," declared Johanna firmly.

With a shrug, Gervase strode ahead so she was forced to grab a fistful of her skirt and hasten after him along the rich dark brown of the narrow sheep track.

He waited amused, knuckles at his belt, legs apart, the wind gently playing with his cloak. "I could challenge you to a rolling race down the hillside but it might shock our escort and confuse

the horses," he called, and paced on again as if he knew that, like
Eurydice, she would follow to a different world.

A tiny harem of ewes fled from them, save for a curious lamb
that knew no fear. The silly creature bleated up incongruously at
the man's great height and ambled off most tardily.

Despite her pretence of contrariness, Johanna was truly enjoying
the rarity of the excursion, inwardly marvelling at everything.
Even a dead lone tree, its roots cluttered with scree, was striking
in its gaunt beauty. A weathered rabbit skull saddened her and
she looked away, all her senses, all her joy centering on the man
who stood beside her.

"Where are we going?"

"To gaze out over your demesne so that when you leave Conisthorpe you can tuck the memory in with your veils and kirtles
like a sprig of rosemary."

He led her up a cleavage in the curving hills to where the land
fell away so she might watch the clouds throwing their shadows
across the moors. The dappled beauty of the dale was set before
her like a feast for her pleasure. She felt his hands upon her sleeves
as he stood behind her and wished that every day might be like
this. The man's fingers lifted her veiling, set her braids aside and
kissed her shoulder. Below in the valley, the river hurried, but time
paused and waited on their pleasure.

"I have never told you how beautiful you are."

The unsought compliment startled her. She suspected calculation on his part and glanced sideways at him for affirmation. There
was charm in the tilt of his mouth, but it might have been the sky
he was addressing.

"No, nor should you have. It would have been mere flattery."

"You underrate yourself."

Like a goshawk, his gaze soared over her lips and slowly down
to hover where her cloak had fallen back above the rise of her
breasts.

The mournful cry came.

"That was a curlew," he laughed and turning her, caught her
to him by the waist. As if he sensed her antipathy still, his lips
pressed briefly upon hers with the lightness of friendship. Then,
taking her hand, he led her around the contour of the hill, the
churlish wind testing the strength of their apparel, tugging at his

beaked hat, prying beneath her skirts, billowing their cloaks into flapping boat sails.

She was glad when they turned inward again to the calm shelter of the upper valley. Here she could feel the sun's warmth. He let drop his stallion's rein and unslung his baldrick, but kept the scabbard close to hand as he sat down upon the moss.

Yet last night lay unresolved between them. At a loss, she glanced around her undecided. Did Eve feel so when Adam had tasted the apple and gazed upon her with a new understanding in his eyes? The air was quiet, the sounds about them God-made; they could have been the only people on Earth.

Ignoring her diffidence, Gervase smiled, lay back, clasped hands behind his head and closed his eyes. "It is too pleasant here to hasten back," he observed, leaving her with no choice but to spread her cloak beside him. She sat for a while in her own silence, listening to the thin song of a soaring skylark. Her companion might have been asleep so she eventually settled onto her front, letting her fingers pluck idly at the grasses, but her glance caressed his face.

"Gervase?"

An eyebrow twitched. "Hmm?"

"The judge is very angry with us. He must have heard from my lord Despenser."

"I know, poor fellow." Her companion rolled onto his belly and rested his chin pensively upon his crossed wrists. "However, let us admit, he still has the power to send you back to Enderby— that is, if he has the courage to thwart a certain high personage and risk demotion."

"Do not be sorry for him." Johanna sat up. "William de Bedford has his price."

"What do you mean?" He eased himself onto his uninjured side, propping his head upon his elbow to study her, his fingers playfully stroking the edge of her cloak.

"Mother—well, she finally admitted to me last night that all along she was expecting the verdict to be eventually in our favour."

That made him abandon his loverlike manner and sit up with a frown that was more than skin-deep. "How so?" he asked abruptly.

"Believe me, I never guessed. Apparently she made a point of informing him on the second day of the hearing that she is the god-daughter of my lord of Canterbury and would be writing to his grace shortly." Johanna had expected merely surprise and relief, not a string of Anglo-Saxon expletives.

"Why in God's Name could she not have told me before we were bidden to Richmond? Did Stephen de Norwood know of this?"

"But if Judge William is not venal, it will make no difference," she added swiftly to appease him. "The verdict could still go against us." She watched the knuckles of his fist continually waste themselves against his palm but his face gradually lost its ill-humoured expression.

"No, the Despensers always prevail. They have a way of knowing the way beneath a man's armour no matter how much he buckles on to guard himself," he answered. "But it is all one so long as your marriage is annulled and all of this has been to some avail."

The cry of another curlew bruised the silence between them.

Gervase observed the bird's flight, but his words were for her. "What are we to do about us, Johanna?"

"Us?" She could scarce keep the tremor from her voice.

"It has gone beyond friendship, has it not?"

"H-has it?"

"Yes, you cannot hide it." His fingers gently turned her face towards him. "My poor confused darling. Is it just a babe you want from me or more than that?"

Tears sparkled upon her lashes. "Am I so transparent?" she whispered ruefully, staring disconsolately at the sky above his shoulder, not daring to read what must be rejection.

"Oh, Johanna, I do not want to betray you. I have too much respect for you." He smudged away the droplets from her cheek. "How can I promise more than I can give?"

"I have been hurt already. Your kindness cannot harm me."

His mouth twisted, and he let go of her. "I have heard both the act and feeling called many things, but never kindness. Love is selfish, my lady."

"Then in God's name, let us be selfish!" she exclaimed, rising to her feet. "If you so wish!" Her hands were curled into exasperated fists as she turned and faced him. "What do you want, Gervase? The interest that you mentioned the day you came to Conisthorpe?"

He ran his hand ashamedly across his chin. "I cannot believe how loutishly I behaved. Is it too late to apologise?" At the shake of her head and the laughter springing in her eyes, his expression grew roguish. "Would you like me to kiss your shoe beaks in all humility?" He was shuffling towards her on his knees, but she realised as he halted within grasp of her skirts that his eyes were far from recalcitrant. "And I thought hitherto that women were frail, sheepish creatures. *Say you want me, Johanna.*" The words were uttered in a different voice. The blue gaze drew her, deep water to drown all inhibition.

A man, this man, on his knees to *her*. Shaken at his mercurial capacity to surprise her still, Johanna gazed down bereft of words. But the decision had been already made on yesterday's eve, the bow drawn; it was the true reason behind it that had been omitted.

What he was asking, she could not answer. Not yet.

"It is not too late to apologise," she whispered, hazarding fingers to touch the golden hair, and then with a sob his face was against her body, his arms encompassing her kirtle skirt.

As if she stood on quicksand, Johanna's limbs melted and she sank to her knees within the safe keep of his embrace and wrapped her arms about his neck. His kisses were on her hair, her brow, her cheek, her throat, her parted lips.

"I swear, lady," he told her, drawing breath, his brow stern, "that you are liking this more than a virtuous woman should."

It was because she loved him. The revelation hit her as if God had suddenly unveiled the writing in the sky. There was no revulsion, no recoiling from this man's touch.

Geraint watched the deep green eyes go light with surprise like a startled wood creature's.

"You called me a whore once," she protested with exquisite coyness.

He gathered her to him, laughing. "Oh, your pardon, so I did. But, lady, if I hold you a moment longer . . ." He watched her lips tremble with a virginal modesty. "Bid me let you go or, believe me, I shall consummate this adulterous match of ours." His hands were upon her back, gentle clamps to prevent her sudden bolting.

"Here?" she asked nervously, not meeting his gaze, her breathing becoming unsteady. "We have already tarried too long." She blinked at the horses as if they might interfere but they were delicately feeding.

"There is no one to see. Our people will stay for us." Already his hand was easing up her skirt to garter height. "Would you like the magic again—Joanna!" Her hands were guiding him to the lacing behind her and her eyes were dark with mischief. "Why, you witch," he murmured, his words drowning against her lips as he loosened the bodice of her gown.

He pulled her slackened kirtle down, immobilising her forearms and freed one of her breasts, stroking his forefinger round the dark surround of her nipple until he knew, watching her face, that she yearned for him to touch the nub, but it was his mouth that took possession.

"W-why now, Gervase? When you refused last night."

He lifted his head. His lady was thinking still, not yet subordinate to her body's craving; her mind's needs must be sated first. "I am a free spirit, my darling, not a stallion to be led by the bridle in to breed." His face grew taut and he looked at her with an emotion as old as Paradise, sliding his hand beneath her innermost skirt. Tenderly he parted her with the skill of a loving journeyman as he sought out the sensitive answering that he had found before.

"Ohh."

He watched with satisfaction her exquisite breasts rise and fall as her breathing quickened. With a prayer of thanks, he knew he had won her. The gate that must let him in was opening and the dew that the troubadours sang of with knowing smiles was moistening his fingers.

Johanna was truly his, her breathing ragged, her body arching. She was tangling her fingers tightly in his hair and drawing his face down to her willing lips. At last he had her past thinking, past caring and his enchantment of her was seeping along her body to her fingertips, up her spine. He loosened his own clothing. Soon his lady would feel the waves coming closer but . . .

Johanna gasped. "Why have you stopped?" The spellbinder had left her deliberately unsated, on fire.

"I wish to pleasure you, my dearest lady, but my own pain needs answering too. Would you have me enter you? If not, then we must cease at once . . . for I desire you beyond all reason. I cannot in all honour—"

"Give quarter, I beg you," she whispered. "Set me free!"

Gervase understood, his hand came back to her, teasing and caressing, until she was again at the mercy of the pleasure he aroused in her. He entered her so easily, as if he knew the door and owned the key. And her body never clenched in rejection as it had against Fulk's battering. She banished comparisons. This was different from anything else. He moved inside her, filling her comfortably as his finger stroked her further. The double sensation was almost unbearable. The sorcery struck her again, as if everything had drawn into a tight fist and let go with a great shuddering toss. She cried out, her body needing him and with a triumphant gasp he found release, filling her with his seed.

Johanna opened her eyes and saw him smiling down at her.

"Now you know why it is sinful, why lust drives men to Hell."

"Was I lustful?"

"Lustful! Venus would not compare." Geraint kissed her nose.

It had been a compromise of course. Not merely his skill as a lover that had ensured her surrender, but her desire to give, to please, to thank him for making her smile again, for valuing her.

"I wish . . ." she murmured, rearranging the tumbling golden hair back from his forehead, but said no more. Wishing would fragment the enchantment.

"All things must end," he told her solemnly, tugging her to her feet. He slung his swordbelt on and with his arm about her waist, he whistled the horses to follow and steered her back towards the open pasture. Maybe, she thought, it was also a beginning.

"How long will you remain after the verdict—if it is not against us?"

"As long as is seemly. A week perhaps. Before the 'miserable Mallet' comes knocking on Conisthorpe's gate like a bad-tempered bailiff."

A week, only a week!

Johanna wanted to tell him that she had fallen in love with him and that if he left her she would wither and die. But he was not hers; he never had been. God had sent him to her for a little space. The man had been honest, never making a secret of his intent to leave as soon as he could and if he now loved her, surely he would not show such eagerness to depart. No, she must make the best of this very moment.

Sensing how much she was drawing on her inner strength to steel herself against his leaving, Geraint carried her palm to his lips.

"You are whole again, my lady, and shall be free of both your tiresome husbands. I will at some future day send you word that Gervase de Laval is no more. Perhaps the Scots will have stuck a dirk in him or he will have died ignobly from dysentery."

"Please, do not talk so." *Not after what we have just shared.*

"You will fall in love with some local lord."

"With your babe within me."

"I doubt it, lady. One coupling does not make a child."

And yet today he had deliberately exposed her to that possibility. Last night he had been angry, today compliant. Was it merely a question of who made the decision, that as a man he could not let it be to her ordering?

"If . . . if you have impregnated me, could I deign to ask the name of the child's father?"

"Why, Gervase de Laval." It was a prompt answer.

Geraint was going to kill Gervase to free her. Some miserable, much-travelled letter would arrive, deliberately sent to some foreign port and commissioned to return, so that no one would be able to doubt the veracity. His motives had to be selfish, fragrant in sweet-smelling altruism; he had to free her in order to stay free himself.

"Shall I carry you? I did not think the way would be so rough."

The upper valley had funnelled and the path was tumbled with fallen boulders, unblessed by sheep turds. A veritable river of stones, it became hard walking for Johanna's thin shoes, a matter of wobbling and avoiding a turned ankle, and she could almost touch each side of the chasm with her fingertips.

"It is limestone," he told her as she ran her fingers over the surface. "See where the tree roots are splitting and loosening the . . . slabs." His whole manner changed and he froze, holding up his fingers almost in a blessing for her silence.

She thought it was some wild creature, and then he stealthfully drew his sword and slowly unlooping the narrower baldrick from his shoulder dangled the horn for her.

Holding her breath, Johanna took it. He signalled her to raise it to her lips and mount the horse on his signal. Letting fall his hand, he flung himself round the blind angle of the chasm.

Johanna blew as hard as she might and screamed as a soldier flung himself down the bank, cutting her off from the horses. Running to Gervase, she found him beset on the perilous rubbled ground by three swordsmen. One he had already dispatched, and he had a jagged wet wall of limestone at his back.

Johanna put the horn to her lips again, but the fourth man dashed it away and grabbed her by her braids. She went heavy in his arms, flopping forward like a cloth-stuffed doll, nigh oversetting him by her weight. Before he could right her, she grabbed a rock and whammed it into his face. He shrieked, reeling back with blood like rivulets plunging forth between his steel mittens.

"Get her!" snarled Edgar de Laverton. He drove his blade at Gervase. A second swordsman came towards her, his breath rasping, his sword tip bloodied. Backing away, Johanna went stumbling, lost her footing and, hindered by her skirt, struggled to right herself, turning onto her hands and knees. Grabbing rocks with two hands, she hurled them at his shins, trying not to be distracted by the strained breathing of the fighters beyond and the vicious clang of every blow that missed and struck the wall.

Gervase was taunting Edgar, "And tell your foul master that I have just pleasured my lady up on the sword."

Edgar gave a hissing laugh. "Then I had better geld you before you do it again," and he lunged at his loins and drove below his guard, but Gervase spun out of the way. He had bundled his cloak about his left arm as a crude buckler.

The second man's boot caught Johanna in the belly and she fell back with a scream as he held the sword across her neck.

"Surrender or he will cut her throat," Edgar roared. Gervase leapt back, watching his opponent but uncertain.

"What? Slay the Lady of Enderby? Then you will hang for certain!"

"I thought you wanted me alive, Edgar," Johanna purred. ·

"Hold her!" her old enemy rasped, readjusting his hold on the sword handle as if his fingers were spasmed.

"Let her go!" Sir Geoffrey, his sword drawn, stood above the chasm and from either side the Conisthorpe men came running.

Johanna, her head pressed sideways by the sharpness of the blade suddenly knew real fear. She was the talisman to freedom.

Edgar backed up until he was flanking her. "Over there all of you!"

The Conisthorpe men slowly grouped themselves to the upper side and Edgar, watching Gervase, edged down the path. His companion, holding Johanna, was slowly feeling his way with his heels, hauling her with him.

"Perhaps you would like me as prisoner instead?" Gervase flung aside his sword.

"No, we cannot enjoy you in the same way, though we could try," snorted the other man. It was then that Sir Geoffrey took the risk and hurled a rock down at the back of her assailant's neck. The man's sword arm jerked forward and in that instant Gervase sprang, kicking Edgar out of the way with one foot and knocking the sword out of the other man's loosened hold. With a swift re-action that astonished herself, Johanna brought up the side of her right hand and sliced it across the bridge of her assailant's nose. He fell back with a scream, blood gushing, struggling to keep hold of her but she scrambled free, gasping, as her mother's men came slithering down the rockface.

With a roar of victory, the Conisthorpe men hauled their captives down the path. In the field behind the church, Gervase waved them to halt.

"Give him his sword. I want to kill him."

"No!" exclaimed Johanna, trying to fling herself between them, but Sir Geoffrey grabbed her back.

They were equally matched; while Gervase had height and greater strength, Edgar de Laverton was agile and light upon his feet, dancing around his opponent, showing his true mettle now that they fought on even ground. Johanna hid her face in the older man's shoulder, not bearing to watch.

"Take her into the church!" she heard Gervase yell, but she would not be led away. Every rasp of steel against steel sent shivers of fear streaking down her spine. The shouts and groans of the Conisthorpe men told her how the battle waged back and forth. Dear God, if Edgar won, Gervase would be dead and the candle that lit her world would be blown out. If Edgar won, the church court would deliver her back to Fulk and he would tie her to her bed at Conisthorpe and—

Around her the men were roaring in bloodlust and then it was over. She uncovered her face and saw Gervase staggering, alive, though blood was streaking down his cheek and his sleeve was torn and dripping. He cast his bloody sword aside and flung himself to the ground, panting air in great gulps.

"It is all right, lass." Sir Geoffrey kept her aright as she stepped unsteadily forwards and, falling to her knees beside Gervase, gathered him into her arms. "Oh, my love, my love!"

IT WAS AS WELL AGNES HAD BEEN RETURNED ELSE SHE MIGHT HAVE had her throat slit in vengeance at Edgar de Laverton's slaying. Geraint was heartily glad there had been sufficient witnesses on both sides to testify that it had been a true fight.

"About as clever as walking into a Grimsby whorehouse without a dagger," Sir Geoffrey muttered later as the men shared a barrel of ale in the keep. "If I and the lads had not been there . . ."

"But you were, sir, albeit a trifle tardy."

"Pig's vomit," exclaimed the older man with reasonable amiability. "I wonder about you, boy, I really do. Lady Johanna—"

"—is good in a fight. I am thinking of having her properly trained in combat practice. Once the news reaches Robert the Bruce, he will declare a truce instantly and King Edward will have to knight her."

"You," growled Sir Geoffrey, "are a menace to my sanity and so is your ruddy esquire."

BECAUSE THE WHOLE REALM AND HOLY CHURCH ESPECIALLY WAS preparing for the most solemn festival of the year, Agnes's interrogation early next day was mercifully brief. The examiner departed to confer with the judge and Geraint received word from Sir Ralph that he had put one of Fulk's men to the question and the man had confessed Edgar's part in the abduction of Agnes. Judge William de Bedford must have been wishing himself well away from Conisthorpe. Within the hour he announced that he had read all the witnesses's depositions and since the case was no longer being contested, he would announce his verdict. A messenger was dispatched instantly to the castle to fetch the petitioner and defendant, and by the time the Conisthorpe party arrived, the church was packed with townsfolk. Thankfully none of the Enderby company were present, nor was the husband-hunting widow, Lady Maud.

Judge William de Bedford was looking sour as a crabapple and his tone in addressing them could have whetted butcher's knives.

"The decision of this court is that the marriage between Gervase de Laval and Johanna FitzHenry is lawful." The lady in question tried to keep her features grave and composed, but she felt like whooping. In accordance with his part, Geraint put an arm round her and kissed her cheek. His relief was sincere. He felt like crowing at Stephen de Norwood. *Three years! How wrong you were.* But the pious Judge William had not finished with them.

"Since, however, the said man and woman are living as man and wife, and in order to prevent any further claims against the said defendant, it is hereby ordered that the plaintiff shall presently wed the defendant before witnesses at the church door and that the marriage shall be straightway consummated."

"Oh, dear God," whispered Lady Constance, masking her mouth with her glove.

IT WAS THE COURT'S REVENGE FOR INTERFERENCE. IT HAD DONE what Hugh Despenser had requested, but it had a little power left to see that the laws of Holy Church were followed. If Gervase de Laval petitioned for his alleged marriage to be upheld, then here was his answer. Justice was heaped onto his platter with a vengeance.

"I object." Father Gilbert strode forward, his vestments flapping. The court had robbed him of a soul to be garnered for God. Then, seeing Johanna's horrified face, he relented, floundering to avert suspicion. If he informed on them, he would be restricted from holy office for at least three years—or excommunicated. "I-I object with all respect to Father Peter officiating. As the lady's chaplain and confessor, I beg permission to hear their vows."

Behind Johanna, her mother let out her breath. "Put a good face on it, for God's sake, Gervase," she pleaded during the hubbub as the two priests stepped forward to the bench.

"I am delirious with happiness." Geraint was smiling though his teeth. There was nothing that he could do but try to look as if it was his namesaint's day and he had been given a cartload of gold.

Judge William addressed the court. "Father Gilbert's request is granted. This court will adjourn until after Eastertide."

"Madam!" With eyes chillingly mocking, Gervase bowed to Johanna fulsomely and offered his wrist. Johanna felt as though her heart would break. She had never dreamed it would end like this.

"Look merrier, both of you," warned Lady Constance.

He led her out into the churchyard, stepped round her so that he was on her other side and, with a hand to his waist and a flourish so vigorous that it swung his sleeve up over his arm, held out his hand to her again so they were facing the porch together. Father Gilbert, flanked by acolytes and suitably garbed in borrowed vestments, was positioning himself.

"It is not my fault," Johanna mouthed at Geraint, appalled at the anger she knew to be simmering behind the clenched jaw. Was he married already despite his reassurances? Or was he betrothed elsewhere and this match would kill his chance of obtaining a rich heiress?

"She is marrying Gervase de Laval." Her mother spoke softly, coming between them. "You can arrange his death, surely?"

"Oh, I certainly can." His tone could have scythed an oak. With a defiant toss of his head, he glared at the rump of William de Bedford's horse as it departed with its virtuous rider. "If I ever lay hands on that son of a dog . . ."

"But he thinks it is the right thing and so it is, if we are not liars."

"This was never the bargain."

They stepped forward together awkwardly like carthorses out of step. It was the second time she had knelt in misery to whisper a trothplight. She should be feeling joyous, but the friend had fled and in his place stood a cold, indifferent man. Would his heiress know him like this, a businesslike bridegroom who had not made the match out of any affection?

"Let the marriage be consummated this very hour," declared Sir Ralph, bussing her on the cheek and ushering them out into the sunlight, "not that it is anything a young couple like you have not managed already."

The mayor had already summoned the town musicians and Johanna and Gervase were preceded in procession by their capering, while her mother sent orders for her great bed to be furnished with fresh sheets. Yolonya was enthusiastically scattering fertility herbs upon it when the bridal party entered the bedchamber.

"Put 'em to bed," ordered Sir Ralph. "I never in my life was so glad to see an end to this business. Put 'em to bed and all will be fair and square."

The women were all about Johanna, unplaiting her hair and undressing her. She sent Gervase an imploring look, willing him to send them away, but it was as though he was made of unfeeling rock. Sir Geoffrey and Sir Ralph were doing the same to him, lifting off the tunic she had embroidered for him, peeling down his hose. Surely he must stop them; the deputy sheriff would see the telltale scars, but the man seemed like a statue, without will. There was a gasp as the jagged edges of his wounds were displayed and Sir Ralph met his steady gaze.

"You are a soldier then," he declared. "I think you *will* be going north against the Scots."

"Now that the case is settled, why not? Shall we get this over?"

They fell back from Gervase and he faced Johanna, forced to look at her against his mind's reason. Clearly he was despising her for this. And even if the forced partnering was with the human being Johanna adored above all others; even if behind his stubborn visage he shared her embarrassment at being exposed to the common gaze, she stood alone. The lustrous mantle of her hair afforded her some modesty, but it was not long enough to hide her gender or stay chastely unparted over her breasts. The humiliation of this public coupling was appalling, but worse still was the indifference in his eyes.

She could sense Sir Ralph's admiring gaze, heard the mayor swallow salaciously. Father Gilbert cleared his throat and gave a blessing for her fertility, not her happiness.

The tester was drawn back and she and Gervase were urged to their respective sides of the high bed.

"You will place your leg against your wife's," ordered the mayor and Johanna felt Gervase's cool skin alongside her thigh. This was how they betrothed princesses to distant bridegrooms, the proxy had to set his naked leg against the bride's and the marriage was witnessed as being insoluble.

"Satisfactory!" boomed Sir Ralph, then, addressing Lady Constance, "This must be a relief to all at Conisthorpe."

"I should say so," exclaimed Sir Geoffrey pointedly, compensating for Father Gilbert's sour demeanour.

Gervase reached for the coverlet and dragged it up to hide their nudity. "Perhaps you will leave us now to bring this joyful occasion to, I trust, a fruitful conclusion."

Johanna waited until the door had closed behind Yolonya, who had insisted on tucking them in like a pair of siblings, and then she clouted him.

"I do not believe in violence," she said firmly, scrambling out of bed and grabbing the wine jug, "but you have had that coming for a long time." She poured herself far too much wine and, swirling it, drank half before he grabbed it from her. Standing before her, confident of his own fine body, he set cold palms upon her haunches.

"I might as well have some pleasure out of this," he said haughtily.

"No, not a bit of it," she protested, slapping his hands away. "You have been treating me as if this enforcement was my fault. Well, I am very sorry for you, but I am not to blame." She stood before the clouded window, her back to him, sipping her wine more slowly. "Is she beautiful, your heiress, or do you just hear the coins drop instead of salivating?"

"Johanna!" It was a whispered protest, a vain rustle against the door that had been closed upon them. Turning her head, she could see that some humanity was beginning to return to his blue eyes, as if they were no longer painted on some flat board but hid a soul behind them.

She studied him blatantly, wondering whether her revulsion would return if he was cruel to her now. She had journeyed far with his tutoring, but this man could rip her fragile wholesomeness to ragged pieces if he chose.

Geraint sighed. He longed to smash his fist into Hugh's almond eyes and strangle the judge until his eye sockets bulged, and curse and curse until the Devil rubbed his hands, his victory over another soul assured.

At least Johanna could not be made lawfully to share Fulk's bed again. But it was this enforced consummation, being told to perform, that he resented, and the complacent smirk of William de Bedford that he was perceived as Hugh's tail and could be pulled this way or that to annoy the beast in Despenser. At least, he thought maliciously, the verdict would make Hugh ropable.

It would be easier on him if Johanna found herself the equivalent of a figleaf, but his true wife of less than an hour seemed to be behaving like Eve before she developed a taste for apples. The wench was standing, unconscious of her nakedness, before the window, like the embodiment of Earthly Pleasure, the light illuminating her skin to resemble unflawed alabaster. And she was his lawfully, whether he would or no, to be enjoyed and treasured, but not by him.

"Do you believe in Hell?" It took an instant for Johanna's voice to reach his understanding.

"If there is good, there must be evil," he answered hoarsely as she turned to face him. Her breasts jutted out between the silken filaments of her hair, firm and alluring. Was this his Johanna, this dark-haired seductress?

"Why?" She turned sideways, brushing her dark curls back across her naked shoulder.

"If God exists, the Devil obviously can."

"But there is good and evil in every one of us, so perhaps God and Lucifer are part of the same entity." Her eyes were translucent as gems, mysterious as she stared at him, willing him to come to her. The game was as ancient as the barred gates of Paradise.

"You are free now," he observed, turning his back and retying his drawers about his waist as if the soft linen could staunch his growing ardour. He wanted her, but it was a matter of principle. If he took her now on her terms, he would become her dazed lover and leaving would be the harder. Fulk would be hammering at the gates to evict them, and in any case he could not take her home. Indeed, home was somewhere he had not been for years.

He sat down on the bed but he had reckoned without Johanna's swiftness to apply her learning when it suited her. She knelt behind him, her silken thighs encompassing his, her cheek like a butterfly's wings soft between his shoulderblades as she slid her arms about him.

"I love you," she whispered the words against his skin. "I will let you go and go you must, but give me these few days to warm my heart against the wintertide, against widowhood."

He would have freed himself abruptly and stood, but her fingers stole beneath the soft linen folds between his legs.

"Lady," he groaned. "Be at an end."

"You find this unpleasing, sir?"

He could not think any longer; the aching in his loins needed fulfilment. She had loosened the breechclout and her fingertips teased him, stroking slowly across his sensitive skin. She drew him back across the bed, performing the labour that was the weft and weave of dreams.

He let her seduce him, understanding at last that this was what she needed—for once to have the ordering of the universe, and that it did not matter anyway. And sin for once was thwarted, for was this not marriage and if there was a child, then was this pleasure blessed.

She set her legs astride his thighs and took him into her, letting him reach out and touch her breasts, giving in the act while demanding his surrender also. As the exquisite flood of pleasure overwhelmed him, his shout was exultant, a roar as animal as any great beast's.

He eased her to his side afterwards, drawing the sheets up round them, nestling her into the curve of his body, his face against her hair.

He laughed softly, pressing a kiss upon her shoulder.

"I am forgiven?" she whispered.

"No, not yet, or rather the forgiving is incomplete. A few days of pleasure, lady, despite Eastertide. We have a lot of forgiving still ahead of us, I think, before I leave."

Twenty-eight

GERAINT REMAINED A FURTHER WEEK AT CONIS-thorpe, agreeable to escorting the ladies and their movables south as far as Ludlow and their demesne at Blessington FitzHenry. And there were welcome tidings. Edmund wrote that he was taking ship for France as soon as he might safely do so, which left Geraint a free lance, if the term could be applied to an unemployed esquire, until he fulfilled his promise to Hugh. Agnes experienced her monthly blood flux and cheered up. Finally, Dame Christiana decided she would accompany them south; Fulk was the kind of man to ignore her pious reputation and accuse her of witchcraft. She had no wish to be tossed into the river trussed like a spitfowl.

His wife, he needs must call her so in truth now, had been trying to show a cheerful face. She had received the astonishing summons to attend the queen's household and that had distracted her somewhat from their imminent parting, but clearly she had been hoping he would either remain with her at Blessington FitzHenry or let her share his travels. It was hard not to be honest with her, to tell her that her fears that he had a commitment to another woman were groundless, but he dared not let her loving spirit enmesh him further. She had a different future now. It was the best he could do for her.

To be with him, Johanna, for her part, would cheerfully have thrown away her chance to serve Queen Isabella, despite the fact that her admiration for the royal lady was great.

"Dedicate yourself to the queen's service, Johanna," Gervase lectured her on the long journey west to Manchester. "She will treasure someone who will understand how a wife can suffer."

"Ha!" She was not thinking merely of Fulk.

"Johanna, I cannot provide for you. I have no land, no income and I have a sworn oath to fulfil. I am expected to serve in the Scots campaign, but until the autumn those who gave me shelter and employment when I fled from the monastery require my service."

"And after the Scots drive you shamefully home like a herd of swine?"

"You grow too disrespectful. I will not rest until this kingdom is cleansed of poor government."

"How noble-hearted!" she snorted. "So you will take on the Despensers single-handed? I imagine an heiress's fortune will strengthen your hand. That is what you intend."

"Johanna," he framed her face in his large hands. "At court you will learn that your little world in Yorkshire was but a fraction of the kingdom. In time, you will understand."

She recoiled. "Perhaps the peace of Shaftesbury Abbey would please me better since you think me so small-minded."

"That is your decision."

She had too much time for thinking; since they stayed overnight at religious houses she was deprived of the comfort and distractions of his body. But by the time they reached Chester, she had decided that she must educate herself in the affairs of the royal court so that she might become his equal and his helpmate in this political crusade of his. And there must be some way of discovering who he was and what burr had been stuffed beneath his girth to drive him so. Some noble's bastard, she suspected.

By the time they reached the city of Shrewsbury, her courage left her and she retreated crablike into her shell, for it was but three days riding now to Ludlow.

Geraint intended some business of his own at Sugwas outside Hereford with the man who had originally secured him a position in the Mortimer household—Adam Orleton, the Bishop of Hereford. It was in the morning at Church Stretton that he announced he would be leaving their company a few miles south of the town. Ludlow was Sir Roger Mortimer's demesne and he might now be recognized. It was better if he took a more circuitous route.

The news jolted Johanna. She thought that at least they might manage one last night together. Instead she suffered him to lead her palfrey's reins aside from their half-dozen household wagons to listen, no doubt, to a practiced speech of farewell, and they dismounted and stood together beneath a freshly leaf-garbed oak, happily bereft of pig dung around its roots, looking out to the treeless western horizon that the local people called the Long Mynd. The slaty-hued clouds betokening a heavy shower were a portent to Johanna of the loveless years stretching ahead—despite its glory as it lit the hillside, there was no kindness in the sky.

"I shall send you a white rose each Lammastide and by that you shall know I live." It was a sop to Johanna's appetite for love, but she wisely kept her own counsel.

"A rose of charity and discretion." *With plenty of thorns.* Her sarcasm clearly inconvenienced his sense of occasion.

"No, do not speak so shrewishly, lady. I dare say you would prefer a blossom of carnality, red as blood, but I think that unwise."

Unwise! Such male conceit! So, he would not wish to mislead her. How very considerate. A husband from the hiring fair that now sought employment with a wealthier mistress. Was the talk of duty just a bluff? Sensibly, she did not goad him. "Why at Lammas?"

"Because I have heard of a place in Ireland where at harvest feast marriages are made that last but a twelvemonth until the next Lammastide. Then the couple reconsider their vows and if they do not wish to continue, they stand back to back and walk away from each other."

"I will wager Holy Church has naught to do with it."

"True, it is a bard who blesses the handfasting. So, we shall have our own rite, you and I. A rose each Lammastide. A way to keep our hands in touch without commitment." He turned her towards the west. "Look, a rainbow. God's peace between us."

Perhaps the archer's bow of colours, elusive above the green-gold land, was drawn to remind them that their destinies were preordained. It might be God's peace; it was not hers.

"You may not know where to find me." Her voice had the edge of treason.

"I shall, believe me. Now, practicalities. I will arrange for you eventually to be sent a letter with tidings of the death of Gervase de Laval. Should you desire to marry and wish instant widowing, send to me in London at the Old Swanne brewhouse in Thames Street west, Vintry, not far from London Bridge. I may not be in England so it could take time to find me, but I shall do what is within my means. And Johanna, if ever you are in hardship, likewise send a message there."

"And if I have need to write to you there, which of your many hats will you be wearing?"

"Now do not be peevish, darling dear. Gervase de Laval shall suffice, believe me."

"I would I knew your true name," she growled.

"And be married to a named traitor."

"Ha, but you are not anymore, are you, Gervase? Some strange bargaining was done in dead of night at Richmond."

He held his hands at face level in surrender. "I was acquainted with someone there, yes, but I managed to talk my way out of that particular difficulty so that there is no danger to you or your family. Just be thankful that you do not know more. There are some secrets better kept locked. So I will leave you." He took her fingers in his.

"You have more speech rehearsed."

"Of course. Your fingers are cold." He carried them to his lips, and breathed on them before he kissed the tips. The intimacy of it scalded her as if he had left her with words of abuse. She wanted to throw her arms about his neck and plead with him to stay, but it was kinder to make a clean cut if that was what he wished.

His eyes were bereft of wizardry as he cleared his throat and grinning, began: "I wish you more happiness than ever it was in my power to give you, I wish you love of a worthy man and children, and a roof that does not leak—"

"Stop, stop, I pray you, this begins to sound more like a Greek curse. I could end up a nursemaid."

"I warrant you shall end up better than that." He turned her hand over and scuffed his calloused thumb sensuously across her palm. "See, here destiny crosses life and the crosses of fortune. You shall walk with the mighty, my Johanna." He looked over his shoulder. "The rain comes." And with a last kiss, he set her back in the saddle.

Johanna travelled on to Ludlow, helped her mother settle the poor incoherent, ailing creature that was her father in their castle at Blessington FitzHenry and gloomily prepared with Agnes to leave for London. Her father died three days before her planned departure. Guilty and saddened, Johanna would have stayed back after the funeral, but her mother, resilient as ever, insisted she must leave.

"Go to Westminster," she advised. "Rise high in the queen's favour. Times change, the old leaders die, others rise up to take their place and those who share Gervase's cause may gain power eventually."

"A gauche country creature like me to hold her own among the courtiers?"

"You will find a way, my darling, believe me."

PART TWO

1326

Four Years Later

Twenty-nine

September 1st 1326, the Feast of St. Giles

"DEAREST, YOU ARE NOT GOING!" LADY CONSTANCE set down the sheaf of daisies she had cut from their garden at Blessington FitzHenry to lay on Father Gilbert's grave. "The roads will be unsafe if a war is in the offing and I truly doubt the queen stands any chance of over-throwing the Despensers."

Johanna scanned the royal letter again. Isabella had written from Hainault, or rather her secretary had, that she had promise of arms and men and would be sailing for Suffolk within the month.

"But I owe her so much, *Maman*."

Indeed she did. Queen Isabella's trust and need of her had helped her find new purpose. True, the first months with the queen's constantly moving household had been an ordeal; not only had she mourned the loss of Gervase, but Edyth had swiftly smeared her reputation before she had even set foot in the royal presence and it had taken Isabella months to recognise Johanna's true mettle. Her skills in embroidery and her ability to adjust a kirtle's seam to add shape and interest slowly earned her the other noble ladies' respect. In her scant leisure time, she had improved her reading and writing, becoming useful to Isabella as an aman-uensis and pleasing her royal mistress by setting up a network of useful informers through the clothing guilds. Above all, she had proved a sympathetic friend to Isabella, a neglected, beautiful woman snared in a miserable marriage.

"I know you miss the cut and thrust of being at the heart of the realm, so to speak," muttered Lady Constance, "but it is two years now since the Despensers dismissed you from the royal household and I do not think you should risk returning until the peace is restored between King Edward and the queen."

"But, *Maman*, I had help from you and Gervase when I was desperately in need. Surely we cannot deny our sovereign lady our support when she is risking everything to free the kingdom? Please let me take her as many men as can be spared. The harvest is in now."

Her mother scowled. "It is not just the queen, is it? You are hoping this rebellion will bring *him* home. If he is bothered, he will seek you out when all the hurly-burly is over—that is if the queen succeeds—but I suppose she has Sir Roger Mortimer to help her. Oh, dearest, you promised me to keep away from the Despensers. I will send some men-at-arms to Suffolk, but you must stay here. Army camps are no place for a noblewoman."

Which was true, but in addition to a sense of duty, Johanna felt the pull of fate. And she certainly intended to keep as many leagues as possible between herself and the Despensers.

I never want to set eyes on you again, the old earl had said to her. It had been the feast of St. Bartholomew, in a room adjoining the king's painted chamber at Westminster Palace two years before.

She could remember every detail of that meeting: Despenser the younger sprawled in a chair of estate reading a letter, his booted feet propped upon the table; the paraphernalia of correspondence missing; only a wooden coffer waisted with iron, the length of a man's forearm, sitting upon the table's demesne in ugly dominance.

Having positioned Johanna before him, the guards stood back, banging the ends of their halberds down on the floor in vicious unison to jolt her. If the king's favourite summoned you, God have mercy on your soul. Could this be some mischief of Gervase's . . . but surely he was still in France?

"Good morrow, my lord," she exclaimed bravely and tried to behave as if he had invited her over to show her the exquisite tapestries. She knew he was not reading his letter.

"Lady Johanna," he cooed mockingly. The catlike stare slid up her slowly. He missed nothing—neither the scuffed patch where she had mopped fiercely at some spilt pottage nor the tiny rip where her veil had snared on someone else's ring.

He tossed the paper aside as if the entire world bored him. "You know I appointed you to the queen's household?"

"I-I found out eventually, my lord, I thank you." She had never discovered why he had been so generous to her.

"I am informed it made life difficult for you in the early months, but you finally became Queen Isabella's confidante." Icy fear streaked down Johanna's spine. Had his spies uncovered her schemes to prosper the queen's cause? Would he force her to give evidence against her royal mistress? All the world knew he wanted Isabella completely devoid of power. God protect her, this monster could order her limbs broken, one by one.

"If you have summoned me to report on my liege lady, save your breath, my lord. I am not afraid of you."

The polished heels returned to the expensive pelt beneath his chair and he leaned forward upon the table, his hands clasped beneath his chin. "No? Upon my soul, I think I had best consult my mirror and change my face then, for you are the only person in England who does not fear me." He lifted the bunch of keys that hung from his belt onto the table and spread them out.

Have I entered an elfin tale? she wondered, looking at the arcs of lashes lowered over those almond eyes. If I choose the wrong key, must I spin a barnful of gold for him by evening?

His gaze sprang up at her like a beast, claws out. "Why are you *not* terrified?"

Recovering from her recoil, Johanna drew her lips together consideringly. "I have neither property you covet nor, truly, information to interest you." *Do not look away*, her common sense told her, *stare him down*. She swallowed and added, "I respect that many of the changes you have made for the realm have been for its good, and some instinct tells me you mean me no harm." That was a fist aimed in the dark.

He seemed inexplicably moved by the scant praise and Johanna, not for the first time, regretted that so intelligent and capable a man should betray his nobler nature by greed and depravity.

He regarded her uncertainly, his eyes narrowing. "Upon my soul, I am not sure whether I am talking to a cunning vixen or— Ah, come in, my lord."

She heard the door creak behind her and shivered, wondering incredibly if it was the King of England who stood observing her, but the athletic Edward did not breathe heavily from climbing stairs.

"My lord father." Hugh vacated his chair for the taller man, barrel-shaped from overfeasting, who halted panting beneath the lintel.

"This is Johanna FitzHenry?" The Earl of Winchester's voice held no overtone of menace as she gravely curtseyed to him.

"Yes, my lord, I have been trying to terrify her."

With a grunt, the earl seated himself and set bare hands, large as Gervase's, upon the baize. "Has he succeeded, my lady?" The older eyes were circumspect. "Have you shown her?"

"Not yet." Effete in comparison, his son leaned before him and threw back the lid of the coffer. Reposing on the crimson padding within were two rolls of unbleached cloth, one blotched with age. Hugh lifted out the roll nearest the lock with extraordinary care and set its contents before her upon their sides.

An involuntary gasp burst from Johanna. Two grotesque waxen figures, the white of mistletoe berries, lay like hurdled victims with pins stuck through their heads, bellies and genitals. Tufts of human hair were fixed into the head of one and a fingernail paring was inserted into the chest of the other like a half-withdrawn sickle.

She fought down her nausea, her fingers clutching for her necklet cross. Surely they did not think . . . She could already smell the smouldering faggots they might light beneath her.

"God in Heaven," she whispered, crossing herself. "You believe I did this, my lords? I may be a woman but I am not a village idiot."

"You recognise them?" It was the earl who asked, his voice edged with fear. He did not look at the awful monstrosities.

Johanna forced herself to examine them again. "Is one of them the king?" No, there was no flaxen hair. Her gaze rose to the few streaks of golden brown in the earl's beard and passed beyond him to the nut brown hair delineating his son's pointed jaw. She looked back at the other rotund image.

"You, my lords? They are . . . re-repulsive." She swallowed. Her practical curiosity bested her discretion—it could have been taken amiss. "Has . . . has any of it worked?"

"No!" The old earl slapped the table.

"Oh, that is wondrous to know," she babbled swiftly, her fear rising sufficiently to almost choke her. "You . . . you really should tell everyone it is nonsense and then foolish people will not do such evil things."

"*Tell everyone?*" Hugh's scorn turned into a hiss of bitter laughter and he moved round the table towards her.

The old earl's lip curled slightly. "We have already dealt with one instance of necromancy against us." Yes, she knew—two men in Coventry, she had heard about that. The magicians had been tortured and dealt with.

Her mind flicked fearfully through a whole book of possibilities before she raised her chin to Hugh. "Dear God, my lords, I hope you do not think the queen—"

"No! Look!" The older man, his great fingers trembling, drew out the second roll and dragged it free of its burdens, revealing two similar figures save that one was clearly a woman—both with pins thrust through the ugly oversized genitalia. A lock of dark hair was embedded into the head of the female; the manikin, larger than the others, had tiny shavings of blond hair, which might have been wiped from a razor, blended into the wax.

"Permit me." Hugh Despenser reached out deft fingers to set Johanna's veil behind her. Wordlessly she lifted the female doll and held it against her plaited hair.

"See, Father, I thought so." God's mercy, the other doll was Gervase. She must have swayed for Hugh swiftly set a stool behind her and gently pressured her down onto it. "Help us."

She could sense the hatred in the fingers that had formed the images and knew there was only one answer. *Edyth.*

"Let me deal with the matter," she whispered.

"You? This is not some idle meddling. We can all die because of this."

"Only if you believe it, my lord." But her golden cross was warm within her hand. "Do you?"

The earl separated the dolls. "These of you are for personal reasons, my lady, but ours," he stared at her, "could have been commissioned."

"No," exclaimed Johanna, loathing the implication. "The queen would not do such a thing."

Hugh lifted the glittering chain from his shoulders. The reliquary, twinkling with amethysts and pearls, lay across his palm. "I know you, my lady, for a great oathtaker and a damnable perjurer to boot, but here—I swear on the soul of he who sold it to me—is a splinter of our Saviour's Rood, brought from Jerusalem during the Crusades. Vow by the living Christ that you believe your mistress had no hand in this."

Johanna reached out her hand without hesitation. "I so swear."

"Would Fulk de Enderby's sister have done this on her own?"

So they had been found in Edyth's possession. Her forehead was beading. They were giving her no time to think. "Y-yes, I am sure of it. Be merciful, my lords. Let me tell the foolish creature she must recant her wickedness and cast herself on God's forgiveness."

Hugh Despenser shook his head.

Johanna froze. "What will you do?"

"I, nothing."

"Your minions then, my lord?"

He answered after a moment's thought. "The woman Edyth shall be bidden north to Conisthorpe. At Borehamwood, brigands will attack her party."

"God forgive her."

If she shut her eyes, would they vanish, would they, please God, vanish? But the Despensers were still watching her and the images still lay between them, the colour of human skin and malevolent as demons. "Wh-what shall you do with those?" she asked finally.

"I think we should make a decision, each on our own behalf," answered the earl, fingering his with a grimace.

"If we cast them on a fire in prayer, will it destroy them?" she asked.

My lord of Winchester's eyes held fear. "No, I dare not. Hugh?" His son shrugged, pacing to the window, hands on his belt.

"Do I make a decision for my husband too?"

The earl looked towards Hugh's rigid shoulders and back to her. "Yes, perhaps you should."

"Then let his and mine be buried deep in the ground, for so we shall all be one day." She placed them face to face and rolled them back into their cloth.

Winchester's eyes met hers with a familiarity that was a blessing. "Aye, amen to it."

Hugh turned. "As for me, gold may not purchase me the allegiance of the sea and the wind but I can defy this crone." He picked up the doll meant for him. "A curse on her who did this! May her soul know all the fires of Hell. I do not believe she had any power but ill will." He tugged out the hair until none was left, pulled out the pins, ripped the doll in four and flung it into the brazier. "It only harms if we believe it," he said firmly. "Father?"

"Let mine be buried also." The earl dropped the cloth with its ghastly contents back into the coffer. He turned the lock, flung the key inside and slammed it shut, his chest heaving. "King Edward has commanded that most of the queen's household is to be dismissed, yourself included."

"No, my lords, that is unjust!"

The earl towered over her. "You have meddled too much, young woman. Besides, if your presence could mean my death because of that," he thrust a finger at the coffer, "I will take no chance on it. I want you out of Westminster before the sun sets this day. Oppose me further, Johanna FitzHenry, and I will ruin your family. I never want to set eyes on you again."

Nor had he. Johanna had been escorted back to Blessington FitzHenry and here she was still. But the queen needed her now. It was time at last to leave.

September 30th 1326, the Feast of St. Jerome.

"Ma brave! Bienvenue!"

Johanna knelt, somewhat muddied by Suffolk puddles, before the queen in the hall at Walton Manor, and marvelled at the change in her royal mistress. Isabella's spirits had been at a nadir when they had parted two years before—her French attendants sent home and almost all her household dismissed in the wave of anti-French sentiment that Hugh Despenser had used against her. But now everything about the queen, her proud stance, the happiness in her lovely face, exuded purpose.

"My gracious lady, it is a joy to see you in such good spirits. I bring you what men-at-arms I have. Would I had more."

Sir Geoffrey and a dozen footsoldiers in the scarlet surcotes with the golden rampant FitzHenry lions, knelt in the wake of Johanna's soles. So too did Agnes, who had insisted on accompanying her mistress—especially since her husband, Matthew, the fair-haired groom she had long lusted after, was now one of the men-at-arms and not to be trusted out of her sight.

Queen Isabella's Parisian accent was stronger than ever. "Friends, we welcome you with all our heart to help us vanquish those who wish to destroy us and our dear son." Her azure sleeve caught the light like an iridescent birdwing, and her lanky fledgling stepped dutifully forward. Johanna had always liked the boy; the Prince of Wales's eyes had ever been honest and he was smiling at Johanna and her men as if he were truly heartened by their coming.

"Lady Johanna, sirs, you are right welcome to our cause." The thirteen-year-old's voice was husky, no longer the reedy warble of a boy.

Our cause. Johanna's glance met Isabella's and both women smiled in mutual understanding. King Edward and the Despensers had been outmanoeuvred. They had made the mistake of sending the prince to do homage to King Charles of France for the disputed lands of Gascony and Ponthieu. While it might have averted an inconvenient war between the two realms, it had given the queen—already in France negotiating a settlement—the most precious piece on the board, and Isabella cleverly had taken herself off to Hainault and told the count he would need to provide ten ships and a troop of mercenaries if he wanted the next queen of England to be his daughter, Phillippa. Such offers were rare in Hainault and the bargain was made.

"*Mignonne*, I have missed you." Clasping Johanna's forearms, Isabella compelled her friend to her feet and flung her arms about her. "See, Mortimer, here is my Johanna restored to me."

"My lady." So this must be the famous Sir Roger Mortimer who had managed the incredible—escaping from the Tower of London. He inclined his head, his gloved hand a courteous curl of superficial devotion at his breast. It was not Christian to make instant judgments, but here was a rainbow bubble of vanity if ever Johanna saw one. She neither trusted Roger Mortimer's aqua gaze beneath the auburn flick of fringe nor did he light a candle in her heart with his grinning mouth of almost flawless teeth. *Hair the colour of earwax*, Gervase had said.

Isabella drew her aside. *"Viens!* Let me look at you. No babe yet?" she teased, setting a palm against Johanna's flat belly. "No tidings from that *méchant* husband?"

"I understand you have done my liege lady much service," Roger Mortimer interrupted, impatient for their attention, a goblet in each hand. Possibly he felt excluded, for Isabella was holding Johanna's hands like an affectionate sister, and their heads, glistening jet and opulent gold, were almost touching.

Johanna tactfully drew him in as she took the offered wine. "And I will do so again, my lord. I truly wish I were a man so I might lead my company myself."

"You think we would look stunning in breastplates, Roger?" The queen thrust back her shoulders.

"Madam, you embarrass me." He glanced about, enjoying a pretence of anxiety, before letting his eyes return to caress Isabella's beautiful neck and the lustrous pearl above her bounteous cleavage. "Can I say no? The enemy would be so diverted at such pretty treasures that the rest of us unworthy followers could creep up unawares and throttle them." He had moved behind the queen as he spoke and his fingers stroked down her throat and settled upon each shoulder. Clearly his hands had ventured further in privacy.

"See how I am adored," she purred.

It was not that Johanna did not want to see, although their happiness together made her conscious of what she lacked, but she had no choice; the intimacy of the relationship was proclaimed by their every gesture and it dismayed her. If Isabella was now fulfilled as a woman, it seemed she was just as besotted with the handsome Mortimer as her husband was with Despenser.

"Madam, the Earl of Kent is come."

Throwing off Roger Mortimer's hands, Isabella laughed and sped to the open casement.

"Have we truly not met before?" Mortimer asked. His appraising look implied he was already assessing her worth as a reward for someone.

"No, my lord." She stepped back slightly, giving herself space.

"And you are widowed, I understand?"

The practised lie rose readily; she was not prepared to make inquiries yet. "I am not certain, my lord. My husband fought in the campaign against Scotland four years ago, but since then I have heard nothing." Except for a rose each Lammastide and the letter three years ago.

"You have surely inquired?" The expected patronising assumption that every woman's mind moved at snail-speed.

"Oh yes, within my limited means."

"Hmm, we shall have to decide what is best done for you."

We! As though he and Isabella were handfast. She must be doubly careful with this man.

"Mortimer! Come, let us greet my dear brother-in-law."

Johanna took a deep breath of relief as he left her, his tail wagging to do a mistress's bidding. She had forgotten how treacherous the quicksands of court might be.

Was Gervase here? This was the cause he had cherished. Her eyes desperately scanned the men's faces and marvelled. Certes, there must be more great lords here than with King Edward.

"I hear you are joining us again?" Cecilia de Leygrave, one of the few ladies attending the queen, slid an arm through hers and propelled Johanna over to meet a young woman called Elizabeth Baddlesmere who had just arrived and had not yet made her obeisance to the queen.

Baddlesmere! Johanna gazed on freckles, springy cinnamon hair and a nose tip pinkened by a summer cold. Was it not Elizabeth's father who had been cruelly executed in the aftermath of the king's victory at Boroughbridge?

"I had hoped my husband would have sailed with the queen." Elizabeth also was sending sideways glances at the knights about them.

"Husband?"

"Sir Edmund Mortimer. His son." She lifted her chin towards Sir Roger Mortimer. "But they say some of the exiles have not taken ship yet."

Johanna's jaw slackened. *Edmund Mortimer!* The hammer hit the anvil.

Elizabeth was staring at her with irritation.

"Y-you are Bartholomew's daughter?" Johanna managed.

"Yes," asserted Elizabeth, obviously out of patience with people trying to be delicate. "There is someone behind you. Do you know him?"

Fingers jabbed Johanna in the ribs.

"*Miles!*"

"Where is your armour, Captain Jo? I see you have brought old Geoffrey out of wrappers. Is not the poor sot past all this?" His tone was affectionate.

"Yes, it is good to see you too, little brother, and no, Sir Geoffrey does not need his horseshoes taken off yet awhile," she added dryly and bestowed a kiss on his bossed cheek. He grimaced, rubbing at it.

"I was sorry to hear about poor old Father Gilbert, God rest his soul. Mother wrote that it was inflammation of the lungs. Was it?"

Johanna nodded, her feelings still raw. It was just over a month-mind since the chaplain's death and the household was not the same without him. He had forgiven her for not taking the veil but she knew her choice to serve the queen instead of God had gravely disappointed him.

"So my lord of Richmond has come south to the queen's banner," she declared, steering the conversation onto steadier ground. "Oh, Miles, let me look at you."

He was a head taller than her and, save for the pustules that marked the passage through his fourteenth year, almost winsome with his dark curls and roguish eyes. But he was no longer smiling once Elizabeth had moved away.

"I am displeased you have come. This is not a women's pilgrimage. Upon my soul, you are not hoping Gervase de Laval will turn up, are you? That will be a spectacle since my lord of Richmond has had word that Fulk has changed allegiance and is on his way to join us and I have not the means to keep you safe if he makes trouble for you. I suppose you have heard nothing from Gervase. I know you still carry a fondness for him, sister, as I do too, but we must look to the new order of things. Our family needs to reassert itself. You have to find yourself a proper husband. Upon my soul, Jo, there should be some knight here with a reasonable income who will take you on."

She did not tell him that a travel-stained letter announcing the death of Gervase de Laval had arrived three years before to free them both. She had told no one.

*   *   *

"AH, JOHANNA," ISABELLA EXCLAIMED, LOWERING HERSELF INTO THE hot water of the Prior of Barnwell's bath, some three days later. "It is like old times between you and I, except that I am no longer *triste*. You frown, *ma brave*. If the king spent years frolicking with Gaveston and now plays with that *malin* Despenser, can I not indulge in a little pleasure with Mortimer? *Tiens!* I am thirty-one and have given England two healthy princes."

Johanna sighed. Since they could be overheard by the queen's other ladies, it was necessary to select a tactful answer. "Of course, my dearest lady, you deserve happiness. It is just that if I were in your shoes I might not be so wise as you and I am sure I should find myself falling into the same errors as the king and be in danger of making my other noble counsellors jealous."

The queen drew her mouth into a small, petulant rosette, but then she relented and sent a flick of bathwater good humouredly over her friend.

Love makes us such fools, conceded Johanna silently, berating herself that she was still gulled by its memories. Even if Gervase arrived by ship from France, he would not want to be embroiled with her. She must not hope; the rose each Lammastide had been a sign of friendship, nothing more.

The knocking on the bathhouse door at length aroused her from her reverie. "My liege lady, my lord Mortimer's son has arrived."

"*Dis-donc*, I must get out and greet the dullard," muttered Isabella, "but I suppose it is for the best that Sir Edmund takes after his *maman*; the world could not hold two such as Mortimer."

At last, thought Johanna, in trepidation as she helped Isabella to dress. If Mortimer's heir was the same Edmund who had fled Boroughbridge, the waiting might be over.

A THRONG OF NEWCOMERS WAS CLUSTERED AROUND THE QUEEN IN the priory guesthouse by the time Johanna had clothed herself and joined the gathering. Isabella's delighted shrieks following her formal speech of welcome betrayed that she was well acquainted with the arrivals.

Heavy-boned Edmund Mortimer was depressingly as the queen had described him, a man likely to bruise his partner's toes when dancing and bore her afterwards. The other knight, stepping forward to take the queen's outstretched fingers, was a destrier to Edmund's rouncey, with broad shoulders tapering to a far slimmer waist and—Christ Almighty!—Johanna stepped back with rare clumsiness, knocking over the royal chessboard. Gervase!

For an instant, her husband turned his head. An indifferent stare swiftly assessed her before he returned his gaze devotedly to the queen who was enthusing so loudly that no one noticed Johanna's confusion. It was Elizabeth Baddlesmere, irritated at being similarly ignored, who steadied her. Together they bent to retrieve the pawns and court pieces. Johanna tried not to stare at him, but it was like bidding the waves to stop lapping the shore. He looked older, yes, tired with travelling, but as alive as the candle flames she had lit day after day for his wellbeing.

He was bending his knee, his lips upon Isabella's scented hand. His smile would have melted the hoary frost off hedgerows, while she, Johanna, was reeling from the wounding message that he would not acknowledge her as his wife.

In defiance of fate, she smiled bravely at Elizabeth while time stretched the present moment. As the laughter splashed around her, she stood precariously on a tiny jutting rock trying to find a balance of rational understanding, an equilibrium based on hope. Oh, she had rehearsed this meeting a dozen times in her imaginings and never once had she permitted herself a happy ending— but the reality was now a juddering, hurtful shock after four years of longing.

"I suppose I must wait my turn," growled Elizabeth as the newcomers were made comfortable on stools before the queen, "but it is quite unjust. I have not seen my husband for nearly five years. He did not even notice me."

"Be patient a little longer," Johanna warned, trying to staunch her own frustration and pain.

"What lotions does she use? I mean, yes, she is beautiful but at her age. . . ." Elizabeth stared enviously. The two men were answering the queen's questions, their gazes idolising her. "Not much alike, are they, the Mortimers?" the girl added bitterly, as if she suspected everyone admired her father-in-law and disparaged her husband. Johanna obediently dragged her glance up but her gaze was drawn desperately to her husband's profile before she discovered that Roger Mortimer, positioned, as always, behind the queen's chair, was watching her like a tawny owl. There was no curious benevolence in his face, only covert interest. She coloured, uneasy, praying that he had not seen the hunger in hers.

"At last!" fumed Elizabeth, and swiftly moderated her voice to sound meek and wifely. "God greet you, sir. I trust you had a good crossing."

Johanna was neither watching the formal reconciliation nor listening to Sir Edmund's account of being seasick.

"Introduce us," said her husband and Edmund Mortimer drew him before Elizabeth. "Madam, my one-time esquire and companion-in-arms, Sir Geraint de Velindre. And?" Edmund gazed at Johanna blankly. Could this be the man that her mother had sent to Petronella for safekeeping?

She did not wait for Edmund's gauche attempt to discover her name but elegantly reached out a hand to Gervase. "Velindre, is that in Laval?" Flirtation laced her voice. Her gaze slid provocatively from his steel sabatons up over the azure livery, halted in brief astonishment at the rearing lions counter-combatant that had been added to her mother's design, and met his wintry stare with parted lips. His eyes glittered warningly at her.

"No," guffawed Edmund. "Wales!"

"An unusual name, *Geraint*. Wales, hmm. You must know the Despensers well."

Her husband dropped her hand as if she had burnt him, his expression condemning her for a featherheaded idiot. "Of course, I know them well, my lady," he sneered. "Like every other man here. I should hardly be lifting a sword against them if I did not. Your servant, mesdames." With a click of spurs, he curtly bowed and strode off in the direction of Miles, no doubt to terrify him into silence as well.

Johanna shook inwardly.

Sir Edmund was studying her with a droll expression. "Your pardon, my lady. He is always like that when someone mentions the Despensers. Has some personal feud with them. Never would say why. Over land or who knows? Maybe Hugh Despenser propositioned him when he was younger."

"Excuse me." Johanna turned away from the disgusting tactlessness. A sea of faces swirled before her and the moist heat of the chamber threatened to suffocate her. The queen's giggling laugh had become oppressive. Leave to quit the royal presence had not been granted, but Johanna could not face Isabella. She was past caring as she fled for the chapel.

Save for a young pox-scarred brother tending the candles, the priory church was a quiet womb that gave nourishment to Johanna's world-weary soul. She knelt, seeing again the disgust in Gervase's face at her frivolity, and tried to let the bitterness of rejection seep from her bones down into the flagstones. Tears overwhelmed her and she tried to muffle her weeping, but even here she had no privacy for her grief. The young monk came loping across to her with the exuberance of a dog that had espied a bone and Johanna retreated politely, angered that there was nowhere that was safe for a woman's solitude. In despair, she paused outside. Now it was night, the shadowy cloisters could offer peace, but instinct told her she was not alone. She took a few steps from the door of the chapel and hesitated. The wall cresset that had lit the distance earlier had been extinguished.

The sudden movement in the darkness made her hope that it was Gervase who waited there, but it was Sir Roger Mortimer who flung a hand either side of her. She recognised the soft, sibilant laugh.

"You intrigue me, Johanna FitzHenry. A hint of the nun within that alluring body. You withold yet offer." His hand curled about her neck, the ball of his thumb seeking her lips. "I saw the desire in your eyes tonight."

God defend her! He had recognised the languishing she had tried to hide and thought it was for him.

"My lord, I fear you are—"

"You like teasing, do you?"

"No, and you are taken, my lord, and so fare well."

"One kiss, little temptress, and I will let you go." It was a mistake to let his mouth descend on hers. She showed him she did not appreciate the experience but unfortunately he took her indifference as a challenge.

"No, my lord, please no . . ." It took the grip of both hands to force those persistent fingers away from her body.

"Oh, so I mistook the signals, did I, or do you want to make an ass of me?"

"This is a misunderstanding, I assure you."

"A malicious word or two in the queen's ear and you will lose the favour you have so diligently acquired."

"Then have me sent away, my lord."

"Too late for that, you tease." He grabbed her hand and forced her palm down to his engorged member.

"My lord, the queen . . . I will not betray her trust."

But he was already loosening his clothing. "Hush, yield to me now and I shall do you no harm." He licked his finger and ran it along her lips. She jerked her head back but the unforgiving stones pressing into her back allowed no further recoil. As his forefinger meandered from her mouth down between her breasts and over her belly to fasten and grab between her thighs, the old fear threatened to paralyse her, but she forced it back. Wait, wait, she told herself, then jab your fingers into his eyes or up his nostrils.

"I want you now, woman, and what Roger Mortimer wants, he usually gets." His hardness jabbed at her belly and his mouth came down relentlessly on hers as his hand tugged up her skirts.

"Father?" An unfamiliar voice called from the head of the cloister.

"Go away, damn you!"

"Father, the queen is asking for you."

"Tell her, Edmund, I will be with her in a moment." Johanna felt the laughter hissing against her mouth. "Tell the queen I am coming."

But the door was thrust further open, two shadows stood aside and a vicious rectangle of light fell upon Mortimer's boots against her bordered hem. The queen's lover loosened Johanna swiftly with a stifled oath, his hand warningly upon her mouth as he thrust her further into the unrevealing darkness.

"Yes, yes, go to, lad. I will attend her now."

Adjusting his clothing, he swaggered towards the cressets and the heavy door creaked to behind him leaving Johanna in merciful night.

"Are you the only concubine besides the queen or is he working through a list?" remarked the nearest column. If she had not known Gervase's voice, she would have mistaken the jagged edge to it for humour.

"God defend me, it is not what you think."

"What I think does not matter anymore."

So after all the waiting, it had come to this. Johanna wanted desperately to see his face but knew that sentencing was already given.

"Dear me," he continued, his beloved voice offensive with sarcasm, "do God and his angels sleep once more? Are the wicked times of King Stephen and the Empress Maud come again to bother England?" He seemed to expect an answer and when none came, he added with brittleness, "Suffolk was full of complaints about assaults on wives and property. It seems we shall exchange the king and his aging catamite for a whore and her old lover. Is he not a perilous proposition considering he already has a wife— oh, I was forgetting—and a beauteous queen for a concubine?"

Her reply was choked as if she no longer could work her voice's mechanism. "I . . ." she swallowed, "I h-had a yardstick once but he is long gone. Gervase—"

He appeared before the night sky, his great shape, at last substantial after the years of yearning for his presence, eclipsing the misted moon. "De Laval? Not anymore," he answered, his voice light and chill as frost. "Geraint will suffice."

It was an effort to strap on her meagre armour against him and try bravery. "You have been brawling against the French in Gascony, sir?"

"Ah, so you do not want to talk about the illustrious Mortimer."

"To you? Have I asked you how many women you have enjoyed, how many hearts you left broken on the cobbles next morning?" He did not answer and she faltered on. "I-I cannot believe that you of all people can condemn me without a hearing but as it is so, leave my reputation there in shards also."

A deep sigh reached her eventually. "Better so. Who knows what this war may do to us?" Even a goosehead could not mistake the bitterness in his voice. He broke the further silence between them by sounding as though he was working through an agenda.

"Miles told me about Father Gilbert. I am sorry. Your mother is in good health though?"

"She is fending off a pair of suitors. I think she will take one of them come Yuletide. You have other questions, sir? Would you like me to enumerate our present household?"

"That will not be necessary," he retorted icily. "Did all the roses reach you?"

"Yes, all four. I thank you." A pox on this formality! Let Satan make a guest of him, whoever he was, and welcome!

"And the letter also?"

"I have not made the contents of the letter known." Johanna's tone grew harsher with each breath. She understood that he wanted her to hate him. It made it easier to cut her loose and let her sink. But why now when the rebel cause held such hope?

"I see." Did it take him just two words, angrily muttered, to destroy all hope of happiness? Oh, she had been right to dread meeting him again; there were no crocks of gold for her to find at the end of this particular rainbow.

He had not finished with the list. "Perhaps it would be wise if you told me your latest proclamation on Gervase de Laval."

She wanted to feel for his left hand in the darkness and confirm the presence of an alien band of gold. She could accept that he might be bound to another woman even if the truth gave her heart-ache, but if the rogue was dismissing her from his life for no good reason then she would be utterly destroyed.

Her voice was increasingly difficult to come by. "The . . . the an-swer for the common hearing has been that reports on Gervase de Laval are inconclusive. But rest assured, tomorrow it will be an-nounced that the Scots have set him free to plague the English and he is gone on pilgrimage to Jerusalem to give thanks for his release. I shall have him eaten by a bear on the return journey."

"Thank you." She did not anticipate the heaviness in those two brief words. "It seems you expected a comfortable resolution even-tually. How sensible and tidy."

"Yes." The word was wrung out of her.

"Is that an absolution?" He sounded too eager.

With a sigh, she dealt him the answer she thought he needed. "It is whatever you wish, sir."

It was hurting too much. Just an exchange of words and God had snatched her up and wrung all happiness out of her. Her soul was unrecognisable, tortured, twisted, colourless. Without hope, she was a nothingness, and yet she cared too much to be falsely weighed in Gervase's scales and found wanting.

"I shall not embarrass you in any way, sir, except there is one condition."

"Only one." His soft laugh lacerated her. "A bargain then. Name it."

"Believe that I have no truck with Mortimer. He waylaid me just now like a highway thief." The answering silence persecuted her. "I will swear so on six cartloads of saints' bones."

"Since you and I are damnable perjurers, Johanna, I can hardly accept that." He turned away from her, the profile she had adored now that of an enemy. His words were a sigh upon the wind. "Is it so important to you what I believe?"

A despair so foul that it had to come from Hell itself crawled up through her body.

"It was . . . *yesterday*," Johanna answered softly.

GERAINT LET HER WALK FROM HIM IN A PROUD RUSTLE OF TAFFETA. Her perfume lingered longer. Then that too was wasted on the restless wind that industriously herded the fallen leaves on the courtyard path. Despising himself, he gripped the stone rail in his gloved hands and banished the memories that threatened to enfeeble his resolve. It had to be done. Afterwards, if he survived, he might make amends, providing she could forgive him, but better she hate him now in case they dragged him from his horse and hanged him. The sorrow blinded him, manifesting in tears that ran down his tanned cheeks to splash onto his velvet mantle, and he cursed his name.

Thirty

IT WAS EASY TO AVOID JOHANNA THE NEXT DAY AS THEY rode southwest to Dunstable, their numbers sufficient now to ride against London, but news came that the royal fox had fled to Hugh Despenser's demesne in Wales.

"Well, here is a sight for a jaded taste. You look as happy as a bald Medusa."

A fist thudded Geraint unexpectedly between the shoulderblades, sending the ale in his leather cup spilling onto the ground. His hand fisted instinctively, only to discover a slight figure standing arms akimbo behind him. For an instant he thought it was one of the horseboys and then his dulled mind cleared. This man had bells stitched to the three liripipes of his hood and a bladder at the end of a stick. His tightfitting jupon and hose were pied scarlet and yellow and so bright that he could have been stuck up in daylight as a clifftop warning beacon.

"Jankyn!" Geraint swung the jester up. The bells rattled angrily.

"Nay, do treat me more honourably than a wench, you great oaf." Set down, the little man tidied his tunic sulkily like an outraged old maid.

"Jankyn, I do not believe it! Whence came you?"

"With my lord Henry, Earl of Leicester—and of Lancaster, I should say, if all was well with the world."

"Why, that is wonderful news. Here." His erstwhile master refilled the beaker from the leather bottle in his saddlepack, and with his arm about the jester's shoulders, led him a distance from the campfire.

Earl Henry had been expected daily, for the queen was his niece and it was well known he was enraged that the king had not allowed him to take his dead brother's title as Earl of Lancaster.

"No surprise there, eh?" Jankyn chuckled, once they were free of eavesdroppers. "Since our mighty king topped my lord Thomas and gave most of his estates to the Despensers, my lord Henry has no trouble with his conscience. I shall not say the same of you. I have seen lepers look more cheerful. Are you reunited with my lady Johanna?"

"Yes, but . . ."

"Goats butt, great one, butt you should not. What's amiss? Is her heart given to another? Is yours? Has she acquired a crookback and an accursed tongue?"

"I cannot explain."

"Will not, you mean."

"Aye, question me no further, Jankyn."

"Pooh, I had liefer lie with a poxy whore than try shovelling common sense into the space betwixt your ears." He cocked his head towards the tents that had been flung up. "Hear the carousing. My lord of Leicester is feasting the queen and prince. You spurn merriment, great one?"

"Aye, I do. Should you not be there providing the entertainment or do jesters these days have apprentices?"

"I wish it were so! Rest easy, I shall do my duty shortly. My lord Henry is in fine humour. As luck would have it, we spent last night at Leicester Abbey and who should be there but one John Vaux, a creature of the Despensers, transporting Hugh the Elder's treasures."

Geraint's lip curled. "More spoils for Isabella and Mortimer."

"My, my, you are grown surly." He jabbed his wand of foolery into Geraint's belly.

"Jankyn . . ."

"Nay, purge yourself, dear cuckoo. There is a worm within the spit landed from your beak. I can play the friar and give you Hail Marys aplenty for your sins."

"Can you see matters improving? What do we do if we snare the king? Force him into more promises he will not keep?" He looked away sourly to the sky as if seeking an answer. "Kill the Despensers? And what happens after that? Oh, Jankyn," he

searched the other man's face, "since Boroughbridge I have waited
for such a time as this." His gaze took in the scattering of the
army's twinkling campfires stretching out across the field. "But the
reality . . ." He shook his head. "When I served in Mortimer's
household as an esquire, I thought he was the sun and moon but
this . . ." he sneered, gesturing towards Leicester's noisy tent. "I
am disappointed. The more I saw of him in France the more I
realised he is not the man to lead this kingdom. Despenser has a
keen grasp of administration but Mortimer is merely an opportunist. He takes each day as it comes. They all do except Bishop Orleton. He seeks to guide them now, but will they listen? Oh, it is so
easy to find fault with them and I would not be in their shoes for
all the gold in Hugh Despenser's coffers but . . ." Another wave of
guffaws reached them. "But empty pots make the most noise."

"What think you then of the prince?"

"I like the boy, Jankyn. He does not bluster like Miles FitzHenry
and the other lads his age, pretending he knows it all. Instead he
listens and watches but keeps his own counsel."

"There is your hope then."

"True, but when? He will be but fourteen come November and
the King Edward is still hale and like to make old bones."

"Sir, while you cannot hold back the tide, it would be folly
indeed to swim against it. Be patient."

"Oh, I know, but when you see short-term greed everywhere
around and no one with a thought for aught but their own interests it is hard."

"That is your monastery training for you, lad. It taught you to
look at the secular world from the backside of the mirror. Whoa,
here comes the Holy Church in a flapping of vestments to shrive
us or perhaps his holiness has gone to the great pulpit in the sky
and you are bidden to Rome . . . oh, my lord bishop, good even to
you."

The bow was obsequious, but Bishop Orleton gave the jester a
perfunctory nod. "Better behaved tonight, thank the Almighty," he
observed, surveying the dark huddled shapes around the campfires.

"That is because their heads ache too much already," muttered
Geraint. "Have you had enough of the back-slapping, my lord?"

Adam Orleton's silvering hair blew into his eyes and he brushed it back, the great episcopal ring of Hereford catching the firelight. "You think to escape? Oh, but I play the messenger. The queen desires you to sing for her. Is that how you spent my money in France?"

Geraint ignored the questioning stare from Jankyn. "Must I, my lord?" he growled. "This carousing turns my belly. Here we are on the verge of a bloody civil war and the queen desires a song. Besides, I have turned lily-livered. My abandoned wife will tear me to pieces with her fingernails."

Jankyn's lugubrious face shone with gravity. "Warble for forgiveness to the raven-haired Johanna then. Music stills the soul. Oh alack, your pardon, worthy bishop, I stray within your cloister."

The older man stared down his patrician nose at Jankyn but his answer was friendly. "The fool is right. Give them a song to sober them for the morrow, Geraint. You will do it?"

So he must face his demons and give his values some utterance. "Have I ever ignored your advice, my lord?" He stared across at the man who had directed his life ever since the sergeants-at-law had dragged him before the bishop as a recalcitrant runaway novice. He owed this man everything. It had been Adam Orleton who had requested Sir Roger Mortimer to take him on as an esquire all those years ago. It had been Orleton who had supported him through his exile in France and in return he had given the bishop information and the loyalty of a loving son. They understood each other well.

The hooded eyes swept over them both and perused the jester. "I should have liked to have seen you as an esquire, Master Jankyn, but I hear you proved incompetent at robbing ladies."

Geraint watched the fool's jaw slacken.

"And who was the gossip pedlar?" retorted Jankyn, recovering to scowl at his large friend. "You, you braggart, or does the lithe Johanna now make confession to bishops? Ha! Guilty!" He shook the bauble of his trade accusingly.

A shriek of laughter assailed them—the Earl of Kent in full whinny.

"Songs can pierce stone walls better than Greek fire," Adam Orleton mused and began striding back, his white vestments flapping like ghostly draperies.

Jankyn capered after him, "Aye, it was Blondel's song that found Richard Coeur de Lion."

The bishop paused, half-irritated. "That, my dear fool," he declared over his shoulder, "was not necessarily a good thing."

Jankyn grinned after him and then turned. "*Geraint*, is it? Dare I ask again what your true name is? A Marcher, are you, or did your fair-haired mother fall in love with some thieving Welshman?"

"I was baptised Geraint, and born east of the Welsh Marches. Be content with that." He unhooked the bottle from his belt. "Here, you finish this and, upon your oath, do not go gossiping to Lady Johanna. Let her think Gervase de Laval is the greatest whoreson in Christendom. She may be grateful one day."

THE VERMILION SILK BUBBLE, FETID WITH THE ODOUR OF MELTING candle wax and the vinegary smell of the men-at-arms' tunics timbred by musk and ambergris, was peopled with mellow, rebellious nobility, high as London kites on Bordeaux and local ale. Queen Isabella, her feet on a tasselled footstool, a jewel-encrusted goblet between her fingers, held out her hand for Geraint's homage and he was briefly tangled in the wondrous blue of the forget-me-not eyes. Beside the queen, secure behind the costly French velvet and saffron taffeta sleeves cascading from the royal elbows, he sensed his wife stirring with irritation on her cushion like a glittering asp.

Praise of her had beset him on all sides—the most intelligent of the queen's ladies, the woman who had cajoled guildsmen all over England to write gossip between the humdrum lists of goods available so she might keep her liege lady informed of their enemies' activities; the lady who had risked the Despensers' wrath and constantly counselled the queen to be stalwart and patient until the time of opposition was ripe.

Queen Isabella broke his reverie.

"I have missed your enchanted voice, dear Geraint. Sing for us now."

He forced himself to smile at the queen, but Johanna's pained intake of breath whipped out at him like a claw.

"I fear I am melancholy, my gracious lady."

"Nonsense, such modesty in one so large," exclaimed Johanna

mercilessly, rising like a phoenix from beside the royal skirts. She held out a psaltery to him. "The queen desires you to play, sir."

Then play he would, and make her weep.

One of the queen's pages set a folding stool for him. He clowned, assessing its sturdiness, and earned guffaws from his audience. Making himself comfortable, he angled it so he could observe his wife's face. Then he stretched out one crimson-hosed leg before him and positioned the broad triangular instrument with its short side lowest.

"This," he began, tuning the strings as he spoke, and the queen clapped her hands for silence, "this is dedicated to a lady . . ." Here, he let his gaze slide over the female faces, "a lady who has doubts about herself and her lover."

"Is she real, this lady?" It was Edmund, still sober and smirking, damn him, who asked. "For do we not all know how fair ladies need our reassurance that we value them."

"I assume so, Sir Edmund. It is a song to tell such a lady that if she frowns, she hides her beautiful soul from men's eyes."

> *Little does any man know*
> *How secret love may pain,*
> *Unless a lady he follow*
> *Who knows where love has lain.*
> *And her love for him will not last long,*
> *She asks too much and blames him long.*
> *Ever and ever, is he in woe aloft*
> *When he thinks on her that he sees not oft.*

Some of the lords and ladies joined him in the chorus with that half-hearted drone of people who are not quite sure of the words. His mouth twisted in a tight half-smile towards Johanna, but she was not deigning to look at him. He drew back the bow of music further and let go at her.

> *He would name her today*
> *If he dared at all,*
> *A maid as fair as May*
> *Peerless withal.*
> *But unless she loves him, she does him ill.*

He loves her true who loves her still.
Ever and ever, is he in woe aloft
When he thinks on her that he sees not oft.

Oh, he had her attention now. Her lips were parted in sadness and her brow was clouded. His handling of her had been graceless and he feared it was too late, the windlass had been cranked. The voices sharing the chorus with him faded and for a moment there was a gentle silence and then the queen led the applause, leaning across to give him her hand. On the other side of her, Johanna's face was unreadable. He had hoped she might understand.

"You sound as though you sing from unrequited love," Isabella teased.

"Of course, my liege lady, dozens of them." His mouth was a wry twist of humour.

Mortimer snared the queen's other hand. "Ah, but he does, doesn't he, Edmund, my son? What of the tale Sir Geraint told you in his cups about pretending to have a precontract with a young wife so she might dispose of her ancient husband?"

Damn Edmund to blazing Hell! The wretch had promised never to divulge that. He dared not look at Johanna, but he sensed if she had kept a catapult at hand she would be loading it with a rock the size of Conisthorpe keep.

He set down the psaltery with unnecessary care. "No, my lord, it was just a tale that I heard."

"Tell us again, Sir Geraint," Johanna breezed into the argument, "for I have heard such a jest also and would know if it is the same tale."

May a thousand demons carry her writhing to do the Devil's pleasure!

"I think mine would be different." He gave his one-time mistress a look of appraisal that was meant to silence her—it had at Conisthorpe—but his little waif's hide had hardened.

"Then what is so special about yours?" she purred, with a little shake of her shoulders that drew attention to her low-cut neckline and was calculated to reduce him to silent fury. It worked. He did not like her behaving like a wanton. Only a visor of amusement kept his feelings hidden.

"Pretty siren, I keep one version for private telling."

"Woohoooooo," whooped their audience, enjoying the joust.

Mortimer, predictably, entered the lists on the lady's side. "Yes, because it happened to you, sirrah. You were the knave in the tale. Deny it if you can. Edmund says you were cavorting with someone else's wife and made a right cuckold of the old Menelaus."

Geraint shrugged, thanking the saints that dear old hoary Fulk had not yet arrived to skewer him through the entrails, and grinned at the Mortimers. "I actually esteemed my Helen's virtue."

"Ahhhhh," chorused his listeners.

"What and never laid her?" guffawed the Earl of Norfolk.

"Oh yes, I laid her." He lowered his gaze with studied complacence.

"Then you did not esteem her." Elizabeth Baddlesmere coloured as he looked up; she had not expected the remark to carry.

"And left a cuckoo egg in her nest?" chortled Mortimer.

Geraint stood, shaking his head, but Queen Isabella rose and folded her arms, facing him, her fingers tapping aggressively on her blue velvet sleeve. "In the tale which Lady Johanna and I heard, Holy Church approved the marriage of the lovers. What became of them in your story?"

"I never heard the ending." God protect him! Had Johanna confided in the queen? How many more gossips knew the story? "Acquit me, if you please, gracious lady."

The royal mouth twitched playfully. She circled her victim frowning, then she stopped in front of him consideringly, patting her fingertips.

"I see the mote within my own eye reflected, sir. I cannot judge you, and since your song pleased us right well, sing again and you shall go unfettered." She held a hand out imperiously behind her for the instrument. Johanna stubbornly made no move and it was Elizabeth who set it in the royal hands. "Here, play for her whom you wronged."

"Very well, for her. May wisdom and forgiveness be her bedfellows."

"And not you, sir?" Johanna quipped, but behind the challenging glint of fire in her eyes, he glimpsed the aching.

"Not if she is wise, sweetheart."

At that parry, she faced him for an instant, drawing breath, beauty armoured in scarlet, poised to demolish and destroy. Keep silent, he subtly warned, and his dangerous glance, so swift and for none but her, disarmed her answer and forced her down.

Barred from taking what was his, he turned calculatingly towards his other amassed prey, cooped and waiting. They expected more lovesick warbling, easy to digest. He sensed Adam Orleton's blessing touch him and knew this would have to be good, nay, the best he could offer.

Softly his fingers plucked out a cadence which usually betokened a verse of unrequited love, but beneath his agile fingers the melody marched into a song that had only been heard where all were sworn friends; King Edward had hanged the writer for sedition.

He observed the interest heightening in the men who recognised the forbidden chords.

> Listen to a sermon by four wise men
> Why England is brought low.

Standing not far from his mother, the king's perceptive son frowned, anticipating the dangerous, subversive words. Yes, lad, thought Geraint, it is a song against your father and a lesson for your mother and her lover. Let them listen!

> The first sage said "I understand
> No King has ruled well in this land
> Under God Almighty,
> Save that a king is not a fool
> If he can rule
> Each man with justice.
> But might is right,
> Night is light,
> And fight is flight.
>   Since might is right, the land is lawless,
>   Since night is light, the land is loreless,
>   Since fight is flight, our land is shamed."

His palm slapped against the resonant wood. Hear the harness! See the pennons! March behind the silver crosses!

The second man said these words full good:
"Whoever rows against the flood,
Of sorrow he shall drink,
Also as misfortune bade
A man will have but little aid
In his struggle,
Now one is two
And happiness woe
And friend is foe.
    Since one is two, this land is weak,
    Since happiness is woe, the land lacks mercy,
    Since friend is foe, the land is loveless."

That third man said "It is no wonder
When they inherit land, these lords go under;
Proud and haughty, they start to boast
And help not those who deserve the most
And give nothing to them.
Now Lust has licence
Thieves are made reeves
And Pride wears sleeves.
    Since Lust has licence, this land lacks truth,
    Since thieves are made reeves, this land is penniless,
    Since Pride wears sleeves, the land knows not charity."

The fourth man said that "Anyone's mad
Who lives to meddle in the flood
For gold or aught,
For gold or silver or any treasure,
Hunger or thirst or any pleasure,
All shall go to naught.
Now Will is rule,
Wisdom's called fool
And all good is dead.
    Since Will is rule, the land is in misery,
    Since Wisdom's called fool, the land is in wrong,
    Since all good is dead, the land is sinful."

The chords faded, his palm thudded a slow funeral rhythm and
faltered to a telling silence. There was no happy ending. Like the

war against the king, it lacked conclusion. Appeased at having declared through music the bitter words that it was not politic to speak, Geraint looked up in surprise as a counter tenor pierced the silence.

> And then spake a child
> With strength of heart,
> "By God's mercy mild
> I shall play my part.
> Right shall be might,
> The Wise shall go free,
> The Light is the sonne.
> > Right shall be might, England shall have law,
> > The Wise shall go free, England shall have good,
> > The Light is the sonne and the two become one."

Not a breath was heard. In his element, Jankyn met Geraint's mouthed congratulations with a swift exultant glance. The fool held every one of them now like feathered seeds in the palm of his hand. Curious, spellbound, they saw him cap his right hand down walnutlike upon his left. His magician's eyes fixed upon his hands, and they all watched with him, transfixed, as he drew his treasure towards him. Mysteriously he took his right hand away and slowly lifted his remaining upturned palm to his lips. Then suddenly, with one swift violent breath, he blew the invisible seeds away and with an anarchic whoop somersaulted through the tent to land in a neat ball at the startled Prince of Wales's feet and spring up with a deep bow of obeisance.

The silence was like the still air before a thunderstorm. Then Adam Orleton began to clap, and turning, smiled across at Geraint as the rest of the throng applauded.

The folding stool fell away behind Geraint as he rose, shocked. The flashing armoured breastplates, the jewelled flesh, swirled in a great rainbow maelstrom round him and he almost reeled as he realised the sinful enormity of what had just occurred. Set the prince up as king and force Edward of Caernarvon to abdicate? No, surely Orleton would not dare! There was no precedent. Had Jankyn intended this?

It seemed he had. The jester, kneeling at the dazed prince's feet, stretched forward and kissed the beak of his right shoe. Then before the disarmed boy could praise or curse him, the fool agilely thrust himself backwards, hands first, and tumbled like an acrobat, head over hands, to land neatly before Queen Isabella's furred hem. He bestowed a kiss on her shoes too, pulled a forelock at his new master, Leicester, and arched his eyebrows in disdainful astonishment at Geraint, still standing with the psaltery in his hands.

"Jankyn!" chuckled Earl Henry, stepping forward to buffet him on the shoulder.

"Have my secretary take down every verse," the queen declared huskily, her eyes seeking out her son. "I want them sung now throughout this kingdom."

Orleton, his arm around the prince's shoulders, walked him to her. And Roger Mortimer, not to be outdone, stepped forward to flank the boy upon the right. Church and State smiled at each other in mutual understanding.

You cannot hold back the tide. Thrusting the psaltery into the lady Elizabeth's arms, Geraint set his hands beneath Jankyn's underarms and hoisted him to straddle his shoulders to further cheers.

"Well done!" The long ecclesiastical fingers plucked at Jankyn's sleeve, bidding him stoop. It was safe, given the hubbub, for Orleton to murmur, "I think we have just changed the course of England's history."

The queen bussed her son on either cheek, and beaming, straightened, joining in the continuing applause, but her look was distrait as she stared up in puzzlement at Jankyn.

It was a mistake then for Geraint, in his confusion, to look for and stare, alienated and despairing, at his severed wife. And Johanna, misty-eyed from unleashed emotion like everyone else, was struggling to arrange her features simultaneously in a heart-given smile at Jankyn and a look of angry bewilderment at him. The circle was joined and the queen saw.

"THIS," SHE SAID TO JOHANNA NEXT MORNING, JABBING HER SIGNET into the orange seal ribboned to the deed, "is in thanks for your loyalty."

Mortimer, who had barged into the privacy between them and stayed like an unwanted smell, sniffed.

The queen looked up. "You disapprove, my lord?"

"Aye, madam, it is unwise to go making promises of lands you do not hold."

"These are Despenser manors and if God is good they shall be within our gift right soon. You had rather we gave them to you, my lord?"

"God forbid, madam, there will be plenty for all of us. No offence to this lady but you have an army at your back, madam, lords who have journeyed miles to follow you and more nobles are on their way. Are you not being hasty with this?" He whisked the deed from the cloth. "One of the men out there may have held these manors and, besides, this lady lacks a husband to properly defend her lands. Believe me, Lady Johanna, I do not question your honesty"—the suspicion was loaded for the discerning—"but I think you have been gulled by some philanderer. I have never heard of this Gervase de Laval."

But he served you, mayhap he saved your son's life. The temptation to blurt out the truth beckoned like the Devil. Yet to what avail? Foisting herself on a man who no longer cared?

Isabella saved her from answering. "But I have. Are you questioning my judgment, Roger? Are you?"

Johanna set a respectful hand on the queen's arm. "My liege lady, I have no wish to be a bone for you two to fight over. Question Lancaster's jester. He was once my husband's esquire."

"A jester," jeered Mortimer. "Upon my word, this story will grow horns and a pointed tail. What sane knight employs a jester as his esquire?"

The queen scraped back her chair upon the flagstones. "I shall have no more wrangling. Give her the deed!"

Johanna noted the resentment flicker in the earl's eyes and little doubted he would continue the battle of wills with Isabella in private by more subtle means.

He gave it to Johanna with a fulsome flourish. "You are become an heiress, my lady. I congratulate you." The leather creaked as he clicked his heels together and bowed to Isabella with frosty hauteur. "By your leave, madam."

Isabella busied herself sorting the letters, but she watched him go, her lower lip folded in pensively. "Do not let him trouble you, Johanna. He likes to bare his teeth occasionally to remind me I am just a woman."

"Mayhap he is right about the grant, my liege lady. This kindness may make wranglings. Are you sure you do not wish to reconsider this when the campaign is over?"

"No," Isabella replied firmly. "And do not let Mortimer put you down. You laboured long and hard on my behalf and, by the Blessed Virgin, I cannot see why you are less deserving. Keep it. Sometimes he needs to be reminded that but for my gender, I would now be ruling France." She sank down again upon the chair with a sigh. "But I do love him, Johanna. I know I am a fornicator or whatever other dirty labels Holy Church can nail on me, but I need him and he is risking his life for my cause."

"It is a just cause, my lady, and no one despises you. All the bishops save Walter Stapledon have come to pay you homage. They respect you as their sovereign lady."

"Only while I am useful. I know I should not be sharing my bed with Mortimer but no more of that. Now, let us be cheerful. Read the deed." She pinched Johanna's cheek. "I want to see you smile, *hein*." She took another letter awaiting signature from the pile.

"My gracious lady, this is too much." Johanna looked up in tearful happiness.

"*Attention*, darling goose, you will make it blotchy."

Johanna shook her head. "I understand why you are doing this and your kindness is beyond thanks."

The queen leaned her chin upon her hand. "It was Gervase de Laval who sang last night, *oui*? Gervase and Geraint are one. Why will he not own you as his lady? Is there something or someone he fears?"

Johanna stared bleakly up at the wall-hanging of Christ healing the blind upon the road from Jericho. "I do not know," she answered sorrowfully. It was a relief to air the wound. "It is as if some canker is eating him."

Unhappily, the queen took her meaning at skin surface. "*Quel horreur! Bah, non!* He looks hale enough to me. There is no evidence of lung rot or any outward manifestation of disease, no rash or leprous marking."

"No, madam, I mean his soul is bitter."

"Ah. Well, mayhap he will turn cheerful when he hears that you shall be rich once *le mauvais* Hugh and his abominable father are in their coffins."

Johanna grimaced. It was not pleasant to think her future prosperity depended on Hugh Despenser's death, and if the queen thought Gervase's love could be bought with manors, it was because she did not know the man. But then, thought Johanna sadly, nor did she. Not even his true identity.

Thirty-one

THE QUEEN'S STAY AT GLOUCESTER WAS MEMORABLE for two things—the ghastly delivery of Bishop Walter Stapledon's head in a canvas drawstring bag and the tidings that the king had moved on to Hugh Despenser's castle at Chepstow and had given orders that all the loyalist troops were to assemble in Bristol under the command of Hugh Despenser the Elder, Earl of Winchester. With her men anxious to see battle, Isabella took repossession of Berkeley Castle and, advised by Mortimer and Leicester, resolved to lead her army towards Bristol next morrow.

The move exacerbated Johanna's short temper. It was not only the constant travelling that irked her but also the fact that Roger Mortimer had told his gossipmongering son about her prospects. Since then she had been pestered by a swarm of land-ravenous fortune hunters who did not give a fig for her feelings or opinions. Every time she caught sight of Gervase's azure-plumed helm as he rode with Bishop Orleton's company, her bad humour flamed up.

What might have been—what could be—but for Gervase's cold-heartedness, threatened to choke her. If only they were not constantly treading the same ground; the very air between them was a brooding thunderstorm and the lightning glances she sent him were returned in full measure. What ailed the man?

"Make him jealous," advised Isabella, locking her jewels into her small travelling coffer as they were about to leave Berkeley. "I will see you down in the courtyard in a thrice."

"I cannot," muttered Johanna. She seized the ring handles of the box containing the queen's perfumes and lotions and was halfway down the spiral stone staircase when one of the knights, bounding upwards, barely saved them both from tumbling headlong.

"Oh, it is you," she growled. Gervase, Geraint—whatever he was damnably called—was blocking her way like an irritating rockfall, all sharp armour and hard edges. There was no convenient landing at hand to let him pass, so she turned with an oath to mount the stairs again only to find his arm insinuate itself around her waist and whirl her to face him.

"Do not struggle unless you want us both to topple."

"An excellent idea!"

"*Johanna.*"

"I do not know you, sir. Let me go!" She wedged the coffer stalwartly between them.

His gaze searched her face. "I love you."

"Love me!" Johanna exclaimed, nearly letting Isabella's precious fragrances smash over their feet. "Love me! God help us, sir, your disease is tardy. It would not have anything to do with the epidemic of land grants, would it?"

"What in God's Name are you babbling about?"

"The Devil take you! Ha, you come sniffing at my heels, whining of love because your precious Mortimers have blabbed that I shall have manors in plenty. Your wretched, poor wife whom you scorned, Gervase de Laval—or whatever poxy name your mother gave you!"

"God ha' mercy, do you think I give a toss what you are worth?"

"Yes, you lying dog! Or do you change like the wind? 'Today I think I shall love my wife,' " she mimicked. "Oh, go and be hanged!"

"Very well, have it on your terms!"

To add to her woes, she arrived down in the bustling courtyard only to discover a newly arrived contingent of sweaty knights and horses adding to the confusion. The air was ripe with Northumbrian and Yorkshire curses—and a voice she had lit candles and said a thousand prayers never to hear again: Fulk de Enderby, snarling at his men.

* * *

BRISTOL, LIKE LONDON, WAS CAUGHT BETWEEN APPEASING THE LORD in charge of its fortress and its instinct for choosing the winning side. The moment the queen's army was sighted from the walls, the mayor and his aldermen rode out to offer their sovereign lady the city's allegiance. Meanwhile, Hugh Despenser the elder, Earl of Winchester, stood on the ramparts of the castle and refused to surrender. The queen, bivouacking with her troops and tents, prepared to lay siege. She ordered the setting up of trebuchets, mangonels and belfries. Engine-makers and those knowledgeable in mining were summoned to discuss how best the walls were to be breached.

Geraint, in full armour, stormed into Edmund's tent. The matter had been pricking him like a stone in a shoe since Berkeley.

"I have a quarrel with you!"

Edmund was at a disadvantage. One of his esquires was wrapping shinbands, strips of blanket, round his worsted hose.

"You are not still maddened because I suggested you toss a leg over the porter's daughter at Berkeley."

"Johanna FitzHenry tells me you have been spreading gossip of her becoming an heiress."

Edmund frowned. "It is not a rumour, Geraint. My father was there when the queen gave her a deed promising her some of the Despenser lands in the Marches. Mighty foolish he thinks it too, giving the manors to an unprotected widow. What of it?" As Geraint made no answer but a growl, Edmund looked round at him. "Ho, so you reckon there lies your answer, an heiress, eh? Well, go and wag your tail around her skirts along with the rest of 'em. Lost cause, I reckon. The wench is still claiming her husband is—"

The thunderous expression on Geraint's face must have betrayed him for Edmund, not usually so fast in such matters, suddenly added up the sum of things. "Oh, upon my father's soul it is Lady Johanna! She's your . . ." In a stride, Geraint had grabbed him by his shirt.

". . . embroiderer," croaked Edmund placatingly.

"Sirs!" yelled the esquire, wriggling out on his hands and knees from between the two men.

"Out!" Geraint snarled at the youth. "You whoreson, Edmund, if you dare blab one further word about Johanna in any way whatsoever . . ."

"Ho! So she definitely is—"

"I told you hold your tongue!"

"You go too far. Remember who I am, Geraint de Velindre. My family gave you board and lodging at Bishop Orleton's request, else you would have starved. And my father is about to knock the bloody Despensers into the ground or had you forgotten!" Released, he straightened his shirt. "Anyway, what is the matter with you, man? Since we arrived back from France you have had a burr beneath your saddle. Is it this Johanna? She is better favoured than my Elizabeth and probably complains less, so why do you not poxy well take her back and have done, especially if she is going to be rich, and do not give me one of your lectures—ouch!" Geraint had grabbed him about the wrist.

"Because of your meddling, Edmund, she thinks I only want her for her money."

"Well, she has none yet."

"That is not the point."

"Sirs!" The esquire charged back into the tent. "Guess what's afoot! Old Hugh has surrendered. The Bristol garrison's rebelled."

Edmund gave a whoop, freed himself from his astonished assailant, buffeted the esquire and charged out of his tent, the strips of blanket unwinding foolishly from his knees.

Snatching back the canvas flap, Geraint swore as he watched the footsoldiers cheering and leaping onto each other's backs as if they had won a great victory. *Geraint de Velindre.* He was no more that than de Laval or the other names he had used. With an oath he shut out the celebration, helped himself to Edmund's supply of Bordeaux and drank deep.

After supper Johanna excused herself from the queen's presence and stood outside the gaudy tent between the gye ropes. Tomorrow they would ride triumphantly into Bristol Castle and old Hugh would be tried by Mortimer, Leicester and William Trussell, one of the Boroughbridge rebels who had been in exile in France. It was Trussell's bloody utterances on what he would like to do with the Despensers that had driven her from the royal tent.

"Well, well."

Her former husband—greyer, balder and quite as terrible—stood between her and the tent entrance. In the four years since he had abused her, Johanna's scars of memory had faded. He was not forgiven but it was a different lady—at ease, confident and worldly—who faced him now and she astonished herself by being charitable.

"I was sorry to hear about Edyth's death. She did not deserve so cruel a fate."

For an instant the man was floored by the admission and then he rasped, "Hypocrite! You wished her dead."

"No, not true, sir," she answered honestly. She had lit candles for Edyth's salvation—out of guilt and pity. But why should she defend herself to this beast in human guise? "Have you buried poor Maud yet?" The wealthy widow had snared Fulk within a few months of the court hearing.

Always that snide, arch look. "No, she is at home with my son."

It was foolhardy but she had to say it. "*Your* son, Fulk?"

"Strike her, b . . . bully, and I will k . . . kill you this time! Give you good day, Mallet."

Had the millennium come? Johanna caught at the gye rope as if the world had turned ethereal. Time could have gone into reverse, except her younger husband was reeling.

"And you preferred this to me?" sneered Fulk. "I will not take advantage of a drunkard but your time will come, boy. I will deal with you, be sure of that." His smile for Johanna was as nasty as a venomed arrowhead. "Still barren, I hear." He adjusted his helm beneath his arm. "You poor strumpet, between two stools, you fall to the ground." With that, he directed a gobbet of sputum at her feet and strode away.

She let her breath go in a soft sigh. "Upon my soul," she whispered, as Gervase stepped back heavily. Since the canvas wall failed to support him, he sat himself down with a mumbled curse. The mitten flopped back from his wrist as he attempted to prop his chin upon his hand. "You look abominable. Drained a firkin, have you?"

Geraint groaned and rubbed his chin. "That is not an honest question for a drunkard, my lady." He was convinced he was quite sober, especially if he remained as close to the ground as possible. "Aye, but you are right, Johanna. I need a shave and my mouth is as dry as the road to Jerusalem."

He blinked up at her. The dying sun's blood red light reflected on the gold cross upon her breast and enhanced the pollen yellow of her kirtle. A stone monument, his Johanna. No, not his. She was looking at a wrecked man, like to crash on the rocks at any moment.

"Do you . . . do you think you could lower yourself for a moment." Surprisingly she sank down onto the October grass beside him, disconcerting him by being amenable; ironic that she must prefer him with a sail missing and despair settling in like fog.

For a moment they watched a pair of gulls soaring. "Wh-what think you of the news?" Did his voice sound as weary as he felt?

"I met him only once. Old Despenser," she explained, unperturbed by his fierce scowl. "About two years ago. Edyth—someone had . . ." She must have read his confusion for she waved her hands as if to wipe away the words. "Oh, to be brief, he and his son warned me to cease my work against them."

"D-did you?"

"Since they threatened not only to harm my mother and Miles but you as well, I did. Why do you smile?"

"Smile, Johanna? No." He buried his face in his hands for an instant, summoning up his courage. "My love, I have no right to ask anything of you, but—"

"No, you have not!" Wise grey-green eyes evaluated him before she finally stood up. It was tactful and necessary to stay at her feet where the world seemed steady, for she had sprung mentally ahead of his soused mind. "I take it you still want me to declare you dead, sir."

He might as well be.

"What you will but . . ." Perhaps he should exert the paltry authority she needed. He clutched at the gye, thought better of it lest his weight bring the tent down and stumbled unsteadily to his feet. The ground still heaved beneath his soles. "I . . . I want you to leave at first light. Make any excuse. Go back to . . . B-Blessington FitzHenry. I will arrange with Bishop Orleton for you to have an escort."

He had to wait several heartbeats before she finally answered.

"Why? Because of Fulk?"

"No. I do . . . I do not want you arguing, lady. There will be things happen that no woman should see. I . . ." He rubbed the bridge of his nose and tried to clear his mind. "Believe me, Johanna, you have no idea what men can do to each other." He closed his eyes painfully; the light on the tent was blinding him.

"Do you think I should not like to leave here, sir? Do you think this constant carting thrills me? You know what I want? Not to go back to my mother. No, I want a hearth and a hall to call my own and a babe in a cradle and . . . but you would not understand. Good night, Gervase."

"*Geraint*, my name, Johanna, is Geraint."

She halted and turned. "Yes, Geraint of some little obscure hamlet in Wales and Bishop Orleton is your father. It is too late for the truth." The winter words, bleak and unforgiving, requested no answer. "I understand why you could not trust me, but there are others who do. My place is with the queen and I shall not leave her now. She at least needs me."

HAD PONTEFRACT BEEN LIKE THIS FOR LANCASTER'S TRIAL? DID THE Romans lick their lips and queue from sunrise to see the Christians eaten? The throng of gaping faces, the hunger for barbaric entertainment in a people that claimed to believe in Christ's forgiveness, terrified Johanna.

Hugh the elder looked closer to four score years than sixty-four when they marched him into the great hall at Bristol castle. Unshaven, red-eyed, stooping, his sparse silver hair unkempt, his wrists and ankles shackled, he looked defeated—a tired officer of government, the accomplice to his son's hunger for wealth. A scapegoat almost. Why had he foolishly stayed behind in Bristol while his son and the king fled to safety? Surely he must have known the opinions among his men, that the city and garrison would not stand? Johanna frowned as realisation dawned. Dear God in Heaven! The old earl was buying time for them.

For an instant, the prisoner seemed to recognise her as she stood behind the queen's chair. The images! Upon her soul, it was not her fault he drooped there in chains. This was not Edyth's doing nor hers, but there was nought in his face now save bleak acceptance as his accusers and judges were one. They sat across the dais like archangels on Doomsday.

"You counselled our lord King Edward to set aside the laws of this land," thundered Mortimer, "and you deprived Holy Church of its rights."

The Earl of Leicester was sad and grave in his utterance: "You executed my noble brother, Thomas, Earl of Lancaster, without justice and for no true cause."

"You committed robberies and depredations," bawled red-faced Trussell, his saliva flying midge-like in the motes of morning light.

They allowed the old man no response. He deserved none; he had given Thomas of Lancaster no right of reply.

"Have you reached a verdict?" asked the queen, sitting like God, her chair on a plinth behind the judges.

"Madam," Mortimer bowed. "We declare him guilty." He handed her the judgment.

In the hush, the noise of the parchment unrolling between Isabella of France's fingers seemed incongruous. Johanna reached out a hand to steady herself against the back of the royal chair.

Isabella rose. "Hugh Despenser the Elder, styling yourself Earl of Winchester, you are found guilty and sentenced as follows: you shall be drawn for treason, hanged for robbery, decapitated for the crimes you have committed against Holy Church and your head shall be taken to Winchester."

Old Hugh Despenser seemed to give a great sigh.

"Is the gibbet prepared?" asked the queen.

"Madam, it is," barked Trussell.

"Then let it be proclaimed that all are to assemble to see justice done. The prisoner is to be executed at the next hour bell."

A great cheer rose and the crowd spat and jeered as the old man was cuffed and hauled out.

Isabella's face was stony. "And I will have the rest of this unholy trinity."

JOHANNA REFUSED TO GO TO THE EXECUTION.

"What is the matter?" exclaimed Isabella, sending her a warning glance indicating the prince's presence. "I will have no sympathy for any Despenser."

"No, madam, the man is guilty, but I think the punishment barbaric."

Elizabeth Baddlesmere nodded. "The Despensers and the king did the same to my father, but I agree with Johanna, I should not wish this on any man."

"I want this to be a lesson, mesdames. There shall be no more

Gavestons, Despensers or Thomas of Lancasters. Let them learn," the queen thrust a finger towards the hall of nobles where Mortimer's laugh was recognisable, "that if any one of them dares to usurp the powers of a king, he will die a foul and bloody death."

"Without exception, mother?" The Prince of Wales's voice broke through the women's argument.

"Without exception. Remember that, my son."

"I will remember."

JOHANNA HEARD THE ROAR OF THE MOB AND KNEW IT PUNCTUATED each dreadful, painful stage of the old man's death. Elizabeth had been ordered out to watch by the Mortimers. Of the royal household, only Agnes remained with Johanna within the keep, the silence compatible between them. Was she being cowardly? Were her principles a rationalisation, a failure to accept that people could inflict such suffering on each other? Even in the castle solar, she could smell the smoke, or was it just imagination that made her want to retch?

The rest poured back into the keep an hour later. Isabella and the other women were sternfaced and white as ashes. The Prince of Wales was green and declared he could not face dinner in the hall. Mortimer, ebullient, chided him but the boy turned on him. "My lord, it pleases me not to do so."

The room fell silent, everyone not exactly embarrassed but rather uncertain, and Mortimer, no less astonished, his dignity a little grazed, bowed. "As my lord prince pleases."

A page tugged at Johanna's sleeve. "My lady, my lord of Leicester's jester stands without the hall and begs you will go and speak with him."

Jankyn, for once unsmiling, bowed and took her hand. "Come."

She and Agnes followed as he circumnavigated the ale spills, piss and vomit of celebration in the courtyard. He led them into one of the towers and up its spiral stairs to the ramparts.

"Jankyn! Where—"

He put a finger to his lips. " 'The fuller the cup, the more careful you must carry it.' There lies your way. Come, fair Agnes, you and I must play sentry, for Paradise is turned inside out like an old cote."

For an instant she did not see the man prostrate, hidden by the curve of the tower. His face cradled in his arms.

"Gerv—Geraint?" *A full cup?* Was he drunk again? Her fault? No, surely . . .

"Sir, did you send for me?"

"Johanna." It was a plea.

"Are you hurt?" She stooped beside him, reaching out a hand to smooth away his tumbled hair so she might see his face.

"Jo . . . I-I . . ." He struggled up onto his elbows, his cheekbones limned with tears. He swallowed, too choked to speak.

Shocked, she eased her kirtle, knelt and waited until it pleased him to find his voice.

"D-Despenser? Did you see?" Was this what ailed him? Disgust of mankind?

"No," she declared stoutly, "I refuse on principle to watch men behave like savages."

"Oh dear God, Johanna." He tried to laugh and smudge away the tears, but his mesh mitten was useless. "Only you could . . . I love you so much."

"Here," she dragged her veil round. But before she could lean down to dab his cheeks, he buried his face in her lap with an anguished howl, his shoulders heaving.

Johanna eased her enigmatic husband up into her arms and rocked him like the babe she never had, stroking his beloved head while his tears wet her bodice. This grief was not the harvest of unrequited love unless the execution had somehow exorcised whatever demons struggled within him. "Hush, hush, my darling, my dearest lord, all will be well."

"No! No, it cannot be! I should not have sent for you." He was shaking his head from side to side, tormented.

"Gerv—Geraint," exclaimed Johanna firmly, gripping him by the shoulders. "Will you for once explain to me what is going on in that deluded head of yours? It is time you trusted me! Understand!" She shook him to make sure he did. "I am your wife. I will share your joy and your troubles. Trust me."

"Lady, I fear to do so. You will hate me."

"Of course I shall not."

"Johanna, it is my father."

"Yes, Orleton. I guessed."

"No!" He pulled back from her and angrily brushed the salt-water from his upper lip. "It is my father they have pulled apart and thrown to the dogs out there." He pointed beyond the wall, his hand shaking.

Thrusting a knuckle to her lips, Johanna stared at him in horror. He broke away, his fist slamming against the wall, as if the pain could assuage whatever guilt or sorrow raged within.

"Now you will hate me." His face was against the harsh stone, hidden from her.

Touching his cheek, she tucked the damp golden hair back behind his ear. "Why would I hate you, sir, when I love you beyond all the world?"

She waited. Had he heard her? Was he too deep within the well of his own misery to reach the firm ground she offered him? But turn he did.

"Oh, my Johanna," he reached out a hand to take hers. "How can you love me when I have been so callous, leaving you to make your own way and not protecting or acknowledging you as a husband should? But all the while I loved you. Do you understand now why I could not be honest?"

"No, I do not. I cannot see that being the Earl of Winchester's bastard should make any difference to us now."

"I am not his bastard."

"But . . ."

His blue eyes were awash with sorrow and pity at her confusion.

"I am his youngest son, Johanna. I am Geraint Despenser."

Thirty-two

HE WAS DESPERATELY SEEKING ABSOLUTION IN HER face. "Geraint." It was spoken softly as one might soothe a creature frantic with pain. "It is a good name."

"And the other? Men spit on it. My brother is the most despised man in England since King Harold's mourners cursed William the Bastard."

"So . . ." Johanna was careful as she chose her words. On one side lay the quagmire of pity; on the other, the laughter of madness. *Despenser! She had married into the Despensers!* "So you disowned your family?"

"My father disowned me when I refused to return to the abbey. You must think I am always running away. I fled from you once, did I not, dear heart?"

"With good reason. Perhaps it is as well you left the church. You would have made a most rebellious bishop. And I thought you were a saddlepack babe."

Geraint's expression lightened. "Adam Orleton's? No." The anguish had weakened and he eased himself back against the wall and tucked her possessively into the crook of his arm. "I might have stayed at the monastery. As I told you before I loved the learning. It was because of the master of novices that I ran away. You should have seen the way he looked at young boys, Johanna. It would have made your flesh crawl. I refused to play his unholy, his unnatural, games. A murrain on him! If I had a silver penny for every time he had me scourged . . . So, I sent word to my family, and Hugh, my splendid brother whom I had always idolised, visited me on his way back from the court and raised the matter with the abbot. Of course they were anxious to refute such a grave charge and since a Despenser was a wealthy acquisition for an abbey, they had no intention of losing me." He stared up at the clouds with a sigh. "In a nutshell, Hugh sided with them. He told me I must stand up for myself. I ran away within the month.

"They set the sergeants-at-law on my trail and it was in Hereford that they caught me. The matter was reported to the new bishop, Orleton, and he ordered me to Sugwas and there questioned me for several hours."

"Did he know who you were?"

"Oh, I poured it all out to him. He lent me parchment to write to my father and let me stay in his household until the answer came. My father replied he would disown me if I did not return to the abbey. I refused."

"That was a great step for you."

"My cursed family already had an evil reputation for exploiting others and seeking earthly riches. The abbey opened my mind to that at least. Bishop Orleton suggested I should start anew, style myself differently and disdain my kin. The Mortimers owed him a favour so he wrote to them at Ludlow, saying I was his protégé, requesting that they give me a place in their household. I thought it a great jape, perfect revenge on my family."

"Because of the feud. And do the Mortimers know who you really are?"

"Upon my soul, no! But I wish I had come clean with them years ago. It is too late now. Anyway, I was made esquire to Edmund who was a few years younger than me. I loathed it at first, especially as I was older and larger than the other esquires. Like a great bumblebee." He smiled wryly down at Johanna. "Is this a devious method to calm me? Making me babble on like a market-place gossip?"

"No," she declared candidly, snuggling in further to his shoulder. "It is an explanation long overdue. So it was your own brother who summoned us to Richmond?"

"Yes, he could have made an end of me, but he wanted me back in the family fold. We made a bargain. In return for your divorce and appointment to the queen's household, I agreed to serve him in the Scots campaign. You are catching flies, Johanna."

She closed her lips. So it had been Gerv—*Geraint* who had arranged her future.

"The rest you may guess at. The war was a failure. We quarrelled again. He desired me to work for him, use his methods, threaten, force, extort and all for short-term greed, no thought of Heaven. He wanted me to spy on Orleton, play a double game. I refused. I had fulfilled my part of the bargain. In any case, I had resolved to keep my oath and set my former lord, Roger Mortimer, free. I helped with his escape and fled with him to France. You realise it was because of Edmund Mortimer that your mother made me play your husband?"

"Why did you not confide all this to me at Conisthorpe?"

"Lady, I was with you scarcely a month. I had no prospects. Does it make a scrap of difference? If you had counselled me to throw my lot in with my brother, I might be a wealthy baron by now but, like him, hunted and like to die." He unlooped his arm from about her and sat forward. "You see why I cannot acknowledge you until all this foulness is over and men are sane again. If they discover I am a Despenser . . ."

She rested her cheek against his back. "Be rational, Geraint. You have to be guilty of something."

"Tell that to a mob. Their brains are in their arses." He stared stonily ahead.

"Then be silent." She knelt beside him, her hands curling comfortingly around his arm.

"And endure not being able to hold you, touch you. You are mine, Johanna, I shall not let you go. You are my comfort and my joy."

"Then be my suitor. Can you hide your grief and play the part?"

The translucent blue gaze blessed her. "I may be rusty but, would you believe, I have had experience . . ."

IT WAS A RELIEF TO LEAVE THE STENCH OF BRISTOL AND ITS SATIATED dogs. Geraint, by permission of Sir Roger Mortimer, was gone king-coursing in Wales with the forces of Leicester and John of Hainault. It was better so. Even for Johanna's sake, he could not kick his heels while they tracked his brother with hunting dogs.

The remainder of the army, led by Mortimer, swarmed north, the queen protected within its midst, to be feasted by Orleton in the shadow of his cathedral at Hereford.

Johanna, alone and unacknowledged still, but for reasons she now understood, counted the days as the wind tugged the leaves off the trees around the bishop's palace where the queen's ladies were comfortably housed. Had she wished, she could have sought Adam Orleton's permission to visit the fine library. Yesterday she had stood with Elizabeth before the wondrous Mappa Mundi and marvelled at all the realms shown there, but she soon fell to thinking of the man who filled her own small world, and instead went and lit candles in the cathedral at the shrine of St. Ethelbert, praying for Geraint's soul, and for those of the newly acquired kinsmen she had laboured to destroy.

And if the queen's men caught Hugh Despenser? What then? Would Geraint try to save him and be caught in the same net or would he have to stand by and watch the barons slay him? Did he hope Hugh would escape? Or recognising his brother's irrepressible greed and the unabating hatred all held for him, would he cheer them on?

After four years to have her lost love unfettered in her arms only to let him go again was torment for Johanna. Every one of her fears seemed gargantuan. Supposing King Edward mustered sufficient Welshmen to turn on his enemies? Would Hugh slay his brother for treachery?

The waiting seemed endless. It was nigh on two long weeks when Leicester's messenger came galloping through the city gates exultant with the news. The hand of God had turned against the king. He and his favourite had tried for two weeks to sail to Despenser's Isle of Lundy, but the wind had refused to change. Every day their boat had been forced back to land. Finally they had gone from abbey to abbey claiming sanctuary until they had been caught at Neath. My lord of Leicester had taken the king for safekeeping to Monmouth Castle, but he was sending Despenser to Isabella.

Five days later Johanna heard the horns sounding and knew they were bringing Hugh through the jeering streets to Hereford Castle. And where was Geraint? Would he be with them? She was

hard put to elbow her way through the surging throng of onlookers in the old Norman bailey as Leicester's men dismounted.

"Sir." She had to thump against Geraint's backplate to be noticed. He was haggard, crescent shadows pouched his eyes and a
half-grown beard covered his chin.

"No, my love." He unclasped her arms from chaining his neck.
"I stink like a London sewer." Pain was webbed like spider lace
across his face. Beyond the gatehouse, the shouting escalated and
the crowd around them gave voice like dogs taking up the chorus
as the cart came in.

"Oh, Christ Almighty!" she muttered, looking across his shoulder.

Two prisoners were manacled by the ankles to iron rings in the
wooden floor of the tumbril. Despenser's lieutenant, Simon de
Reading, his bald head spattered with filth and excrement, stood
full square. The slighter, younger man was unhealthily pale, his
eyes closed. Only his wrists, shackled to the rail of the wain, kept
him upright.

Was this the king's chief minister whom she had last seen
adorned in velvet and miniver, his fingers glittering with gold and
lodesterres? The once-fine shirt hung half out of Hugh's breechclout which showed, stained and unkempt, above the sagging
hose. Dribbles of spit spattered his clothing and drips of ordure
tributaried down all over him. The brown hair was plastered to
his brow with fresh piss and he could not even wipe away the
human dung that was sliding off it to clog on the luxuriant lashes
and running down his unshaven upper lip and over his mouth.

"He has not touched food or water since they caught him." Geraint's voice was cracked as he fingered her hands upon his shoulders.

"The queen intends to have him taken to London, to be tried at
Westminster."

"No chance of that, my love. It will be over tomorrow, believe
me."

THEY STOOD LATER IN THE DUSK IN THE BISHOP ADAM'S HERB GAR-
den. A nightingale, unbidden, sang a descant over the sounds of
the hall that eddied around them and the waves of the Wye lapped
hungrily at the bank as a fisher boat rowed past.

Johanna leaned back against an oak's trunk, her arms cradled across her breasts, trying to keep out the unhappiness. Just being alone with him for a few precious moments was insufficient reward for the longing that had lain with her as a bedfellow, but now she needed to send him away again for his own sanity. "Why do you not leave tonight?" she repeated. "You cannot want to watch." She did not want to tell him of Edyth's waxen images.

He stood pensively, his elbow leaning upon his folded arm, his forefinger stroking across his upper lip. "And compound suspicion. Of all people, Fulk, curse him, saw me talking with Hugh. A pitiful snatch of words, but . . . he saw me set my hand on his arm."

"Forgive me, I should not judge, but that was foolhardy of you."

"Yes, a bad mistake. I have not changed, have I? Too impulsive for my own good." He groaned, placing his hands in the small of his back, and stretched. "Do we have to evaluate everything from self-interest, Johanna? You think I should not show some compassion for my own brother?"

She folded her lips and tried to find words to repair their lives. "Yes, of course, but you were risking our future. His you cannot change."

His grin was not particularly reassuring. "My practical wife."

The words garlanded him, barring him from her like a funeral wreath. Was there no tomorrow to share?

"Did you have time to make your peace with him?"

"I asked forgiveness, yes."

"*You* did." Was she hearing aright? "I know you will despise me for saying this but why?"

"Because he is my blood." The blue eyes were stern. "You think that wrong?"

"No, but . . ."

"Oh, aye, I opposed him but I do not hate him."

"You misunderstand me," she told him gently. "I . . . I, try as I might, do not dislike him. He has such a charm about him." She turned away. "What am I saying? The serpent of the tree of knowledge was charming and so, they say, is the Devil."

"Certes, he is charming. Put a blade to poor Nell de Clare's throat, Johanna, and she will tell you she loves him still."

"Do you?"

"My brother is a greedy miser, Johanna, worth thousands—all with the Italian bankers, and not a penny given to the poor. I despise him but I do still care for him even if his soul is black as Hell."

She rested her head against his back. "It is too sad. His abilities misspent."

"Sodomy and extortion. What an epitaph. The idiot! He thought if the barons rose against him, it would be merely the matter of arranging for a ship to carry him to France or Ireland. He thought he could arrange everything."

"Except the wind."

"Yes." His laugh was bitter.

"Then after tomorrow?"

"Still harping on the future, sweetheart. What if there isn't one?"

She dragged him round to face her. "You were a rebel at Boroughbridge, remember. We all know Kent and Norfolk have fought against their brother the king but they are not beating their breasts in remorse."

"Only because they cannot even spell the word." He set her from him. "Do you not see? I cannot make any promises."

"But I will have income. Come with—" Dear Heaven, that was the wrong thing to say. Her riches depended on Hugh's execution. "Your pardon. I . . ."

Geraint's fingers caught her chin. "I suppose the irony of it is that it *is* my inheritance in a sense and if I want to have it, I have to dance to your tune."

Johanna jerked her face away. "How dreadful for you, my lord. I suppose you would prefer to play the tourneys until you finally grow feeble like a rogue dog and lose with a lance through your helm and," she blew on her fingers, "out goes the candle and what is left? Nothing." She caught his hands. "Come with me tonight. I want you to hold me in your arms and give me a child, our child."

"So you love me, Johanna, in spite of everything?"

She felt the rough bark pressing against her back as his fingers slid under her veil.

"No, I hate you heartily." Her arms slid up around his neck and she drew his head down towards hers, wishing it daylight again so she might see his face. He was pulling her down, down onto the rough ground and his lips were demanding her surrender.

"I want you, Johanna. We have no bed, no privacy. Will you let me take you here on the ground, shamefully like a beast?"

There were half a dozen dead acorns hatching beneath her but Johanna was past caring. She needed possession, to know that he was hers. She felt his mouth upon her throat and his hand upon her breast.

"Every night I was in France, every night since we parted, I have lain burning for you."

"Liar," she whispered. "Perjurer."

"Is that a no then?"

"Yes."

"Perjurer. I am your husband. The law requires that certain duties should be carried out."

"Ha!"

"I DO NOT CARE IF YOU DO PUKE, ELIZABETH BADDLESMERE," snapped Isabella.

Elizabeth typically was in rebellion and Johanna set an arm around her shoulders. She did not want to watch the execution either but she was going to do so because she knew Geraint must and it was necessary to be cautious for his sake; a second refusal to attend the queen at an execution might rouse suspicion.

The Queen and her ladies rode their palfreys to the market square in the High Town where a stand for the royal spectators had been swiftly thrown together. It was opposite the gibbet, if one could call it a gibbet. A horizontal beam, hoisted in the night, was half thrust out of the upper window of the highest house in the square like a giant phallus. Knotted around the deep groove near its tip was a hangman's rope and alongside it, propped against the roof, were two thatchers' ladders, each at least fifty feet high.

"Does Hereford breed the tallest crowd in England, my lord bishop?" chortled Mortimer. "At least no one will complain they cannot see."

"It was the best we could manage in the circumstances," apologised Orleton, assisting the queen to her chair beneath the scarlet canopy. "But it may be recorded that the greediest man who ever lived was hanged on the highest gibbet ever built."

"I hope this will hold, my lord bishop." John, Lord of Richmond, tested the rail of the stand as the ladies slid along the form behind the queen and Prince Edward.

"Feeling queasy?" It was not the sort of question Mortimer should have asked the royal lad, but he liked pulling tails. Isabella set a hand on her lover's knee to hush him but the boy, wedged between his mother and his host, gave Mortimer an almost sly look.

"I uphold the law, my lord," he answered.

"I shall be sick, I know it," whimpered Elizabeth, and Mortimer, who was sitting in front of her in a jupon that would have bought three destriers, swivelled round and gave her a menacing look.

Boisterous as a choppy sea, the crowd was being thrust back against the walls of the stand as more people fought their way in. There must have been hundreds, cramming up through the Shambles, and filling every other street and alley leading in, packing all the casements, pigeoning the roofs. Thank Heaven it was November. The stench of sweaty villeins and the omnipresent odour of the city sewers was sufficient to make the queen vigorously waft her nosegay of dried lavender.

"Shall we have this over with?" asked Orleton, and at her nod gave the signal. The nearby trumpeter blew a summons and the crowd hallooed gleefully. An answering horn came from St. Ethelbert Street, sending a message to the castle that all was in readiness. The crowd waited in anticipation and then Johanna heard the distant jeering. A river of kettle-hatted soldiers could be seen forcing the crowd back with their halberds, and finally two galloping horses hurtled into sight, jarring the hurdle over the stones and cobbles of St. Owen Street.

"God ha' mercy!" whispered Johanna.

The crowd shrilled and whistled. The two prisoners bound to the wicker panel were covered in filth and bleeding from the stones cast at them. No wonder the horses had been whipped to go fast; the executioners wanted their victims conscious. One of Simon de Reading's heels was almost skinless, his blood already colouring the yard. He had not been able to draw it clear of the cobbles.

Naked except for underdrawers, Despenser's body was gaunt, almost unrecognisable. His rib cage made furrows of a body suffering from self-imposed starvation and his hollowed belly and the crown of nettles rammed down across his brow gave him the mien of a martyred saint instead of a rich extortionist. Strangest of all were the ink writings all over his body.

"What is it?" asked the prince.

"Scriptures, my young lord," answered the bishop. "This evil creature will carry God's words to the grave with him," and he signalled to the chief executioner to untie Simon de Reading.

Dear God, thought Johanna, he was to be the first course fed to the crowd and Hugh Despenser would have to watch and know that he must suffer the same agonising death. She craned to see where Geraint stood, but despite his height she could not glimpse him.

He was brave, Simon. He spat at the jeering faces before they forced him up the ladder, but only halfway, sufficient to set the noose around his neck. Johanna had seen men hanged before, murderers and thieves condemned by her father. She knew how long it took, what might happen. Before the executioners' assistants could force him off the rungs with their steel-tipped pikes, Simon flung himself off the ladder with such violence that they only just grabbed his thrashing body in time. His attempt to thwart them had failed and they lowered him down to the brazier and the knives.

Johanna could not bear to watch the agonised contortions of the man's face and the shudders of his body as the chief executioner set about his appalling duty. She saw Hugh had his eyes closed. His lips moved as if in prayer, but he must have smelt the burning flesh and heard the tormented scream. The stink of the victim's flesh reached the stand.

Elizabeth fainted into Cecilia's arms and another lady started retching. Against all common sense, Johanna rose and fought her way to the edge of the stand to find Fulk barring her.

"Despenser lover!"

"Get out of my way!" she snarled, fearful that his hatred of her might make him turn the crowd against her, but the people about them were too intent on relishing the traitor's agonising demise. It was impossible to force a way through the throng or to return to her place. She could only cling precariously to the stand and try not to be shaken off into that sea of bodies. Fulk's face was menacing. He could easily unpeel her fingers from the rail and toss her down to be trampled, or stick a dagger in her when they dispersed.

"Lady Johanna, for the love of Heaven, stay where you are!" John, Lord of Richmond's voice reached her. Too far within the stand to protect her, at least his warning checked Fulk. She forced herself to face down the living blight upon her life.

With a roar the crowd surged forwards again. A couple of brawny men at arms were thrust up against the rail between her and Fulk as they tried to keep the apprentices from climbing the stand and the pressure of the mob from threatening the wooden supports. Johanna's knuckles whitened, it was all she could do to hold on and not be swept out.

It was Hugh's turn to die. There at least was a confessor beside him as he was hauled to his feet to sag between his guards. He tried to speak to the people but the jeers were deafening. Even the drummers could barely be heard.

Where was Geraint? Could he too feel the hatred emanating from the whole square, fetid and ugly? Had God sent an archangel to intercede, it would not have saved Despenser.

Fifty feet high. Dear God, pardon all sinners! Geraint's brother was paying for Gaveston's sins too and for twenty years of rule by an unworthy king. Hugh was as much a scapegoat as a scoundrel. No one dared drag a king to a public execution; the precedent was too dangerous.

"Sodomite! Catamite!" hissed hundreds of voices. Johanna hid her face, trying to block her hearing with her arms, not caring who saw her cowardice. The pattern was horrible. Each ugly, hoarse shout from multiple throats followed a terrible silence as they all strained to hear the victim's anguish.

"My sweet, gentle Johanna."

Strong, protective arms enfolded her. With a tiny cry of relief, she hid her face against her husband's silken surcote.

Holding her like a talisman, a cross against terror, gave Geraint strength to endure his older brother's agony. He kissed the parting of her hair and stroked her neck beneath the linen veil as a distracted parent might soothe a child, but his eyes were on Hugh's face so that he would know when that tortured soul was finally severed and freed. Could it take so long? Tears blurred his vision and the bitter awareness of what might have been soured him. The waste of such talent. His brother could have been the greatest counsellor a king ever had, if it had not been for his sinful love of money. *You fool, Hugh!* A few years of luxury bought by eternity in Hell.

"Look at me, Johanna." She was his anchor to sanity.

"Is it over?"

"Not yet, but he is gone. Hold me with your gaze, my darling. Do not let me look anymore."

"I love you," she whispered, her gloved fingers touching his cheek. "I could never stop loving you." The laughter, the awful laughter drew him—they were tearing Hugh in four—but her fingers gripped him. "Fulk knows who you are. You must leave Hereford."

"Fulk has lost Conisthorpe to me." He broke the news to her now, trying to keep his consciousness from recording what they were doing to his brother's body.

"Dear God! Look at me! Keep looking! You mean—"

"I went to my lord of Richmond. It was Miles's suggestion, and I told him everything—our marriage and the estrangement from my father. Fulk has been dismissed. I am the new constable and I am going to take you home." One of the women in the crowd close to them whooped and she felt his great frame shudder.

"Upon my soul, Geraint, no wonder Fulk is baying for your blood. We must be gone from here today if the queen will give me leave."

"My darling, Fulk is nothing. I have Orleton to vouch for my loyalty."

"No, believe me, that monster is like a wasting disease waiting to destroy us."

Geraint stared over her head to the bloody cobbles and the wain with its ghastly staked cargo. She looked then and saw the executioners with their spattered leather aprons cleaning their knives and hooks.

Her bloodless lips spoke as if she was entranced by some magician. "Christ protect us! The wax images! I saw him tear himself."

He was unaware of what she meant but held her close, his face against her perfumed hair, trying to keep the smell of his brother's blood from his breathing, striving to be unaware of people fighting to dip cloths in the bloody puddles for mementoes.

"Geraint, listen! I could not bear to tell you before. Edyth made images of him and your father and he tore his and threw it in the fire just like . . ."

She shook with the horror of what might still happen to them both, trying to concentrate her gaze on Geraint's face.

His hands on her forearms kept her upright. "It means nothing. Believe me, my love, it was not ripping his own image but his actions that doomed Hugh long before you encountered him."

"But they are both destroyed now, Hugh and your father."

"God's will, Johanna."

"But I never told you. There were two other images. *Yours and mine.*"

For an instant, Geraint stared at her.

"It was Edyth's doing. Your brother had her killed for it."

He let go of her with one hand and crossed himself. Was there no end to it, he thought? Another sin left for him to deal with; yet another reason for Fulk to want him hurdled to the scaffold.

"Johanna, you do not believe such nonsense?"

"I am trying not to." Her lower lip trembled.

"Trust in God, dearest." He gathered her to his heart once more as the crowd dispersed around them. "Does not your mother still stoutly swear that it was God who brought me to the wild wood?" He watched her knuckle the tears away and nod. "Then be not afeared, my love."

Curses or foolish images caused him no dread, but madness was another matter; for he saw Fulk watching them and read the crazed hatred in his face.

TO HAVE LAIN ALONE THAT NIGHT WITH THE MEMORY OF HUGH'S dreadful death and fears for their own future haunting them would have been anathema. Geraint bespoke them a bed in a merchant's house hard by the bishop's palace in George Street. The messuage backed onto a tavern but even the drunken brawling in the yard did not keep them awake.

Agnes's shriek woke them. "It is Sir Fulk, my lord." The girl had entered their bedchamber and was struggling to bar the door.

Expecting some assault, but not so soon, Geraint flung himself out of bed and drew his sword. Johanna sprang up to help Agnes, but a half-dozen soldiers thrust the door open, with a mob of townsfolk behind them, the terrified merchant and his wife held in their midst.

Fulk, his sword drawn, pushed through. "That's him, Despenser's brother, and bring his whore as well. We shall hang them both."

"Out the window!" Geraint bawled at Johanna, slashing at his nearest assailant. Agnes thrust her towards the casement. "Come on, madam!"

It was the only way to find help. Johanna flung open the latch, squeezed through, and trusting, sprang out. She landed on a thatched outhouse. Agnes thudded into her and the impact sent them skidding off the roof to land sitting in the muddy inn yard. Somewhere a horn was blowing.

Johanna stumbled to her feet. "Fetch Bishop Orleton, Agnes! I will go to the queen. Make haste!"

"But, my lady—"

"Go!"

Not worrying about the straw snared in her unbraided hair, or the mud spattering her chemise, Johanna ran barefoot across the yard, and hid behind the wall as they dragged Geraint out struggling. There were some twenty of them.

She sped across the street to the bishop's palace. One of Fulk's soldiers saw her and gave chase.

"You cannot enter here!" bawled one of the startled royal guards, not recognising her.

"Grab her. She's gone berserk!" puffed her pursuer. The royal guard swung out his halberd to bar her but she ducked beneath it.

"Where is the queen?" she demanded, bursting into the royal apartments and shaking Elizabeth on her pallet. "Is she at mass yet?"

An astonished Elizabeth blinked at her.

"Still abed, but—"

"Get Sir Edmund!" exclaimed Johanna, jerking the blanket off her. "The mob has seized my husband."

"But—"

Johanna pulled her up and thrust a cloak at her. "He saved your

husband's life! Tell Edmund the mob is about to execute Geraint—
or is it Gervase—but for God's sake, fetch him!"

She ran towards the door of Isabella's bedchamber and beat
frantically upon it, shaking the iron handle. Cecilia tried to drag
her back.

"There she is. Arrest her!" yelled the men-at-arms, bursting into
the room.

Strong arms seized her by the waist and jerked her flailing from
the door. "She is crazed. Find a rope!"

Johanna fought. Her shift tore in the man's hand and she broke
away almost naked. Evading the tentacles that tried to seize her,
she wrenched a cloak from one of the beds and ran out the side
door that took her back down the staircase. At least she knew the
way to the bishop's rooms.

Orleton! He would save Geraint. But they must think her lunatic. A noblewoman with straw in her hair and no kirtle.

In the hall, the bishop's secretary caught her by the forearms.

"Lady Johanna, God ha' mercy, what is amiss?" He held up a
hand to stay the men-at-arms.

"Father, the rabble, they have my husband. Geraint, Gervase.
He's the bishop's man."

"Yes, I know him. But my lord bishop is attending mass in the
cathedral and so I told the other demoiselle."

"Then, I pray you, any of his officers will do."

"They are all at Prime. Come, let us go there, my daughter. Wait
here! I shall look into this," he exclaimed to the soldiers, but—
Heaven protect her—there were one of Fulk's men, three Mortimer
retainers and four men-at-arms with halberds following them as
they ran across the cobbled yard to the cathedral.

"They think I am mad."

"My lord is in the chancel. We cannot interrupt the Eucharist.
Wait out here," ordered his secretary. "I will see what can be
done."

She could hear the shouting in Broad Street. "My husband will
die."

"God must be served. Have faith!" He left her shivering in the
portal.

"Seize her now!" yelled one of the Mortimer men-at-arms. They had ventured across the yard. There was no alternative but to take refuge in the cathedral. Inside, the nearest faithful hissed at her.

"Is this a whore for penitence?" One of the sergeants-at-law at the back of the congregation seized her by the shoulder. "She's 'sposed to have a taper."

"I am lady-in-waiting to the queen. My husband's life is in—"

"Oh aye, woman, and I am the Holy Roman Emperor and this here is his holiness the pope. Take her—oh strike me dumb! Here's trouble!"

A trio of Mortimer retainers had entered the cathedral and were dutifully sheathing their swords.

"That crazed woman tried to force her way into the queen's bedchamber!" one exclaimed.

"Crazed, eh? Help yourself!"

She managed a scream of protest that cut across the Latin and echoed up the Norman nave. "Someone, save my husband!" For only a heart beat, the priest's voice faltered.

"Aye, if she has one. Yesterday must have unhinged her mind." The tallest soldier stooped, sticking his face into hers as if she were a child. "Who has your husband, lady?"

"Fulk—Fulk de Enderby. They will kill him."

"Who, Fulk?"

"No, you fool. Ger—"

A hand from behind came down across her mouth and before she could protest, he pulled down her jaw and forced a rag into her mouth. "No more screamin', darlin'. Slide the rope round her easy like 'fore she does 'erself a mischief."

"Shall we take her straightway to the city madhouse?"

"Aye, and then best talk to his lordship." They hustled her out. Without her hands free, she could not keep herself covered as she struggled.

"Aye, she's frenzied," muttered one of the men admiringly, pulling the cloak further aside, exposing her body to the foggy air and the others' leers. "We might have some pleasure afore we deliver her."

Johanna slammed his shin with the sole of her foot. Cursing her foully, he drove his boot into her calves. She collapsed to her knees, and he grabbed her by the hair, jerking her head back.

"Behave, darlin'!"

"Let her go!"

Agnes flew like a fury at the man, scratching at his eyes, and suddenly there were people everywhere.

HE HAD EXPECTED RETRIBUTION FROM FULK BUT THIS FULFILLED HIS bloodiest nightmares. They were set on dragging him towards where they had hanged his brother. Town shutters were drawn back at the furore. Geraint yelled for help to a couple of men he knew in Leicester's livery and struggled so hard that it took a dozen of the whoresons to hold him. They had him above their heads by the end of Broad Street like debris upon a human river.

Geraint was saying his prayers as a pole above a shop came his way, and instinctively he grabbed it. The momentum helped him swing himself up and he gripped the nearest casement and found himself above the astonished mob. Within an instant they were ramming the front door, and bawling for ladders. If he could just stall them until some help arrived. Pray God Leicester's men would come back with reinforcements.

"I have no quarrel with any of you save him!" He thrust a finger at Fulk. "This is a private quarrel and I will fight him in combat."

"He is a Despenser! Deny it on the Rood!" bawled Fulk.

Boards shook behind Geraint's back. They were trying to force the shutters open.

"I serve the Mortimers."

"A spy in their household."

"Send for Sir Roger Mortimer and ask him."

He could see three horsemen and a score of men-at-arms running up Broad Street.

"Shoot him down!" snarled Fulk and the man-at-arms beside him primed his crossbow.

"Geraint!"

Jankyn had appeared at the edge of the crowd and sent a knife spinning through the air into the shutter. Geraint prised it out and edged to one side of the casement. They were driving a blade between the flats to force him off the wooden sill into the mob.

"Get him!" As Fulk swung round to order his men to grab Jankyn, Geraint threw himself on the older man's shoulders and sent him smashing back onto the cobbles. There was a risk they would drag him off before help came, but the crowd was groggy-witted from the night's carousing. They stumbled back as the two men went rolling towards the central gutter.

Fulk had pulled free his dagger. Despite his age, he was not only fit but strengthened by hate and anger. He spat into Geraint's eyes, and tried to strike home while he was blinded. Cobbles bit into Geraint's back through the thin lawn and Fulk's sabaton kicked into his shin, but inch by inch he forced the armed man over onto his back and plunged the knife down.

Leaderless, the crowd hesitated and then it was too late to drag him to a hanging. Henry, Lord of Leicester drew rein, and his men dispersed the mob.

Geraint caught Jankyn to his breast, his eyes awash.

"I expected it, but not the manner. Is Johanna safe?"

A VELVET CLOAK, ITS FOLDS REDOLENT WITH MUSK, ENVELOPED JOhanna and Elizabeth's fingers freed her from the gag.

"Agnes, where is my husband?"

"Hush, my lady, let us untie you first."

Johanna stared at the circle growing around her. Orleton, mitred and resplendent, had emerged from the cathedral with a half-dozen clerics at his heels. The queen, a fur cloak cast over her silk wrap, was hastening across from the bishop's palace. Behind her, Roger Mortimer was striding after her as best he might in slippers.

People were pouring in from Broad Street. Soldiers in Richmond's livery were carrying in a body, heavy and tall, slung on some mired canvas.

"No!" Johanna broke free and ran across. They set it down and she sank to her knees in horror, tears blinding her as she reached out a hand to disclose the face of the man she loved. But it was Fulk de Enderby's corpse that stared, open mouthed, at Heaven, fresh blood welling from the blade wound in his throat.

"Johanna."

Geraint stood upon the path, flanked by Miles and Jankyn, and held out his arms to her. For an instant, she was transfixed as if it was beyond belief that he was safe and alive, then with a sob she ran across to him and he lifted her high within his arms and swung her round.

"It is all right, my love. It is all over." Tucking her against his shoulder, he flung his other arm round Jankyn's shoulders and hugged him anew.

"Geraint, what in God's Name are you about now?" Sir Edmund Mortimer arrived out of breath, gazing in astonishment at the notables gathered around his one-time esquire.

"Shall you tell them, my lord bishop?"

Orleton nodded and Geraint, not letting go of Johanna, moved across to his protective arm.

"Most gracious sovereign lady, I present to you by his true name your most loyal servant, Geraint Despenser, the youngest son to the late traitor styling himself Earl of Winchester."

A buzz of consternation greeted Geraint as he knelt. Johanna tumbled to her knees beside him.

"*You* are a Despenser?" The queen's lips parted in astonishment.

"Yes, madam, although I have fought against my kinsmen oft enough as my lord bishop will bear witness."

"I shall require more explanation of this, sir," exclaimed Isabella stiffly. "Could you not trust us with the truth?"

"My liege lady, forgive me for deceiving you. I barely escaped a hanging this morning because of my despised name."

The queen's gaze fell thoughtfully upon her lady in waiting. "And you acknowledge the lady Johanna as your wife?"

"Yes, madam, and there is yet more I would say. Have I your leave to address Sir Roger?" Given permission, he rose to face the man in whose household he had served. The earl was looking as taken aback as Edmund. "So, my lord Mortimer, will you now bury your kin's feud against my blood or will you see me hanged for this?" He gestured to the body and then glanced round at all the onlookers. "Is it over now? Have you great Marcher lords been satiated or is this to continue until the next generation too? Must Hugh's son be at war with you, Edmund? Must my children be at war with yours until the umpteenth generation?"

Johanna tugged at him warningly. His imperious manner was dangerous in challenging these barons, yet she loved him all the more for it.

Edmund, at least, had the grace to look abashed and shake his head, but the earl his father was clearly annoyed at the deception.

"Do not think to gain anything from your kinsmen's lands. Your father's and brother's estates are forfeit," Mortimer snarled.

"No, my good lord, I shall make no claims of you. Am I exonerated from this slaying?"

"He saved my life, Father," Edmund intervened, "and yours too, helping you escape from the Tower. Surely there has been enough killing?"

"I will stand surance for him," declared the bishop. "He has always been to me as a son."

John, Lord of Richmond coughed and stooped to cover Fulk's face. "*Mea culpa*, madam, God forgive me but I believe I precipitated this slaying. Sir Fulk's wife, Maud, warned me that he was no longer always in his right mind and I deemed it best to replace him as Constable of Conisthorpe. He wanted Sir Gervase, your pardon, Sir Geraint Despenser, dead for many reasons. May his soul be at rest."

The queen sneezed. "Amen to that! *Dis-donc!* Are we fools to be standing round in the November wind? Have the body coffined and carted to his widow at Enderby. See to it, my lord!" The new Lord of Conisthorpe bowed, hand on heart, and the royal entourage hurried off to warm its hands before the bishop's hearth.

Geraint watched his wife draw breath and touched her lips with his fingers to silence her.

"Yes, I know. It was a close thing."

"Aye," exclaimed Jankyn. "There are fools and more fools, taradiddle."

"Oh, Jankyn," exclaimed Johanna, holding out her arms to him. "Forget the taradiddles."

He chortled and drew her hand to his lips. "It is the taradiddles that make the world go on. Go to, my lord, you let your lady's feet become the colour of woad." Which was why, a short time later, Johanna found herself back in the hired bed with a bowl of hot pottage sitting on a broad platter in front of her.

Beside her, Geraint yawned, his hands clasped behind his head upon the pillow. "I do not think I shall be able to manage to survive as Lord of Conisthorpe, not to mention, owning those manors you have gained in the Marches, since I am used to deception and being a natural born rebel."

"Fie, you are telling me a fairytale," Johanna argued but she licked the spoon thoughtfully. He had spent his life rebelling—against his family, against Holy Church and against the king.

"That could be." Geraint lifted the empty bowl from her hands and set the platter upon the floor. "Though I tell you this, my lady wife, I need an heir. Shall we test the illustrious Hildegard of Bingen's hypothesis that two loving parents can beget a worthy son?"

"Being a rebel, you would not agree with her."

"Johanna, I hate to admit it, but I could be wrong." His loving gaze embraced her. "Would you care to find out?"

Postscript

SOME OF THE HISTORICAL CHARACTERS IN THIS STORY did not survive long afterwards. Edward II was forced to abdicate and in February 1327 the Prince of Wales was crowned as King Edward III. During the boy's minority, the kingdom was ruled by a council of regency under Henry of Leicester. The deposed king died at Berkeley Castle. It is not known whether he was actually murdered with a heated poker by the orders of Isabella and Mortimer.

Because of his intimacy with the queen (the young king's guardian), Roger Mortimer enjoyed great power but became increasingly disliked for his greed and ostentation. An ignominious campaign followed by a treaty which recognised the independence of Scotland brought him further unpopularity. His insubordination and opposition to the royal council finally forced Edward III, by then eighteen years old and a father, to arrest his mother's lover secretly. The earl was brought before Parliament, declared guilty of treason and hanged. Banned from the court, Queen Isabella lived comfortably at Castle Rising, Norfolk, until her death in 1358.

Geraint's friend, Sir Edmund Mortimer, died in 1331 but his son by Elizabeth Baddlesmere retrieved the family honour and was one of the first knights of the Order of the Garter.

Research for this novel took me to Yorkshire where Richmond Castle, Bolton Priory, Knaresborough, Boroughbridge and the moor above Conistone provided much inspiration. At Boroughbridge you can turn off the old Great North Road at the town bridge and stroll along by the River Ure to the site of the ford where Lancaster's men were driven back in 1322. At Richmond Castle, Scolland's hall is a silent ruined casing but the view from the walls is lovely and the great keep still stands. Up on the moor near Conistone, above the narrow lanes where small cushions of moss grow luxuriantly upon the limestone walls around the living churches, it is not hard to imagine horsemen outlined against the sky.

Of course, the voices in Yorkshire are different now. In 1322 Johanna's family would have conversed in Norman French. Most people of noble class could speak English as well but it was not until later in the century that English began to replace French completely. Queen Isabella would have spoken Parisian French rather than anglicised French, so in the story in order to emphasis that she is of a different nationality, I have peppered her speech with the occasional French phrase.

As for the use of surnames in 1322, most nobles were generally called after the place they were born. King Edward II, for example, was also known as Edward of Caernarvon. Tradesmen, however, would have been tagged with a name that showed their calling, for example, Peter Weaver. Hugh Despenser was more correctly known as Hugh Le Despenser, but to avoid situations like "the Le Despensers" I have, pardon the pun, dispensed with "Le."

In many of the records written in anglicised French, "de" does not have an apostrophe so in this story Sir Fulk de Enderby's name is written as "de Enderby." Married women did not take their husband's name; the wife of Hugh Despenser was often referred to by her unmarried name, Eleanor de Clare.

Anyone wishing to read a much more authentic version of the song "Unter der Linden" by Walther von der Vogelweide will find it in the anthology *Medieval Song* edited by James J. Wilhelm (Allen & Unwin, 1971). The other songs, "An Unfortunate Lover" and "Four Wise Men on Edward II's Reign," are loosely based on poems in *The Oxford Book of Medieval Verse* (Oxford University Press, 1970) but Jankyn wrote his own verse.

Acknowledgments

THE INSPIRATION FOR THIS "MEDIEVAL GREEN CARD" arose out of a conversation with University of Sydney lecturer Carol Cusack. We were discussing the status of women and she was telling me about a particular medieval divorce case. The court case in *The Knight and the Rose* has metamorphosed a long way from the original example, but, Carol, here it is and thank you.

The burgeoning of social history and women's history studies since the 1970s has provided a wealth of information in books and journals which has made the research into medieval divorce far easier than it might have been some thirty years ago. I should particularly like to thank historians R. H. Helmholz, University of Chicago, and Jeremy Goldberg, University of York, for replying so promptly to my questions on medieval marriage disputes.

It made a lot of difference visiting the battlefield of Boroughbridge, and discussing where to set Conisthorpe. Alison Hodgson, a fellow history student from undergraduate days, and her husband, Bill, not only provided wonderful hospitality but took us to Durham and Richmond and on a wonderful walk up the Swale valley. Then there was Pam Robbins, the kind curator at Pontefract, who unlocked the exhibition hall in the castle grounds on that bleak, cold day; and Yorkshire-born Jill Fulford who lent me all her books on the county.

As always, my fellow writers have been very supportive, especially Elizabeth Lhuede for her welcome comments on the completed manuscript; Chris Stinson who always kindly checks the

French in my novels and en route offers other pertinent advice; and Delamere Usher for her astounding advice on breaking locks. Romance Writers of Australia have provided much helpful advice over the years and I am proud to be among their ranks.

Thanks to: Anne Phillips and Angela Iliff for the use of their "libraries" and for being there when discussion was needed; Michael Spencer of Berowra, Sydney, consultant in heraldry, for inventing coats of arms for Geraint, Johanna and Fulk; Peter Davies MD for enthusiastically sharing information on abscesses, strokes and cracked ribs; John Chappell for his advice on Yorkshire dialect; Paul West of St. Albans (UK) and Emma Tolhurst of Bristol for chasing up queries; to my father for suggesting Yorkshire as the best place to set the story and to my mother and daughter for their constructive comments. Thanks also to copy editor Amanda O'Connell. Again, my gratitude to the Transworld Division of Random House Australia, and especially to Christine Zika, my editor at Berkley, who believes that Johanna's story is worth the telling.

Finally, this book would not have been completed without my husband's continual encouragement and his contribution, not only in trailing around battlefields and castles but also in earning the frequent flyer points that made it possible to be in England in a most beautiful, mild spring.

Isolde Martyn
Sydney, Australia